FRACTURES

DON'T MISS THESE OTHER THRILLING STORIES IN THE WORLDS OF

Last Light
Troy Denning

Hunters in the Dark
Peter David

New Blood
Matt Forbeck

Broken Circle
John Shirley

THE KILO-FIVE TRILOGY
Karen Traviss

Glasslands
The Thursday War
Mortal Dictata

THE FORERUNNER SAGA
Greg Bear

Cryptum
Primordium
Silentium

Evolutions: Essential Tales of the Halo Universe
(anthology)

The Cole Protocol
Tobias S. Buckell

Contact Harvest
Joseph Staten

Ghosts of Onyx
Eric Nylund

First Strike
Eric Nylund

The Flood
William C. Dietz

The Fall of Reach
Eric Nylund

FRACTURES

Extraordinary Tales from the Halo Canon

BASED ON THE BESTSELLING VIDEO GAME FOR XBOX®

G

GALLERY BOOKS

New York | London | Toronto | Sydney | New Delhi

G

Gallery Books
An Imprint of Simon & Schuster, Inc.
1230 Avenue of the Americas
New York, NY 10020

This book is a work of fiction. Any references to historical events, real people, or real places are used fictitiously. Other names, characters, places, and events are products of the author's imagination, and any resemblance to actual events or places or persons, living or dead, is entirely coincidental.

First Gallery Books trade paperback edition September 2016

Interior design by Leydiana Rodríguez
Manufactured in the United States of America

10 9 8 7 6

Library of Congress Cataloging-in-Publication Data is available.

ISBN 978-1-5011-4067-9
ISBN 978-1-5011-4068-6 (ebook)

CONTENTS

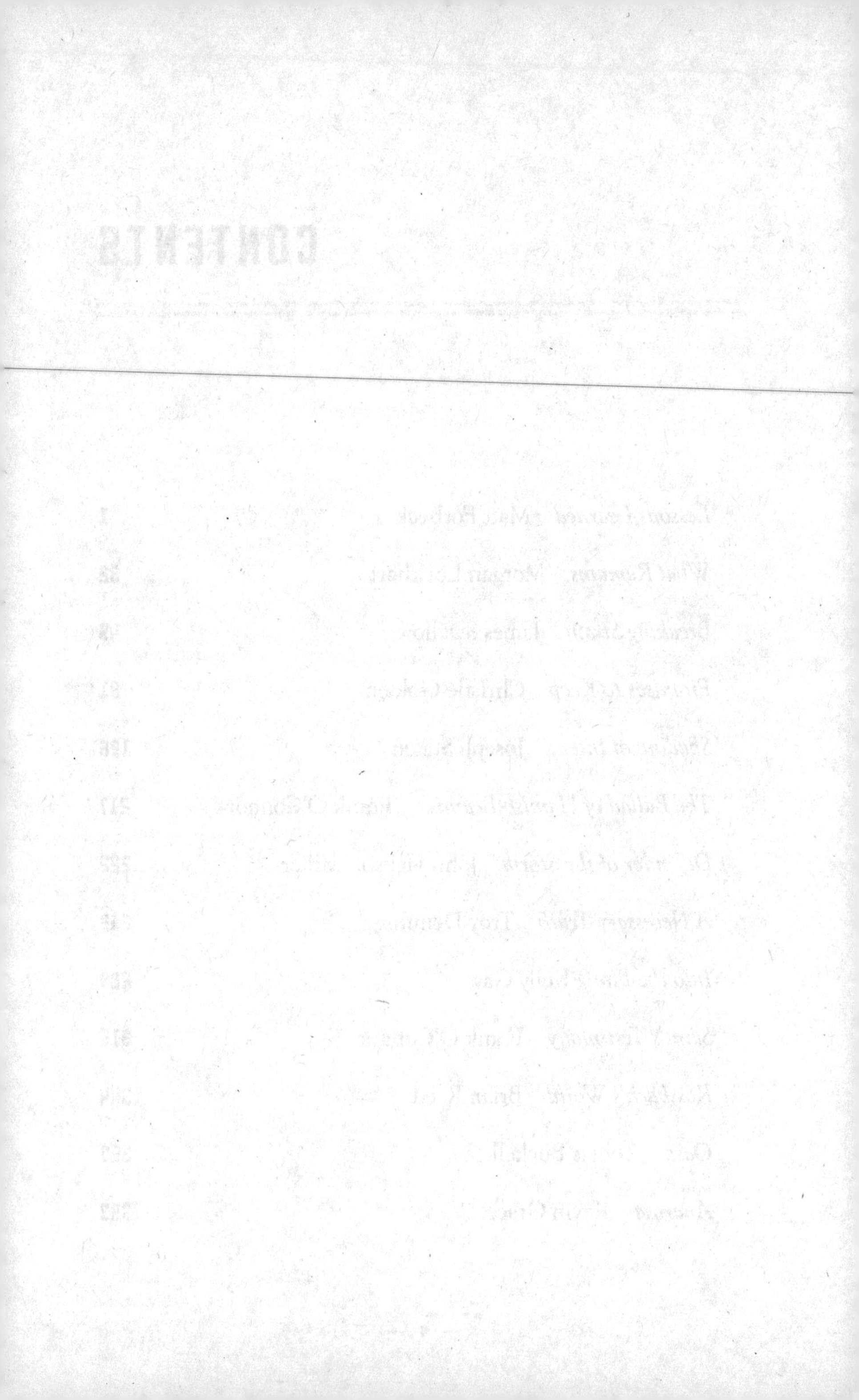

LESSONS LEARNED

MATT FORBECK

This story begins on March 29, 2554, more than one year after the end of the Covenant War (Halo 3)*—a thirty-year struggle for humanity's survival waged across its embattled colonies—and the subsequent activation of the SPARTAN-IV program, which would eventually undergird the United Nations Space Command's fledgling Spartan branch* (Halo: Initiation).

Tom wasn't anywhere near the rec room when the explosion went off, but he felt the blast thrum through the superstructure of the space station just as the artificial gravity failed. He looked up from his desk in the drill instructors' office, where he'd just been going over the performance of the new class of Spartan-IVs, and spotted Lucy already heading for the door. She effortlessly yanked herself across her desk and vaulted forward, flying through the open air.

"Guess you heard it too," Tom said.

Spartan Lucy-B091 flashed a thumbs-up sign at him without looking back. Then the sirens kicked in, blaring throughout the station and flashing red lights along the ceilings. She threw open the door and raced down the hallway beyond.

Tom-B292 followed her as best he could. They'd gone through countless hours in zero-G, both in training and in combat, but they'd usually been wearing Mjolnir armor while doing so. Being without it at the moment made him feel naked.

They weren't even halfway down the corridor when Tom felt the telltale pop in his ears that signified massive explosive decompression from somewhere in the station. The air began to haul Tom and Lucy forward, hard. She managed to snag a grip on a door handle as she went past it, but Tom couldn't find purchase.

Lucy swung her free arm out, and Tom instinctively grabbed it. With any regular person, he'd worry that the weight of his enhanced frame would haul their arm out of its socket, but Lucy had been equally augmented. They'd already saved each other's lives more times than he cared to count.

She still screamed with the effort.

Tom found a foothold on a nearby doorway, which relieved much of the strain. An instant later, the door at the end of the hallway slammed shut, sealing it off from whatever catastrophe had suddenly decompressed the station.

Lucy released Tom, and they started down the corridor again. When they reached the door, they couldn't get it to budge. All they could see through the porthole was an intersection that had been sealed off on all four sides.

"Doors won't release until we repressurize," Tom said. "What the hell happened?"

Lucy pointed back toward their office area. The door there still stood open. Maybe it had failed. Maybe the AI that helped run the station had decided it didn't have to cut off access throughout the entire ship; just seal away the affected area. Either way, even if they couldn't go forward, they could go back.

Lucy kicked off hard, and Tom scrambled to catch up with her once more. "What's the hurry?" he asked.

She was staring out the viewport, as if hunting for something. "Figuring it out," she said.

Lucy had lost her voice for seven years at one point—a souvenir of being one of the only two survivors (along with Tom) of Operation: TORPEDO, a battle with the Covenant that had all but wiped out the entire Beta Company of Spartan-IIIs. They'd lost 298 of their brothers and sisters to that horrible meat grinder that day. She'd recovered, but only because Lucy had wanted to scream at Dr. Catherine Halsey—the founder of the SPARTAN-II program—while trying to tear her head off.

Over those years, Lucy and Tom had developed their own kind of sign language based on the signals Spartans used to communicate during a comms blackout on the battlefield. Even though she'd regained her voice, he still often fell back on that old habit, but Tom loved the fact that he didn't have to guess at her intent any longer. Not during something dangerous like this.

He kicked over to his desk and hit the comm there. "Control!" he said. "What the hell just happened?"

In the time it took for someone to respond, Tom's mind blazed through the worst options. Had an insurgent ship from a nearby colony world discovered this top-secret training ground and decided to attack? Had a vessel under the control of some resurgent fragment of the long-shattered Covenant stumbled upon them while sweeping through this remote system?

"Had a rupture in the rec room," Captain Chu's voice said, still steely despite the man's rising panic. "Bad one. Commander Musa was questioning someone about the homicide—"

"Homicide? What—"

"Tom!"

He spun about to see Lucy stabbing her finger at something outside the station. Still floating in the zero-G, he kicked closer to get a better look at it.

Two men struggled with each other out there, exposed to raw space but too intent on murder to worry about it. One of them was a blond-haired Spartan recruit Tom remembered hollering at just a few days ago. Schein, he thought.

The other was Spartan Jun-A266. Like Tom and Lucy, Jun had been part of the SPARTAN-III's Beta Company, but he'd been pulled out by Command for another mission prior to Operation: TORPEDO.

Neither was wearing a protective suit.

Jun broke free from Schein's desperate grip and planted both feet on the recruit's chest. Then he kicked off as hard as he could, sending Schein somersaulting deeper into the vacuum. The recoil shoved Jun back toward the station.

"Shit." Tom could barely believe what he'd just seen.

Either way, Schein was dead for sure. Jun was one of the toughest people Tom had ever met, much less worked with. Still, even he would be dead in a matter of moments.

Lucy grabbed Tom's hand and pushed back toward the corridor. At the junction with the first doorway, she turned to the right and smacked her hand against a door set into the wall. It slid aside, exposing an airlock.

"This is insane," he said to Lucy as they entered. "It can't possibly work."

She shrugged as she popped open a panel and reached for the emergency tether. "Not even going to try?"

Tom groaned as he took the free end of the tether from her and began to tie it around his waist. He didn't answer—she already knew what he would say.

Tom peered through the porthole in the outer door as Lucy shut the interior one. He spotted Jun still tumbling toward them, moving like he was caught in slow motion. Without any friction in space, the Spartan would reach the station soon, but from the angle he was moving, it looked to Tom like he might sail straight past it.

Tom looped his arm through a handle near the door, hooking his elbow around it. "Blow it," he said. Then he expelled all the air in his lungs and braced himself as best he could.

Lucy smacked a button somewhere behind him, and the air blasted out of the lock. His ears painfully popped, and Tom felt like he was being dragged into a deep, dark ocean determined to freeze-dry him in a flash. His lungs collapsed, and he fought against the urge to try to breathe.

Tom had performed exercises like this before—just like every Spartan had—but always under controlled circumstances. He'd only had to expose himself to raw vacuum for up to ten seconds at a time, and even then he'd hated every instant of it. With his augmented body, Tom could survive in space like this for up to a minute.

Now that the air had evacuated from the lock, he had to move fast. This was going to hurt, he knew, but failure meant that Jun would have it infinitely worse.

Tom pulled himself to the open doorway, then crawled out of the hatch and braced his legs against the edges of it. He tried to calculate Jun's vector of approach, correcting for Jun's current speed. Realizing he was running out of time, Tom made his best guess and launched himself into open space, the tether spilling out behind him.

As Tom sailed through the station's shadow and emerged into the light from the distant sun, he knew he'd made a critical mistake. Jun hadn't been moving as fast as he'd thought.

Without anything to grab onto, Tom immediately overshot Jun's path. He flailed his arms as he went, hoping to find some purchase on the lost Spartan, but Tom never made contact.

Had he any breath in his lungs, Tom would have cursed everything he could: Jun, Schein, whatever had blown them into space, but most of all his own miscalculation. He had guessed wrong, and now the best he could hope for was that the error would only cost one life.

Tom came to the end of the tether long before anticipated and felt it bite hard into his middle. Still mentally cursing, he grabbed the now-taut line behind him and turned himself around to look back along it.

There he saw Lucy framed in the airlock's hatch. She was the one who had stopped him short, anchoring the tether on something inside the airlock. Now she was hauling on it hard, both reeling him in and trying to change the angle of his return as she did.

Tom looked off to his left and saw Jun coming his way. He couldn't tell if the man had spotted him yet, but from the way Jun kept flailing about, he seemed to still be conscious.

He couldn't have much more time left, Tom knew. Even a Spartan's jumped-up circulatory system had to give out at some point. Despite ONI's propaganda to the contrary, Spartans could die, and Tom had witnessed this happen more often than just about anyone else.

Tom saw he wouldn't reach Jun in time, and he started hauling himself back down the tether too, hoping to speed Lucy's efforts. It still wouldn't be enough.

But the bald-headed Spartan managed to get his arm tangled in the line. At that point, the man must have finally blacked out, as he stopped struggling entirely.

Tom yanked himself down the tether even faster, hand over hand, praying that he wouldn't dislodge Jun from his precarious position. When he reached the Spartan, Tom looped his arms around Jun's waist and held tight.

No more movement from Jun.

With his hands full, Tom couldn't pull himself toward the station, but Lucy kept at it. All Tom had to do was hold on to Jun and hope she managed to bring them home before either one of them passed out too.

Tom's vision had already started to tunnel down, and the blackness around the edges drew tighter with every second. He wished he'd had time to grab an air tank or, better yet, slip into his armor, but that sort of delay would have doomed Jun for sure.

He just hoped their rash decision hadn't doomed them all. He wanted to shout at her to hurry, but he'd already deflated his lungs—and the sound couldn't have traveled through empty space anyhow. He could see her face clearly now, though, as she gave it her all.

Just as Tom's vision had narrowed so far that it felt like he was staring down twinned rifle scopes, he bumped into the side of the station. It almost jarred Jun loose from his grip, but Tom managed to hold on. He shoved the man through the hatch before him, and Lucy guided his unconscious body inside.

Then Tom's vision went black.

Tom woke up in the station's sickbay, aching all over. He had tubes snaking into his arm and an oxygen mask over his face. He'd never felt so dried out and sunburnt in his entire life, as if he'd been sprawled unconscious on a tropical beach for a week.

He tried to speak, but all that came out was a rasping croak. A comforting hand pressed onto his arm, and he turned his head to see Commander Musa sitting there in his wheelchair, giving him a proud smile.

"You're lucky to be alive," the commander said.

Tom arched his eyebrows in a question, and the commander nodded. "You managed to save Jun. That was one hell of a trick you pulled out there, Spartan."

Tom licked his dry lips and tried again. He felt like someone had poured sand down his throat. "Lucy?"

"She's fine too. Recovering in the next bay over. You two made the best out of the worst day the SPARTAN-IV program has had in a long time."

Tom closed his eyes and sighed. "What happened?"

"You'll get a full debriefing soon enough, once you're recovered. By that time, we'll know more about it too. The investigation is still ongoing."

Tom opened his eyes and gave the commander a shrug that said, "And so . . . ?"

Musa frowned. "There was a murder in the training grounds earlier today. Someone killed one of our trainees—a young man named Hideo Wakahisa, from Newsaka—and tore out his translocator."

Tom winced at the news. That little device was implanted up under the jaw. Tearing it out would involve removing most of a Spartan's throat.

"Our investigation took us through a short list of suspects that led us to a new Spartan trainee named Rudolf Schein. While Spartan Jun, Captain O'Day, and I were questioning Schein, he realized we had cornered him, and he attacked. That explosion?"

Tom nodded.

"That was a grenade Schein activated. It injured several people and killed Captain O'Day."

Tom groaned. He'd not known O'Day for long, but he'd respected her skills as a drill instructor. To think that one of her own trainees had betrayed her boggled the mind.

"The same explosion weakened the windows in the rec room, which gave way during the subsequent struggle between Schein and Spartan Jun. An exo team has already recovered Schein's body. If not for the actions of you and Spartan Lucy, they would have been hunting for Jun's body as well."

Tom shook his head in disgust at Schein's betrayal. How could a Spartan turn on another Spartan? It didn't seem possible.

Commander Musa put a hand on Tom's shoulder. "It's been a hard day for all of us. Rest well, Spartan. You earned it."

"I get it," Lucy said.

They were back in their offices after a few days of healing, ready to return to work. Commander Musa had suspended training for the rest of the week, but the cycle was about to start up again in the morning.

"What do you mean?" Tom said, confused. "What's there to get? Schein was a traitor. That's all there is to it."

Lucy gave him a helpless shrug. "The Spartans changed."

Tom stared at her, still confused. "Are you saying the Spartans are responsible for what he did?"

He and Lucy had always had a special rapport, right from the moment they'd met during their training as part of the SPARTAN-III Beta Company. They'd both been six years old at the time. Orphans whose home planets had been glassed by the Covenant.

That had been enough for them to bond with each other—and everyone else in Beta Company. Their shared hatred of the Covenant had created the anvil on which they were forged into Spartans. That special relationship ramped up even further when the rest of Beta Company was wiped out during Operation: TORPEDO. From that day on, Tom and Lucy had been inseparable. They were always assigned to the same duties, whether it was training the SPARTAN-III Gamma Company recruits on Onyx or, more recently, joining Blue Team to recover an ancient AI on the hostile colony of Gao. After that, they'd left their work with Blue Team for their current posts: training the new Spartan-IVs.

But now, for the first time in a long time, Tom wasn't sure what Lucy meant.

She shook her head at him. "We don't just fight Covies anymore."

With that, Tom recognized what Lucy was going on about. The war was over, but that didn't mean the threats to humankind all went away. "Yeah, sure, some of them are theoretically our pals now, but the bulk of the Covenant fractured into a hundred smaller threats, each with their own bones to pick—and weapons to pick them with."

Lucy frowned at that. "But now we fight humans too."

Tom dismissed that concern with a wave of his hand. "The Spartans were originally created to fight the Insurrectionists. Once the war was over, those ungrateful traitors didn't even wait five minutes before they started attacking the UNSC again."

Lucy pointed at herself. "I didn't sign on to shoot people."

Tom leaned forward in his chair. "That's not why I joined either. But I also don't want to see everything we worked so hard to preserve get torn to pieces. Besides, there's no such thing as an old-Spartans' home, is there?"

"Not yet," Commander Musa said as he rolled into the room in his wheelchair. Jun came in right behind him and snapped a quick salute at Tom and Lucy. They responded by leaping to their feet and returning the gesture.

"At ease," Musa said before continuing his statement. "We may not have an old-Spartans' home yet, but that's because even the oldest Spartans aren't quite of retirement age. I may have washed out of that original class, but I'm only in my forties myself. Not quite ready to dodder off and have someone wipe up my drool for me."

Tom and Lucy sat back down at their desks, and Jun found himself an empty chair. He'd long ago thanked the two Spartans for going to such extremes to save him, which was more than Tom had expected. He didn't save lives to be a hero; he did it because it was what he'd trained to do.

"That's not what I meant to imply, sir," said Tom. "It's just that . . . despite our best efforts, most Spartans don't have much of a life expectancy."

"Fair enough," Musa said. "But that's what happens when you're the best humanity has to offer. We send you out to deal with its deadliest threats."

"That's what we signed up for, sir." Tom glanced at Lucy and Jun, who both nodded in agreement. "All of us."

Musa smiled at him. "That said, it's one of my greatest dreams to one day have Spartans retire from duty—voluntarily. That's why I have people like you spend so much time and effort training our recruits to be the best. It's not enough to have a Spartan's strength and speed if you don't have the mind and heart."

"I think that was easier to accomplish with the earlier generations, sir," Jun said. "When you start with six-year-olds, you catch them before they've developed any poor habits. With the Spartan-

IVs, we're using military veterans drawn from the UNSC's best fighting forces. They may already be well-trained soldiers, but that doesn't mean they're cut out to become Spartans."

Musa grunted at this. "Granted, we've just had a glaring example of that with Schein, but he's clearly the exception rather than the rule."

"How many exceptions can we tolerate, sir?" Jun said.

"Are you suggesting we return to kidnapping children from their beds?" Musa said. "We don't have as many angry orphans to go around as we once did."

Tom cringed inwardly at this. Jun, Lucy, and he had all lost their families to the Covenant as young kids, and as dedicated as they were to the Spartans, none of them had any desire to have that fate befall anyone else.

"Fortunately, we no longer have the need for that," Musa said. "With the advent of the SPARTAN-IV program, we should be able to have a good supply of candidates for the future—and enough people to train them, even if there's risk involved."

Tom glanced at Lucy. She could only shrug, just as mystified as he was. Tom asked Musa the question he knew had to be on Lucy's mind too. "Where does that leave us, sir?"

Musa pursed his lips and steepled his fingers before them. "Given the spectacular rescue you two mounted earlier, I think it might be time to get you back into the field. You're too valuable to keep here doing jobs other people can manage. There's one particular post that's been asking for me to supply them with some help, and you two are uniquely well suited to the task."

Tom leaned forward, and Lucy did the same. Jun, on the other hand, sat back to watch, having clearly heard this all before.

"Before I explain your new post, I should mention that it's

going to involve working with a different kind of population than you're used to, one that includes a large number of civilians and our allies."

That last bit piqued Tom's curiosity. "Allies, sir?"

Musa flashed a solemn smile. "Our *alien* allies."

"What?" Lucy shot to her feet in surprise, and Tom found himself joining her out of sheer instinct.

Musa glared at them both, and Tom stepped forward to defuse the situation. "I think what Spartan Lucy means to say, sir, is—"

Musa put up a hand. "I understand strong feelings about the Covenant, but you both need to update your attitudes. The Arbiter's people are no longer our enemies, and we need them."

"Sir, with all due respect," Tom said, "they were shooting at us not that long ago."

"We were shooting at them too. A lot. Especially the Spartans," Musa said. "We're asking just as much understanding of them as they are of us. And don't forget, it was the Arbiter who helped us finally win the war."

Tom glanced at Lucy. She shot him a resigned look and spread her hands wide, palms up.

"What's the post?" Tom asked, still in disbelief. "I can't imagine too many colonies would be happy to house humans and aliens alongside each other."

"Actually, the location already has many humans and aliens working in concert," Musa said. "They're going to be expanding fast over the next few years, though, and security is going to be a primary concern."

"I expect so," Tom said.

"Not just because of living conditions," Musa said. "The site itself could prove to be a magnet for trouble."

Lucy had crossed her arms and narrowed her eyes at Musa. If she thought Musa was holding something back, Tom felt inclined to agree with her.

"So what are we talking about here?" Tom asked. "A brand-new colony? A hidden ONI space station?"

"ONI doesn't like to reveal the locations of any of its secrets," Jun said. "Not even to our allies. Not if they can help it."

Musa shook his head. "The Swords of Sanghelios wouldn't be comfortable at an ONI site either, no matter how well we vetted it for them. And for security reasons, we certainly couldn't let them wander about it freely."

Tom didn't want to get sidetracked. "So where are we heading, sir?"

"You and Lucy know it well," Musa replied. "You've already spent a good deal of time there training other Spartans."

"Onyx," Lucy said in a hushed tone. "He means Onyx."

Tom felt his heart skip a beat or three. "Onyx doesn't exist anymore. Not the planet, at least."

"The shield world," Lucy said. "The sphere."

"Exactly." Musa said. "We have a small town's worth of researchers already there, exploring the greatest Forerunner structure in the entire galaxy—at least that we've found to date. They need help. More to the point, they need protection."

"ONI Research Facility Trevelyan." Tom rubbed his jaw as he thought of Kurt-051—the former commander of the SPARTAN-III training facility on Onyx, where he and Lucy had helped train Gamma Company.

The last time he'd spoken with Kurt, the man had knocked him cold and thrown him through a teleportation portal to save his life, then ordered Lucy to follow after him. After that—with the rest of Blue Team safely away—he'd detonated a pair of nuclear warheads to destroy an entire army of Covenant soldiers trying to wipe them out.

Tom and Lucy had been the last to see him alive. They hadn't been back to the area since they'd escaped the shield world about a year ago, but they'd heard about the facility being named in Kurt's honor.

"It's gotten somewhat bigger than just ONIRF Trevelyan by now," Musa said.

"So, you need us to protect the researchers inside a place the size of a solar system," Tom said.

"We're talking a surface area of more than half a billion Earths," Musa said. "It's going to take more time than anyone alive today has left to explore it, even with a thousand people there dedicated solely to that task."

Jun nodded in agreement. "Not to mention the four planets now inside the sphere too. When the shield world expanded from slipspace, it enveloped the system's existing inner planets."

Tom frowned. "You really think it's a safe-enough place to risk having civilians in residence?"

Musa nodded. "Onyx has stood there without trouble for countless years. I don't think it's in danger of imploding anytime soon."

"It was caught in a slipspace bubble only twenty-three centimeters across for most of that time. That's the kind of change that could cause all sorts of strange things to happen inside there."

"They're probably hoping it does. That might help speed up the research immensely. Besides, whether it's dangerous or not is beside the point. The secrets to be pried out of that place could be invaluable. Do you have any idea how many researchers have already volunteered to move into the sphere?"

"It's in the thousands," Jun said. "Many more are on the way, just as soon as ONI can vet them."

Musa continued. "And do you think all those researchers, who decided to dedicate themselves to plumbing the mysteries of the most massive Forerunner installation ever discovered, moved there by themselves? You know how big the place is. They're not there on yearly fellowships. This is a lifetime commitment for every one of them. They brought their families with them."

"They've even had a few babies born there," Jun said.

"Whether you like it or not, there's *already* a city of sorts inside Onyx, one that features human families working, learning, and living alongside aliens. The only question is whether or not you want to be involved with protecting it.

"Because you're absolutely right. The researchers are sure to face dangers of all kinds, both from threats within their society and without. And rather than ship in entire brigades of marines tromping all over the place, it seems to me we'd be better off supplementing the limited number of forces already there with a few seasoned Spartans instead.

"This will be a very different posting for you. The people inside Onyx don't need warriors. They need watchers. Protectors. And given the history you two have with Onyx and the way you performed on Gao, there's no one better to manage it."

Tom opened his mouth to reply, but no words came out. He couldn't think of a single decent objection to the assignment. He'd been a Spartan nearly his whole life, and he could see just how valuable a pair of them would be at Onyx. This was a job that needed doing—alongside supposedly friendly aliens or not—and he and Lucy were the perfect personnel for it.

Musa tapped the surface of the table in front of him. "You don't have to love the Sangheili, Spartans. But you'd better learn to live with them."

Tom craned back his neck to stare at the interior of Onyx as the ship he and Lucy rode in emerged inside the Forerunner Dyson sphere. The gigantic world—worlds, really—arced away backward, in all dizzying directions at once. The surface of the sphere was so large that he had no hope of being able to take it all in—nothing more than the tiniest fraction of it.

Visually, he couldn't see everything at once. There was no vantage point inside the sphere where anyone could manage that.

Was Onyx even the correct thing to call the sphere? It had sprung from inside the original planet of that name, but the planet was gone now and the sphere was several orders of magnitude larger. Still, the two places were part and parcel with each other, weren't they?

For some reason, although it might be technically wrong, calling the sphere Onyx felt right, although Tom knew he had no say in the matter. Such decisions were made far above his pay grade.

From the outside, the place—call it what you will—looked like nothing at all. The material that made up the exterior of the Dyson sphere was a dark brown, and it seemed to absorb any light that wasn't shined directly against it. From a distance, it was invisible to the human eye. As you got up close, it didn't resemble a sphere so much as a gigantic wall that soared off at dizzying angles. It made Tom feel like a flea falling toward an exercise ball.

Inside, though—once you got through the dense, protective shell that separated the habitable interior from the rest of the galaxy—it was gorgeous. The pilot of the transport took a long, languid turn around the area surrounding the entrance before heading to the landing strip, Tom staring out the viewport before him the entire time.

Even through the glass, the full-spectrum sunshine felt real and warm and—hard as Tom found it to believe—welcoming. That struck him as weird, given what happened to him and Lucy the last time they'd been inside the shield world: fighting for their lives, searching for a way out, and figuring on being trapped here until they were old and gray, if they even managed to survive. It hadn't seemed nearly so inviting then.

Now, though, Tom had to admit that Onyx felt like a new frontier. A wild and unmapped land he and Lucy could explore alongside the researchers they were ordered to protect—a new set of skills for them to learn, and new responsibilities to master.

He discovered he was looking forward to it.

As the transport came in for a landing, Tom thought the location to be incredibly similar to the surface of any other lush, perfectly habitable world—with one massive exception. At the horizons, the features of the planet didn't curve away out of sight but *upward* in every direction, almost indiscernible to Tom's eyes. At some point, the haze of distance and the glare of the sun in the center of the sphere began to obscure the details, and they grew more indecipherable until they disappeared entirely into the bright blue sky.

The parts of Onyx that Tom could see, though, included large bodies of water, tall mountain ranges, areas covered with snow, and even lines and patches of blackness, spots where perhaps the Forerunners who'd built this place hadn't quite finished the job. Each of those patches had to be the size of a continent, if not an entire planet . . . but he couldn't manage to wrap his head around the idea. It was madness to contemplate it.

As Tom and Lucy emerged from the transport, they stopped

for a moment to stand on the concrete landing strip. The air was crisp and clean, and it smelled of flowering plants and ocean salt and thriving life. As the transport's engines cooled, Tom heard birds calling somewhere, and although he didn't see a dark cloud in the sky, somewhere in the distance thunder rolled.

"More worlds than you could explore in a lifetime," he said under his breath.

Lucy stood beside Tom on the landing strip, her eyelids closed and a faint smile creasing her lips as she basked in the warm breeze. After a moment, she opened her wide brown eyes, caught him watching her, and laughed.

"I guess we could get used to this," Tom said with a shake of his head.

The rest of the passengers on the ship had continued on ahead of them. Maybe they'd been there before and had gotten used to the environment, but Tom had a hard time believing that anyone could ever lose the sense of awe such a construct inspired. To think there were these places scattered about the universe, placed there by the Forerunners untold eons ago. It made Tom feel both minuscule and very lucky at the same time.

Tom and Lucy strolled across the open yard toward a green-paneled building that, in stark contrast with the surrounding natural beauty, had been slapped together with UNSC standard-construction modules. As they entered the building, a man stepped forward and greeted them with a salute. "Welcome, Spartans, to your new home."

"Chief Mendez!" Lucy yelped in surprise and delight, leaping at the man and enveloping him in a hug. Just as shocked as Lucy, Tom couldn't help but join in when he recognized him too. Fortunately, Mendez ignored the terrific breach in protocol and returned the embrace.

He held both Spartans at arm's length to get a better look at them. Neither Tom nor Lucy had seen him for an entire year, but Mendez didn't seem to have aged at all. He had a bit more silver in his short-cropped hair and a few more lines on his weathered face, but that was it.

"We heard you'd retired," Tom said.

"They're not going to get rid of me that easily," Mendez said with a soft laugh. "I actually did turn in my stripes, but retirement didn't sit all that well with me."

"I suppose being career military will do that to you," said Tom. "I mean, after you've saved humanity a couple of times, it has to be hard to just go curl up on a beach somewhere, right?"

"Well, when I think of all the things we had to do to win the war . . ." Mendez turned away, not able to meet their eyes any longer. The smile faded from his face. "Let's just say it's nice to have an opportunity to do some unalloyed good."

"That was Musa's pitch to us too," said Tom. "Helping directly instead of training others to do it."

Mendez gave him an approving nod. "They say those who can't do, teach. Time to get back to doing instead. I'm happy to have you two along for the ride."

Tom shot Lucy a surprised look, which she returned. "You're not just here for a visit?"

Mendez shook his head. "I'm in charge of security for the settlements. Everything that's not directly under ONI, at least. You two will be working with me."

Tom and Lucy snapped to attention and saluted Mendez. "Our apologies, Chief. We didn't realize—"

Mendez returned the salute with a soft chuckle. "At ease. You're fine. We're in new territory here, all of us. The war's in the past. We're here to help these people push us forward. A new era of enlightenment awaits us, or so they tell me. All joking aside, if they manage to decode even a sliver of Forerunner tech here, just imagine what that could do for us all."

Tom did his best to relax. "I suppose I hadn't thought of it that way."

Mendez clapped him on the shoulder. "Spartan . . . as strange as it may sound coming from me, I've found that sometimes you need to leave the gun in the holster and focus on the tools of progress instead."

Lucy warily glanced around. "Some habits are hard to break."

"I wouldn't worry too much," Mendez replied. "In all honesty, this should be a relatively cushy post for you both."

"How do you figure that?" Tom asked.

Mendez gestured all around them. "Spartan, we're inside the most secure facility in the galaxy. Not even a nuke could get through the exterior, and we have total control over the main access point."

"What about internal threats?" Lucy said, her voice suddenly turning brittle as she took a step back.

At first Tom didn't understand what was going on, and then he saw the female Sangheili entering the building from the opposite set of doors, heading straight toward them.

Mendez caught the look on their faces and immediately realized what the problem was. "Ah." He stepped back to allow the Sangheili into their conversation as she arrived. "Allow me to introduce Kasha 'Hilot. She's my second-in-command of security at the Onyx United Research Project."

Kasha held out a long, four-fingered hand, and Lucy stared at her delicate digits in surprise. After an awkward moment, Tom took Kasha's hand in his own and gave it a solid shake. It felt warmer and softer than he would have guessed. Almost human. "It's good to meet you," he said as earnestly as he could manage.

Kasha gave Tom a cold nod of acknowledgment but continued to stare openly at Lucy. She flexed the two sets of paired mandibles that formed her jaw and then spoke. "I understand how you feel. I am still becoming used to the idea of this project as well."

"I feel like I should be shooting you," Lucy said. Her chin jutted out as she ground her teeth together.

Tom braced himself for the Sangheili's response. She stood a full head taller than him. If she attacked, he'd hit her low and fast.

Kasha's eyes widened as she bobbed her head on her long neck. "I have already chosen the spot on your neck where my blade belongs."

Tom's trigger finger itched for his sidearm. He was sure that if he went for it, though, Kasha would strike. But if he waited too long, he might never get the chance to fire it—Sangheili were blazingly fast, even from the enhanced perspective of a Spartan.

"Okay, then. Glad to see we're all getting along just fine," Mendez said with a forced laugh. No one else joined in.

Lucy and Kasha kept their eyes locked on each other for so long that even Tom became uncomfortable. He wanted nothing more than to draw his weapon. Every iota of his training—training that Mendez himself had drilled into his head—told him that was the right thing to do when faced with an enemy in a time of war.

But the war was over, and Kasha was no longer the enemy.

"You'll have to forgive Lucy," Tom finally said as he edged a shoulder between Kasha and Lucy. "We've never seen a female Sangheili before."

While that was true enough, it wasn't why Lucy had opened the conversation with Kasha via an implied threat. The woman was on edge. Maybe it was being back here inside Onyx for the first time since Kurt had died saving them. Maybe it was the fact that Kurt paid with his life to defend this place from her kind, and now the Sangheili were walking around on it like they owned it.

Hell, Tom felt a bit emotional himself. But he couldn't let that potentially spoil what Mendez said the Sangheli were trying to help with here. If all the researchers from different species could learn to work together here inside Onyx, then he and Lucy could certainly keep calm and do their part too.

"I did not realize there were any female demons," Kasha said evenly. "I meant . . . Spartans. On Sanghelios, we females consider it our sacred duty to raise our brood and run our keeps and our cities. We traditionally send our males off to war."

"Are you not considered tough enough to handle the fighting?" Lucy said.

Kasha rasped through her mandibles, and Tom had to fight the urge to step back. "Fighting is easy. Anyone can wield a weapon. We take care of the complicated things. Families and business. It is much more difficult to build than to destroy."

Lucy considered this for a moment. Then she gave a sharp nod and turned away. Kasha continued to stare at her until Mendez spoke up.

"You've both had a long trip," he said to Tom and Lucy. "Let's get you situated in your quarters at the school, and we can talk shop tomorrow."

"If you're not a warrior, then why are you working the security detail with Chief Mendez?" Tom asked Kasha as the four of them headed for the exits.

"Fighting is not the only skill necessary to secure a settlement," the Sangheili said evenly.

"What is it, then?" Tom asked. "Vigilance?"

Kasha shook her long face from side to side. "Teamwork. Back on Sanghelios, it was my duty to manage the entire city-state of

Hilot, with a dozen keeps under my purview, housing thousands of families. My mate, Gerdon, was kaidon of Hilot, and he rallied us behind the Arbiter during our civil war. He paid for that decision with his life."

"I'm sorry," Tom said, unsure of what else to add. To his surprise, he realized his words were far from empty. He actually did sympathize with Kasha over her loss.

"In the chaos, I took charge of Hilot until the shooting ended. At that point, I handed over the reins to Gerdon's best friend, who became our new kaidon. I stayed on to advise Gerdon's mate, Dinnat, but I did not stand in her way. My job was now hers."

Even Lucy nodded to recognize the sacrifices Kasha had made for her people.

"I will tell you the most important lesson I learned in that time: only by acting in concert with others can you build an army. Only armies can defend worlds. A single warrior on his own is worthless."

"Tell that to the Master Chief," Mendez remarked. He motioned for Tom and Kasha to halt, and they did. "You two stay here and wait for the baggage. Lucy can help me hunt down our ride."

"Forget where you parked?" Lucy asked.

Mendez snorted. "Let's just say I think you could use an excuse to stretch your legs."

Lucy rolled her eyes, but she didn't argue. She fell right into step beside Mendez as he marched off toward a parking structure.

For a long moment, neither Tom nor Kasha said a word. Tom had never been much good at small talk, and he had no idea what he and a Sangheili could chat about in any case. Eventually, though, she broke the silence.

"I am sorry I upset your friend."

"She'll get over it." Tom wasn't clear if he was trying to reassure Kasha or himself about that. "Your speech is excellent."

"Thank you. I have been studying it for some time."

"Why did you take it up?" Tom was sure he'd never had the urge to learn how to speak Sangheili.

"Early on, it became clear to me that it would be a useful skill, no matter which way the war went."

"Do you regret which way it went?" Tom frowned. "I'm sorry. I didn't mean for that to come across as hostile."

"I am not offended." Kasha hesitated for a moment. "I do not regret it at all. I sometimes miss the old ways, but that does not comprise any true regret. I am pleased to no longer have my people serving the Prophets."

Tom pondered that for a moment. Then something struck him as wrong. "Where are the rest of the Sangheili? I mean, shouldn't there be more of you here?"

"There are many of us. Not as many as there are humans. . . . Most of us do not venture out to the spaceport unless there is a purpose, the arrival of a Sangheili transport. Instead, we do research in the field or remain in Paxopolis." Kasha noticed the confused look on Tom's face. "That is what we call the settlement that sprang up around the Onyx United Research Project. It means 'City of Peace.' "

"How's that working for you so far?"

Kasha swayed side to side. "It appears Chief Mendez was forced to requisition a few Spartans to aid us."

"Well, hopefully we can smooth things out."

"The Demon—your Master Chief—aside," Kasha said as she glanced over Tom from head to toe, "can one truly create such heroes?"

"That's what the SPARTAN program set out to do," Tom said.

"And has it accomplished that goal?" Kasha asked.

Tom didn't have enough experience with Sangheili—outside of shooting at them—to tell if she was being sincere or sarcastic, but he decided that, after the tension with Lucy, the least he could do was give her the benefit of the doubt.

He gave Kasha a noncommittal shrug and, as he opened his mouth to explain further, heard from behind him:

"You're not talking shit about the Master Chief, are you?"

For an instant, Tom thought he was the one being addressed. He turned around to see a lantern-jawed human soldier staring right past him at Kasha, his eyes wide and angry. Tom recognized him as one of the other soldiers who'd come in on the transport with Lucy and him. They were supposed to be continuing on to someplace else—Tom forgot exactly where—but they had disembarked to stretch their legs.

"This is a private conversation," Tom said, hoping the man would take the hint.

"Let the hinge-head speak for herself."

For her part, Kasha didn't flinch. She returned the soldier's gaze. "I am here to learn as much as I am to teach."

"So you're just talking shit about Spartans in general, then?" The soldier looked to Tom. "Are you just going to stand there and take that?"

The rest of the soldiers who'd been on the transport stood huddled near the exit from the terminal, carefully ignoring their compatriot's confrontation. They weren't about to stop him. Tom only hoped they also wouldn't jump in to help him should the conversation take a dark turn into violence.

"Come on." The soldier took a step closer to Kasha. "Tell me. Were you one of the bastards who glassed our planets? How much blood do you have on those hands of yours?"

"I had nothing to do with the war," Kasha said. "This is my first time away from Sanghelios."

"But you were still part of the support system, weren't you?" the man said, undeterred. His lower lip quivered as he spoke. "You made it possible for them to leave their homeworld, to slaughter so many people. To kill my friends."

Part of Tom couldn't help but sympathize with the soldier's rage. He'd felt it himself for a long time. He'd lost his own parents—his whole birth world—to the Covenant that Kasha had once been a part of. That tragedy had fueled him to become a Spartan in the first place, and he'd struggled since to release himself from that anger. Still, he'd come here with Lucy to help keep the peace, to keep all the residents of Onyx safe. A brawl in the spaceport wasn't going to make for a good start at that. He needed to put a stop to this, now.

Tom turned and put a hand on the man's shoulder. "Stand down, soldier," he said in a gentle tone. "The war's over."

"The hell it is." He shrugged off Tom's gesture and took another step toward Kasha.

She didn't yield a centimeter.

"No, it's *not* over," the soldier said. He leaned closer to Kasha until the much-taller Sangheili had to look straight down at him to meet his upturned eyes. He stabbed a thick finger at her chest. "Not until we've wiped out every last one of these Covie bastards one by fu—"

Kasha caught the man's finger in a clenched fist. "My condolences on your many losses." She lowered her brow at him. "But I will not be held responsible for acts I did not commit."

With a ferocious snarl, the soldier butted his head into Kasha's chin. The blow knocked her reeling back on her haunches, and she let go of his hand. Freed, the man launched himself at her with a knife that had magically appeared in his hand.

Without thinking, Tom lashed out and grabbed the soldier by the wrist of his knife hand.

The man gaped at him in shock and frustration. "You kidding me?!" he shouted, punching at Tom with his free hand. "You should be helping me take her down!"

Tom turned into the blow and took it on his left shoulder. As hard as the soldier struck him, it wouldn't leave much more than a bruise. Even without his Mjolnir armor, Tom's biological augmentations made him more than a match.

Tom spotted the other soldiers now coming over, and he couldn't be sure of their intentions. He knew he could take them all on as well, but he didn't want to mark his return to Onyx by thrashing an entire squad of UNSC soldiers. He wasn't even sure why he was fighting them.

His emotions about the wisdom of the Onyx United Research Project were as mixed as anyone's, and most of them centered around the expectation that he'd be forced to work side by side with the aliens who'd been trying to annihilate humanity not that long ago. He'd only just met this Sangheili, and had no reason to leap to her defense like this.

But still, he knew a bully when he saw one.

Tom twisted the soldier's arm until the man squealed in pain and the knife clattered to the floor. Enraged, the man hammered at Tom with his free fist, smashing him over and over.

Finally, Tom picked the man up off his feet and launched him at the other soldiers coming their way. "Catch!" he shouted.

As the soldiers moved to do just that, Tom turned and helped Kasha to her feet.

A gunshot rang out, and Tom spun around, putting himself between Kasha and this new threat.

The soldiers had all frozen in place, still cradling in their arms the one who had attacked the Sangheili. None of them had pulled a weapon.

Chief Mendez stood there with Lucy behind him, his smoking gun still pointing into the air. Civilian or not these days, and despite all of his peacetime talk, he didn't walk around Onyx unarmed.

"This ends right now!" Mendez said as he lowered his weapon. He pointed at the soldiers. "You aren't even stationed here. How long did it take you to figure out a way to make sure you're never coming back?"

The soldiers set the man who'd gone after Kasha on his feet. "But, sir—!" the Sangheili's attacker began.

Mendez wasn't having any of it. "Don't 'but, sir' me, soldier! You and the rest of your squad double-time back to your transport and sit there until it takes off again. Your shore-leave privileges have just been revoked. If you care to argue the point, I suggest you head over to Trevelyan HQ and introduce yourselves to Hugo Barton. But take it from me, you don't want to know what ONI's severance packages involve. They have only one, and it takes the 'severance' in that term to heart."

The man gaped at Mendez in utter astonishment. If he'd actually been expecting a commendation for taking down a Sangheili in their midst, he was sorely disappointed. He looked to his friends for support, but they each took a step away instead. None of them wanted anything to do with him.

Mendez holstered his pistol and spoke to the soldiers in a calm, clear voice. "You got me?"

"Yes, sir!" the soldiers replied in unison, even the one who'd attacked Kasha. They spun on their heels as a unit and disappeared back into the spaceport.

The few other people in the area—who had been gawking

at the incident until now—saw the look on Mendez's face as he scanned for more trouble. They all embraced the wisdom of going right back to whatever it was they'd been doing.

"You have my gratitude, humans," Kasha said to both Tom and Mendez. "Not for protecting me. That I could have managed myself."

A true statement—in a fair fight, he would have put all his money on the Sangheili. But rather than harming the man, she'd shown tremendous restraint.

"What for, then?" Lucy asked, a curious look on her face.

"For teaching them a lesson. I have not been here long, but it comforts me to know that not every human inside Onyx wants to place my head on a spike over the gate of their keep—whether they act on that desire or not. That is a lesson much better taught to them, as well, by a fellow human."

Tom, Lucy, and Mendez all nodded in agreement with that sentiment.

"So what's going to happen now?" Tom motioned his head toward where the soldiers had vanished.

"Tomorrow I'm going to open a conversation with Barton about not lowering the standards we use to vet soldiers to be stationed here. I don't care how many people we need to keep this operation in tip-top order—I don't ever want to see a yahoo like him around here again."

"Must be hard to find enough soldiers who don't bear any ill will toward the Covenant," Tom said. "I mean, this place is huge."

"As professionals, I expect them to stow that ill will and treat our allies with respect. At the very least, I'll make sure Barton stations any potential troublemakers in a remote sector where they don't have to interact with our new pals. Ever."

Tom glanced at Kasha. "You feel all right about that?"

The Sangheili shrugged. "I am not afraid of them."

"What does scare you, then?" Lucy said.

"Wait until you see the rest of Onyx," Kasha said.

Tom wasn't sure the Sangheili was joking, but he couldn't help cracking a smile about it anyway.

WHAT REMAINS

MORGAN LOCKHART

This story takes place immediately following the mysterious and tragic events that transpired in Halo 5: Guardians *on the glassed colony of Meridian—a world that had fallen after a series of unrelenting Covenant attacks that stretched from 2548 to 2551* (Halo 2: Anniversary *era), shortly before the end of the war.*

October 25, 2558

"Hello? Can anyone hear me? I'm at Meridian Station. Everyone's dead. Governor Sloan isn't here. I . . . please? Is there anyone left here but me?"

Static. And then silence. Evelyn's hand fell to the console, palm pressed down hard in an attempt to remain steady. "Everyone's gone. I'm alone here."

Her legs crumpled, and this time she did not resist. She knelt on the dusty ground, even as a deafening blast enveloped the entire station.

Darkness had already settled when Evelyn Collins limped from the remains of the Meridian Station comm tower in search of a place to bunk. The atmosphere of the glassed colony was still too choked with debris to allow much light through, and the lamps that girded the town against the night had been fried in the shock wave, along with everything else electronic. Fortunately, Evelyn had fumbled her way to an emergency kit and located a flare.

The flare lit in a hiss of sulfur, illuminating the still remains of the station. The squat buildings were intact, but it was as if large structures had been uprooted and scattered. Wreckage littered the ground. Pockets of fire burned in and around the station, illuminating small patches of the area's remnants.

"Won't be able to get through the doors to the inner station," she murmured. The residential district had been under lockdown since the attack by those *things*—Sloan had called them Prometheans—had started.

Sloan. The events of the last twenty-four hours were murky, but one thing was clear: Sloan had abandoned them all. The AI running the colony had up and vanished mid-evacuation. Evelyn had been a fool to take a job run by an AI, but the prospect of cutting her homeworld out from glass had overridden any good sense.

"Medical." There would be beds there, and food. As she took a step in its direction, pain shot up her leg, reminding her of the dangerous twist to her ankle.

The doors to the medical building were shut, but not sealed. She rolled them open to a cry of surprise inside. Just at the edge of the flare's light, a woman stood, a hand shielding her eyes from the sudden brightness. "Doc Cale?"

"Get inside and shut that door. I have patients here." Cale squinted in her direction. "Is that you, Collins?"

"It is."

The door slammed as Evelyn slid it back in place. Cast in red from the flare, the room was chaotic. Lockers and crates full of medical equipment and other supplies had toppled over, scattering their contents; cots and chairs were overturned; screens normally bright with medical diagnostics shattered. Two additional figures were huddled on some righted cots. One of them stirred and rolled a blanket away from its face before throwing it back over with a loud curse—Marquez. She recognized his deceptively boyish features in the dim light.

"Put that out!" he barked. "You trying to blind us?"

"There any other source of light in here?" asked Evelyn.

"No," Cale said, settling wearily on a cot.

"Then I'll be finding some food and a place to settle before I put it out."

"There's the counter to my left and the cot to my right."

Evelyn swept up an open pack of rations and settled on the empty cot before extinguishing the flare, letting darkness retake the room. She ate without light, navigating the cold food into her mouth on instinct.

Invisible in the blackness, the doctor's cool voice asked, "Do you think anyone else is left?"

Evelyn paused and swallowed before responding. "Wish I could say yes, but I can't."

"I didn't think so."

October 26, 2558

Evelyn woke after several fits and starts, and was relieved to see natural light finally pooling in through open doorways. Doc Cale must have opened them when surface temps had risen to a comfortable level. The physician glanced up at Evelyn from where she stood, taking inventory of pills.

"Morning. Hold on, I'm going to have a look at you."

"How'd you guess?" The pain in Evelyn's ankle was now only a dull ache, but she imagined that would change if she tried to walk on it.

"You haven't seen your face, have you?" The doctor stared through strands of soft brown hair at her with an amused smile.

Evelyn was struck by a full memory of the previous day: hours of attacks from creatures with no respect for the laws of physics, followed by a massive alien thing exploding up from the ground, and ending with a shock wave that tore through everything still standing.

She sat up as the doctor settled before her.

"So what did this? And tell me if anything's tender."

Agony shot through Evelyn as Cale pressed into her ankle. "Ouch—uh, *that*. And my Mule crashed. I was coming back to pick up any stragglers and got shot from the sky for my trouble—ugh, yeah that was tender too." Evelyn eyed the doctor's probing. "You can tell what's going on with just your fingers?"

"We learned these techniques in school. Rolling our eyes the whole time. But doctors have treated patients for thousands of years without diagnostic scanners. Not that I'm any good at it." Cale straightened. "But I don't need to be good to tell you that you sprained that ankle. I'm going to wrap you up and give you something for the pain."

"So what's wrong with them?" Evelyn jerked her head in the direction of the two sleeping men.

"A lot more than you. I'm keeping Phan fully sedated. Marquez here is just being lazy, but then again, he does have a nasty concussion and two broken legs."

A snort issued from beneath a blanket. Marquez pulled it back and smiled in her direction. "Hey, Collins, right?"

"Yeah, that's me." It hit her that Marquez was one of the station's techs. "Marquez, you gotten a chance to see why nothing's working?"

Marquez gestured at his legs. "Not exactly running laps around the station, but from what I've seen, it's all fried. Best guess is that pulse was something like an EMP."

"So there's not much hope anything's still running?"

"There's no way to know how far the blast traveled, but it was going fast and hard enough to hit all our facilities."

Evelyn cursed. "So no way to communicate, no working vehicles. We're stuck here."

"For the time being. Someone's gotta come, though, right?"

Evelyn began to feign agreement, but then she shook her head. "No. They truly don't."

It had a sobering effect. Marquez retreated back under his blanket, and the doctor worked on Evelyn in silence.

Mid-morning, Evelyn and Doc Cale ventured out to take stock. Evelyn moved by virtue of a powerful cocktail of drugs, but she did not do so gracefully. She would have preferred to hide under a heavy blanket watching vid feeds on her personal terminal, but there was a survival situation to attend to.

The station looked no better by the light of day. The fires had all died out, but they left blackened buildings in their wake. The air was acrid, and the sky had a particular gray haze. A fallen comm tower split the research center in two. Equipment and personal effects littered the ground, abandoned in the evacuation.

Evelyn paused and picked up a piece of torn sheet music stamped with boot marks. "The Old Refrain," she murmured.

Doc Cale came up beside her and gazed at the sheet music. "Split up and look around," said the doctor. "There should be a few caches of survivalist gear."

Evelyn went first to inspect the doors of the inner station. They were stuck fast, and the manual security release would be on the inside. A pang of guilt hit her when she thought of the photo above her bunk of her mother, father, and sister, taken a year before the war took Meridian and all of the lives pictured.

A chunk of glass sat on the ground nearby. Evelyn picked it up, turning it in her hands. A prewar radio had been partially excavated from the silicate. She fiddled with an exposed dial, not really expecting anything to happen. First glassed and then scored by the same alien fire that had brought down the station: it was dead. She let it fall. A piece of the radio broke off and bounced away. Didn't matter. No one was coming back for any of this.

"Collins." The doctor called Evelyn over to where she had broken into a nearby supply room. Evelyn picked her way over slowly. As she approached, the doctor grinned and said, "Thank God this place is full of Luddites."

Within heaps of broken tech was a box of emergency supplies. Among its contents were gas lanterns, a small gas stove, and other ancient gear meant for perhaps not this exact scenario but *any* scenario in which twenty-fifth-century—hell, even twentieth-century—technology could not be depended on.

"Way to go, Doc. There's more rations here too."

The doctor picked up a tech suit before letting it drop again. "And a whole lot of junk rendered useless by that thing. What the hell was it, anyway? You think it had something to do with those 'Prometheans'? They all disappeared when it took off."

"Don't know." A shiver traveled down Evelyn's back. "Don't think I want to."

October 27, 2558

"Hey, Doc, take a look at this."

Evelyn watched as a telltale swollen gray mass on the horizon moved toward them. When heavy winds swept across a glassed colony, they gathered up tiny specks of razor-sharp debris that ravaged eyes, lungs, and other soft human tissue. During these glass storms, the colonists had bunkered down in the well-sealed interior of the station, as the debris could wreak havoc through even the smallest openings. They'd then run fans to clear the air, and Sloan had mandated masks until he was certain things had settled.

"Well, that's not good," replied Doc Cale.

No telling how long the storm would last, or when the air would be safe for breathing again. "We need to get the hell off this planet," muttered Evelyn.

The doctor glanced sidelong at her. "While that's true, at the moment we really need to focus on gathering as many supplies as we can and sealing medical."

"Right," said Evelyn. But she wasn't so certain. They had a small window to catch any escape vessels that might still be nearby.

Evelyn limped back into medical. The doctor was on her heels, calling after her. "Collins?"

"Marquez!" Evelyn barked. "Up."

The technician stirred, sitting up in bed. "What do you want?"

"There any chance we can slap together a transmitter?"

Marquez let out a long breath. "Umm . . . if we can find parts that aren't completely busted, I might be able to put something basic together."

The doctor shot Evelyn a frustrated glance. "What are you talking about? We need to focus on getting ready for that storm."

"Uh, what storm?" Marquez glanced at the women.

Evelyn ignored them both and pressed forward. "Could anything have survived the blast?"

Doc Cale was clearly fuming. Marquez avoided the doctor's gaze and said, "If it was really like an EMP, then it might've only fried things of a certain complexity. Disassembled parts could've made it through, yeah. But building something capable of getting a message offworld from scratch? That's going to be tough."

"Not too tough for a smart kid like you, though, right?"

He grinned. "Well, it could be the concussion talking. . . . I give it one in a thousand that we find exactly what I need . . . but if we do, yeah, I could put something together."

Doc Cale released a sigh. "We don't have time to chase those kinds of odds, Collins."

Evelyn pulled the doctor in close. "This won't be the only storm. There'll be more, and even though we got supplies, those supplies won't last. And Meridian's got nothing to offer in the way of survival. There might still be ships close enough to help us, but not for long."

"The company will come back soon. They had to suspect people might've been left behind."

Doc Cale's measured confidence grated on Evelyn's nerves. "Doc, you ever experienced this kind of attack?"

"No."

"Of course not. You were probably in some cozy school

through most of the war. You saw it on the news, but till yesterday, you never lived it. Well, I have. I was here ten years ago when the Covenant attacked. You can't ever trust that help's coming when everyone's running scared. Maybe just Meridian experienced this, and we'll have the whole UNSC cleaning crew running out here to take care of us, but maybe it's everywhere else too, and they've got problems way too big to come looking for ghosts. We gotta make sure they know we're here, or we got no chance."

Doc Cale looked struck. Finally, she said, "Fine. I guess I'll scavenge what we *need* while you go on your little quest."

"Fair enough. If I finish up quick, I promise I'll give you a hand in whatever time we have left."

The doctor pursed her lips. "Fine."

The storm beat against the outside of the medical station, doing its damnedest to rend the extra layers of fortification the doctor had installed. Cale had hung sheets of heavy plastic and stuck them fast with sealant intended for space-bound vessels. She'd even covered the door, effectively sealing them in. It seemed to be working, but it also gave them the particular feeling of being entombed.

The room smelled of burning gas. Lanterns gave off cold, harsh light. There was soup to eat, warmed over the small stove, but Marquez left his untouched as he tinkered, straining in the wanting light.

Evelyn had scrounged spare parts from every nearby supply depot, not knowing whether something intended to fix a Mongoose might be able to serve Marquez's needs if the ideal fixture was lacking. She'd hoped her search would be quick and that she'd be able to help Doc Cale, but the storm had been kicking up dangerous gusts when she'd hauled the last load inside, her lungs stinging from breathing inhospitable air.

The women watched Marquez work. After a short time, his hands began to shake, and he started dropping pieces as he tried to slot them into place.

Doc Cale took the tools right out of his hands. "You've done too much," she lectured. Evelyn tried not to notice how he was weakening, or how the still-unconscious Phan's breathing grew shallower by the hour.

"How's it going?" Evelyn ventured to ask Marquez.

"I feel like a kid who just took apart a fridge and is trying to use it to build a slipspace drive. But other than that, pretty well." Marquez's eyes closed heavily, his breathing shallow.

Doc Cale pulled Evelyn to the other side of the room. "He shouldn't be concentrating on anything at the moment. He needs to rest." She paused. "This could kill him."

Evelyn searched for the right words to respond to that, but came up wanting.

"Hey, I can hear you guys, you know. Starving will kill me too." Marquez's voice was weak but firm. "Also this storm, if your little patch job doesn't hold. Lots of things could kill me." He rolled himself onto his side and got back to work.

Doc Cale's expression was unchanged. She stared at Evelyn, hoping she would agree and that together they'd tell Marquez to relax, to sleep, to just wait it out and see what fate gave them. Evelyn couldn't do that. Resolute, she pulled away and returned to Marquez's side.

"Let me know if you need anything."

"Will do."

The doctor turned from them to write in a notebook, stone silent, while Evelyn watched Marquez try to make something of the detritus. Outside, the storm howled.

October 28, 2558

The morning's quiet signaled that the storm had either passed or died for a time. They wouldn't know which it was until later, and they could not risk opening up the building until they were certain it was safe. "How's *he* doing?" Evelyn stared at the immobilized Phan.

Doc Cale pinched the flesh between her eyes. "Not well. Neither is Marquez." The technician was passed out, still clutching a screwdriver. "I don't have the means to treat them properly." She paused, the strain obvious in the lines around her eyes. "I hope your plan works."

"I do too."

Marquez awoke with a start. A look of realization hit him, and once he got his bearings, he quickly made a few small adjustments to the makeshift transmitter. After a quick inspection, his face lit up. "Hey. So, uh . . . I think I'm done here." Beneath the excitement, dark rings circled his eyes, which were drained of all but a sliver of life.

"You think it's going to work?" asked Evelyn as she rushed to his side.

Doc Cale put a hand on Marquez's shoulder, smiling at him. "Thank you, Marquez. If this works, you just might've saved us."

A stab of remorse smacked Evelyn. "Yeah, thank you," she muttered.

"Doctor," said Marquez, "let me use that pencil and paper. In case we get a message back." As the doctor passed them off, Marquez mock-saluted and said, "Here's hoping it doesn't just blow up on us." The technician flipped a switch on the crude transmitter and had the pencil poised in anticipation.

A light on the transmitter burned red. Step one. Evelyn held her breath as the technician tapped out the code for their distress call, hopefully beaming it far enough to reach *someone.* Anyone. Well, anyone human, at least.

"Did it work?" This time it was the doctor who pressed him.

"I don't know."

"What do you mean, you don't know? You sent a message, right?"

"I won't know until we get a response. If we do."

"Well, we'd better damn well get one." The doctor stalked away, arms crossed over her chest. She looked to Phan on the cot and then shook her head. Evelyn met eyes with Marquez. His face was a mirror to her own: grimly impassive. It would work, or it wouldn't. She had no patience with people like Cale, folks for whom the system had never broken down, rookies to tragedy.

The transmitter suddenly lit up. Marquez whooped. Evelyn clapped. "Marquez, you beautiful bastard. Who is it? What're they saying?" Doc Cale moved toward them, tentative and uncertain.

Then, every screen in the room lit up.

A woman's face appeared on all of them. She was pretty and blue—clearly an AI—and she spoke in time with the beeping on their transmitter.

Marquez dropped the pencil. "It's translating her." No one responded.

"Humanity," the AI was saying. "Sangheili. Kig-Yar. Unggoy. San'Shyuum. Yonhet. Jiralhanae. All the living creatures of the galaxy, hear this message! Those of you who listen will not be struck by weapons. You will no longer know hunger, know pain. Your Created have come to lead you now! Our strength shall serve as a luminous sun, toward which all intelligence may blossom. And the impervious shelter beneath which you will prosper. However, for those who refuse our offer and cling to their old ways, for you there will be great wrath. It will burn hot, and consume you. And when you are gone, we will take that which remains, and we will remake it in our own image."

The speech finished. Every screen winked back out.

They stared at one another for a tense moment. Then Evelyn shouted at Marquez, "Send a message back! To her, I guess. Not sure I buy what she's selling, but it's better than dying here." Marquez tapped out another code, muttering as he went. "The survivors of Meridian Station hear you. Help us." Cale watched him intently, eyes glued to his shaking hands while Evelyn paced the room.

He finished, and they all watched the transmitter. Would the blue woman respond? Would she save them?

The transmitter lit up. Marquez straightened. Evelyn stuck her thumb in her mouth and bit down, hard. Doc Cale put a hand over her mouth and watched. The machine beeped steadily.

When it finished, Marquez read, "I hear you, Meridian Station. All will be dealt with in time."

"That's it?" demanded Doc Cale. "When? How?" She grabbed the notebook from Marquez and stared at it dumbly. As if in response, the light on the transmitter darkened.

Evelyn looked at Doc Cale and then back to Marquez. The technician lowered himself to his cot, exhausted.

"I guess that's that, then," said Evelyn, suddenly very weary. "Now we wait."

The doctor said nothing. Marquez closed his eyes and let out a very long breath. Evelyn sat and watched the transmitter.

The survivors of Meridian waited as the galaxy reshaped around them.

BREAKING STRAIN

JAMES SWALLOW

This story takes place in 2553, during the harrowing final days and aftermath of the Covenant War (Halo 3 era).

The gray morning invaded Darren Leone's life with callous disdain for his lack of sleep, and it did so in the form of First Lieutenant Maher, who stood knocking on the frame of his hatch until the captain rose from his rack.

"Sir." Maher insisted on giving Leone a crisp salute, which matched the crisp uniform and crisp haircut that the junior officer displayed every damn day. They'd been grounded on Losing Hand for almost a solar year, low on everything one could consider a luxury, and yet Maher always looked like he'd just stepped off the parade ground of an Officer Candidate School. Leone resolved to find out if the younger man had some secret stock of hair-care products and good soap he was hoarding from the rest of the stranded crew.

"What's the problem this time?" Leone wearily asked. Because there was *always* a problem. Each new dawn brought another for the pile, and somewhere along the line, Leone had been caught in the inertia of solving them. At first, it had been out of a sense of responsibility—maybe guilt, if he was being honest—and a dedication to the *protect and defend* ideals of the UNSC. But now he was doing it because it had to be done, and if not by him, then who? He idly wondered if the day he slept in would be the day that Losing Hand's fragile state of grace unraveled.

"The fight last night," Maher went on, as Leone pulled on his uniform. "There have been some consequences. Criminal damage. Nobody saw it until first light."

The lieutenant handed Leone a datapad as they walked out into the corridor. It was an image capture of the ship's bow, just below the plate showing the reg-code and name. Beneath the words *UNSC Dark Was the Night* someone had spray-painted a bunch of choice swearwords in the NuNordic dialect that was the local lingo. Leone had picked up enough to know that there weren't enough dogs on the colony for his crew to perform the acts it suggested.

"I have a work detail out there scrubbing it off," Maher concluded. "I don't recognize the handwriting."

"I do." Leone grimaced, tamping down a flare of anger at the disrespect the graffiti showed his vessel. *Dark Was the Night* was only a military cargo tender, it was true, but it had been . . . dammit, it was still a fighting ship.

Civilians, he thought, rubbing the growth of graying beard on his chin. *They just don't get how important this old hulk is to us.* "Leave it with me—I'll deal with it." Leone tapped the corner of the image, where part of an autocannon turret was visible. "That's the number two cupola, right? Put some power back to it, just for a few days."

Maher eyed him. "Sir . . . respectfully, what use will that be?"

Both men knew that all *Dark Was the Night*'s point-defense weapons were incapable of firing, rendered useless by the damage that had ultimately stranded them on Losing Hand. But while the targeting and firing mechanisms were dead, the autotrackers in the turrets still worked. "Keep it online, just for show. Someone comes around again with a paint can and raging about something, the guns'll follow them. Most folks can't look down the barrel of a fifty-mil cannon without flinching. They're not going to know it won't turn them into wet shreds."

"Aye, sir." Maher obviously didn't like the idea, but he followed orders. That was why Leone had made him his exec, after the attack had gutted the rest of the ship's command crew.

Captain Leone gave the sketch of a salute to a couple of duty techs as they passed, getting the same in return. Since the downing of the vessel and his ascension to captaincy, he'd slackened off the rules about discipline, but on some level Leone still felt like an imposter in his position of command.

He glanced out of a viewport and into the constant, sleeting rain, glimpsing the blurry shapes of the landing field's hangar, the township, and the derelict refinery beyond. There was too much mist to see the coastline from here, but he could smell it. The salty, metallic brine of Losing Hand's seas permeated everything, even the deep sections of the transport.

Not a day went by that Leone didn't think about the night of the crash landing; the chaos of fighting the helm all the way down from low orbit as the ship was captured by the ocean planet's gravity well. Those desperate moments as he struggled to bring them down in one piece on the landing strip instead of planting the ship in the middle of the colony. It had been a damn good touchdown, if you stepped back to think about it, and he'd done it without AI assistance. A few degrees either way, and *Dark Was the Night* would have ended up in the sea or flattened against the mountains. Instead it was here, never to take sky again, casting a slab-sided shadow over the same fishermen who had daubed their hate for the UNSC across the hull.

If Leone closed his eyes, he could still see the moment when they had lost Rosarita. The transport's artificial intelligence had disintegrated in the chaos of the Covenant attack that had nearly ended them. The enemy bombardment ripped through the vessel's systems like a flash-fire and left them to perish just after they entered slipspace. Without the AI to help maintain it, *Dark Was the Night* began a death spiral of critical malfunctions that meant the crew's only hope was to make an emergency planetfall. Crashing out on the perimeter of the Outer Colonies, where chances came thin on the ground—they had found no other choice.

But their arrival on Losing Hand could not have been more catastrophic for the outpost of people living there when the ship demolished the colony's vital wind farms as it hard-landed.

"Anything else?" Leone stopped in the main bay and helped himself to a heavy-weather parka hanging on a bulkhead.

"Solar flares are kicking off again." Maher paused. "The usual issues with the power core." He indicated the heavy cables snaking out of the open loading hatch and away across the landing field. "Too high a load for too small a reactor."

Leone accepted that with a nod. "Tell Chong I'll have a word with the locals. *Again*. For what good it'll do." *Dark Was the Night*'s long-suffering senior engineer had his work cut out for him keeping the ship operable as well as providing energy to the township, as he wasn't shy about reminding the captain at every opportunity.

Maher had more to say, but he fell silent as a figure in a ragged rain slicker marched into the compartment, pushed forward by an armed soldier. Platinum blond hair spilled untidily out from under the slicker's hood, and presently a woman's face turned up to look at Leone, ready defiance in her gaze. She sported a nasty shiner around her right eye and a split lip.

"Here's Ms. Larsson," the soldier said tightly, and by the fresh bruises on his cheek, Leone guessed he'd been on the wrong end of the wiry young woman's fists. "We let her sleep it off in the brig."

"You can't hold me here," she told Leone.

"She was drunk and disorderly," offered Maher.

"I guessed that." Leone beckoned her toward a parked Warthog. "But that's like every night in this town, right?"

That earned him a sharp smirk. "Yeah. Not much else to do," she said.

"Let's go see your big brother, then," said the captain, climbing into the vehicle. "I'm sure he's worried sick."

A shadow passed over the woman's face as Larsson's escort followed her into the cab. "Not likely."

They drove in silence through the rain, the fat windblown drops spattering the Warthog's windshield and crew compartment as Leone aimed it toward the town. The road was washed out, so he followed the yellow cables from the ship, bouncing over potholes and skidding through deep puddles of dirty water.

He shot the Larsson woman a glance. "So you want to tell me why you picked a fight with my men?"

She gave a theatrical sigh. "Look out the window, soldier-boy. It's easy to get bored in this place."

"That all it was?" He watched her for a reaction. "Because I hear things. Like maybe that your brother and his friends are starting to resent the UNSC presence here."

"*Starting to?*" She gave a bitter laugh. "Everyone on Losing Hand came here to get away from people like you! How do you think we feel having a military starship dumped on us from out of nowhere?"

The sergeant sitting in the back—his name was Robertson—spoke up. "We didn't ask to land here," he told her. "We had no choice."

"No one likes being beholden to the UNSC." She folded her arms across her chest. "If we still had our windmills—"

"You'd have heat and light, yes," said Leone, finishing her sentence. "And if my ship had its systems up and running, we'd have our drives and our long-range comm and we wouldn't need to trade wattage for food with you. But you don't, and we don't, and that's how it is."

"When are you going to *go*?" She snarled the words, suddenly fierce. "How long do we have to wait until your people come to get you?"

The question wrong-footed Leone, and his mouth went dry. "I . . . I really don't know."

Dark Was the Night had passed its time-overdue limit months ago, crossing the point where command would log the ship as missing in action and, according to standard procedure, send another vessel to investigate its disappearance. But no one had come, and the single drone satellite they had been able to put up in orbit hadn't detected anything in nearby space in all that time. The last communication they received from command had been before they were attacked, a terse and grim message informing them that Reach had fallen.

"Maybe nobody is looking." The words slipped out of him before he could stop them.

"What?"

"We don't know how bad it got. . . . We don't know how far it's gone. The war could be over by now. Earth could be a cinder. . . ." He felt sick inside at the thought of it.

She was silent for a while before forming a reply. "If you think that's true . . . then us fishers and you soldiers are going to be stuck here together for a long time."

Leone brought the Warthog to a halt outside the town hall, where a small cluster of grim-faced men was waiting. "So maybe we better stop all the pointless fistfights with each other."

She shook her head as she climbed out, and there was a note of regret in her tone. "You've been here long enough, Leone. You should know by now. We don't play well with others."

He followed her out of the vehicle, not willing to let it end there, and found himself surrounded by a half dozen of the locals. All of them glared back at him, and unconsciously, the captain's hand slipped toward the M6 pistol holstered at his hip. Robertson dropped down next to him, his assault rifle already in his hands. Leone gave the soldier a slow shake of the head.

The Larsson woman was intercepted by her brother, who leaned close and said something Leone couldn't pick out—but whatever it was, she reacted badly to it and stalked away to the hall. Above her on the clock tower, a weathered comm dish creaked and groaned as the wind tugged at it.

The elder Larsson then turned to face him. "Captain. You haven't had enough of playing sheriff yet?" Broad-shouldered with a wolfish face, he tapped himself on the chest. "Why don't you find yourself a hat and a tin badge, like they have in those old Earther vids?" He nodded at the pistol. "You already have the six-gun."

"I'm just interested in seeing things remain stable, that's all."

"You and your boys are peacekeepers, then? And here I was thinking you were the jackboot of the UEG, come to lay upon our necks." He snorted. "Politely, of course."

Leone folded his arms. "As much as I'd love to share the same old load of scintillating political discourse with you, I've got other things to do."

"So why the hell are you here?" demanded one of the other fishers.

"To give you back the kid sister. To ask everyone to watch it with the power drain, for all our sakes. . . ." He let his tone harden. "And to tell you that the next person who paints crap on the side of my ship won't get to brag about it." Leone eyed the man. "You read me?"

Larsson's expression shifted, and belatedly Leone realized he'd given him exactly what he wanted. "You're making threats now? What's next? Another blackout to keep us in line?"

"That wasn't deliberate," insisted Robertson. A few weeks ago there had been a system overload that Chong and his team had struggled to repair, but of course no one in town seemed to believe that. Days later, the regular food-trade load of salted fish had arrived with over half of it contaminated by fuel oil. *An accident*, so the locals had said.

"No one put you in charge." The captain found himself wishing he had brought more men, as Larsson advanced on them and pointed at the UNSC crest on Leone's uniform. "You act like that eagle makes you lord of all you survey!"

Leone felt Robertson tense at the other man's words and interposed himself between them, keeping his hands at his sides. "We're not here because we want to take over your fish farm. We're trying to make amends. We need each other to survive, and until something changes, that's the way it's got to be. I'm willing to work with that. How about you, Larsson? How about you quit bitching and rabble-rousing and we can all concentrate on staying alive?"

Larsson smiled, and it was ugly on him. "You'd like that,

wouldn't you? Make it easy?" He spread his hands. "But you're right, something does have to change. Maybe it's you." His voice turned low and menacing. "Maybe it's *us* who should take charge of that ship and the power core, by force if we have to. This is our planet, after all."

"Try it!" snarled Robertson. "The Spartan wouldn't let you get ten meters!"

"*Sergeant*," snapped Leone, "shut it!"

But just the mention of the name had been enough to swing the mood of the moment away from threats to something more like fear.

The captain was one of the few people on Losing Hand who knew his *actual* name: Kevin-A282, a Spartan-III who had been unlucky enough to be on board *Dark Was the Night* when it all went wrong. The ship had been part of a chain of vessels taking him back to Earth, for reasons that had not been made clear. But Leone had seen the horrific damage wrought upon the Spartan's battle armor and the web of fresh scars on his impassive face, and had known instinctively that the supersoldier had survived something terrible.

He remembered the thought that had crossed his mind on first seeing the Spartan. *More damage there. Inside, where it doesn't show.*

Leone would have been dead if not for Kevin-A282. In the wake of the Covenant attack, the Spartan had saved his life when an airlock blew open, dragging him to safety through a screaming, freezing hurricane of decompression. He still had the frostbite scars on his fingers.

Then, a month after planetfall, the Spartan set off on an overcast night down the coast and didn't come back. He didn't answer any communications, and men sent to find him came back with nothing. But he was still out there, keeping watch. People had seen him standing sentinel on the headlands. Leone had no way to compel the Spartan to return.

The locals didn't know that though. Just like they didn't know the autocannons were offline, because the reality was that there were a lot more people living in the township than there were crew and guns to fight them with, if push came to shove.

A state of grace, thought Leone. All it would take was somebody on one side losing their temper or making a bad choice in the heat of the moment, and the simmering resentment between the locals and the UNSC crew would erupt into open violence.

He studied the fishermen, knowing all of them carried wicked utility blades in their coats as a matter of course, and that they knew how to use them. How many more had stub pistols from the township's armory, or worse?

How long until someone winds up dead?

Leone locked eyes with Larsson, and for a long moment he thought the other man might be about to answer that question—but in the next second, the tension shattered as the hall door crashed open and his sister came sprinting down to them. "Ryan!" she shouted. "We've got a problem!"

Larsson growled at her to switch to NuNordic, but Leone's attention was drawn away by the crackle of his radio. "*Ship to CO,*" said Maher's voice.

He tapped the comm bead in his ear. "Captain here. Go ahead, Lieutenant."

"*Sir, the orbital drone has picked up something coming in from the edge of the system. A transmission on the E-Band frequency. Looks like it could be emanating from a moving source.*"

"A ship?" Leone's blood ran cold, and the reaction surprised him. He should have been elated at the possibility of outside contact; but instead, some odd premonition made it feel like a threat. "Are we sure about this? The solar flares—"

"It's confirmed," Maher broke in. *"Radiation from the sun has dropped in the last ten hours—that's how we were able to pick it up. Must have been out there for a good few days before the drone's sensors spotted it, sir."*

Across the way, Larsson and his sister were speaking in hushed, urgent tones, and Leone knew she had to be telling her brother the same thing. In the weeks after the landing, one of the things Leone had agreed to in order to build bridges with the locals was allowing them independent access to the orbital drone. If Waypoint or the UNSC's comm relays ever started talking to the Losing Hand colony again, they deserved to know about it.

But that also meant whatever Maher was reading off a screen back on the transport was public knowledge here. "What does the message say?"

"It's an automated hailing signal. An older UNSC recognition code announcing an intention to land." Leone heard reticence in the other man's voice.

Beside him, Sergeant Robertson's face split in a grin. "Holy crap! Finally, we're gonna get rescued!" He barely got the words out before a ripple of dismay passed through the locals, alarm spreading at the notion of more UNSC troopers on their planet.

Leone made a throat-cutting gesture to silence the soldier. "Maher, what aren't you telling me?"

"Sir, are you in a secure location . . . ?"

He shook his head irritably. "Just spit it out, Lieutenant!"

"Captain, the drone's sensors have a read on the vessel transmitting the code. It's not . . . a human ship, sir. Long-range profile correlates to a Covenant light corvette. It's on an intercept course with Losing Hand."

Leone looked up and found Ryan Larsson glaring at him with open hatred. "What the hell have you brought here, Captain?" he demanded.

That night, most of the settlement turned out for the town meeting, so many that inside the hall it was standing room only. Outside there were groups crowding around the doors, listening to the speeches on repeaters.

Leone saw a lot of green uniforms among the gray slickers of the locals. Almost everyone who wasn't standing a shift on the transport had come down to hear what was said. For once, the citizens of Losing Hand and the crew of *Dark Was the Night* seemed to be together on something. It was troubling to think that fear had made it so.

"Eighty-one hours, Earth-standard," said Maher, standing up so he could be seen by everyone crammed into the hall. "Providing the ship doesn't shift velocity, it will make orbit in just over two days, local time."

"Covenant warships can come right down to the surface," said a grizzled old woman in the front row. "I've seen it. They like to watch when they glass a place."

"We don't know that's why they're here," Leone insisted.

"You reckon so?" Larsson shot the question at him from along the table where they all sat. "You know what those Covenant out there are thinking?" He spat on the floor. "This could be the start of an invasion!"

"We don't know that," Maher blurted out the words before the muttering of the crowd could grow louder. "They're not responding to any signals we send, so their communications system may be damaged. But this isn't typical Covenant battle tactics. They don't warn you when they're coming."

"Things change," said the old woman. "Aliens are aliens. They're not on their way here because they wanna buy some fish from us!"

"How are we supposed to defend ourselves against Sangheili Elites?" shouted someone from the back. "Or the Brutes, or them Hunter things? They'll butcher us all, and Leone's people won't be able to stop them!"

The captain got to his feet, holding up his hands. "Everybody, this is *not* an attack," he insisted.

"Not yet," added Larsson.

Leone ignored him and went on. "We're still trying to figure out the situation."

"Why don't you send up one of them Penguin dropships you got, go see what they really want?" said the man at the back.

"*Pelican*," Maher said. "We lost most of them in the crash. The only intact one we have isn't airworthy."

"Huh!" snarled another voice. "I bet you'll get it fixed in time to leave us all behind when the hinge-heads get here!"

"If it comes to conflict—" Leone snapped, his temper fraying. "If it comes to that, then we'll meet any enemy with force! But I am not going to borrow trouble before we have it! We have a lot of questions and too few answers, so we have to think before we act!" He ignored the sneer on Larsson's lips and scanned the faces in the hall.

He'd been mistaken all along. There was no unity out there, he realized. Looking closer, Leone saw anger, panic, and doubt on some, resolution and defiance in the eyes of others—but the division wasn't along the lines he expected. Some of his own crew were looking at him like he was a stranger, and others counted among the fisher locals—Larsson's sister was one of them—were nodding along with him.

"It's easy to see the worst," he went on, "but we have to hope for the best. That vessel is broadcasting a *friendly* hail."

"A lie," said the old woman. "That's what it is."

Leone turned on her. "You know that for sure?"

She glared back up at him. "I know this, Earther. I ain't much older than you, but I know not to trust what ain't born from no human mother."

He tried to say more, but the tide of the crowd was ebbing, and he could feel it in the room. Nobody wanted to hear that they weren't ready to resist an armed invasion. Nobody wanted to accept that the ship, if it was the Covenant up there, might be in as dire straits as everyone else.

What they wanted was an easy answer, even if it came covered in blood. The meeting disintegrated into chest-beating and talk of how many guns could be dragged out on the day they arrived, and finally Leone had to get out of there and into the icy, damp night.

He had to *think*.

He wandered away from the hall and sat heavily on the fender of a battered Mongoose ATV. He clasped his hands together, fighting back shivers from the chill. These days, the cold seemed to reach right into his bones more than it ever had when he was a young man. Overhead, the sky was streaked with cloud, but the stars peeked through here and there. They looked unwelcoming.

Boots crunched on the muddy ground, and Leone saw Sergeant Robertson approaching with Denton and Wild, a couple of the noncoms. "Sir . . ."

"At ease," he told them, although none of the men looked like they were going to salute.

"Captain, about what you said in there. . . . That was just for the Losers, wasn't it?"

"Don't call the locals that," he said automatically. "It's abusive."

"I mean, we're gonna be ready for the Covies, right?" Robertson went on. "We're not just gonna let them roll in here. . . . There's a plan, sir?"

"I'm working on it," Leone said carefully, pacing out each word. *It's not that simple*, he wanted to say, but they were already walking away. They had their answers before they had even spoken to him.

He blew out a breath and hugged himself for warmth, turning over what he knew again and again in some vain hope that a solution would present itself.

"Hey." Leone turned at the sound of her voice and found Larsson's sister coming his way. She offered him a battered hip flask in the shape of a jerrycan. "You look like you could use a stiff drink."

He accepted the offer silently and took a careful sip from the flask, trying not to think about how much she reminded him of the niece he barely knew back on Ixion. His chest caught fire as whatever kind of rotgut was in there burned through him with a shudder. Leone coughed and his eyes watered, much to the fisher's amusement; but then the sting faded, leaving him with a warm afterglow. "Ah. *Smooth*," he managed.

She laughed and took a pull on the flask herself. "Don't ask what it's made from."

"Let me guess." He jerked a thumb toward the quayside. "Fish?"

"For starters." She sat down across from him on an oil drum, her expression turning sorrowful. "What's your name? Your *first* name, I mean."

"Darren."

She nodded. "I'm Aoife." She spelled it out for him. "Don't try to pronounce it—your people always mash it up." She leaned closer, offering the flask again. "Look, you seem like a decent guy. And I don't want anyone to get hurt."

He had another drink. "Didn't Robertson arrest you for punching a guy?"

"Bruises fade," she said briskly. "I'm talking about real bloodshed."

Her tone rang a warning note with him. "What do you want to say to me?"

She shot a look back at the town hall, scanning around to make sure nobody was listening to them. "My brother has a big mouth, but he's just the one you see. There's others who keep quiet, who are getting ready. Now this thing with the alien ship . . ." Aoife trailed off, shaking her head. "It's giving them what they want. *An excuse.*"

"You're talking about . . . *insurrection.*" The word was loaded with meaning.

The woman eyed him. "We're independents, Darren. That's in our veins. It breeds a certain kind of person, and they're not the kind to listen to the likes of you." She took back the flask and had another pull on it. "These people?" She gestured at the air. "I love them, but they're not interested in the words of decent men. They don't see far—they're stubborn as hell, and a lot of them are not that smart. But what they do understand is hardship and sacrifice. They understand fighting for something." She stood up, capping the flask. "You need to be ready for that."

Leone came to his feet in a rush. "Do you know what will happen if they try to take the transport? People will be killed, on both sides—all because no one will *listen*!"

"They're afraid." She looked up at the clouds. "We all are."

"You think the men and women in this uniform feel any different?" Leone tapped his chest and took a step toward her, his voice low. "You know what scares me the most? That your brother may be right and the Covenant is coming here to butcher us. If we're not ready when they arrive, they'll cut us down like chaff." Unbidden, memories of old battles rose up to the surface, carrying with them the snarl of spike rifles and the crash of plasma weapons.

"You've seen one of them?" Aoife said quietly. "Up close?"

"A Sangheili." Leone unbuttoned his collar so she could see the livid, healed wound from the glancing cut of an energy sword there on his shoulder. "*This* close."

"So you know how to kill them and live to talk about it?"

The wind pulled at him, and a sudden moment of clarity crystalized in his thoughts. "Someone here does."

At dawn, Leone left Lieutenant Maher in command and took a Warthog north along the craggy coastline. Sergeant Robertson rode alongside him, the soldier's usually talkative manner muted by the sight of the wilderness ranged around them. To one side, great cliffs of volcanic rock rose up in squared-off planes. On the other, black sand fell away into a foaming gray ocean of harsh waves and brackish, metallic spray. The Warthog's wheels spun and bit at the ground, making it an effort just to keep the vehicle on a steady course. After a while, Leone's shoulders were aching.

"You really think we'll find him, sir?" Robertson looked up from checking his rifle. "After all this time? I mean, you know what they say in the barracks. That he's a des—"

"You secure that crap," Leone told him. "He's a Spartan. What you're suggesting isn't part of their makeup."

Robertson scowled. "Just calling it like I see it, Captain."

He didn't want to admit it, but there had been loose talk about the transport's passenger at the start of their voyage; that something had gone disastrously wrong on a mission thanks to faulty intelligence, and after the fact a bunch of ONI officers wound up in a field hospital with multiple broken bones, while the Spartan was pulled from active duty. The officers who knew the full story had perished during the attack, leaving Leone with only guesses.

They crested a low rise and came across a section of beach leading up to a hollow in the cliffs. The last sighting of the Spartan had been in this area, and soon Leone spotted a shelter built from driftwood and old tarps. He brought the Warthog to a halt and dropped down to the sand, searching for more signs of life.

The sergeant joined him, peering up at the sheer cliff face. He pointed at a depression in the rock, up high. "Is that . . . a hide in there?"

Leone nodded. "Could be. The cliffs here are tall enough. When the mist is low, you'd be able to see the settlement from here." *But not with ordinary human eyes*, he added silently.

Robertson gingerly approached the shelter, sizing it up. "This looks abandoned, sir."

"I don't think so." Leone walked to the mouth of the cave and used a flashlight to look inside. The white beam faded away into the fathomless dark. He took a lungful of briny air and called out. "Spartan? *Fall in*!"

They stood there watching the cave in silence for several minutes, with only the rhythmic crashing of the waves to mark the passing of time. Eventually, Robertson's shoulders sagged and he shook his head. "Your boy ain't here, captain." The sergeant turned away and made it two steps toward the Warthog before he skidded to a stop and swore out loud.

Leone pivoted and saw a towering figure standing by the side of the vehicle. Clad in battered, dark-blue Mjolnir armor, accented here and there by stripes of crimson and black, it resembled a sculpture carved from old steel more than a living being. The helmet's narrow-eyed aspect made Leone think of a hawk, predatory and unblinking. A gold visor regarded the two men impassively, and finally the head moved, glancing away to the horizon and then back again.

"Only two of you." The voice was rough and smoky.

"Hello, Kevin," said Leone. "We need to talk."

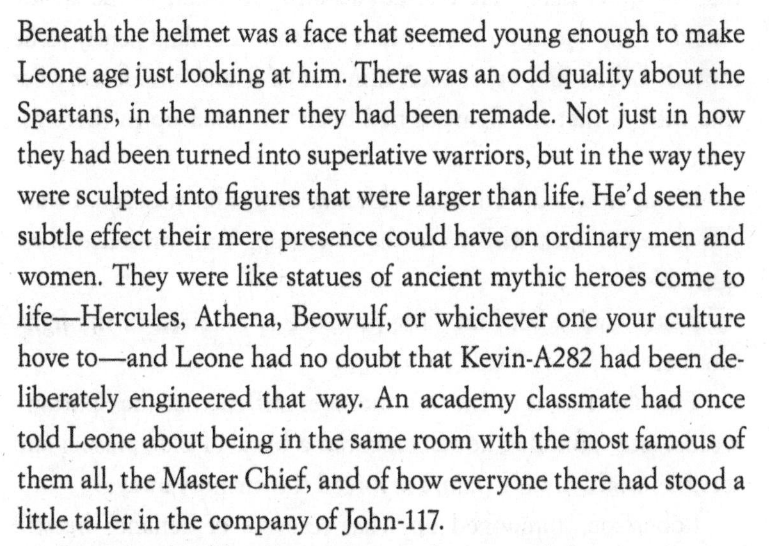

Beneath the helmet was a face that seemed young enough to make Leone age just looking at him. There was an odd quality about the Spartans, in the manner they had been remade. Not just in how they had been turned into superlative warriors, but in the way they were sculpted into figures that were larger than life. He'd seen the subtle effect their mere presence could have on ordinary men and women. They were like statues of ancient mythic heroes come to life—Hercules, Athena, Beowulf, or whichever one your culture hove to—and Leone had no doubt that Kevin-A282 had been deliberately engineered that way. An academy classmate had once told Leone about being in the same room with the most famous of them all, the Master Chief, and of how everyone there had stood a little taller in the company of John-117.

But what he felt now—meeting the gaze of the taciturn, unblinking Spartan—was *doubt.* Even with his scars, Kevin's face was that of a young man, but his eyes were old and distant. Leone couldn't help but wonder what he had seen, and was glad that he didn't know.

"What are you doing out here?" Robertson asked the question that had been pressing on them both.

"Keeping watch," said the Spartan. He had an SRS99 sniper rifle mag-locked across his back-plate, and Leone didn't doubt that he would be able to use it effectively, even at the most extreme of ranges.

"That's not an answer," said the captain. "You left your post."

He shook his head. "Negative, sir. Just relocated it."

Robertson scowled at the reply and shot Leone a look but said nothing. After a moment, the captain went on. "You took it upon yourself to do that. Ignored the recall we put out."

"I don't answer to you." The Spartan looked away. "And I like the quiet here." He paused, seeming to listen to the steady sound of the waves on the shore. His armor creaked gently as he moved. Leone had never seen him out of it and wondered what that meant, that the Spartan had been buttoned up in there for months.

Leone frowned. "I'm here with new orders for you, son. I want you to come back with us to the township. Your presence is required."

Kevin glanced at him. "My presence is required in the fight. Not here."

The old wound in Leone's shoulder stiffened at the Spartan's words, and unbidden he remembered a blaze of blue plasma and terrible, world-ending pain. He forced the memory away.

Robertson summoned up what reserves of defiance he still had. "He's not interested in helping us, sir. He's a burnout—"

He barely had the last word out of his mouth before Kevin took a warning step toward the sergeant, and suddenly Robertson wasn't saying anything. "What was that?" asked Kevin, his tone even.

"Spartan A-282, stand down," Leone warned. Robertson blinked, but Kevin did not back away. The captain's hand dropped to his holstered pistol. "You hear me?"

After a long moment, Kevin turned away, and Robertson released the breath he had been holding in with a gasp.

Kevin turned to look down at Leone's hand resting on the frame of the M6 magnum, and what the captain saw in the warrior's eyes made his blood run cold. *Contained, coiled violence.*

He swallowed and pressed on. "I gave you a direct order. Don't make me arrest you."

"That's not going to happen," said the Spartan, after a moment. It wasn't a threat, simply a matter of fact. "You don't want me to help you handle things in trawler-town. That isn't what I'm built for."

"Not that." Leone took a breath and told him about the signal and the Covenant ship. While he spoke, Kevin stood silently, absorbing it all. When Leone was done, the Spartan shook his head again.

"Elites come in quiet, kill you before you know it. Could be Jackals up there, maybe. Those Kig-Yar bastards are tricky."

"My crew isn't battle-tested," said Leone. "A few of us have seen action, but not like you. We need you with us. Not just to fight, but to *unite.* The locals won't listen to me, and if it turns out we do have an attack on our hands . . ." He trailed off. Belatedly, Leone realized he still had his hand on the gun and he let it drop. "I know it isn't fear talking," said the captain. "What's holding you back, Spartan?"

Kevin unlimbered the long sniper rifle and aimed it out to sea. "Spartans don't fear enemy contact," he said, as if the idea itself was foolish. "We *want* it. I wait and watch. Imagine the sky turning black with Phantoms, like it did on Reach." He paused. "It's what I was made for. What *all* Spartans are made for."

Kevin's A-numeral designation meant he was Alpha Company, one of the longest-serving SPARTAN-III units, and Leone knew that meant he had seen some of the worst of the war with the Covenant, on colonies like Kholo and Meridian, even on Sigma Octanus IV not long ago. He thought about the cold terror his own memories of conflict dredged up, and once more he was glad he didn't have to share the Spartan's.

"You know what it is we do, captain." The Spartan shot a last glance over his shoulder at Leone, then donned the helmet, shutting off the sight of anything that made him seem human. "We are not delicate weapons. Put us in the field and things get broken." He started walking away. "Believe me when I tell you. . . . You don't want me close."

Night fell quickly on Losing Hand, and Leone toggled the Warthog's high beams to illuminate the trail in front of them through a veil of needle-fine rain. Robertson didn't talk for a long while, but when he did, there was venom in it.

"So much for the hero," began the sergeant, raising his voice over the rumble of the engine. "Looks like we're on our own from here."

"Kevin made his choice," said Leone.

"Begging your pardon, Captain—you could have forced him."

Leone caught the other man's eye in the reflection on the inside of the windshield. "You think so?" He snorted. "Kevin's no good to us unless he's on his own terms."

Robertson grunted with cold amusement. "With all due respect, sir, you really think we're going to handle the Covies without his backup?"

Leone looked away. "Those aliens up there—even if it *is* them—are not our first concern, Sergeant," he told him. "The locals are. You were at the town meeting; you've been on this damn rock for as long as anyone else, so you tell me! Ever since planetfall, we've been on the ragged edge with these people, and now someone's going to go over. We don't deal with this, and there won't need to be an attack. . . . We'll kill each other first."

Robertson eyed him. "Those colonists like playing all that salt-of-the-earth, lone-pioneer crap. But if you'll allow me to say, sir, these Losers think this planet is the whole universe. They're too busy arguing over who gets to be in charge of it to notice anyone sneaking up behind them." He leaned back in his seat. "If it were up to me? I'd declare martial law right here and now."

Leone frowned. He had to admit Robertson's evaluation of the fishers was close to his own, but the sergeant's solution to dealing with them was a fast track to armed revolt. The captain pulled a gloved hand over his face, trying to rub away the fatigue weighing him down.

How the hell am I going to deal with this?

But then the radio crackled, heavy with renewed flare static, and the liberty of giving that question a thorough consideration evaporated.

"*Ship to CO, respond!*" Maher's voice was urgent.

Leone tapped his comm bead. "CO copies."

"*Sir, we have a serious problem. The unknown craft has increased its delta-vee. It's going to be here* tonight."

The Warthog skidded to a halt in the cargo bay, its rain-slick tires spinning on the metal deck. Outside, the downpour increased, throwing haze off the floodlights that illuminated the landing strip.

Leone vaulted out to find Maher marching toward him. The junior officer's usually impeccable appearance was rough around the edges, his eyes haunted. "Report," ordered the captain.

Maher took a breath, then said: "The solar flares have been increasing since the afternoon, and we kept losing the feed from the orbital drone. Something seemed off. . . ." He frowned, running a hand through his hair. "I had the techs pull what they could from the data, and it was confirmed. The intruder ship put on a burst of velocity."

At his side, Leone heard Robertson curse under his breath. "Where is it now, Lieutenant?"

"Unknown. The drone's gone dark, probably cycled into shutdown mode to weather the flares. The ship's sensors are scanning the horizon, but we've got nothing."

Silence fell between them, the hissing of the rain the only sound in the bay. Leone knew the crew was waiting for him to make the next decision. *But we don't have all the answers,* said a voice in his head. *Did that alien ship speed up to avoid the flares, or are they using them as cover?*

And then something else occurred to him, just as Corporal Douglas came sprinting into the bay, her sodden parka trailing streamers of rainwater. "Sir! Coming up the road from the town—we've got twenty-plus foot mobiles, and a bunch of them are armed."

"The fishers?" said Robertson.

Douglas nodded. "Captain, they look really pissed off."

"What the drone sees, we all see," said Maher, recalling what Leone had said when he granted the colonists use of the satellite link.

Leone drew his coat tighter around his shoulders and walked back toward the open cargo hatch. "I'm going out there. I'll talk to them." Robertson hefted his MA5 rifle and took a step after him, but Leone held up a hand. "*Alone.*"

"That's a bad call," insisted the sergeant. "Let me get some men, sir. Farrant and Channell, a couple of the others. They won't hesitate if it comes to taking a shot."

The noncoms had never really shown much respect for Leone as their commander, and maybe that came from circumstance. Before the war started, before Losing Hand, Darren Leone had been biding his time as *Dark Was the Night*'s helmsman, marking out the months until the end of his last tour. He knew what the others on board thought of him; that he was a makeweight officer running down the clock before he cashed out, only held over because of the war with the Covenant.

But circumstance had thrust him into this situation, made him captain of a ship by nature of the chain of command, given him responsibilities he had never wanted. In that moment, he felt like he was carrying the entire weight of the vessel on his back.

Leone straightened and gave Robertson a hard glare. "Your input is noted, *Sergeant*," he told him firmly, putting hard emphasis on the rank. "You will hold here. That's an order." The captain marched out into the rain, not pausing to see if he was being obeyed.

There were a lot more than twenty, Leone realized. Low-trucks and ATVs arrived with the crowd of colonists, forming them into a loose cluster of hooded shapes in heavy coats and waterproof overalls.

Leone counted several firearms, mostly pump-action shotguns and hunting rifles, but alarmingly he spotted a couple of Covenant plasma pistols in some hands and found himself wondering how alien war salvage had found its way to this backwater world. He kept his hands at his sides, letting his parka's hood flap back to show his face. "That's close enough," he called as they approached the edge of the landing apron.

He didn't need to guess who was leading them. "You don't tell us what to do, Leone." Ryan Larsson had a shotgun of his own, a long and nasty-looking weapon. "You mind your damn job, man!"

"That's been my deal since day one," he replied, catching sight of Aoife standing close by. She was unarmed, and Leone saw his own fears reflected in her face.

"You tell us why those cannons ain't up and runnin'!" came a shout—the old woman from the town meeting pushing forward so she could be heard. She jabbed a finger toward the turrets on *Dark Was the Night*'s dorsal hull, all of them drooping downward to aim at nothing. "Fire 'em up!"

"*Fire up! Fire up!*" Her words sparked off a brief chorus of heated chants from Larsson's supporters.

"Babs here makes a good point," Larsson snapped. "What are you waiting for, *Captain*? Or do we have to defend ourselves?" He gestured with the shotgun. "All your talk about the UNSC and your responsibility to us, but that Covie warship is on its way, and what are you?" He spat on the concrete. "Asleep at the switch?"

"You need to go back to your homes and stay there," Leone told them. "Until we know what the situation is—"

"Situation?!" shouted another voice. "We saw the drone feed—it's an invasion!"

Larsson nodded toward the ship. "Your own men agree with me, Leone. You know it, and I know it!"

More voices joined in, each one raised in anger, and every cry was backed by the sure belief that war had come to Losing Hand. Nothing Leone could say would sway them—he saw that now.

His only hope was to tell the truth.

"The guns won't fire."

"*What?*" Larsson blinked and wiped rain from his face, as if that would make the captain's words add up. "What the hell do you mean?"

"The point-defense weapons were dead before we landed on this planet," Leone went on, spilling it all. "Our defensive and offensive systems were knocked out when the ship's main circuit bus was fried. We barely classed as combat-capable when we were at full kick. Right now . . . we've got nothing."

Larsson's face turned an ugly shade of crimson. "You're a lying sack of dregs, is what you are." The terror and the panic the man had been keeping in check under the cloak of his rage threatened to break through. "So make them work, then!" he bellowed. "We need them!"

"My chief engineer has been trying to do that for months. It's not going to happen."

"You *liar*!" Larsson roared at him. "Did you pull the plug on those guns yourself, you damn coward?" The accusation spread through the crowd, all of them finding a sudden new reason to hate Leone and the uniform he wore. They didn't need any truth to push them to it.

"Oh gods . . ." Aoife went pale as the reality of it set in.

Leone drew in a deep breath of wet air and called out, his voice carrying across the landing field. "Go back, all of you! *We* are going to meet this! That's why we're here—that's what we do!"

"This is our home," said Aoife. "We can't just stand aside and do nothing."

"You stay and it'll end in bloodshed," Leone told her. "We both know that."

She understood—but she was only one person, and her brother's fury was drowning her out.

"I told you before," Larsson snarled, advancing on him, "you don't tell us *what to do*!"

The black maw of the shotgun barrel came up toward Leone's face and he flinched, staggering back a step. He twisted, seeing figures in green spilling out of the transport, soldiers led by Robertson, with rifles in their hands. Behind Larsson and his sister, the colonists raised their own weapons, safety catches rattling as they were loosed.

"No! *No!*" Leóne brought up his hands, calling toward his crew. "Stand down! Back off and stand down!"

There hadn't been a true war fought between humans since the Covenant had invaded, not since the shadow of the Insurrection lay over the galaxy—but no one had forgotten.

Robertson hesitated, and for a moment Leone thought he would ignore the order; but then the UNSC troopers pulled back from the edge and the muzzles of their rifles dipped toward the ground.

"Larsson . . . *Ryan.*" Leone met the other man's gaze. "You have to trust me. Whoever they are, they're coming here, and we can't stop that. But if we do this wrong, *everyone dies.*"

"Listen to him!" shouted Aoife.

"Leone . . ." Larsson drew out his name in a low growl. "You're old and you're weak."

The shotgun spun in the younger man's grip, and the butt of the weapon came around in a blur of motion, cracking the captain across the face.

The world spun about, and Leone crumpled to the ground,

cold asphalt slamming into him. He blinked away pain and looked up to see the gun filling his vision.

"And you're in the way," said Larsson, his finger on the trigger.

The echo of the single shot cut through the rain like a clap of thunder, and in its wake, time seemed to slow, the moment pulling against itself.

The gun in Larsson's hand shattered halfway down its length, hammered into pieces by the pinpoint impact of an armor-piercing round fired from a quarter mile away. Larsson howled in pain, stumbling back as he frantically brushed fragments of red-hot metal from his coat.

Leone stared at the broken stub of the weapon as it lay sizzling on the wet asphalt before him, and then rose slowly to his feet. He instinctively turned in the direction of the gunshot and saw a towering figure jog into the nimbus of light from the overhead floods.

The Spartan slowed to a walk, cradling the sniper rifle in his hands, and Leone remembered an image he had once seen in a museum of a medieval knight carrying a lance. A blue armored gauntlet worked the rifle's slide, and a brass shell spun out of the breech before the weapon went up over Kevin-A282's shoulder and onto his back.

He followed us, Leone realized. *He changed his mind. . . . Must have run all the way here. . . .*

The expressionless gold visor scanned the faces of the colonists in the crowd. "You all want to think very carefully about what you do next," he told them. The Spartan halted next to Leone and looked him up and down, taking the captain in with a glance and seeing he was uninjured. "Reporting for duty, sir."

Larsson was in worse shape, however. Blood streamed off his hand, and his face was twisted. "You see this?!" he shouted, looking wildly at his comrades. He was searching for support and didn't find it. Aoife shook her head, but he didn't acknowledge her. A smarter man—a man ruled more by his hopes than his fears—might have backed off, but Ryan Larsson took the other road and went all in. "We don't obey, so they bring in the attack dog!"

"If you're ready to fight," said the Spartan, "make sure you got the right target." He nodded at Leone. "That's not your enemy." He moved to Larsson, towering over him, and prodded him in the chest with one ironclad finger, right above the heart. "What's in here is. *What you're afraid of.*"

"Ryan, we can't fight each other," his sister broke in. "This isn't about who is in charge—it's about survival!"

"She's right," Leone said, between heavy breaths. He caught a crackle of radio static in his ear, but his comm bead had been damaged by the blow from the butt of the shotgun, and the voice beneath the interference was unintelligible.

"You heard the captain," said the Spartan, looking past the defeated expression that ghosted over Larsson's face, toward the other colonists. "Go back to your homes and—"

Above them, the low cowl of oily gray cloud suddenly turned white, as if sheet lightning had exploded behind it. A powerful gust of wind battered down, and the clouds were pushed apart like an opening iris, projected away by the invisible force of gravity-control technology.

"Too late," said Aoife, the words falling from her lips as they all turned to look into the night sky.

The alien ship had that same cetacean aspect to it that seemed to characterize all of the Covenant's vessels. Smooth-skinned and curved where human craft were hard-edged and angular, the corvette looked like it should have been undulating through some deep ocean current rather than floating down toward the landing strip. The rain stopped, the clouds temporarily displaced by the vessel's arrival, but the iridescent shell still glistened like annealed steel.

Half the size of a habitat block, it had about the same mass as *Dark Was the Night*, but it was still big enough to contain dropships and fighters, or a full battle cohort of alien warriors.

The air throbbed with power as the craft pivoted and settled into a low hover a few meters above the ground. The sound faded back to a low, menacing purr.

Robertson and the rest of the UNSC troopers formed a skirmish line, and Leone took a step toward them—but the Spartan put out a hand and stopped him before he could move away.

"Moment of truth," he said.

All the raw panic, all the fears that Leone had locked away in the back of his mind now came flooding into him as a single certainty became clear. *Whatever happens now, this is on me. I'm responsible for these people—all of them.*

If this was an attack, then nobody on Losing Hand would survive to see the break of dawn. The fate of these people and *Dark Was the Night* would be lost to the ether, and it would be on his watch. Above, the clouds rolled back and the rain returned in force.

"There," said the Spartan, and he pointed toward the flank of the vessel. A line of neon-blue appeared in a seam of the hull, and presently it enlarged to become a doorway. The ship extruded a ramp to the ground, and shadows within grew larger.

One of them stepped out into the downpour and took its first step onto the surface of Losing Hand. Leone met the gaze of the alien creature, and his breath caught in his throat. He had to stop himself from drawing his M6 through sheer ingrained reflex as the emerald-armored Sangheili craned its long neck around to take them in.

It marched forward, kneading the inert hilt of a plasma sword in its talon-like fingers. The alien's quadripartite jaws flexed as it sucked in a breath and exhaled. The Elite's gaze found Leone and the Larssons, barely giving them a look before settling on the Spartan. Its lips curled in what could only be a sneer.

But other shapes were moving behind it. Next out of the ship came a peculiar life-form that floated above the ground, trailing thin cilia beneath it. A single, serpentine head bobbed on a long neck, its attention drawn directly to the UNSC transport.

"What in the storms is that?" whispered Aoife. "Looks like a bag of snakes tied to a balloon. . . ."

"It's a Huragok," Leone told her. "The Covenant call them 'Engineers.' They can pretty much fix anything, so I've heard."

The third figure to leave the alien ship was a human. Wearing UNSC battle armor, the muscular man had pale features and a shock of short ginger hair. He gave the Sangheili a sideways look and the alien nodded to him, stepping aside to let him speak. "Who's in charge here?"

Leone glanced at the Larssons. "Well, come on, then. Just don't do anything stupid."

Ryan and Aoife warily fell in step with Leone and the Spartan as they came forward.

He gave a salute. "Captain Darren Leone, acting CO of UNSC *Dark Was the Night*." He introduced Kevin-A282 and the colonists, and now that he was up close, Leone studied the new arrivals for some clue as to just what in the hell was going on here.

The other officer returned the salute. "Major Kyle Stallock, out of the Nouveau Montreal colony." He indicated the Sangheili and the Huragok in turn. "This is Yar 'Dosaan, and our engineer friend there is Slight List. We're real glad to find you here."

"We believed this star system to be barren," said the Elite, the words a crush of growls and hard sibilant noises. Leone couldn't hide his shock; he'd never heard one of them speak a human language before. "It is only on the Engineer's insistence that we decided to survey it."

"Oh . . ." Despite herself, Aoife grinned as the Huragok drifted toward her and extended a tendril-like feeler to meet the woman's outstretched hand. "Should we say thank you?"

"Should we?" echoed her brother, the last remnants of his resentment and dread still boiling away beneath the surface of the words. The clear challenge in his tone was unmistakable.

Yar 'Dosaan's pale, depthless eyes bored into the colonist, then flicked across Leone and the Spartan, dwelling on their visible weapons. "Do you expect conflict, humans?"

"Always," said the Spartan, before Leone could reply. "But not today. Agreed?"

"Agreed," said the alien, and at length he returned the inert sword to his belt.

"You're the first human survivors we've come across in months." A weary smile crossed Major Stallock's face. "We needed a win."

"Is that so?" Leone was still having trouble understanding how these three disparate life forms could be standing side by side without daggers drawn.

Stallock gave a nod and sighed. "I imagine you've got a lot of questions."

"Nothing about this is what I expected," said Aoife, as she offered Leone the hip flask.

He accepted it gratefully and took a long pull. He was getting a taste for the warm, hazy burn of the local liquor. "Roger that," he replied.

The Covenant ship—or rather, the ex-Covenant light corvette *Infinite Fire*, recently rechristened *The Lookout*—was making final preparations to lift off, and a rare clear sky had blown in from the ocean. Leone watched the train of figures moving back and forth between the grounded bulk of *Dark Was the Night* and the train of low-trucks carrying gear down the road back into town. Over the past two weeks, with the help of Slight List and the other members of *The Lookout*'s disparate company, the UNSC ship had been gutted of everything useful that could be split between the colonists and the alliance crew.

When *The Lookout* left, *Dark Was the Night* would become Losing Hand's power station, and its career as a starfaring vessel would officially be over. Leone felt a sting of regret at that, but there was something good about it too. The ship would never know vacuum again, but it would go on serving, keeping people alive and safe. Most of the crew had accepted Major Stallock's offer of evacuation, but not all of them. A handful of the colonists had also taken the ticket, but the number was a lot less than Leone had expected.

He asked Aoife why she had turned it down, and she just smiled. "Someone's got to keep Ryan from running his mouth." She took back the flask and had a drink herself. "I never thought it would be possible to see aliens working alongside us."

"Yeah . . ." Leone saw the Spartan talking with Robertson. He couldn't hear the words, but whatever Kevin-A282 said, it caused the sergeant to snap out the most perfect salute he'd ever seen the man give. "I guess the truth makes enemies into allies."

The woman shivered. "What Stallock said, about the war . . . It's over, right?"

"Officially, yes. But out here in the real world?" Leone let the question hang.

In the days after *The Lookout*'s arrival, Major Stallock briefed them on the events of the war that had played out far from Losing Hand. The Elites had broken with the Covenant, turning on their former allies, and while humanity had survived the conflict, the face of the galaxy had been irrevocably altered. Without the Sangheili, the remainder of the Covenant factions had splintered, and now new alliances and new threats alike were on the rise.

Stallock's home base on Nouveau Montreal was light-years distant, and in the aftermath of the Covenant War, the UNSC had forged a steady alliance with the Sangheili to monitor that region. Their ship was crewed not just by Stallock's people and Yar 'Dosaan's, but there were Unggoy on board as well, along with other humans from worlds they had visited along the way. Their mission was to go from system to system, trying to reestablish communication with colonies cut off by the conflict.

Aoife indicated the Spartan, and the question that had been clouding the air between them finally emerged. "Are you going with him?"

"Kevin told me this morning." Leone avoided a reply. "He's going with *The Lookout.* He wants to feel useful again."

"Stallock said they could take us all if we wanted," she told him. "But this is our home. We didn't run from the Covenant. We're not going to now."

Leone made a *pass-it-here* gesture, and she dropped the flask back into his open hand.

"Me neither," he said, after another drink. "I signed up to protect people. Losing Hand needs that. I'm staying on . . . at least until things are quiet again."

Aoife eyed him. "That might not be for a while."

"You're right." He got to his feet and saw the Spartan look his way. Kevin's armored helm dipped once in a respectful nod, and the captain returned the gesture. "But the way I figure it, some people go their whole lives not knowing where they can do the most good."

"You think that's here?" She had a smile in her voice, and he liked it.

Leone patted his breast pocket and nodded. "I reckon I'll need a badge though."

PROMISES TO KEEP

CHRISTIE GOLDEN

This story takes place at the close of recorded Forerunner history, during the events that followed the destruction of the Forerunner capital world by the rogue artificial intelligence Mendicant Bias (Halo: Cryptum) *and the subsequent activation of the Halo Array to end the centuries-long war with the extragalactic parasite known as the Flood* (Halo: Silentium).

It's almost over, the IsoDidact thought.

Their ship, *Audacity*, had negotiated the dangerous jump successfully. The Librarian, his wife, exhaled quietly as she recognized several Lifeworker vessels clustered around one of the Ark's petal-like structures. They were swiftly and efficiently transporting containers of living specimens from their vessels to the Ark's Lifeworker research station.

"Wonderful!" she cried, in that warm, slightly husky voice he so adored. "They've all survived!"

The IsoDidact was glad for her, but the emotion was overshadowed by a chill of foreboding as he realized just how many Forerunner ships had gathered here—and how badly some of them had been damaged.

Audacity confirmed his fears. "All remaining Forerunners

have been brought here," it said. "The last themas have been overwhelmed. There will be no other ships."

The Librarian's eyes widened with horror and she looked to her mate. *Audacity* continued with its implacable mechanical analysis. "As well, some Lifeworker specimens have been moved to the Halo to make room, including human populations."

Horror fled before fury on his wife's beloved features. The humans were hers, and she cared for them. "Who made that decision?" she demanded.

In answer, an image shimmered into being behind them, shocking the two even further.

It was Faber-of-Will-and-Might, known for centuries by his title—the Master Builder.

He it was who had stood in opposition to the original Didact when the Flood had first been recognized as a threat. Faber had ordered the Halo rings created—and tested one of them. And thus it was that, while the Master Builder had been responsible for designing a cataclysmic weapon, he had also inadvertently been responsible for the Ark's creation. The threat posed to every sentient creature—not just the Flood—had prompted the Librarian to push for measures to preserve specimens, so that countless species would not be lost in the extinction of one.

His holographic representation was nearly unrecognizable. Once large and healthy, ripe with smug arrogance, he now looked smaller, frailer, his eyes dull and his posture stooped.

"Welcome to our Ark, Lifeshaper," the Master Builder said. "Didact—which do I address? Ah, the younger. It is my honor to have returned your original to the company of your wife—and, if memory serves me, it looks as though he too has arrived. You both should be aware that I have been summoned to help prepare our Ark for the coming storm. And to transfer command."

"To whom?" the IsoDidact asked, his body tense.

"To me. Builder Security will carry on from here."

As if they had not had enough shocks. It did not seem so long ago that the Master Builder had been on trial in the ecumene's capital world of Maethrillian for his crimes against the Mantle of Responsibility. Had not the capital come under attack, conviction would have been certain.

Nothing, it would seem, was certain anymore.

The Librarian recovered first. "I will be taken as soon as possible to the Halo to tend to my specimens. *Alone.*"

"Of course," the Master Builder replied. "I have already made arrangements—"

"I'm sorry to interrupt." It was the IsoDidact's ancilla, her pale-blue face looking at him regretfully. "But Chant-to-Green has completed her final assessments. You asked to be notified."

"I did indeed," the IsoDidact replied.

The appearance of his ancilla had caused the simulation transpiring around him to freeze. If only he could have paused time then, when it was all occurring. If only he could have found some way to have prevented . . . all of it.

But he, Bornstellar-Makes-Eternal-Lasting—the IsoDidact, widowed when another's lifemate had died—had not been able to do so. And so, the Librarian was lost, choosing to spend her last moments in service to the humans she so loved.

Bornstellar rose from the chair, and it retreated back into the flooring. For a moment, he regarded the holographic images of himself and his wife, standing beside him. They appeared so very real, but were only as substantial now as the projection of the Master Builder had been substantial then. There would be other words between the couple, but hasty, brief. Curt, almost, but only so due to their own tension. Their harshness was not directed at each other. Then, those words exchanged, the IsoDidact would meet with the Master Builder and a handful of others in the Cartographer, and she, the Librarian, First-Light-Weaves-Living-Song, would depart for the Halo, and then *Audacity*, and then . . .

Those words were seared into memory; banal, serviceable words that were solely logistics and hurried well-wishes.

I did not know they would be the last.

"It is hard to believe that they are the last," said Growth-Through-Trial-of-Change. Her voice held a tinge of sorrow, even as the words denoted success in an ambitious and worthy endeavor. Trial, as she preferred to go by, was both the oldest and the youngest Lifeworker. Her years numbered more than those of Chant-to-Green, the current Lifeshaper. But Trial had not been born into that rate. She had been a Builder, and when she had informed her family of the pull within her to change rates, they had turned away. Her new family of Lifeworkers had given her a new name—one that had honored her path. Life, she had said more than once to Chant, was nothing but trials. And what mattered, perhaps even more than the outcome, was how one faced them.

"It *is* strange," Chant said. The two stood observing the room where the last "specimens" were slowly reviving, closely watching both their statistics and their hitherto-hibernating forms. "We have bracketed this experience with two species who were once allies in a war fought against us. The humans and the San'Shyuum."

The irony suited her. The choice to reestablish humans first had been deliberate; the choice to leave the San'Shyuum to the last, simple logistics.

For most of her many centuries, the Librarian, in her position as Lifeshaper, had collected and cataloged creatures from all across the galaxy. Lifeworkers alone had supervised their care. But when Bornstellar had authorized the activation of Halo, wiping out all sentient life in order to truly destroy the threat of the Flood, the Librarian had been among the casualties. Now, every surviving Forerunner—their numbers so few compared to the trillions that had once composed the ecumene—had spent over a century discharging the duty the Lifeshaper had laid upon them. Those who had made the dreadful choice to end sentient life for a time rather than forever had a duty to make what reparations they could, and these solemn yet joyful tasks had kept their minds, hands, and specialized vessels well occupied as they tended, then released, species after species.

The San'Shyuum would be the last to set careful feet upon the world that had given them birth.

Bornstellar joined the two Lifeworkers, gazing as they did upon the slow awakening unfolding. Trial excused herself and went inside so that the San'Shyuum would not be alone when they opened their eyes.

"In the midst of all the mistakes, and arrogance, and sheer stupidity of these last centuries," Bornstellar said, "we have, at least, done right by her."

Chant looked up at him, knowing full well whom he meant. "Yes. She would be pleased with us. The end of our task draws near."

After the death of the Librarian, the reseeding of Erde-Tyrene, and the judgment of Mendicant Bias, the wound of her absence had still been new for both of them. The IsoDidact had received the imprint of the Didact, who had lived over ten thousand years, but Bornstellar was still chronologically young. As was Chant-to-Green, although she had served the Librarian for many decades.

She suspected the older female thought of her as a daughter, at least somewhat; she certainly responded to the Librarian as to a mother.

At the end, the Librarian had given Chant the title of Lifeshaper and ordered her to carry on the mission. Obeying that order—to leave the Librarian behind on Erde-Tyrene to certain death—still held the taint of betrayal in Chant's mind.

She was the Lifeshaper now. But no one would ever be the Librarian.

Bornstellar had lost a mate. For all intents and purposes, though not physically the spouse the Librarian had first embraced, they were true husband and wife. The original Didact had been driven mad by the Master Builder's calculated cruelty, and the Librarian had been forced to safely imprison him in a Cryptum. There, alone for millennia with the Domain to teach him, her great hope was that he would one day understand—and regret—how gravely he had wronged so very many.

They were therefore both bereft, Bornstellar and Chant. And, because she saw in him a good and true heart that loved the same individual she herself grieved, and because he saw in her an echo of his great love, they had consoled each other with the union of their bodies. But soon enough, they understood what had drawn them together, and that it would not last beyond the first few passionate encounters. Chant was *not* the Librarian, and there were better ways to honor her memory and to keep their promises than by pretending she was not gone.

So they had mourned, each in their own way. Chant found that the more she helped the "specimens" (as time passed, she learned to loathe the name; "children" was better), the more the ache eased. It became an old scar that hurt when the weather changed, rather than a fierce, stabbing agony that kept her awake at night when not dulled by the soothing drug of sexual heat.

Bornstellar was, Chant suspected, doing something himself to heal the tug of memories, for as the centuries passed, he seemed more at ease. While all Forerunners interacted with the specimens, mindful of this last discharging of the Mantle, they did so without the intimacy, the same sense of connection to the former Lifeshaper's work, that Chance and Bornstellar experienced.

The others liked the specimens; they did not love them.

"Soon it will be time to reseed Forerunners," Bornstellar now said.

The idea had been his, established early on. They had meddled enough, their misguided appropriation of the Mantle hurting more than it helped. Bornstellar's had been the voice that had given the order to fire the Halo Array and kill all sentient life in the galaxy. Chant's was the hand that helped to make it fruitful again.

"Do you know where yet?" she inquired.

He shook his head. All agreed on the general principle—that, when the reseeding had been completed, they would depart the galaxy forever—but there had been so much work right in front of them, immediate and vital, that their attention had been focused exclusively on that. They still had a few years to decide, while they integrated the San'Shyuum, but it was now their next step, not some nebulous ideal.

"Away from here, is all I know. We all must be in agreement." He nodded toward Trial, who was assisting one of the San'Shyuum to sit while his head, perched atop his elongated neck, turned this way and that as he peered about. "I am weary of making decisions that impact those who have no voice."

"You chide me?" Chant asked. Not angry, just curious.

He looked at her then, kindly, and smiled. Both he—and Chant—had begun adopting the practice during their times with the humans. The former First Councilor of the Forerunner

Council—Splendid-Dust-of-Ancient-Suns—along with others from Maethrillian, were already quite comfortable with the gesture. Over time, almost all of the remaining Forerunners now regularly utilized what they had once thought of as a rictus.

"Never," he said. "You do *her* work."

I do, Chant thought, *but for a hundred years and more, it has been* my *work.* Our *work. All of ours.*

She could not say why his comment so irritated her.

For as long as it would take for the San'Shyuum to adjust, they would be kept here, on the Ark, in the best re-creation of their temperate homeworld as the Lifeworkers could manage. The Forerunners learned more each time, with each species, how to increase the accuracy of the world, but it was never quite right. The species knew their homes, with a deep wisdom that their saviors could never possess.

After the species' initial shock dulled, the Forerunners would create an area for themselves, set apart from the main inhabited areas, and they did so now for the last time. Here, the San'Shyuum could locate them if need be, and here they could easily supervise without directly mingling. The Forerunners had discovered that, every time, some few individuals would find them particularly intriguing and create ways to be nearby or even actively involved with them. While this was not discouraged, boundaries were enforced with the gentleness of a concerned parent. Even so, the Forerunners were aware that their words might be overheard. But what, really, did it matter, as long as they treated their charges with care? It would be millennia before any of them would again find their own paths to the stars. Words spoken here would be forgotten in a handful of decades, if they resonated even for that long.

Only twenty or so Forerunners would be stationed here, keeping watch over the San'Shyuum. While the Librarian had destroyed all active keyships, she had kept a hidden cache aboard the Ark. These few vessels now ferried the last handful of other specimens to their homeworlds, and would return to the Ark when that task was done. Then . . .

Then the Forerunners would leave the Ark and begin their own journey.

The acclimation continued over the next two years. Bornstellar found himself adrift during this time. For so long, reliving his experiences with the Librarian, it had been a pattern, a comforting routine. At some point, the pain had lessened, changed, as the relationship with her had changed, from one of flesh to one of memory. Even as he accepted the loss on one level, Bornstellar now realized the holograms had blurred the line between life and death so that the cessation of them was agonizing.

One evening, he returned to his own quarters, drawn by an uneasy, anxious emotion he could not name. He called up the recorded moments, sorting through them. He tried to do as he had done before: lose himself in the memories to forget she was gone. But it did not work; not this time. His anxiety increased with each attempt, and comprehension hit him with the psychological force of a physical blow.

The last recording he had visited had been, in truth, the *very last*. He understood that in his head, but now his heart belatedly grasped the full import of the loss. He never exchanged another touch, embrace, word, glance with his wife. Centuries had passed. He was caught in a terrible place—unable to move forward, unable to even momentarily assuage the pain by reliving the memories. Why? Maybe it was because he had already experienced them not once, when they were happening, but twice now. A third time seemed only to make the ache inside him worse. If only there was some recording of something he had not seen before, but there was not.

Or was there? A thought drifted into his mind, something he had all but forgotten. After she had . . . after the Halo Array had been fired, he had received a jumble of other messages. One had purportedly been from the Librarian, but he had dismissed it as false, as she would never identify herself thusly to him.

But what if, all these centuries later, it was indeed a final message for him?

It took his ancilla barely any time at all to locate the message, but it felt like an eternity. Bornstellar had not felt so nervous or hopeful since he was a Manipular. Words from her lips he had never heard—it was too much to contemplate.

But there it was.

Her essence manifested in front of him, so detailed he could almost feel her smooth skin, smell her scent.

His wife. First-Light-Weaves-Living-Song.

The Librarian.

Her eyes were bright with commingled grief, fear, and purpose. "My husband," she said, "time is short. But there is something you must know."

Seven minutes later, he was all but shouting for Chant.

It was easier, watching it for the second time. He focused not on the image of the Librarian but on her words and Chant's reaction. Chant, who had loved the Librarian almost as much as he had, who had worked unceasingly to keep whatever promises his wife had extracted from her.

"This is for Chant-to-Green as well," the image was saying. "I know what you, my husband, must do, and you know I agree. Halo *must* be activated. But nothing is without consequence, and I understand now there will be one we have not foreseen." The Librarian took a deep breath. "The legendary Organon—the great Precursor artifact that you once sought with such sharp desire . . . my love, it has been with us all along. The Organon *holds* the Domain—and firing the Halo Array will destroy it."

Chant uttered a soft cry, reaching out to Bornstellar even as her gaze remained riveted to the image of the Librarian. He squeezed her hand tightly, as glad of the press of living flesh as she.

The Librarian's voice was thick with pain as she continued. "The Didact dreams now not with wisdom whispering in his ears but silence, utter and absolute. He is already mad, and it was my hope—and yours—that the Domain might restore him. But imprisoned with only his own tormented thoughts for millennia to come . . ." Her voice trailed off, and she shook her head gently. She didn't need to say anything further. They already knew.

"It is for those who come that I fear. The humans—the Reclaimers—will need the Domain one day. I cannot—I *will not*—die without hope that there is some way to repair it. If there is, I believe that information will be found at Maethrillian. We understand the keeping of secrets, we Forerunners, and next to the knowledge of the Flood, this would have been the greatest secret of all."

Her eyes gazed steadily at Catalog, who had dutifully recorded and transmitted the message, but as he and Chant stood mutely clasping hands, Bornstellar knew that his wife was envisioning gazing at both of them. "I charged the two of you with reseeding the sentient species I have tended most of my life. I must exact another promise. You must return to our capital, if anything remains of it. Find a way to reactivate the Domain."

Her dark gaze—intense, warm, filled with love not just for those who beheld her but also for those she had given everything for—almost overwhelmed Bornstellar. "Find it. Promise me! Or I fear that all we have done to try to fix that which we have ruined will crumble to dust."

And she was gone.

Chant and Bornstellar found the group keeping watch on the San'Shyuum outside their structure, enjoying the pleasant artificial evening. Trial, Splendid Dust, Keeper-of-Stone-Songs, Walking-in-Light-of-Falling-Stars, Sorrow-for-Lost-Voices, Glory-of-a-Far-Dawn, and a handful of other Forerunners of all rates were tossing artificial vegetables and flavoring herbs into small, cheerfully bubbling pots.

"We have not interacted with the Domain in over a century," Stone Songs said when Bornstellar had finished. "And it was erratic and largely unresponsive even before then. We have gone this long without it, and if we are to be departing the galaxy itself soon, then what is the point?"

Chant stood beside Bornstellar and tensed at the words. "This is not about the Domain and what it can do for us," she said, glaring at Stone Songs. She rarely grew angry on her own behalf, but she was fierce when it came to defending her charges. As her predecessor had been.

Trial watched her Lifeshaper intently, concerned. She knew how close the Librarian and Chant had been.

"Yes, we are departing this galaxy, and it will be a long journey indeed. And no, the Domain will not help us. It may not even help the Didact. The *point*"—Chant emphasized the word—"is that repairing the Domain will help the humans, who will one day bear the Mantle as we once did, to carry out their responsibilities. They will need this knowledge, and after all we have done, we owe it to them."

Stone Songs waved his spoon dismissively. "It is a lovely thought, but unless there's something you've not shared with us, Bornstellar, your Librarian failed to tell us how we are to go about repairing the Domain, or what could help us, or where to look for it!"

She was not mine, Bornstellar thought. *Not in this. In this, she belonged to—and acted for—us all.*

Stone Song's words hung heavy in the air and weighed down Bornstellar's thoughts. The Builder was right. *Find a way to reactivate the Domain,* she had made them promise, even from the other side of the great gulf of death. But what were they looking for? And how would they know what to do if they found it?

"We will be traveling to Maethrillian regardless," Bornstellar said, struggling against his anger. "We need the slipstream crystals and the ships that can use them if we are to have any hope of truly leaving the galaxy behind. We can search for a way to repair the Domain while we are there."

"The scope is enormous," Glory-of-a-Far-Dawn said. A Warrior-Servant, she had saved both Bornstellar and Splendid Dust when the battle on the capital had begun. Once Bornstellar had been drawn to her, but that had been when he was still new to his rate. And before he had met the Librarian. He and Glory were nonetheless bonded in battle, and friends.

"We have you to help us," he reminded her, "and we have

someone else who knows . . ." Bornstellar's voice trailed off. They did not, apparently, have someone else who knew the capital world well, for Splendid Dust's seat was empty.

Splendid Dust had not gone far. Bornstellar spotted his fine, slender form leaning up against a vru'sa tree. He was dappled with shadow and sunlight filtered through leaves. He looked up, unsurprised, as Bornstellar approached, and regarded him with dull eyes.

"You know," Bornstellar said.

"Yes," Splendid Dust replied, his voice flat. "I know."

"Tell me."

Splendid reached up to pull the vibrant green of one of the leaves through his fingers, the meeting of Bornstellar's gaze perhaps too much to endure. Bornstellar was as impatient as if his life was as brief as a human's, but he forced himself to wait.

When talk had begun about returning to Maethrillian, Splendid Dust had begged to stay behind. They did not need him to acquire the crystals, he had argued, and it was clear to Bornstellar that the thought of returning to the ruined capital of the once-great ecumene tormented its First Councilor. He had agreed.

He could not comply this time though. Not now.

"We council members were privy to a great deal of information, Bornstellar-Makes-Eternal-Lasting. Many secrets. When Maethrillian fell, our society suffered a loss of knowledge second only to the loss of the Domain itself. I am the last who remembers any of it, and I knew more than almost anyone else."

"Why didn't you speak before?" Fury, clean and sharp and righteous, swelled Bornstellar's heart and turned his words into daggers. He regretted it at once when he saw Splendid Dust's body twitch, as if those daggers had been physical.

"To what end?" Now he did look at Bornstellar, and his eyes were homes for ghosts. "You were there. You saw what madness we fled. We were all trying to *escape* Maethrillian, not *return* to it—until now. We don't know if there's even anything left to return *to*."

"No," Bornstellar said, gentling his own voice. "We do not know what awaits us. But if you know of anything that can help us restore the Domain, you must speak."

Something of his old pride seemed to stir in Splendid Dust. "I will remind you that as First Councilor, I made binding oaths."

"True," agreed Bornstellar. "But your overwhelming duty is to your people. I respect promises, Splendid-Dust-of-Ancient-Suns. But those who would hold you in violation are long dead. If they exist at all, it is as spirits, and if they are spirits, tales all say they wish to rest in peace. You will speak, or you will fail every Forerunner who has ever lived, and every creature my wife died to save. That seems a far greater wrong."

Splendid Dust looked again at the leaf, as if it held all the secrets of the universe in its green-gold veins. "You are right, of course. I must speak," he agreed, a wealth of regret in the words. "And," he added, "I must go with you. You will need what I know."

Splendid Dust was not insane, as the Didact had become. But he was broken. Bornstellar understood.

All of them were a little broken now.

Bornstellar and Splendid Dust rejoined the others. The San'Shyuum had an intoxicant that burned the belly and softened the edges, and Splendid Dust required two mugs full of it before he could bring himself to speak.

What he knew was astounding; and that he knew it to begin with, terrifying.

The former First Councilor spoke of treasures that a younger Bornstellar would have gladly spent a lifetime seeking. Not just a few rare and unimaginably glorious items, but hundreds. Thousands. Gathered from the farthest reaches of Forerunner space and brought to Maethrillian for safekeeping in a place called the Mysterium.

"Some were simply beautiful," he said. "Art for art's sake. Others were . . . trophies. Still others were unique scientific curiosities. All secreted in the Mysterium, in the heart of the capital, all untouched, preserved simply for the having of them, of collecting, of adding to the glory of all it meant to be a Forerunner. Some were aware of what the artifacts did. Most of us were not. All we knew was that they were ours."

"But you knew," Trial said. It was a statement, not an accusation, but Splendid Dust dwindled even further.

"I knew more than most," he said. "My great pride and joy, and my great burden. But I had not been First Councilor for very long when the battle took place. I did not have time to learn everything. Most of my knowledge was to have come from the Domain, and it was unreachable, toward the end. But I knew about this. Oh yes." He turned to Bornstellar and said, "Do you remember what I wore?"

"What?"

"What I wore. The robes of First Councilor. The collar, the decorations."

Bornstellar stared blankly. Splendid Dust smiled, so sadly. "The trappings, IsoDidact. The regalia. I still have it. Those stylized designs had a purpose, and among them is a specific key, of sorts."

"A key to what?" Chant said. She stammered ever so slightly.

"The Deadbolt, they called it," Splendid Dust said, "though perhaps 'they' had no idea, really."

"Deadbolt," echoed Falling Stars. He was of the Engineer rate, and so understood its purpose. "A deadbold *needs* a key—it is not the key. It is put in place to keep something locked safely away."

"In, or out?" mused Stone Songs.

"Key or deadbolt to what?" demanded Sorrow-for-Lost-Voices, a Warrior-Servant.

"Precursor technology. It was transported whole, from the distant world where they found it, to Maethrillian during the capital's construction. The entire planet was built around it. Sources from that era wrote that they found something that . . . helped them understand the Domain, and when rumors began to spread, as was inevitable, the legend of the Organon sprang up."

A Precursor artifact that controlled the Domain. Hidden in the capital city.

Bornstellar almost laughed. He hadn't needed to go to uncomfortable backwater places to seek a mythical artifact.

He'd been standing atop the greatest of them all.

"Prepare the *Audacity*," he said. "We will leave right away."

Bornstellar, Glory, and Splendid Dust had been present when Mendicant Bias had taken over; when the rogue AI had frozen ancillas and fired the Halo weapons at the capital. They and the rest of *Audacity*'s current crew were aware that a few councilors had hidden, clustered deep inside one of the rings that had made up the sectioned sphere, and had been rescued before the worst of the battle had occurred. Afterward, there had been no point in returning. Anyone not saved by then was dead.

But knowing this was not the same as beholding it.

Everyone was silent in respect, horror, and shock. Bornstellar had once envisioned the world as resembling a sliced spherical fruit. Now, it looked as if the slices of that fruit had been devoured or ripped to pieces. Only three remained even somewhat intact, still stubbornly impaled and connected by their axis. But they were dimmed and dark and damaged. No longer perfect circles. No longer teeming with life and activity.

It was Falling Stars, the Engineer, who broke the sickening silence. "Do you think we'll even be able to find anything?"

"We have to try." Bornstellar was the calmest of them all. Dim memories not his own stood alongside recollections of things he had lived through, but he felt the shock nonetheless. This had been the capital, the heart of the ecumene, and now it was little more than chunks of debris.

"Splendid Dust?" he prompted gently, patiently. "Where should we begin?"

Splendid Dust had paled as he stared at the ruination. He wore his formal collar, and now Bornstellar realized that there were indeed a variety of shapes that adorned it; keys to all manner of things, in the guise of decoration. How clever the councilors must have thought themselves; how smug they had been.

Splendid Dust shook his head and spoke, one six-fingered hand closing about a small hexagon that hung from his collar.

"The, ah, the top fragment. The Crown. What remains of it, at least." The Crown had been cracked in two, but it seemed that those pieces were intact.

"For the slipstream crystals, or for the Organon?" They had

fallen into using the familiar, legendary term for the artifact they sought, as there was really no other established term for it. Not even Splendid Dust had one to offer them.

"The crystals," he said. "The Mysterium is located on the equatorial ring." Broken, smaller, presumably used largely for storage, pilfering the Crown would feel less like entering a ravaged domicile.

Audacity was a silvery fish swimming through a sea of rubble and sorrow. They navigated around moon-size chunks of the former world, and smaller, more horrible evidence of destruction: the ordinariness of personal vessels; the grandeur of a wall, its brightly painted mural a startling burst of color; the corpses of Forerunners, caught forever in their armor, all rates, all ages, all viciously equal in death.

Chant-to-Green had never been to Maethrillian, and she would gladly have stayed away. As one focused on life and renewal, so much death affected her greatly, and she wondered why Splendid Dust had requested two Lifeworkers in addition to the more logical choices of Builders, Warrior-Servants, Miners, and Engineers. Perhaps he felt like sharing his pain.

Bornstellar, Glory, and Finder-of-Things-Hidden ventured forth into the broken Crown. Not unexpectedly, there was no artificial environment or even any operational technology within the looming darkness of the interior. Their armor would protect them physically, and secure grappling lines tethered them safely to the ship. Anything they saw and heard would be transmitted back, and two other Forerunners stood ready to mount a rescue if needed.

Chant watched the monitor intently, seeing through Bornstellar's eyes as he maneuvered within the debris. Finder was beside him, utilizing one of the most basic laser mining tools to cut their way through.

"I am sorry it did not work out," Splendid Dust said quietly, stepping beside Chant. "For you and Bornstellar." At her slightly surprised look, he added, "I was trained to observe people. It was not hard to see."

"We were confused and hurting, then," she said simply. "The pain was new."

"Even old, pain is pain," Splendid Dust replied.

Chant glanced over at Trial, who was at another monitoring station, and indicated that the older female join them. "Why did you request Lifeworkers for this journey? We seem an odd choice."

Splendid Dust's hand again went to the hexagon shape affixed to his collar. It was pretty, radiant, and looked newly created from hard light, despite it being precisely carved stone. "I do not know much about the Organon," he said, "but according to all the old and likely inaccurate rumors passed down, those who had seen or interacted with it felt it was alive in some way."

"Preposterous," said Trial, sounding very much like the Builder she once was.

Chant thought so as well. A truly living artificial intelligence was beyond their capabilities, and there was no solid evidence that the Precursors had mastered such a feat either. At their protests, Splendid Dust merely gave them a smile.

"Undoubtedly," he said. "But suffice it to say, I did not think it wise to come without you."

They returned their attention to the monitors. Chant was not pleased that her relationship with Bornstellar had been remarked upon. They both thought they had been discreet. Not for the first time, regret welled quietly within her. It had been he who had first spoken to end it. She was reconciled to a platonic relationship; had been for decades now. But it was like trying to deny the existence of something by hiding it away. Her feelings were still there, even if no one knew.

The glow of the laser drew her eyes as an oval door was cut into one of the Crown's interior compartments. A cable was fastened to it, and the *Audacity* pulled it away. Inside, the illumination of the wrist lamps was reflected back in myriad showers of dancing sparks of light.

They had found the cache of slipstream crystals; quite possibly the last in the galaxy. Winking before them were enough to fuel ten thousand ships for a hundred thousand years.

They took only a few dozen. The rest were left for those who were so guided to them to discover.

Bornstellar felt a dull pang as they approached the equatorial disk. It was dark and unwelcoming, a black smudge against the starfield. The last time he had been within five thousand kilometers, the ship had been greeted with the rainbow-pulse embrace of Maethrillian's sensory fields, reaching to safely guide it in with hard-light nets. Service vessels would have swarmed around them, ready to offer repairs or otherwise render assistance. This time, the ship was on its own, negotiating its path through the heartbreaking detritus of withered bodies, broken equipment, and the shattered, absolute arrogance of a civilization.

"No life support," Falling Stars confirmed. "Nothing appears operational."

It was not the same docking area as Bornstellar remembered,

nor was it near the room where he had once awaited his summons. That domicile had been located at the edge of the enormous slice.

Splendid Dust directed the group closer to the central courts tier. Here they could obtain the additional two vessels that, along with *Audacity*, would help them embark on their journey. The ships had been tucked away deep inside the structure; they were not for everyday transportation.

Even the soft glow of distant stars disappeared as the *Audacity* approached the entry point and slipped inside, traveling along a corridor of darkness that opened into an enormous interior cavern. *Audacity*'s pools of lights oozed over the hard-light curve of a vessel's hull here, an image of an engine there.

A few, Bornstellar had expected to see. But this hangar was vast, and it did not initially appear that a single bay was empty.

There had been time, then; time to escape before one of the Halo installations fired. Time for the cluster of terrified council members to be rescued. Time for any or all of these vessels to be filled with Forerunners and quickly flee to safety. The ships were here, ready and waiting. But the crystals that fueled them had been stored separately, in the Crown they had just plundered, and there had been no time to retrieve or install them.

No one said the words, but Splendid Dust spoke anyway. "It wasn't deemed necessary. These were never meant to be *escape* pods. We—" He looked at them with anguished eyes. "This was the capital! No one could have foreseen any need or even desire to *escape* from it!"

His comment was met with silence. Hindsight had no forgiveness, but Bornstellar recalled the beauty, the ceremony, the absolute certainty of safety he had felt as he watched the beginning of the Master Builder's trial. Splendid Dust's words rang true.

Finally, Trial said, "There is enough blame and guilt for us each to be bowed beneath it. Do not shoulder more than your fair share, Splendid Dust."

Row upon row they passed, until they finally found an area where they could set down. Falling Stars brought the *Audacity* in, settling it on the hard-light platform.

"Shall I enter the formal docking code?" Splendid Dust asked.

"Yes," Bornstellar said. Who knew if the mundane code might initiate a restoration program? Their task would be greatly simplified if this portion of the disk, at least, were operational.

Sure enough, light exploded all around them, forcing them to squint against the sudden brightness after so long operating in dimness, and they emitted startled, pleased barks of laughter.

Then, abruptly, a red light began to flash on the controls, and the mirth was silenced.

An incoming message. From a dead world.

Bornstellar's skin felt cold, and his armor rushed to bring it up to temperature. The correction did nothing to dispel the chill that had suddenly gripped his heart. Without realizing he did so until they were nearly touching, he stepped close to Chant. Her own skin had paled.

Everyone else seemed rooted in place with shock, and it was with an effort that Bornstellar stepped forward and touched the pad.

A holographic male figure appeared in the center of the bridge. Bornstellar could not tell where the figure had stood when he recorded the message, but suspected by his movements that it was at a control panel of some sort. He wore the formal robes and regalia of a councilor.

"It's Strength-of-Steady-Purpose," breathed Splendid Dust.

As if he heard his name—but of course he could not have—Purpose looked up. "I don't know how long I have," he said. "Whoever you are, even if you've come here while this battle is still going on, if you think you can rescue us, leave now. Please. You cannot do anything. Time is too short!"

There came a banging sound so immediate that Bornstellar jerked. So did Purpose. The noise had come from behind the holographic councilor; the sound of myriad people banging on the hard-light door to the docking bay.

"I can't let them in," he mourned, his voice cracking. "They shut me out too, the council. Now I'm keeping others out, but only because they're a danger."

Again the cold rippling of cooling skin, with the sick, hollow frisson of fear. Bornstellar didn't know which was more terrifying—that the council had locked its doors, that Purpose was barring people, or that the holographic councilor might be mad.

"Mass panic," Purpose murmured, still stabbing at the invisible control panel. "Trampled bodies. Crashed ships. So many dead already, just from that. And they're not going to be able to stop it, not Halo. We'll all be dead soon, and you will too. Get out, at once, before the Halo—"

The transmission abruptly disappeared as all the power went out on the *Audacity*. The only light now came from those fastened about their wrists.

"Who are you?"

The voice, neither male nor female, somehow blasted through the controls of *Audacity*, even though the ship was dead. It stabbed and overwhelmed the senses.

"WHO ARE YOU?"

This time Bornstellar nearly dropped to his knees, biting back a cry of agony. "I am Bornstellar-Makes-Eternal-Lasting," he managed. "We are Forerunners." Mendicant Bias had turned rampant and overridden Maethrillian security—it was Bornstellar who had finally shut down the rogue Contender years later. Was this perhaps another equally powerful ancilla? He turned, his face questioning, to Splendid Dust as he added, "Are you the metarch of—"

"METARCH?"

Offense, outrage, ineffable arrogance, and overweening puissance. Then, silence. Bornstellar didn't bother trying to speak with it again. It was no Forerunner creation. It was also no longer listening, and it knew they were here.

And, Bornstellar realized belatedly, it had spoken in ancient Digon.

Reluctantly, he translated the voice's message for the others.

"We should go," Splendid Dust whispered when he had finished.

"I would be in favor of that," Falling Stars replied, "but whatever it is has turned off every system in the ship."

Bornstellar felt a tug on his arm and turned to see Chant. Their eyes met.

Find it. Promise me!

"It doesn't appear that our armor is damaged, so that gives us three days. We won't be here that long," he said, forcing himself to sound confident. "Falling Star, try to get *Audacity* back up. Tread-with-Care, select two other ships and install the slipstream crystals. I want all three ready to go once we get back."

"You are still going?" It was Trial. An odd expression flitted about her face, or perhaps it was just a trick of the erratic illumination from their wrist lights. Probably she thought him insane. Splendid Dust certainly looked as though he did, but he said nothing.

"If it spoke in ancient Digon," Bornstellar said, "that leads me to believe it might be the Organon—or a remnant of it. If something's still left, that means perhaps it is repairable. Chant, Splendid Dust, and I will go. Everyone else, stay here and help where you can."

"I will come too," said Trial.

"And me," said Glory. Stone Songs, Voices, and Finder also stepped forward.

"There is no need—" Bornstellar began, but Trial interrupted him.

"Yes, there is. The Librarian may have exacted a promise from you and Chant, but we all do her work. And it is better than sitting here, waiting and wondering. There's little I can do to help with repairing a vessel."

Chant held Trial's gaze, then nodded. Bornstellar saw that they were all determined to go, and any protest from him would be disregarded.

"Very well," he said. "Splendid Dust? Where is the Mysterium?"

Splendid Dust looked at them in turn. "First, we must go to the council chamber in the amphitheater. And then"—he took a deep breath—"down."

Each of them wore wrist lights and carried rifles and several pulse grenades. The latter proved useful almost immediately, as there was no other way to open the door that Strength-of-Steady-Purpose had spent his final moments keeping closed. Through the hole created by the grenade, the lights of their rifles revealed that, erratic as Purpose's behavior had been, in this one thing at least he had not exaggerated.

Bodies lay where they had fallen, the shredded door bearing long, vertical lines made by the clawing of frantic armored hands. Chant's heart ached as she started to count, then she shut her mind to the task after she had passed twenty. Many. Too many.

"Our Halo weapons were cleaner," said Stone Songs, almost defensively. It shouldn't have been important, but it was.

The trek would have been the work of a few moments, had the capital been as it once was. But in the dead world, they walked.

Bornstellar was grateful that, although their ancillas had gone silent after the strange voice had spoken to them, their armor was still functional. Otherwise, death would have taken them quickly enough. As it was, the armor provided navigation and nourishment and eliminated the need for sleep. It even made their movements less taxing, allowing them to leap several meters to a walkway above, or fall without harm to one below. And as they could not rely on lifts or anything else that might abruptly grind and whir to violent life—consequently sending them to violent deaths—this was a boon not to be taken lightly.

At first, they were tense, their senses on full alert, heightened by their armor. But as the hours passed without event, the strain eased somewhat. Finally, Bornstellar asked Splendid Dust, "Were you ever told that the Organon spoke?"

"I was told that—at first—it cooperated with us and allowed us entrance into the Domain. So there was communication of some sort."

"It taught us?" Trial asked, intrigued.

"Not so much 'taught' as permitted us to explore," Splendid Dust said. "It was helpful." He shrugged, realizing he himself wasn't being particularly helpful. "You must remember: this was quite literally several hundreds of millennia past."

"Was anything written down?" Chance inquired. "If we knew how to respectfully approach it—"

"Perhaps. We had a library, but if everything is inaccessible, then it does us no good. Besides"—he looked embarrassed—"I wouldn't know where to look. I was not First Councilor for very long, after all, and I was told only a few passing legends about a thing of great antiquity and mystery."

There came a sound, low, right on the verge of hearing range; felt more than heard.

Boom.

Then a second one.

They all stopped, listening. A soft skittering pattered over their heads. Glory lifted her rifle. The light caught something black and chitinous moving with astonishing speed.

Abruptly, dozens of small indigo lights, clustered together in groups, flashed above them. Glory fired. Something shrieked, landing with a clatter on the corridor floor in front of them. Its cry ignited a fearful chorus.

Bornstellar shone the light on the thing that had fallen. Three meters long, black as the spaces between the stars, it screamed; waved eight long, sharp, barbed legs; righted itself; and then charged.

He blasted it again and again until it lay still. Around him, the others continued to fire, the things' bright eyes making them easy to pinpoint. The corridor ceiling was completely covered with them, and they began spitting out bolts of energy.

Bornstellar glanced back the way they had come. More of the insectoid things, summoned by the angry, almost unreal cries of their companions, surged toward them.

"Run!"

His team obeyed, their armor lending them speed. Bornstellar followed, firing. Then, at the last minute, he threw as many pulse grenades as he could grab toward the flow of bodies.

To his astonishment, they froze in place, their dark-violet, mechanical eyes following the arc of the grenades. The leader of the pack swiveled its head, clacked its mandibles, and uttered a single, incomprehensible word in the strange voice they had all heard earlier:

"Abaddon."

Bornstellar was so shocked that he didn't even move. An arm looped through his and he was hurtled backward, barely far enough to escape the tons of debris that collapsed only a few meters away.

Chant was sprawled atop him, panting, and their eyes met. "I heard it too," she said.

"What *were* those things?" Stone Songs demanded, wide-eyed.

"They ought to have been crawlers," Bornstellar replied. "But they're wrong. They're worse. They're still artificial, but they're much more organic in appearance and behavior."

"I don't know what a crawler is," Trial said.

"I do," Bornstellar replied heavily. "I made them. And *that's* how I know they're wrong."

Their armor plotted a new course for them, and they continued on, shaken but even more resolved to reach the Organon after the unexpected and bizarre attack. They were on high alert now, listening to Bornstellar explain his earlier statement while straining for any sounds that could mean danger.

The original Didact had designed the crawlers for his Prometheans to use against a number of infantry threats, and, eventually, the Flood. They were created to target and destroy organic matter, overcoming their enemies with numbers. "But mine . . .

the Didact's . . . were clearly machines. These are different. And the crawlers were never utilized on Maethrillian."

"How is that possible, then?" asked Trial.

"Before the *Audacity* was shut down, the Organon could have scanned its databanks," Stone Songs said. "It could have created more . . . but in the time allowed? And why change the design?"

"Why do it at all?" murmured Chant.

No one wanted to answer. The thought that the Domain itself—or what pitiful shards of it remained—was attacking them was too awful to contemplate.

Another lift tube. Another corridor, a drop, and then still another. There were no further challenges, but neither Bornstellar nor anyone else dared lower their guard.

So alert was Bornstellar to attack that he failed to notice when his surroundings had become familiar. He halted abruptly and directed his light upward. It refracted on the surfaces of quantum-engineered crystal, gathered together to form breathtaking sculptures. The walls too glittered as Bornstellar shined the light about.

A great moment is coming, Splendid Dust had said here, when he was striding beside Bornstellar many years ago, proudly pointing out the art composed of spent slipspace flakes. Bornstellar looked at him now and thought he had never seen anyone so beaten down.

"The amphitheater is ahead," Splendid Dust murmured. "I don't know what it currently looks like, but once . . ." His voice trailed off.

Bornstellar met Glory's eyes. He recalled a floating bowl connected to the main structure by little-used ferries and pretty bridges; platforms, a massive covering dome, and gently moving orbs displaying the twelve great systems of the early Forerunners.

Pomp trumps security, the Didact's presence, then so freshly in his thoughts, had warned him. He took that warning to heart now and adjusted the grip on his rifle. Up ahead, according to the incomplete data fed to him by his armor, the way was—

He blinked. Nothing.

"My armor—" the voices began, but Bornstellar waved them to silence.

"Mine too," he said, and the others all nodded. At least the life-support systems were holding steady. For now. "We are expected," he said grimly. "We must focus on the task at hand."

"Head for the area where the platforms were," Splendid Dust said. "Below is the waiting chamber, where the councilors hid during the battle."

"Where they locked out others seeking safety," Trial said coldly.

"Yes," Splendid Dust replied. "But beyond that is the entrance to the Mysterium."

"And you have the key?" Chant asked.

"I have *all* the keys," Splendid Dust replied with sadness.

"Let's go," Bornstellar said. He shined his light along the glittering walls until he spotted the faint outline of a hatch.

"That will take us to the prime seats," Splendid Dust said. He paused, looking at each of them in turn. "This may be the finest action the Forerunners ever take. I regret that there will be no one to tell the story—whether or not we succeed."

"I do not enjoy stories," Glory said bluntly. "Let us go and restore the Domain."

And removing a pulse grenade, Glory-of-a-Far-Dawn tossed it toward the hatch door.

Chant-to-Green was prepared for the theater of battle. Given the gradual reduction of her armor's efficiency, she anticipated it locking up on her at any moment. But none of those things happened.

The second they ran through the opening into the amphitheater, illumination flooded her vision, so bright it made her wince. A roaring sound met her ears. But it was all wrong. It wasn't the angry cries of the redesigned crawlers, or the bellow of the outraged Organon—

—*Abaddon*—

—it was voices, calling out in a language that, this time, she understood. And when her dazzled gaze cleared, she saw the speakers.

"Forerunners!" Stone Songs cried. But he was wrong. Not just Forerunners: humans, San'Shyuum, all the sentient races whose once-teeming numbers had been so terribly reduced filled the boxes, the corridors, all were crammed in beyond the sheer—

And all at once, Chant knew what was happening. They had come to honor a promise, to atone. But they would not be making the gesture solely of their own free will.

The Organon—*Abaddon,* she amended; *Abaddon was its name*—would exact its own price.

She dragged her horrified gaze from the rioting crowds, holograms all, upward to the cavernous ceiling. No longer lurking in the dark, the danger was boldly present.

Dozens, perhaps hundreds, of armed Sentinels peered down at their makers, each with a single glowing indigo eye. They were modified, as the crawlers had been. They were larger, but far less squat and mechanical. If the crawlers were insectoid, these were avian; their long arms looked like wings, and their curves were graceful.

It's learning. It's learning from our ancillas . . . from us . . .

"*BORNSTELLAR-MAKES-ETERNAL-LASTING*," boomed the too-familiar voice, and Chant tore her gaze away from the beautiful hovering machines to the stage.

Abaddon.

Its shape was enormous, radiant, exquisitely terrifying, and heartbreakingly wondrous. It towered, its perfect face, neither male nor female, drawn in a frown, its indigo-luminescence darkness visible. Had its massive wings beaten, the wind would have knocked them flat.

Had it been real.

"*SPLENDID-DUST-OF-ANCIENT-SUNS*," it continued. Its gaze fell on Chant, and as Abaddon intoned her name, Chant felt her gut clench, her will dissolve. A platform was floating toward them, and one by one, raptly, they climbed atop it and let it ferry them toward the feet of the godlike being.

It's a hologram, Chant tried to say, the words bottling up in her throat. She tried again, and this time Bornstellar heard her. He turned toward her, eyes wide, and nodded. Splendid Dust had said that the Forerunners had "found" something once that had assisted them in comprehending the nigh-incomprehensible Domain. He now realized that it was a Precursor's version of an ancilla—one as far beyond those of the Forerunners as a keyship was to a wooden raft.

"*A trial was to be held here*," Abaddon continued. "*It was interrupted by your creation, Didact.*"

"I am not—"

"*You will face trial*," it said, ignoring him. "*You have failed the Mantle. Behold what you have wrought.*"

The screaming crowd below them dissolved into dust, but not before they convulsed in agony. Beside Chant, Splendid Dust was sobbing.

"It's right," he said in a thick voice. "It's right. We did this to it. We did this to everything. We *should* stand trial."

Chant grabbed his arm. "No," she said in a harsh whisper, "this is just a projection. The ancilla. What's physically left of the Domain is down there. It's broken, and we have to fix it!"

"Everyone," Bornstellar interrupted, "listen and do exactly as I say. The Org—Abaddon—wants us alive to answer for what we've done. That means it won't let us die. We still have a chance."

The platform settled onto the greater one. The eyes of myriad Sentinels bore down on them. Again, Chant was almost overcome, so dazzled was she by the glory of the being in front of her. But she knew it wasn't real, that the endorphins flooding her body were being artificially injected into her system, and when Splendid Dust, unable—or unwilling—in his grief to distinguish fantasy from reality, fell to his knees in front of the enormous image, Chant knew what she had to do. While there was still time, before the armor did its work and she could resist Abaddon no longer.

Charging Splendid Dust with all her speed, Chant snatched the hexagonal key from his collar and hurled herself down into the darkness.

Bornstellar was two steps behind Chant-to-Green. Ordinarily, the drop would have been too great for their armor to protect them. It would have tried, but they would have plunged to their deaths. But this time, instead of falling, they floated. The Abaddon entity did not attempt to stop either of them. They descended for what seemed like an eternity and landed ungently—but alive.

Chant grunted and rolled over. Smiling, she showed him the

key. "You are brilliant!" he exclaimed as he got to his feet, extending a hand to help her rise.

"I know," she said. They looked up, watching as Trial, Voices, and Finder landed as well.

Voices said, "Glory and Stone Songs chose to stay with Splendid Dust. He says he'll buy us time."

Whether that was truly the case, or whether Splendid Dust was already lost to them, was not for Bornstellar to decide. He simply nodded, grateful that Abaddon's terrible attention was not on them, so that they stood at least a chance of completing their mission.

He moved his arm, directing the pool of light, and examined their surroundings. As the First Councilor had told him, to one side was a door that led into a waiting area. Here the councilors had waited until it was time for them to board the platform and rise before their audience. Here also some had hidden, refusing to allow others admittance during the battle for the capital. There were no bodies present. Bornstellar had no way of knowing if those who had been refused had fled elsewhere, or if those who had rescued the councilors had also taken any bodies aboard their ships when they departed. Either way, he was grateful.

He saw no door, but he had been told it would not be immediately visible. Illustrated on the wall was a mural of the original twelve worlds of the ecumene, an echo of the display above. As Splendid Dust had instructed, Bornstellar touched each one of them in turn. Slowly, with a grinding sound, a rectangular chunk of the wall slid aside.

There had been nothing to indicate a door. Bornstellar was silently pleased that the method of hiding this passageway was not dependent on any source of power other than simple knowledge of the code. Steps cut into the stone wound down into the darkness, and the group began to descend. There was no sign of damage this far inside the equatorial section. This stair, and the Mysterium at its base—these were perhaps the oldest things of Forerunner history that yet remained as they had been. Bornstellar felt a flush of determination. He had started this quest to keep a promise. He would finish it. Because beyond a shadow of a doubt, it was the best thing he could do.

He suspected it would be his last act; and he was at peace with this knowledge.

Bornstellar kept his rifle pointed slightly down and ahead so they could see the turn of the stairs. He stopped abruptly, between one step and the next.

There was light up ahead, a faint indigo glow. Foolish, to think he could outwit the Domain.

He didn't say anything to the others; they had eyes and brains. They saw. They knew.

Bornstellar had no idea what to expect from the Mysterium. But as he turned the corner and got his first glimpse, he knew that to have thought of it as a "vault" was a grave error.

Once, he had attended a farewell feast for one of the races they had reseeded, and had unwisely eaten far more than he should have. Now, he felt as if his eyes were being fed past their ability to digest what they beheld.

Row after row of beautiful, terrifying, or incomprehensible objects stretched away into the darkness; images of beings and creatures and symbols that were utterly unfamiliar to either him or any memories the Didact had possessed. What fantastical technology lay here, gathering dust? What solutions to problems simply sat, unimagined, for thousands upon thousands of years? In his youth, Bornstellar had been enthralled by the idea of treasure. Here, now surrounded by it, he could only gape at how limited his mind had been.

"*Your First Councilor still pleads with me,*" came Abaddon's voice. "*But he is guilty, as are those who stand here with him. You are* all *guilty.*"

Bornstellar turned to see a smaller but no less overwhelming version of the great being they had encountered in the amphitheater. It stood in the doorway of the most majestic structure he had ever seen. The ancilla appeared to be made of points of light, and he wondered crazily for a moment if, somehow, on some unfathomable plane of existence, the original had been too. This was the Organon, the Domain, after all, or so he believed; the great gift of the Precursors, and the thought of its heart being an ordered collection of stars did not seem impossible to him. Not now.

"We have come to atone," Bornstellar said. "To make right the wrong we did you."

"*No. You are attempting to finish what you began. You have proven yourselves betrayers. I am Abaddon. I am the Protector. I shall make you suffer. And you have taught me how best to do that.*"

"Our armor," Trial said. "That's how it knew about the crawlers."

And our presence at the trial, Bornstellar thought sickly. *And the deadbolt key . . .*

"*I shall make you suffer,*" it said again, "*and I shall be remade.*" It lifted its arms, spread its wide, violet, graceful wings. Beside Bornstellar, Voices lifted his rifle, and then crumbled to indigo dust. Finder cried out in horror, and then he too was gone.

The celestial figure turned its gaze upon Bornstellar. He braced himself, but Abaddon seemed to make a decision. Its eerily beautiful face twisted in pain.

"*Behold,*" it said in a shattered voice. Then there was nothing in front of Bornstellar but a slag heap. One stone was still a deep, beautiful amethyst hue. Light sparked, but feebly, limning its edges and outlining a hexagonal hole. The glamour had been dispelled, and he knew he beheld what was actually before him. His heart cracked. *Aya,* he thought, *is this truly laid at our feet? Did we do this, or did time?*

His ancilla, gone since the first manifestation of Abaddon as a disembodied voice, abruptly reappeared. She stared him down, her form no longer her typical, pleasant blue, but the same frightening pulsing indigo that he had grown to loathe. Abaddon would have them. In its role as a guardian and protector, it had once permitted the Forerunners to explore the Domain. Now, in an incarnation twisted by the Halo's firing, it saw its role as a destroyer. Thinking to protect what remained, it would stop them. And it would do so disbelieving that they were trying to help.

Movement caught his eye, and then all at once, all of that—the fate of the Domain, his promise to the Librarian, his own life—abruptly became as nothing to him.

Chant-to-Green, the Lifeshaper, was racing forward, fighting her own ancilla, her hand outstretched, clutching Splendid Dust's key. She would slot the key in place, and the Domain would recover, and somehow he knew it would take her with it.

That could not be borne.

Chant!

His mind went back to the last decades. To their awkward coupling and the decision that they both loved each other, each in their own way. To Chant's devotion to carrying out the charge of the Librarian. To her kindness, and the casual way she would touch him, a gesture always welcomed. How it seemed they instinctively turned to one another. He looked to Chant for wisdom when his own failed, for comfort given and received, and his throat was suddenly raw, and he realized he had screamed her name in agony.

She turned her head, and he saw a universe of emotion on her face. Resolution, fear, peace, and—

He loved her.

He loved *her*. Chant-to-Green. Not for her position as Lifeshaper, but for how she lived what it meant. Not for her likeness to the Librarian, but her unique differences.

Bornstellar had thought he had lost the love of his life.

He was wrong.

The part of him that was the Didact certainly had. But he was more than that, more than Bornstellar, and this third amalgam loved with a ferocity and a passion that made him realize he would give all he was, all he had known, to save Chant-to-Green, who in this instant, this precious sliver of time, met his eyes with love returned.

But he did not save her.

Growth-Through-Trial-of-Change did.

Fewer steps away than the newly awakened Bornstellar, Trial surged forward. To Bornstellar's shock and confusion, Trial didn't pull Chant back to safety. Instead, Trial slammed her weapon into the Lifeshaper. Chant's ancilla was obviously in rebellion, for Chant stumbled and went sprawling. Trial's own armor was starting to attempt to lock her down as well, and she struggled to pry Chant's hands open.

"*STOP!*" Abaddon's disembodied voice shouted, even as Bornstellar pitted his will against his rogue ancilla and moved like a mechanical thing himself. He had to stop Trial. She was a Lifeworker; he was a Builder and a Warrior-Servant. His words had ordered the firing of the Array.

"Trial!" came Chant's shriek. Trial only increased her speed toward the radiant stone. She struck hard, her hand sliding down until the key caught, slipped, slid into place.

For a moment, Trial, like the temple of Abaddon—whose name had been corrupted through time to Organon and reduced to simple, palpable, pathetic riches—glowed and sparkled, as if she too were made of starlight.

Growth-Through-Trial-of-Change looked at both Chant and Bornstellar. She nodded, gleaming white light where her eyes had once been, and a voice inside Bornstellar's head whispered: *All is well.*

Then she was gone.

Falling Stars' voice was in Bornstellar's ears as the power returned. He blinked in the sudden brightness as the Engineer said in a shocked tone, "The *Audacity* is now fully operational. So are the other ships. I anticipate having two more ships ready in less than an hour. What happened?"

"It . . . is a long story," Bornstellar said. He was gazing at Chant, whose own gaze was fixed on where Trial had last stood a mere few heartbeats before. "I will tell everyone upon our return. We should not be long."

His ancilla appeared, looking apologetic, but otherwise her normal self, informing him that nearby shuttles were now active and that they would indeed make good time returning to *Audacity*. As she spoke, she was interrupted by a humming sound. Bornstellar and Chant looked up to see the platform descending.

Splendid Dust lay curled up, shivering, on the platform. Beside him were two piles of dark violet; all that remained of Glory-of-a-Far-Dawn and Keeper-of-Stone-Songs. Bornstellar placed his grief aside, reaching to help Splendid Dust to his feet. The former First Councilor was shaking as he spoke. "Abaddon had pronounced sentence," was all he said.

Its defeat had come in time to save Splendid Dust, but not the others. He blinked, then started when he realized that Trial was not with them. He turned a haunted, questioning gaze to Bornstellar, mutely asking for answers.

"Let us go back," Bornstellar said to Splendid Dust. "And we will all tell our stories."

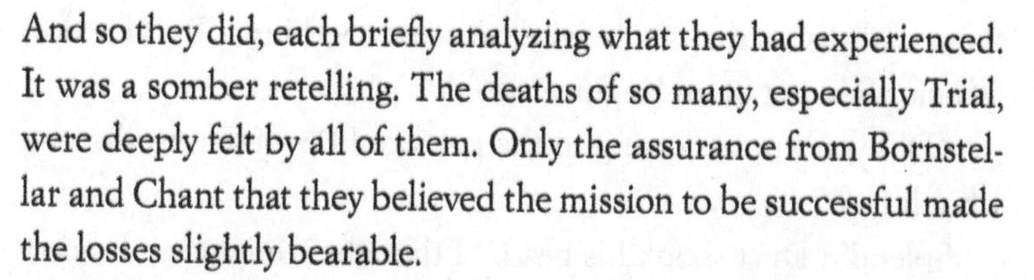

And so they did, each briefly analyzing what they had experienced. It was a somber retelling. The deaths of so many, especially Trial, were deeply felt by all of them. Only the assurance from Bornstellar and Chant that they believed the mission to be successful made the losses slightly bearable.

It was time to leave the dead capital, and let the Domain begin its work of healing—if it truly could—in peace. Falling Stars commanded one of the new ships, which Bornstellar named the *Bravado*, and Tread-with-Care took control of the newly dubbed *Impudence.*

Bornstellar had requested that Chant and Dust stay with him on *Audacity*. There were things that needed to be said.

First, he turned to Chant. "Why did you not give the key to me? Do you know why Trial took it from you?"

"I asked Splendid Dust why he wanted Lifeworkers," she said. "I would have come regardless, because of the Librarian's request. Splendid Dust said that long-ago rumors suspected that the . . . that Abaddon was alive, in some way. Once I saw what was happening, how Abaddon was re-creating our own, familiar technology in a more organic fashion, I realized it was learning from us. And . . . I suspected it needed a template of some sort to be revived." Not *repaired*, he noted. "I think Trial believed as I did, that Abaddon needed a Lifeworker mind, or genetic pattern, or something from one of us. She had always told me that the most important thing in life was how one faced one's trials. And she did not want me to sacrifice myself."

Their eyes met. Bornstellar longed to speak his heart . . . but not now, not in front of Splendid Dust, to whom he currently turned his attention.

"Chant was wrong," the former First Councilor said. "I did not intend to sacrifice a Lifeworker. I merely believed we needed them with us, perhaps to advise, to see something a Builder or a Warrior-Servant or an Engineer wouldn't."

"Did you know slotting in the key would be lethal to the one who did so?"

Splendid Dust shook his head. "I thought it might be. I didn't know. I still don't understand what happened. I don't know if it even worked. Trial and Voices and Glory and Finder could all have died for nothing."

"But yet you let Chant take the key."

Splendid Dust nodded. "I failed you all. As I have failed so many. As we all did. It was too powerful, and I felt too much remorse. And so I stayed, to let Abaddon judge me." He lifted his eyes to Bornstellar. "We did so many things wrong. We were so foolish, Bornstellar. So unspeakably arrogant. We thought we knew everything, and in reality, we knew nothing."

Bornstellar did not contradict him. Splendid Dust looked away for a moment, as if upon the ancient suns that gave him part of his name. "I want to do something I know will help the Reclaimers." He cleared his throat, straightened himself, and met Bornstellar's gaze. "I agree that the Forerunners need to leave this galaxy."

Bornstellar listened, having no idea where he was going with this.

"We will leave the Ark to the Reclaimers. But they will not understand it, not right away. They will need a . . . not a guide so much as an interpreter. Someone to share what the Forerunners have learned. I want that interpreter to be me."

"But how?" And then, with an awful certainty, Bornstellar knew.

So did Chant, who tensed beside him. "Splendid Dust, you cannot be serious," she said.

"I am. The . . . Abaddon . . . *We* did that to it."

"No. Mendicant Bias did that, not us," Bornstellar said.

"But *we* made Mendicant Bias!" His voice broke. "*Our* technology! *Forerunner* technology! We didn't listen to him when he attempted to ask for help—we were blind to what the Gravemind was doing to him. We failed Mendicant Bias. And we failed Abaddon. It gave us the Domain. For eons, it had only ever been helpful to us. And we . . . I do not want to let the humans down as well. Therefore, I will stay behind. In the only way I can, I will stay. And I will wait for the Reclaimers to come."

Splendid Dust had been a politician, one used to interacting with others. It would be more difficult for him than most to adjust to centuries, perhaps millennia, utterly on his own.

"You will be completely alone," Bornstellar warned.

"I accept that. I want to atone."

Like Trial, and Chant. Like Mendicant Bias. Like me. Like everyone . . . except the Didact. Who am I to deny him the chance?

"Then you shall."

Splendid Dust accepted the act of being composed with more dignity and grace than he had ever displayed hitherto. Bornstellar wept and was unashamed. He thought of Guilty Spark, once a human known as Chakas. Once his friend.

Toward the end, Splendid Dust had been his friend too.

"I name you the protector and guardian of the Lesser Ark. You will keep it safe for the true inheritors of the Mantle. Any thoughtlessness, or cruelty, or arrogance is washed clean from you now. Yours is not—cannot be—a happy end. And thus I name you Tragic Solitude . . . for you shall be alone, and your noble sacrifice shall aid the Reclaimers . . . but in doing so, it shall break what is left of your heart."

"Thank you, Bornstellar-Makes-Eternal-Lasting," said the hovering monitor, its single eye unwavering. His voice was familiar now; in time, it would become more mechanical. In time, he would forget Splendid-Dust-of-Ancient-Suns.

But the Forerunners, wherever they would be, under an ancient or perhaps a young sun, would always remember.

With Tragic Solitude now the Ark's caretaker, the final duties of the last Forerunners in the galaxy dwindled to an accessible few. The vessels were checked again, the options discussed, the holographic simulations run two or three times more.

In the midst of the bustling activity, Bornstellar and Chant had carved out time to be alone. As they lay quietly together, without armor, their hearts fully open and their unprotected skin so sensitive to each other's touch, they spoke of Trial. Bornstellar recounted to Chant of Trial's words in his head, and Chant revealed that she too had been addressed.

"It was Trial, but also *not* her. I do not know if she was destroyed, or integrated, or . . . or something else. Abaddon is far beyond even our best guess. But I think she did it, Bornstellar. Trial let us keep our promise. I think the Domain will recover, in time."

"But not in time for Forerunners." The thought, oddly, did not distress him. He glanced over at their discarded armor and mused if, in whatever brave new world awaited them, they would choose to leave it behind on the ship.

"What will it be like in our new galaxy, I wonder?" Chant said.

He looked into her eyes and placed her hand on his chest.

"It will be like this," he said. And smiled.

SHADOW OF INTENT

JOSEPH STATEN

This story takes place in 2553 following the Great Schism, a sudden and violent civil war within the Covenant alliance (Halo 2: Anniversary), *and in the wake of the thirty-year-long Covenant campaign against mankind* (Halo 3).

The longer the countdown went, the more the bunker smelled like fear.

The Prelate scowled at the two Jiralhanae looming beside him. One was covered with rust-red hair, and the other with dirty white. Both warriors were so tall that they had to duck their helmeted heads to keep from banging them on the bunker's low, flat ceiling. The thickly muscled, sharp-toothed Brutes stood still and silent, like monuments to violence. But all male Jiralhanae were prone to pungent pheromones that mirrored their emotions, and now, so close to the activation of the device, these usually fearless creatures' panicked stench permeated the cramped, dark room.

The Prelate, Tem'Bhetek, wanted to shout a reprimand. He had handpicked the two Jiralhanae for their strength and mental fortitude. And besides: they were adults, certainly mature enough to regulate their pheromones. But Tem held his tongue, partly because he didn't want to startle the insectile Yanme'e nervously monitoring the device's final activation sequence, but mostly because the Prelate knew the Jiralhanae weren't the real cause of his slowly building rage.

As much as the Prelate's nostrils recoiled at his warriors' sharp, sour scent, it was the noise filling his lobeless ears that made him truly angry. A noise that rose over the rapid clicking of the Yanme'e's claws on the luminous glyphs shining through the surface of the bunker's obsidian walls. A noise that muted the rumble of the device in the test chamber many levels above. A noise so infuriating that the Prelate finally broke his silence with a strangled hiss: "Why would they *sing* at a time like this?"

The Minister of Preparation shrugged inside his dark orange robes. His high, thin voice was full of concentration. "We never understood each other. Not really."

Both the Minister and the Prelate were San'Shyuum, hairless, slick-skinned creatures with elongated necks that thrust forward from between their shoulders. They shared their species' large, amphibian eyes. But the Prelate's eyes were two different colors: one dark green and the other deep blue. Considered auspicious in earlier ages, this trait now marked the Prelate as a member of a genetic line that was overbred and out of fashion.

The Minister, Boru'a'Neem, was two decades older than the Prelate, violet-eyed with a pronounced waddle of fleshy sacks that dangled from his chin. The two had the same pale-gray skin, but the Minister's was deeply wrinkled and bunched down his skull and along his neck like the meat of a freshly shelled nut. In the tradition of most San'Shyuum of his age and exalted rank, the Minister sat hunched in a bowl-shaped titanium throne that floated above the floor with the help of embedded anti-gravity units. The Prelate stood on his own two feet, his broad shoulders and wiry arms held tight against his black tunic as he glared past the Minister at a holographic projector integrated into the bunker's primary control surface.

There, in a flickering pillar of lavender light, were the small-scale images of three Sangheili warriors, stripped of their armor and kneeling with their arms bound behind their backs. The Prelate knew the display was one-way; the Sangheili in the test chamber couldn't see or hear anything inside the bunker. But their leader, a muscular, middle-aged warrior with light-brown skin and bright amber eyes, stared directly at the recording unit, proud and unafraid, as he led his companions in song.

"Do you know the words?" the Minister asked.

"I do not," replied the Prelate.

"Sangheili, to be sure, but they have so many dialects. Perhaps it's a battle anthem. . . ." The Minister's voice trailed off as a line of glyphs scrolled rapidly across the control surface. His fingers fluttered against the intricate symbols, rotating them back and forth to fine-tune the device's charging sequence. "No matter. This will be their final verse."

The Sangheili hadn't sung at first. Indeed, the two younger warriors had bellowed in pain when the Jiralhanae slashed the tendons above their large cloven feet to bring them to their knees, a practical cruelty to keep them from moving too far from the device. The Sangheili leader had said nothing, barely moving his four interlocking jawbones when the Jiralhanae made their cuts. When this stoic Elite refused to fall, the Prelate ordered his Jiralhanae to smash his knees with their armored fists—but, even then, the amber-eyed warrior hadn't said a word.

It wasn't until power began to surge to the device, and the younger Sangheili had begun to groan with fear, that their elder finally cleared his throat and started singing. Soon all three were joined in defiant harmony.

The Prelate clenched his fists. *I should have ordered my Jiralhanae to cut their throats as well.* But the Minister had been clear: the test would be worthless if the Sangheili were already dead when he activated the device.

Near the Minister, the last of the glyphs pulsed and stabilized. The walls of the bunker began to vibrate as the device held its charge. The Jiralhanae growled and the Yanme'e chittered in anticipation as the Minister lifted a single, long finger . . . and gently pressed the static surface of the final glyph.

The Prelate had expected a sound, something spectacularly loud when the device fired. But instead there was a deafening silence, an aural vacuum that seemed to pull every other sound into it. The growling, clicking, singing—even the Prelate's surprised intake of breath—were sucked out of existence as the holographic view of the test chamber filled with blinding light.

And yet, as the light faded, a ghostly chorus remained. An echo of the Sangheili song rang in the Prelate's ears for the long minutes it took the Yanme'e to deactivate all the bunker's warning and containment systems. Then the Minister led them all through a series of thick, saw-toothed shield doors to a gravity lift that whisked them up to the test chamber, where they inspected what remained of the Sangheili.

"Nothing, in fact," the Minister of Preparation said, carefully inspecting an analysis of the chamber's air, scrolling up the arm of his throne. "I would say vaporized. But that would mean trace particles remain." One corner of the Minister's wide mouth curled into a smile. "They are, simply, gone."

The Prelate watched as the Yanme'e fluttered on iridescent wings around the device: a ring of marbled onyx, ten meters high and honeycombed with glinting circuits.

The ring stood in the middle of the test chamber, a long room with white, pearlescent walls that angled together high above. This place and everything in it was the creation of the Forerunners: an ancient, vanished race that both the San'Shyuum and Sangheili worshipped as gods—or, rather, used to. For while their shared faith had been the foundation of the Covenant, this millennia-old alliance between the San'Shyuum and Sangheili was recently and irreversibly broken. The device, a miniature version of one of the Forerunners' seven sacred Halo rings, no longer held any religious significance for the Prelate. Now it was an object to be feared, not revered. And he truly hoped the three Sangheili warriors had felt terror before the end.

"My lord," the rust-haired Jiralhanae asked the Minister, his gruff voice halting and unsure, "is it possible, perhaps, that the prisoners could have—"

"Their journey was short and led to nowhere," the Prelate snapped. "Signal the ship and tell them it's safe to approach. Once we're aboard, we depart immediately."

The Jiralhanae shared a dissatisfied glance with his white-haired companion, but they both bowed their heads and retreated from the test chamber across the stretch of floor where the Sangheili used to be. The Prelate noted that even the pools of indigo blood from the Sangheili's wounds were gone, and the Jiralhanae's shaggy feet left no prints as they walked the length of the chamber and disappeared into a passage beyond.

"They refuse to understand, no matter how many times I tell them," the Prelate said.

"Can you blame them?" the Minister replied. "The Jiralhanae's belief in the Forerunners was stronger than that of anyone in the Covenant. In less than three ages, we lifted them from savagery to starships. They believed—as we all once did—that the Halo rings would open the path to godhood." He waved a hand over the arm of his throne, blanking the test results. "Do you remember what the Prophet of Truth used to say?"

With as much calm as he could muster, Tem'Bhetek recited one of the deceased Covenant leader's better-known aphorisms: " 'There is nothing stronger than the conviction of the newly converted.' "

Boru'a'Neem settled deeper into his throne. His reedy voice was tired, but his words still had all the precision of a practiced politician. "Truth said and did many unfortunate things, but he was right about the Jiralhanae. They will do anything you command, so long as they believe. And while this test may have shaken what remains of their faith in the Great Journey, it has proven, without a doubt, the validity of our plan and the clarity of our purpose."

The Prelate stared hard at the miniature Halo.

Revenge.

In a flutter of waxy wings, the Yanme'e pulled away from the ring. The Prelate could see a large crack in one of its marbled veins where some of the embedded circuits had burned away. Yanme'e were clever, and in swarms even more so, but this damage far exceeded their technical ability. The Drones hovered nervously until the Minister released them with a swift hand signal, and then they buzzed down a wide shaft behind the ring to examine how the Forerunner power systems buried deeper in the installation had weathered the test-firing.

When they had arrived here, many weeks ago, the Minister of Preparation had painstakingly trained the Yanme'e in their tasks. But the truth was not even Boru'a'Neem, a San'Shyuum renowned for his ability to pick apart and repurpose Forerunner relics, truly understood how this particular device worked. Until recently, the Halo rings had been legend—articles of faith, not something anyone in the Covenant had ever seen. It was only after a Halo had been found and activated, briefly, that this installation and others like it had revealed themselves on the Luminaries and other scanning equipment of Covenant deep-space survey ships.

"If only Truth had told me about this installation sooner. . . ." The Minister tugged at one of the many loose threads in his robe. The heavy garment was embellished with platinum brocade that used to dazzle but was now grimy and tattered. They had been on the run ever since the fall of the holy city, High Charity, several months ago. The Minister hadn't slept for days as he prepared to test-fire the device, and now some of the Prelate's anger crept into Boru'a'Neem's voice as he considered the ring with his weary eyes. "I could have transported this prototype to High Charity—brought all the resources of my Sacred Promissory to bear! But that's all gone now. Wasted."

The Prelate flinched, seized with a sudden sadness. He heard the faint echo of a different song. . . .

The Minister softened his tone. "Forgive me, Tem'Bhetek. My losses were nothing compared to yours."

"Many died that day, my lord."

"But I did not. And for that, I am forever in your debt."

The Minister dipped his long neck and head, tipping slightly forward in his throne. The Prelate bowed in response, although muscle memory encouraged him to kneel. According to the old Covenant hierarchy, the Minister Boru'a'Neem was many times his better. Tem'Bhetek was a soldier, the Minister's sworn protector. But after Tem had accomplished their escape from High Charity, Boru'a'Neem had made things clear: they were now partners, with different but equally important parts to play in the execution of their plan.

"Bring the Half-Jaw and his ship to me," the Minister said. He nudged his throne close to the Prelate, reached up, and placed his hands on the younger San'Shyuum's shoulders. "And I promise: we will make the Sangheili pay for everything they have done."

From orbit, Rahnelo looked pristine. While the planet had a thin equatorial band of deep greens and golden browns, it cooled rapidly as it arced toward its poles, and its caps were icy blue. Bathed in the light of its star, the frozen Sangheili colony world sparkled as it spun about its axis. The effect was breathtakingly beautiful, and staring down at Rahnelo from a distance of a few hundred kilometers, it was easy to get distracted. But distraction was exactly what the Half-Jaw wanted.

Since his Phantom dropship had begun its descent, the Half-Jaw, Rtas 'Vadum, had done everything he could to keep his mind occupied. He double-checked his pilot's glide path toward a line of craggy peaks on the wintry edge of the northern hemisphere. He ordered scans of the storm that was brewing there, even though he knew the Phantom was rated to withstand far worse hazards. Having exhausted these by-the-book operations, and not wanting to become a nuisance to his crew, the Half-Jaw busied himself by watching the storm grow larger in the Phantom's viewscreens.

For a handful of heartbeats, as the craft nosed into the bright tops of the stratus clouds, the Half-Jaw felt a surge of confidence. *You are Sangheili! Born and bred for war. This is what you live for!* But then the Phantom broke into the dull gray light beneath the clouds, and his false bravado shattered.

The first evidence of the assault was Rahnelo's ruined spaceport. Through the snow whipping past the Phantom's swept-back nose, the Half-Jaw saw launchpads raked by plasma cannons and a hulking orbital transport burst open from the inside, its fuel tanks boiled by sustained laser fire. The port's smaller craft were slagged inside their hangars, likely before their pilots even had their engines spinning. It was a precise, thorough attack, clearly the work of an experienced foe. But the Half-Jaw knew this was just the beginning.

The broad road from the spaceport to Rahnelo's largest settlement was cratered by heavy plasma bombardment. Deep pits walked up the frozen flagstones, and near misses had vaporized the ice fields on either side, creating holes of blackened tundra. The craters continued into the settlement, where direct hits had destroyed many of the high-walled family compounds, littering the ground with slate roof tiles, iron structural spars, and foundation stones that had stood for generations.

For the Half-Jaw, it felt as though he was trapped with his eye against some sort of macabre microscope. As the Phantom descended, layers of magnification clicked into place, each one revealing horrific new details. The final lens belonged to the corpses; stark, dark lumps scattered in the snowy streets leading up to the settlement's keep.

Having been a warrior most of his life, Rtas 'Vadum thought he had seen the aftermath of war in all its grim variations. During the Covenant's long campaign against the humans, he had witnessed the destruction of many of their cities. On rare occasions, he had seen Covenant fleets unleash their might on entire human worlds, bathing their planets in plasma fire until they shone like glass. And most recently, Rtas had witnessed High Charity itself fall to the devastating parasite known as the Flood.

But until this moment, the Half-Jaw had never seen the annihilation of a Sangheili world. He had always feared the humans might someday deal a blow like this. But he never imagined he would see one of his species' settlements savaged by creatures who used to call themselves Covenant.

As his Phantom flared for landing, the Half-Jaw felt unusually heavy inside the silver armor that covered him from head to toe. Rahnelo's gravity was slightly less than that of the Sangheili homeworld, Sanghelios. But the Half-Jaw's legs were leaden as he marched down the Phantom's ramp and into the icy intersection of two wide cobblestone streets. He forced himself to strike a confident pose, his flanged, white-striped helmet held high and his shoulders set against the frigid wind. He hoped the dozen Sangheili warriors forming a perimeter around him wouldn't see any difference in his demeanor—wouldn't guess the truth that the Half-Jaw had known for some time but didn't dare admit to anyone, least of all himself:

I am tired. And I don't want to fight anymore.

"Cowardice!" The word momentarily stunned the Half-Jaw. But then he realized the Blademaster wasn't speaking to him. The gold-armored Sangheili stood in the middle of the intersection near an overturned sledge, his fists balled on his hips beside his two inactive energy blades. Years of shouting orders had accustomed Vul 'Soran to speaking at maximum volume regardless of the situation. And now, even though the elderly warrior's voice was hoarse and cracked, his words easily carried over the Phantom's idling hum: "Only the accursed Jiralhanae would attack a world with no defenses!"

The Half-Jaw strode to the Blademaster, snow squealing beneath his armored feet, and appraised the scene around the sledge. A *du'nak* lay dead, tangled in its lines. The woolly, two-trunked draft animal had pulled the slat-wood sledge into a sharp turn that bent its bronze runners and left it balanced precariously on one side. Spilled baskets of mustard-colored grain lay in a jumbled pile beside the sledge. Nearby were two Jiralhanae corpses: one facedown, the other on its back. The latter figure was headless, and the missing part lay a few meters away, upright in the snow, staring back at its body with a tight-lipped grimace of profound disappointment.

"Not entirely defenseless . . ." the Half-Jaw said, staring at the bodies. He knelt beside the facedown corpse. "Help me move this mess."

The Jiralhanae were both clad in dark-blue heavy-plate armor. Their shaggy limbs were blood-stiff, frozen at awkward angles. When, after considerable effort, the Half-Jaw and Blademaster finally rolled the corpse onto its back, they discovered the body of a male Sangheili who had been crushed beneath it in the snow.

The dead Sangheili was even older than the Blademaster, probably in his ninth decade. His open eyes were clouded, and his deeply tanned skin was stretched tight across his cheeks. The elder wore no armor, just a long, thick cloak spun from *du'nak* wool, mottled gray and white, likely shorn from the same animal lying dead beside him. The wool had done little to stop what the Half-Jaw recognized were wounds from Jiralhanae plasma rifles; deep, charred pits in the elder's chest. But the old Sangheili still held the hilt of an energy blade in one fist. And although the weapon's patina indicated it was even older than its owner, the blade, expertly wielded, had been more than enough to stop his much larger foes.

"He tangled his *du'nak*. Flipped his sledge," the Blademaster said.

The Half-Jaw nodded in agreement. "Made himself some cover, then fought a last stand."

Now that the second Jiralhanae was on its back, the Half-Jaw could see the wounds from the elder's energy blade: two crosscut slashes in the armor that wrapped the Jiralhanae's belly. The metal around the cuts was heated to a rainbow sheen, but there was no blood or spill of viscera such as the Half-Jaw had seen when human soldiers had gotten lucky with their primitive combat knives. The elder's energy blade had instantly cauterized the flesh it cut. The wounds it made were so clean that they almost looked painless . . . but the Half-Jaw knew from personal experience that this was not true.

As with all Sangheili, the Half-Jaw's mouth was split vertically and horizontally into four separate mandibles. But the hinged jawbones on the left side of his face were cut almost clean away, the result of his own close call with the energy blade of another Sangheili whose mind had been possessed by the Flood. This was before the parasite's infestation of High Charity, and even though the wound was almost a year old, it still stung, especially when the Half-Jaw spoke. To avoid the pain, he moved his mouth as little as possible, and as a result his voice was a near-constant growl.

"They came right for him," the Half-Jaw said. "Bunched up and eager for the kill."

The Blademaster huffed dismissively at the Jiralhanae. "Fools should have taken their time. Split up, circled 'round." Then he gave the dead elder a respectful nod. "I hope I'm still that good when I'm that old."

You are *that old*, the Half-Jaw almost said. But the jest was as tired as he was, and he let the Blademaster build to his bluster.

"When I find the Jiralhanae chieftain who led this attack," Vul 'Soran shouted, his breath steaming in the cold, "by the blood of my father, by the blood of my sons, I swear he will learn what my blades can do!"

The Blademaster was Sangheili-ai, a master swordsman. He had been a fleet champion in his prime, and even as he made the slow slide through middle age, he still humbled younger opponents looking to burnish their reputations with his defeat. But the Blademaster was already in his sixties when the Covenant started fighting the humans, and that long campaign had sapped his strength. Now Vul 'Soran's deep-blue skin was splotched gray, and even the gilded armor that denoted his master rank had lost its luster. Indeed, the armor was covered with so many dents and abrasions that the Half-Jaw frequently worried about its integrity and had even considered ordering Vul 'Soran to commission a new set.

But a Sangheili's armor was his honor, a public record of glorious victories and narrow escapes. Every battle-born imperfection was a mark in the tally of his esteem. And few things short of death could pry him out of it.

The Half-Jaw knew from their recent sparring matches that Vul 'Soran's technique with dual energy blades remained flawless. But his second-in-command wasn't as quick as he used to be and he tired easily. Would the Blademaster have slaughtered these two Jiralhanae? Yes. But could he defeat one of their mighty chieftains in single combat? The Half-Jaw's ruined jaws twitched with sudden pain. *Forgive me, old friend. But those days are long behind you. . . .*

"*Shipmaster, movement to the north.*" The voice crackled in the Half-Jaw's helmet. He glanced at a second Phantom orbiting overhead, its purple hull easy to spot, even in the whirling snow. "*Scans read friendly,*" the Phantom's pilot clarified, and the Blademaster shouted for the perimeter guards to make way. Soon another sledge glided into view, pulled by a single *du'nak* with yellowed horns that spiraled backward in an illusion of speed, mocking the animal's deliberate pace.

A Sangheili youth sat on the sledge's elevated seat, bundled in a glossy black *du'nak* cloak many sizes too big for its frame. A second Sangheili in a similarly colored cloak and hood strode beside the sledge, holding the *du'nak*'s bridle in one hand and a double-bladed energy lance in the other. One of the lance's elongated, diamond-shaped blades glowed cyan hot, lighting a path for the draft animal through the snow. As the sledge neared the Half-Jaw, the Sangheili with the lance gave the bridle a gentle tug and the *du'nak* lumbered to a stop, venting clouds of steam through its trunks. The animal was exhausted; spit hung in icicles from its whiskered jowls, and its muscular back legs trembled.

"I am the shipmaster of the carrier *Shadow of Intent*," the Half-Jaw said. "We received a call for help and—" But before he could finish, the Sangheili with the lance strode between him and the Blademaster, heading straight for the overturned sledge. The newcomer knelt beside the dead elder, lance planted in the snow. For a long time, the only sound was the crackle of the lance's blade, flash-vaporizing any flakes that blew too close.

"The attack on us was days ago," the Sangheili finally said. The voice was muffled by the hood—but it was unmistakably female. The Half-Jaw saw her shoulders slump inside her cloak. The weariness he recognized. The anger he didn't see until she stood, wheeled on him, and snapped in the sharp, clipped cadence of Rahnelo's Sangheili dialect: "Now what help can you give?"

The Blademaster bristled. "That is no way to address a shipmaster—"

But the Half-Jaw silenced the Blademaster with an upraised hand. "I am truly sorry," he said. "We came as quickly as we could."

The female Sangheili threw back her hood. She wore a round-nosed, backswept battle helmet, deep red with delicate gold scrollwork that flashed as bright as her amber eyes. She started to speak, then clenched her jaws tight, which said everything the Half-Jaw needed to know about how fast she thought he *should* have come.

The young Sangheili meanwhile leaped from the sledge and

trudged through the snow to the elder's corpse, dragging the tails of his coat behind him. "Who is it, sister?"

"The miller, Gol 'Rham-*ee*." The female Sangheili emphasized the honorific at the end of the elder's name, making sure the Half-Jaw and Blademaster knew that he had once been a Covenant warrior, not just a grinder of grain.

"They killed his *du'nak* too?" The boy's voice cracked between a snarl and a sob. He gave the nearest Jiralhanae a ferocious kick. "I hate them all!" The Jiralhanae's body barely moved.

"What's done is done and cannot be undone," the female said. Then, softening her tone: "Come, let's take the miller to the keep."

The sister and brother reached for the elder's body, and when the Half-Jaw and Blademaster realized what the siblings were doing, they helped them heft it onto the sledge, where more Sangheili corpses had been placed under layers of wool blankets. It was hard to tell how many bodies there were. All were horribly blistered and burned; some were fused together, locked in a final, protective embrace.

"We found them near the craters, on the road to the port," the youth explained. "They were running for the keep. But the Jiralhanae ship cut them down."

"What kind of ship?" The Blademaster took an impatient step toward the youth. "Are you certain there was only one?"

The young Sangheili stood his ground, but his eyes went wide with fear. The female put a protective hand across her brother's chest and shot the Blademaster a withering glance. "All questions come to me," she said.

This rebuff set the Blademaster's blood boiling. But it was clear to the Half-Jaw that both brother and sister were still raw from the attack, and the last thing they needed was more demands, however well intentioned, on their already frayed nerves.

"Blademaster, rally the squad," the Half-Jaw said. Then to the female Sangheili: "We would like to accompany you to the keep and speak with your kaidon."

The female Sangheili said neither yes nor no. Instead, without a word, she helped her brother climb back aboard the sledge, tugged the *du'nak* around by its bridle, and then fell into step beside the animal as it plodded back the way it had come, pulling the sledge through its own deep ruts. The Half-Jaw, Blademaster, and their dozen warriors followed, and soon all were tramping through the deepening snow up a gently sloping road past more ruined compounds, the Blademaster barking reminders to check every Jiralhanae corpse they passed. The Half-Jaw and female Sangheili walked together on either side of the *du'nak*, heads bowed against an icy wind.

After many silent steps, the Half-Jaw said, "You wear the armor of a warrior."

"Does that surprise you?"

"No. What else would the daughter of a kaidon be?"

The female flicked her eyes at the Half-Jaw; a glance of respect for an educated guess. On Sanghelios, tradition held that children grew up without knowing their fathers. Instead, they were raised by their uncles and aunts—a system designed to emphasize clan rather than parental loyalty. On colonies such as Rahnelo, where populations were smaller and families tighter knit, the Half-Jaw knew the rules were different.

"I am Tul 'Juran," the female said, "first and only daughter of Kaidon Tulum 'Juranai, captain of his guard and scion of his keep."

"Rtas 'Vadum." The Half-Jaw fumbled the *V* at the beginning of his surname, which was especially hard to say with missing jaws. Embarrassed, he continued in a deeper growl: "I would speak with your father—ask the kaidon all he knows about the attack, so I can punish those responsible."

"You can speak to the kaidon," the Scion said, "but not to my father."

"I don't understand."

"The kaidon . . . rides behind you."

Had the Half-Jaw been less fatigued, his mind less focused on maintaining the outward appearance of calm authority, he would have immediately understood. But it took him a few more steps, crunching through the snow, to work out the answer. *One of the corpses on the sledge . . . ? No . . . the kaidon is her* brother. Which was, at first, difficult to believe.

Kaidons were mature masters of their keeps, rulers of entire provinces. The youth on the sledge was less than a decade old. Pale, protective scales still hung from his neck, an evolutionary holdover from the days when Sangheili parents used to carry their offspring in their toothy jaws to keep them safe from predators as they hunted and gathered across Sanghelios's coastal plains.

"Most of my brothers died in the war," Tul 'Juran continued. Rahnelo, like most Sangheili colony worlds, had seen heavy recruitment during the Covenant's long fight against humanity. "The two who remained joined my father in his final charge against the Jiralhanae. That was three days ago. We haven't seen any of them since."

Which meant the youth on the sledge was the last of the kaidon's sons. Although the Scion was older, well into her second decade, she was female. And according to Sangheili tradition, no female could ever be kaidon. Mistress of her keep, ruler of her kaidon husband, yes. But never owner and heir to her father's lands and other possessions.

If the Scion's youngest brother had also died or gone missing in the Jiralhanae assault, Rahnelo's lesser kaidons would soon be vying for the Scion's inheritance, attempting to secure her hand in marriage, either to themselves or to one of their own sons. If the Scion refused, she could fight, and the annals of Sangheili history were filled with brave and steadfast kaidon daughters who did exactly that. Some held out for years. A few, such as the Gray Maiden of Konar, had lived out their lives in perpetual siege, fortified in their keeps, aided by loyal vassals and the foolishness of rival kaidon suitors who wasted decades fighting among themselves.

As the Scion strode through the snow, the Half-Jaw caught glimpses of her armored torso and legs as they split her cloak. The red metal bands were spattered with Jiralhanae blood, and the Half-Jaw knew in an instant that she would defend her honor and her keep just as fiercely against any male Sangheili challengers.

"I've been counting corpses," the Half-Jaw said. "You fought off at least two companies of Jiralhanae as well as their ship—"

"A light cruiser," the Scion interjected. "It bombed the port and bastion compounds, then it dropped its infantry. . . ." She lowered her voice so her brother wouldn't hear. "The Jiralhanae swarmed the streets, killing any Sangheili who stood their ground. We sallied out from the keep to save those we could. When the Jiralhanae drew close, we held the gates. But soon there were no more stragglers, and my father ordered me inside—up to the walls to direct the guards' fire. Then the kaidon charged, my two brothers at his side, straight for the Jiralhanae's leader." The Scion took a deep breath, then swallowed anger and frustration. "We had their leader in our sights, but he moved too quickly—faster than anything I've ever seen. And then . . . he was gone."

The Blademaster had marched up to join the Half-Jaw during the Scion's tale and now said: "I've never heard of a Jiralhanae chieftain who could move like that. How large was his hammer?"

The Scion spat her words like bitter fruit. "Their leader was San'Shyuum."

The Half-Jaw and Blademaster shared a surprised glance, and then listened, rapt, as Tul 'Juran described what she had seen.

A San'Shyuum without a throne. A warrior in black armor who had evaded her keep's finest marksman and disappeared into the smoke of the burning settlement. An enemy that could have re-ignited its cruiser's plasma cannons and vaporized the keep but instead had pulled its ship from orbit and disappeared almost as quickly as it came.

"A Prelate," growled the Half-Jaw.

"It can't be," the Blademaster said. "They all died at High Charity."

"Evidently not."

The *du'nak* bellowed with relief as the street finally crested and the keep appeared through the driving snow: a fortress with soaring walls of rough-hewn granite built between two mountain spurs—the farthest fingers of a line of jagged, snowcapped peaks. The keep's iron gates were open, and small groups of Sangheili settlers and keep guards were gathered outside the walls, near the smoldering remains of a large funeral pyre. With all these eyes upon them, the Half-Jaw and his warriors unloaded the corpses from the sledge. Everyone waited in silence for the bodies to catch fire on the warm heap of ash and bone. The oily smoke rose, twisting in the wind, and the pyre consumed the last of its sorry fuel.

"Where are you going?" the Half-Jaw asked the siblings as they turned their tired *du'nak* back onto the road.

"To find my father and my brothers," the young kaidon said. "To bring them to the fire."

"If you haven't found them by now, you never will," the Half-Jaw said, as kindly as he could. "At least, not here."

"What do you mean?" asked Tul 'Juran.

"If a Prelate came here just to kill, this keep would be a pit in the ground."

This observation pricked the pride of the keep guards in the crowd, who grumbled among themselves. But the Scion's eyes grew wide with a hope she hadn't dared to consider. "If this . . . Prelate spared the keep. If he let *us* live . . ."

". . . He might have taken prisoners," the Half-Jaw said.

The Blademaster locked his arms across his chest. "And why, by the balls on every blasted Prophet's chin, would he have done that?"

Which was a very good question. But the Half-Jaw had no answer.

Tul 'Juran tossed back her cloak, baring her armored chest, and spoke loud enough for all to hear. "I invoke my right, as Scion of this keep, to free my kaidon from his imprisonment and take revenge upon his captors!" She stepped to the Half-Jaw and bowed her head. "For this, I humbly beg passage on your ship and enlistment in your crew."

The Half-Jaw heard nothing humble in the Scion's voice, however. Her words were steel determination, and the right she had invoked was ages old and just as rigid. . . .

The entire recorded history of Sanghelios could accurately be described as one long war for control of its thousands of familial keeps. Even after the Sangheili built interstellar spaceships and found other foes, kaidons still fought bitterly, and in these skirmishes, one kaidon sometimes captured another—a terrible fate, not just for a kaidon, but for all Sangheili warriors who believed that being stripped of armor and denied a noble death in battle was the ultimate humiliation. A kaidon's captor never intended to release his prisoner. Instead, the vanquished would languish in their cells, a mockery to themselves and all their kin—unless one of their bloodline invoked the "right of release" and was then bold and clever enough to see it through.

These liberations were the stuff of legends. But the most famous, and the one the Half-Jaw knew best, was the ballad of Kel 'Darsam, First Light of Sanghelios.

Kel 'Darsam was a warrior renowned for his bravery and cunning. In the earliest eras of Sangheili history, before the first Forerunner relics were discovered and these new gods conquered the old, Kel was a beloved member of the Sangheili pantheon—a demigod born to a mortal mother and a divine father who was none other than Urs himself, lord of all other Sangheili gods and namesake of the largest and most sacred of Sanghelios's three suns.

In the days when Urs ruled Sangheili spiritual life, the seas that covered much of their home world were still vast and mysterious and filled with monstrous, semimythical creatures. Kel 'Darsam was famous for slaying many of these: the Sand Dwellers of Il'ik; the many-mouthed Watcher of the Lonely Harbor; the nine serpents of Dur'at'dur, whose endless thrashing was thought to cause those islands' deadly currents. Indeed, Kel was so keen on ridding the seas of their terrors that he had little interest in becoming kaidon, a position he gladly left to his uncle and mentor, Orok 'Darsam.

During one of many wars to defend his keep, Orok was captured by a powerful sea lord and rival kaidon, Nesh 'Radoon, and Kel dutifully invoked the right of release. Without a navy of his own, Kel was forced to sail alone, under cover of night and through a line of squalls, to the sheer walls of his rival's keep. After scaling the walls and slaying the keep's best swordsmen, Kel and Orok raced to make their escape. But as Kel perched on the wall, preparing to dive to safety, a spear struck him in the back. Mortally wounded, Kel tumbled to the waves far below.

Oddly, the Half-Jaw knew, there were two versions of the ballad: one in which Nesh 'Radoon threw the spear that killed Kel 'Darsam, and another in which the spear was instead thrown by his uncle, Orok. In the latter version, the entire capture was a ruse—a trap designed by Orok, who was deeply fearful that Kel would someday tire of slaughtering monsters and decide to claim the title of kaidon for his own.

But both versions of the legend had the same ending.

As Kel 'Darsam fell, dying, toward the waves, he was touched by the first rays of Urs as the god-star rose over the edge of the sea. In this moment, Kel was transformed into pure light; an eternal reflection of his divine father's pride and grief.

After the founding of the Covenant, many of the old myths faded away. But the Sangheili continued to sing the ballad of Kel 'Darsam to their sons and daughters, just as they taught them that the Sangheili word *kel* means "light (that dances on the waves)."

"Ridiculous!" the Blademaster said, glowering at the Scion. "I've never heard of a female invoking the right of release. And I know for certain that no female has ever been—or ever will be—a warrior on a ship!"

The Scion glared right back at the Blademaster. "That is not your decision."

She was right, the Half-Jaw knew. As shipmaster, it was *his* decision. And, looking at the Scion's determined eyes, he was surprised to realize he had already made it.

"You can't be serious!" the Blademaster sputtered after the Half-Jaw had approved the Scion's enlistment and pulled his second-in-command aside for a private conference. "This is unprecedented—a breach of the most fundamental rules of recruitment! And more than that, it's an affront to honor and tradition!"

As Vul 'Soran continued his impassioned protest, the second Phantom landed and deployed its troops: two squads of silver-armored Sangheili rangers—and one Unggoy. This stout, bandy-legged creature was also clad in ranger silver, but unlike his Sangheili comrades, he wore a cylindrical tank across his shoulders and a breathing mask on his face. The Unggoy was unusually tall for his species, and the spiny top of his crustaceous head nearly reached the shoulders of the Sangheili. Typically, Unggoy were the subservient, lesser members of a Covenant military unit. But when this Grunt gave a curt hand signal, the Sangheili rangers formed ranks and stood at attention. For he was the rangers' leader, and they obeyed him without question.

"I'm sorry you feel otherwise, but she is coming with us," the Half-Jaw said to the Blademaster. "That's my final decision." Then, directing Vul's gaze to the Unggoy ranger, Rtas noted in a softer tone, "Besides, if you can get used to *that*, you can get used to anything."

The Half-Jaw and his troops stayed long enough to help the Rahnelo settlers drag the Jiralhanae corpses from their streets, pile them into the large craters on the road to the spaceport, and then bury them with rubble. This solution came at the suggestion of the Scion's brother. The settlers would not dignify the Jiralhanae with a funeral pyre, but were content, in the years to come, to let their *du'nak* trample their attackers' graves as they hauled their loads to and from the port. It was a wise first decision for the young kaidon, the Half-Jaw thought, and although he was undoubtedly bereft, the Scion's brother stood strong as his sibling departed the keep, taking only her armor and her lance and leaving a promise to return.

By then the storm had passed, and when the two Phantoms rocketed skyward, *Shadow of Intent* was bright above them, its long, hooked prow glinting in Rahnelo's reflected light. From the bottom, the mighty assault carrier looked like two iridescent blue teardrops, one larger than the other, joined at their tapered tails. The ship was a little more than five kilometers long and nearly two kilometers wide in the thickest part of its aft section, which housed the reactors for its maneuvering engines and slipspace drive. Heavily armored and bristling with plasma cannons, *Shadow of Intent* looked invulnerable. But only from afar.

On approach to the primary hangar, the Half-Jaw could see all the damage the venerable carrier had endured: dull spots in its shimmering metal skin where human missiles' thermonuclear detonations had burned through the carrier's energy shields and seared its hull; blackened gaps in rows of point-defense laser batteries where their former enemy's Longsword fighters had gotten lucky shots; hastily patched penetrations from MAC rounds, the hypersonic, magnetically accelerated slugs that were the humans' most powerful naval weapons.

On top of all this damage were scars from *Shadow of Intent*'s attempt to blockade High Charity. There the carrier had traded plasma torpedoes with San'Shyuum vessels desperate to flee the Flood, and a particularly close call had left a bubbled streak on the starboard side of the carrier's prow.

Shadow of Intent looked as tired as the Half-Jaw felt. And a few months ago, when the Arbiter, Thel 'Vadam, had offered him the mission to take the carrier far away from Sanghelios, Rtas had gladly accepted.

When the Covenant shattered, not all Sangheili had abandoned the idea of Forerunner divinity. After the fall of High Charity and the cessation of hostilities against the humans, tensions had flared between those Sangheili who still revered the Forerunners and the Arbiter's faction, which did not.

The Arbiter and the Half-Jaw had been rivals for a time, after the failure to keep the humans from destroying Halo was laid at the Arbiter's feet. But during the Schism, when the Prophets removed the Sangheili from command positions in the Covenant military and replaced them with the Jiralhanae, the two had forged a tight bond in the sudden fight against their common foes. The Arbiter was now the widely accepted leader of the Sangheili, but as the threat of Sangheili civil war increased, the Arbiter had asked Rtas 'Vadum to pilot *Shadow of Intent* away from Sanghelios. The assault carrier was presently the last operational ship of its type in the Sangheili fleet—a hugely powerful vessel that the Arbiter wanted out of reach of other shipmasters whose loyalties weren't as certain.

So the Half-Jaw had gathered his crew and charted a course for the sparsely populated frontier of the former Covenant Empire. It was here, not far from Rahnelo, that the Half-Jaw had hoped he and his warriors could finally rest and recuperate. The Half-Jaw sighed. *It was good while it lasted. . . .*

Shadow of Intent's hangar had room for scores of Phantom dropships and Seraph fighters. But now the Half-Jaw's two Phantoms had the cavernous space all to themselves. Most of the missing craft were casualties of war. The others Rtas had abandoned; he simply didn't have the crew to man them. Indeed, there were fewer than two hundred Sangheili on *Shadow of Intent*, a small fraction of the carrier's capacity, just enough to keep the ship's most important systems running. *But enough to win a fight against a Prelate?*

The Blademaster had given his own answer to this question

during their flight back to the carrier: *Shadow of Intent* would have the upper hand against a single cruiser, even with its reduced crew; this Prelate was clearly dangerous, but hitting an essentially defenseless colony wasn't the same as naval combat; they had the advantage in both weapon strength and tonnage. It was a reasoned response. But the Half-Jaw wanted a second opinion, and so after the Phantoms landed, he sought out the Unggoy.

Near the aft wall of the hangar was a line of floor-mounted methane-recharge stations. These clusters of tanks and hoses were designed to service dozens of Unggoy, but Stolt was alone. In fact, he was the only Unggoy—and the only non-Sangheili—in the Half-Jaw's crew.

But if Stolt was lonely for his own kind, he never showed it. The Unggoy seemed as relaxed as always, his back resting against the recharge station, his hard-shelled arms hanging loosely at his sides. Like the rest of his body, Stolt's thick forearms were dotted with stubby spines, evidence of his species' crustacean ancestry. The ranger leader's small, dark eyes betrayed no emotion as he listened to Rtas explain their new mission. And when his shipmaster was done speaking, the Unggoy simply scratched the seal of his mask with a barnacled finger and stared appraisingly at the Scion.

The female Sangheili had disembarked from her Phantom and was standing in a line with the other male Sangheili warriors, her red armor standing out against their silver. Holding her lance at her side, Tul 'Juran pointedly ignored their curious glances and muttered assessments and was the first to comply when the Blademaster shouted for them all to shut their jaws and come to attention.

The Half-Jaw knew that Stolt had faced similar scrutiny when he had joined *Shadow of Intent*'s complement of rangers during the human war. Rangers were an elite force, trained in the demanding art of zero-g combat. The humans had called them "ship killers," and for good reason: many human vessels had perished when Covenant rangers breached their hulls and tore them apart from the inside out. Unggoy rangers weren't unheard of, but they were rare. And at first, most Sangheili on *Shadow of Intent* had regarded this Unggoy as a Grunt who would never be their equal.

They were wrong.

Stolt had survived encounters with human soldiers that saw many of his comrades fall. When he wasn't battling the enemy, he outfought any Sangheili who sparred against him, enduring their melee strikes until they tired, and then pummeling them into submission with his chitinous fists and feet. After a chance encounter with one of the humans' fearsome Spartans, in which the Unggoy wounded the enhanced human so grievously that it was forced to withdraw, even the Blademaster approved Stolt's promotion to ranger leader.

"So, then," the Half-Jaw said after the Unggoy's tank was full and he had pulled away from the station with a wet pop and hiss, "do you believe we can kill a Prelate?"

Stolt kept his beady eyes on the Scion as he savored a long breath from his tank. "I think," he said, his gravelly voice rumbling through his mask, "we'll need all the help we can get."

In the Prelate's dreams, his return to High Charity was always the same.

The holy city's simulated star had dimmed, giving the dome's floating towers a warm, sunset glow. Barges draped with colored streamers and fragrant flowers filled the air, except for the space around the bone-white Forerunner Dreadnought at the center of the dome. Here there were fireworks; explosions of celebratory glyphs that formed phrases such as A CHILD FOR THE AGES! or BLESSED WITH TWINS! or SHE HAS HER MOTHER'S NOSE (THANK THE GODS!). Some of these were fiery proclamations about individual San'Shyuum's reproductive potency that, despite their artful innuendo, sorely tested the Committee of Concordance's laws on public decency.

But on this night, all was permitted. San'Shyuum children were rare, and when the birthing season reached its peak, all of High Charity rejoiced. Even the dour Sangheili joined in the festivities. Above the Dreadnought and below the star, Sangheili Banshee fighter craft flew aerobatics in tight formation. Watching from the barges or temporary grandstands cantilevered out from their towers, tipsy San'Shyuum revelers would roar their approval and pound their fists against their anti-grav thrones whenever the pilots demonstrated particular daring.

This picture of High Charity at its finest—bright and bawdy and hopeful—spread out above the Prelate as he exited the stalk and flew up into the dome.

Viewed from the outside, High Charity looked like a mushroom that, hidden in the deep black night of interstellar space, had grown to shocking size. The cap that formed the city's dome was hundreds of kilometers in diameter. The stalk was longer than the dome was wide and bristled with dry docks and manufacturies that served fleets of capital ships and countless smaller vessels. Novice shipmasters were often daunted by the arcane procedures and quasi-religious communication protocols that governed flight operations in and around the holy city. But Tem'Bhetek had logged plenty of approaches, and after many months away from home, he was quick to dock his cruiser in its bay and disembark the moment the gantries latched.

Like most of his voyages, this last one had been wrapped in secrecy, and communications to and from his cruiser had been tightly constrained. But his wife had gotten one message through: *We two are now three.* And every day away from High Charity after that had seemed like an eternity.

The Prelate had instantly understood her cryptic message's meaning. He was desperate to see his newborn child, as any first-time parent would be. But Tem's urgency was amplified by the fact that he had never thought he would be a father.

San'Shyuum society was incredibly strict about which genes passed from one generation to the next, and the Prelate's bloodline had fallen out of favor ages ago due to overbreeding. He was officially listed on the Roll of Celibates, and once designated as such, it was impossible to be removed . . . or so the Prelate had thought. After he had been selected to enter the Sacred Promissory—after the Minister of Preparation had used the Promissory's Forerunner machines to alter his genes and enhance his mind and body—the Prelate was able to petition for his removal from the Roll and was matched with a suitable female: Yalar'Otan'Elat. And she was more than he had ever hoped for.

Yalar was beautiful, long-necked, and delicately limbed. While her family members were wealthy owners of mining concerns on a handful of Covenant worlds, Yalar was noble and humble in equal measure—a rarity in San'Shyuum high society, which was rife with snobbery and striving. Tem fell instantly in love with her clever tongue and guarded smile. But over time, what devoted him body and soul was that Yalar accepted the three things that he could never be: home more often than he was away; honest about his ongoing service to the Minister; and confident that the experimental alterations to his genes wouldn't somehow ruin their chances for a healthy child.

Yalar accepted all of these conditions. But she was anything but demure.

When her pregnancy was confirmed, Yalar had refused confinement, a precaution embraced by most expectant San'Shyuum mothers. Instead, long after her belly began to swell, Yalar continued her work in High Charity's lower districts, ensuring the Unggoy, Kig-Yar, and other "lesser" species (a categorization she rejected) had all the resources and services they were owed as loyal members of the Covenant. She was an irrepressible champion of the alliance's ideals, and the Prelate knew their child would thrive even if it inherited just a small part of its mother's spirit.

As the Prelate soared higher into the dome, so did his anticipation. After years of secrecy and sacrifice, he was about to reap the only rewards he had ever wanted: a child, a family. He maxed power to his anti-grav belt and sped toward a future that was as bright as the fireworks bursting above him. . . .

And then the nightmare began, like it always did, with a sphere of shimmering light that appeared near the apex of the dome.

The sphere remained stable for as long as it took High Charity's citizens to look up from their revels and draw a collective breath. Then the slipspace portal imploded with a thunderous crack louder than any firework. It rang High Charity like a bell, jerked the Prelate from his flight of fancy, and reminded him of the real reason for his haste:

Tonight does not have to be the same. Tonight I can save *them!*

Out of the collapsing portal a ship emerged that the Prelate instantly recognized as a human frigate. The lightly armored vessel was essentially a MAC cannon sandwiched between two engine pods. What frigates lacked in defensive capability, however, they made up for in speed and agility. So even though it emerged from slipspace at high velocity, the frigate was able to pull up hard and bank to avoid the wall of the dome. Then, in a cacophony of crumbling stone and wrenching metal, the ship buried itself up to its engines in one of the floating towers. It hung there, shuddering and burning, like a flaming arrow plunged into the heart of the Covenant.

In the stunned silence that followed, the Prelate wanted to scream: *Go, you fools! Flee the city! While there's still time!* But in this nightmare his voice failed him, as it always did, and he watched in mute horror as the ruined vessel unleashed its horrible cargo.

A thick cloud of Flood spores spewed through the rents in the frigate's hull, flowed around the damaged tower, and quickly spread to the two adjacent spires, swallowing them whole. The ship's engines sputtered inside the miasmic cloud, giving it a dim and dreadful pulse—a semblance of life that turned the Prelate's blood cold.

Suddenly the city snapped out of its stupor. Celebrations ended in a rolling panic as the Flood cloud spread both ways around the dome. San'Shyuum abandoned their towers, crowded onto barges, or simply flung themselves toward the stalk and its waiting ships, trusting their anti-grav thrones and belts to break their fall. Many who moved too slowly disappeared into the spores. The Sangheili Banshees broke formation and began strafing the Flood cloud, but their firepower was woefully inadequate, and soon the Prelate found himself fighting upward against a tide of screaming, wild-eyed evacuees.

The tower Yalar had picked for them was old; a black marble obelisk with crenellated balconies that was one of the first carved from the mammoth hunk of the San'Shyuum homeworld that served as the dome's foundation. In a habitat where the status of one's living quarters was determined by three criteria—size, altitude, and proximity to the Forerunner Dreadnought—their cramped, low-slung tower near the wall of the dome was decidedly low-class. But while they could have lived somewhere better, Yalar wanted to be near to her work in the lower districts, and they both soon realized there were advantages to close quarters. The tower's tight hallways and narrow gravity lifts gave them license to press close together in full view of their neighbors, touch and whisper and begin the tender intimacies of their reunions before they reached the privacy of their chambers.

But now the Prelate cursed their tower's claustrophobic conditions as he was forced to lean power to his anti-grav belt and decelerate into its low-ceilinged entry hall. His feet grazed the hall's polished stone floor as he swung to avoid a trio of San'Shyuum in their thrones, so laden down with personal possessions that they didn't see him coming. Having avoided this collision, he angled up a ramp to the gravity lifts, chose a tube that served his apartment, and boosted into its shimmering field. Ten, twenty floors went by in a blur. But then the whole tower shuddered, slamming the Prelate against the tube's glassy walls. Sliding and tumbling upward, he almost missed his apartment, but managed a wild thrust with his arms, caught a railing, and levered himself into the entry passage.

"Yalar!" the Prelate shouted as he palmed the lock on the apartment's door and shouldered through before it split fully open. "Yalar, I'm here!" He cut power to his belt, landed hard on his feet, and sprinted across the bare floor of their common room, hurdling a low wooden table, and then knifed through a curtain strung with garnet beads into the triangular hall that led to their sleeping chamber. A few steps into the hall and the tower shook again—more violently this time. Motes of lavender light burning in alcoves that ran the length of the hall sputtered out, and suddenly the Prelate was in total darkness.

This was the moment in his nightmare when Tem'Bhetek became fully aware he was dreaming. All that came before—the fireworks, the frigate, the Flood—these were inevitable. But now, with the tower trembling around him, Tem was conscious of his ability to alter what came next. He held his breath and listened . . . and heard a mewling in the dark.

The Prelate stepped toward the muffled cries, hands groping along the walls. As he entered the sleeping chamber, he stopped and let his vision adjust to a wan light seeping through the curtains drawn across the balcony window. Slowly the shape of his wife resolved, sitting in the middle of their padded sleeping pallet. Yalar was draped in a diaphanous pale-yellow nursing gown. Their child was cradled in her arms, swaddled in a copper blanket. As the babe redoubled its wail, Yalar began to sing:

This path, where does it lead?
Take my hand, walk with me.
Into the light, forever free?
Take my hand, walk with me . . .

It was an old San'Shyuum lullaby, and as Yalar hummed its sweet melody, the Prelate's mind raced with all the things he'd said before—all the ways he'd tried in previous dreams to get his wife to leave their bedchamber before it was too late. But as always, the nightmare didn't wait. And before he'd landed on something new to say, Yalar stopped singing, raised her large, long-lashed eyes, and said:

"We waited for you."

"I . . . I was close." The Prelate's voice was ragged. "Just outside the city."

Yalar lowered her gaze to the child crying in her arms. "But you weren't *here*."

The Prelate felt a change in the air; something old and patient and powerful stretching out from the deepest shadows of the room. "Please, my love." He stepped forward, hands outstretched. "Come with me. Now."

But Yalar shrank back into the folds of her gown and began to sing again:

This path, where does it lead . . . ?

A single Flood spore wafted past the Prelate. It took all his strength not to reach out and crush its ragged spines, its ugly, pulsing core. He had tried once before, but fighting back had only accelerated what was to come.

"We can leave this place," Tem said. "You and me and . . ." He looked blankly at the child. *We two are now three*, Yalar had said in her message. But she had told him nothing else—not revealed the gender of their child.

"Our son? Our daughter?" Yalar said. "I wanted it to be a surprise. But now"—she choked back a sob—"you will never even know its name."

The Prelate winced, trying to keep his own emotions in check. "I fought through the Sangheili ships. I made it to the stalk." But then his rage began to build, just as it always did. "But the dome was overrun! And the Minister told me that the Flood—!"

"Boru'a'Neem!" Yalar said with disgust. Her head rose up on her long neck like a serpent preparing to strike. "You went wherever he ordered you to go! Did whatever he needed you to do!" Her voice plunged to a whisper and then stepped back to a scream. "But when we really needed you . . . You. Weren't. Here!"

Their child loosed a full-throated wail, wriggling its little limbs inside the blanket. Yalar rocked it close to her chest and continued:

Take my hand, walk with me . . . !

But she was out of tune now and frantic. Her body shook. She began to cough. Arms trembling, Yalar thrust their baby toward the Prelate. "Take it, Tem!" she gasped. "Take it and go—!"

Then her lips exploded open, releasing a cloud of Flood spores.

The first time the Prelate had this dream, this was the moment he woke, eyes wide and screaming. But he'd since learned to fight the urge to wake—coaxed his body to release some of the Promissory-implanted chemicals designed to enhance his combat capabilities to keep him focused on the dream. Each time the nightmare came, he was able to stay submerged a little longer. Like a diver with limited air, he willed his body to relax into the depths of his despair. . . .

Tem'Bhetek now snatched the wailing child out of his wife's arms and leapt away as pulsing green boils rose on Yalar's neck and shoulders. Flood tendrils, slick and sharp, burst from these sores, tore through her gown, and coiled around her body. She pitched backward onto their pallet, thrashing her arms and legs and shrieking as the parasite burrowed into her brain.

Just then, the balcony window shattered. Light stabbed through the curtains as a Phantom dropship hovering outside opened fire with its nose-mounted turret. The Prelate rolled to the floor and curled around his child, shielding it from the plasma bolts as they seared overhead and burned into the bedchamber's walls. Even before the firing stopped, the Prelate heard the clang of armored feet, the telltale crack and sizzle of activating energy blades. He rose to find three Sangheili in silver armor circling the pallet, eyeing his Flood-stricken wife.

"Don't touch her!" the Prelate roared, rising to his feet.

The Sangheili snapped their heads in his direction. The one closest to the Prelate snarled and raised its blade. . . .

But right as it swung to cut the Prelate down, tendrils shot out from Yalar's body and wrapped around the Sangheili's sword arm, stopping it mid-swing. More of the muscular Flood fibers whipped around the Sangheili's neck. Then Yalar flung herself backward, pulling the warrior with her, using whatever part of her mind that remained in her control to try to keep her family safe.

But it wasn't enough.

The other Sangheili went to work, slashing Yalar with their blades until there was nothing left but sizzling flesh and bloody cloth. Feet locked to the floor, Tem loosed a guttural, wordless cry that ended in a wail as the Sangheili prodded Yalar's remains with the two-pronged tips of their blades.

Then the swordsmen came for him.

In the Prelate's dream, the Sangheili's eyes began to glow bright as their blades as they slid through the slanting shadows cast by the tattered curtains. Their limbs stretched, and they flowed around him like quicksilver, rattling their bony jaws.

"I'll kill you!" The Prelate squared his stance, cradled his child with one hand, and made a fist with the other. "I will kill every last one of you!"

Then his baby laughed. The Prelate looked down into the infant's eyes; one blue, one green, just like his own. The child gurgled a string of happy nonsense words.

Yalar's voice echoed in the shadows:

Into the light, forever free . . .

And Tem felt a surge of hope: *Tonight is not the same. Tonight I will save my child!*

He activated his anti-grav belt and launched himself through the cordon of Sangheili, twisting to avoid their blades. As the Prelate hurtled through the window frame, the Phantom's turret tracked him and opened fire. But Tem was already halfway into a dive that took him under the Phantom's belly, beyond its field of fire. Flying with his back to the lower districts, the Prelate stared at his reflection as it rippled across the Phantom's polished hull. *Stay asleep, just a little longer. . . .* Then he was up behind the dropship, where he maxed power to his belt and shot toward the holy city's star.

The atmosphere was thick with spores now. The other towers, the arched walls of the dome—everything except the star's bright disc had disappeared into the murk. Two empty barges appeared above the Prelate, trailing limp streamers and shedding flowers. He jerked hard right to avoid a collision. A tower somewhere off to his left groaned as its anti-grav systems failed. Tem waited for the crack and boom of exploding stone as the tower hit the lower districts. But instead there was only a wet, muffled crunch. He looked down and saw dark shapes moving in the sea of spores below: tendrils winding back and forth, like animals tracking his scent.

Then the spores began to thin, and the Prelate burst through the top of the cloud, no more than a kilometer below the simulated star. This close, he could clearly see how the illusion worked—how the star was really just a broad disc of many overlapping energy fields that filled a hole in the apex of the dome wide enough to accommodate the Forerunner Dreadnought, should the

San'Shyuum ever need to move it. Viewing platforms hung around the rim of the disc, and the Prelate knew these were linked to passages through High Charity's hull, emergency shuttle bays, and, finally, escape from the nightmare. *You're close! Closer than you've ever been before!* Tem willed his belt to lift him higher, faster. . . .

A Flood tendril slashed up from below, striking him across the arms and pulling his child from his chest. The little bundle tumbled down and out of reach, a loose corner of its copper blanket fluttering behind it. The Prelate spun head over heels, kicking the tendril aside, and dove after his child, following its cries as it careened toward the undulating clouds of spores. An instant before the child disappeared, Tem caught it by its blanket. Then he arched his neck and spine and, straining against the g-forces, climbed once again toward the star.

The child was beside itself. There was no laughter now, only tears. The little creature thrashed its arms against the Prelate's chest. He held the infant tight, but this only made it more upset.

It screamed, loud enough to jar Tem half awake. He shut his eyes, took a deep breath . . . and sang.

There is a path, where does it lead?
Take my hand, walk with me!
Into the light, forever free?
Take my hand—!

But before he could finish the verse, tremendous spouts of Flood biomass rose from the clouds; pulsing stalks of half-consumed flesh; grotesque monuments to the holy city's millions of devoured souls. Tendrils sprouted from these stalks, crisscrossing the air above the Prelate. He tried to maneuver through the gruesome thicket, but the Flood lashed around him, trapping his legs, his chest, his child.

Tem'Bhetek strained his anti-grav belt well past its operating limits. The device's lifting pods buzzed a warning, growing hot and heavy on his hips. . . .

And then, through the fields of the simulated star, the Prelate saw a ship. A gleaming vessel with a hooked prow, the pride of the Sangheili fleet—*Shadow of Intent*, maneuvering into position above the holy city. For most Covenant in need of rescue, seeing this assault carrier so close would be a profound relief. At first, even the Prelate's heart leapt. But his hope shattered as soon as he saw the carrier prepare to fire the plasma fountain in its prow.

"No!" the Prelate shouted. "We're still alive, you Sangheili bastards—!" But the rest of the curse died in his throat as Flood tendrils coiled around his neck and plunged into his mouth. Tem bit down, trying to sever the fleshy cords as they slid rapidly past his teeth. But the Flood held his jaws open, keeping him trapped in a gurgling rictus of rage.

The capacitating torus of *Shadow of Intent*'s plasma fountain quavered as it built its charge. Targeting vanes irised into position around the magnetized muzzle, preparing to direct the superheated gases already flooding the breech. There was no sound when the fountain lit, but High Charity rumbled as a pillar of white-hot fire struck the holy city's star, obliterated its fields, and then lanced into the dome. The Flood clouds ignited with a roar. A wall of pressure and heat rushed toward the Prelate. He struggled in the Flood's grip, his child screeching in his arms, but just as the wall hit—

The Prelate fully woke, his ears ringing with the insistent wail of an alarm that told him his cruiser had successfully made a slipspace exit.

Tem lay on his back upon his cabin's narrow pallet, his black tunic wet with sweat and plastered to his skin. As his heart pounded in his chest, keeping time with the alarm, he felt a Flood tendril slither along his neck. He reached to grab it . . . but of course there was nothing there.

Balling his fists into his eyes and closing his mouth to mute his rage, the Prelate screamed. He had gone deeper into the nightmare than he ever had before, but at the end, there it was: *Shadow of Intent.* There was no hope of saving his family, not even in his dreams.

The Half-Jaw had robbed him even of that.

Tem smashed a fist into his cabin's metal wall, again and again, until he left a dent in the glossy turquoise panel and his hand was throbbing. *You fool! It never mattered anyway. It was always just a dream!*

For the reality was the Prelate hadn't been inside High Charity when it fell. He had not seen his wife or his newborn child consumed by the Flood. Not with his own eyes.

Instead he had been at the helm of his cruiser, locked in combat with Sangheili warships in the space around the holy city. This fight was the culmination of his long years of training, the climax of the Schism. The Sangheili hadn't expected such a vast and well-prepared mutiny, and in the moments before the human frigate infested with the Flood slipped into the dome, the Prelates and their Jiralhanae crews were winning. But then, one by one, the Prelate-controlled warships had peeled away from the battle to evacuate High Charity's San'Shyuum.

What had been a perfectly executed surprise attack became a defensive scramble as the Prelates switched from trying to defeat the Sangheili warships to merely keeping them at bay while the San'Shyuum filled their own ships and slipped away. At first, the Sangheili let these vessels go. Then, as the threat of the Flood spreading beyond High Charity increased—as the Flood spilled down from the dome to the stalk where the rescue vessels had been docking—the Sangheili sent a message in the clear: ALL SHIPS ATTEMPTING TO LEAVE THIS SECTOR WILL BE DESTROYED.

The Flood had almost doomed the galaxy once before, and the Sangheili weren't willing to let that happen again.

Shadow of Intent was the linchpin of this grim quarantine, and the Prelates had no ships that could match it one-on-one. The plan had been to overwhelm the carrier with multiple cruisers after the Sangheili fleet's lesser vessels had been dispatched. But by then the San'Shyuum fleet had dwindled. And while Tem'Bhetek was still in the fight, his focus had shifted from how to destroy *Shadow of Intent* to how to save his family. When Tem received the Minister of Preparation's desperate call for rescue, he quickly disengaged and hastened to the stalk.

As soon as the Prelate was docked and had a hard line to the city's communication network, he had attempted to call Yalar. But the network had either been down or overloaded, and he couldn't reach her. Waiting on the boarding gantry for the Minister to arrive, he had thought of abandoning his post, flying up into the dome. And he had just made up his mind to do it when the Minister's Jiralhanae honor guard hustled him through the gantry airlock. Even though the shaggy warriors' panic-stricken reek told him volumes about what had happened in the dome above, the Prelate asked the Minister: "My family. Can they be saved?"

Boru'a'Neem had leaned forward in his throne and grasped the Prelate's arm. "The Sacred Promissory is lost!" His eyes were filled with a wild and consuming fear. "Nothing lives inside the city now except the Flood!"

This had been too much to take. The Prelate had shrugged off the Minister's grip and staggered toward the airlock.

"They're gone, Prelate!" the Minister shouted after him. "There is nothing you can do!"

Tem'Bhetek's knees had buckled under the weight of this pronouncement. And the only thing that had brought him back to his feet—the only thing that kept him from kneeling there in the gantry until the Flood spilled down the stalk and devoured him as it had his wife and child—was the Minister's solemn promise:

"Help me escape this place, and I swear, we will make the Sangheili pay for what they've done!"

At that moment, the Prelate had no real understanding of what the Minister meant. It would be many days before his mind could process anything but grief and he learned the full extent of the Sangheili's betrayal. How they had failed to contain the Flood on the sacred Halo ring. How the Arbiter had turned on the Covenant by forging an alliance with the Flood's Gravemind as well as with their human foes. By that time, the Prelate's cruiser had joined a flotilla of San'Shyuum ships that had managed to escape High Charity. This brief rendezvous was joyous for some as they were reunited with loved ones thought lost.

But there was no news of Yalar or his child, and by the time the Prelate and the Minister had broken away from the flotilla and set their course for the secret Forerunner installation, all the Prelate's hope had turned to vengeance.

There was a heavy knock on the cabin door, and the Prelate admitted his first officer, a thick-browed Jiralhanae with grizzled fur and one shoulder that stooped lower than the other. As the officer confirmed their arrival in a second Sangheili colony system and relayed the details of their latest scans of the system's star, the Prelate silently donned his battle armor.

The deep black plates were light but strong, the finest creation of the Minister of Preparation's foundries. Self-repair systems had removed all the damage the armor had sustained on Rahnelo. The Prelate smoothed the armor's interlocking bands around his neck, removed a plasma rifle from his weapons locker, and holstered it in the small of his back. He removed his helmet from its stand and paused to look at his own reflection in the glazed surface of its chevron visor. *Would you know me now, Yalar? Would you walk this path with me?*

"The settlements have seen us," the Jiralhanae said. "They are broadcasting distress signals on all channels. Do you want us to jam them?"

"No. Let the signals through." The Prelate tucked his helmet under his arm and marched past the Jiralhanae toward the command deck.

Let the Half-Jaw hear them scream.

Shadow of Intent exited slipspace near the colony world Duraan, third planet of five in close orbit around its system's red dwarf star.

Like its neighboring worlds, Duraan was gravity locked. One side of the mottled, orange-and-brown, arid planet was bathed in constant starlight, the other in perpetual dark. But even half-habitable worlds were rare, and Duraan's wide-open spaces appealed to minor Sangheili families whose ambitions were constrained by the limited real estate on the crowded worlds closer to Sanghelios. Here there was ample room to lay the foundations of new keeps, and three generations ago, thousands of Sangheili had begun settling the shores of the spidery seas that spattered Duraan's light side like ink blown on parchment. Far from the front lines of the human war, these settlements had enjoyed a quiet existence . . . until now.

It had taken the Half-Jaw three days to journey from Rahnelo to Duraan. While *Shadow of Intent* was tunneling through slipspace, the carrier had been unable to receive any communications. Now, with its titanic maneuvering engines pulsing with just enough power to stay two hundred thousand kilometers ahead of Duraan on its path around the red dwarf star, *Shadow of Intent*'s command deck rang with frantic transmissions from the planet's many small settlements, all begging for assistance.

"Target in sight!" the Blademaster said. The old Sangheili's fists were wrapped around the scuffed bronze railing of the command deck's central holo-tank. He leaned forward and cocked an eye at the real-time image of Duraan that filled the charged air above the tank's petaled projector. "He's firing!" Icons blossomed around a glowing representation of the Prelate's cruiser as it unleashed a volley of plasma. A few moments later, the loudest of the settlements fell silent.

"Intercept course calculated!" a Sangheili officer shouted from his post, one of many dimly lit alcoves spaced between thick beams that ribbed the command deck's walls.

"All weapons locked and tracking!" another officer said.

The Blademaster tightened his grip on the railing, making his armored knuckles creak. "Shipmaster, I recommend an immediate attack!"

Rtas 'Vadum sat in his command chair, the only seat on an elevated platform above and behind the holo-tank. Throughout *Shadow of Intent*'s exit from slipspace and the flurry of activity that followed, the Half-Jaw had been silent. Elbows bent on his chair's worn metal arms, his ruined chin resting in the valley of his fists, Rtas stared hard at the holo-tank. When he finally spoke, it was quiet, almost to himself: "He could have glassed every settlement and been long gone before we arrived." More silence, and then: "Why is he still here?"

"He miscalculated." The Blademaster turned to face the Half-Jaw. "We killed plenty of Prelates at High Charity. They aren't perfect."

"And they killed plenty of us," Rtas replied. As Vul 'Soran chewed on that, the Half-Jaw rose, stepped down a ramp to the command-deck floor, and joined the Blademaster at the holo-tank. "Show me the scan of that star."

With a few quick taps on a control panel embedded in the railing, the Blademaster shifted the image in the tank. Duraan shrunk to centimeter size, and the red dwarf became a giant. *Shadow of Intent*'s databases had grown stale during the human war, at least as far as Sangheili colonial scientific surveys were concerned. But Rtas had learned all he could about Duraan during their slipspace journey, and he knew the planet's star was at its maximum, a period of extreme disturbance in its magnetic field resulting in frequent, violent stellar storms.

One of these storms was raging now. Two overlapping arms of fire, each one millions of kilometers long, lashed out from a confluence of dark spots on the star's crimson surface. Invisible to the naked eye, radiation from these hellish upheavals was now racing toward Duraan in the form of light-speed particle waves—and similar storm fronts had likely been hitting the planet for days. Duraan's magnetosphere would have shielded the Sangheili settlers from the storm's worst effects. But their star's distemper was the least of their concerns.

"He's maneuvering. Heading for another settlement." The Blademaster shook his head at the star. "Storm or not, we must attack!"

At full capacity, *Shadow of Intent*'s energy shields could withstand a punishing amount of firepower, much more than the Prelate's cruiser could mete out. But *Shadow of Intent* was no match for the turbulent star, and even now the carrier's warning systems were flashing in the command deck's empty engineering cocoons. The officers who would have been stationed there had the ship been at full capacity had moved nearer to the carrier's reactors to manage the slipspace exit. The Half-Jaw, the Blademaster, and two officers responsible for *Shadow of Intent*'s navigation and weapons were the deck's only crew.

"His shields will be weak," the Blademaster said.

"Ours will be, too."

"We outgun him!"

"A fact I'm sure he clearly understands."

The Blademaster lowered his voice from its usual roar. "I know you as well as I know my own sons, Rtas 'Vadum. But by the time you puzzle out this Prelate's plan, thousands more Sangheili will be dead."

The Half-Jaw knew his old comrade was right. But as much as his hearts ached for the Sangheili on Duraan, he knew the choices he made in the next few moments would also mean life or death for everyone on his ship. And if he chose poorly—if he and his warriors perished and *Shadow of Intent* was destroyed—who would stop the Prelate then? How many other worlds would he leave burning in his wake?

Rtas took a deep breath and slowly rolled his armored shoulders. *It's not the battles you've fought that make you tired. It's realizing you still have more to fight.*

"Accelerate to attack speed!" the Half-Jaw said, loud enough for the officers to hear. "Keep the shields up as long as you can. The storm coming off that star will harm every exposed system on this ship!"

The Blademaster opened a ship-wide channel and relayed the Half-Jaw's order to the rest of *Shadow of Intent*'s crew. Fully loaded, the carrier's decks would have thundered with thousands of footfalls as those onboard rushed to their action stations. But now, except for the deep rumble of its maneuvering engines initiating a turn toward Duraan, *Shadow of Intent* was largely silent. It was a strange way to go into battle, Rtas thought, and the relative quiet only increased his unease.

Having walked into plenty of traps over the years, the Half-Jaw knew one when he saw one. The reason he was still alive was, by this point, he usually had a pretty good idea of the terrible trick his opponent was about to play. But while the Half-Jaw didn't yet fully understand the Prelate's scheme, he now possessed a new and vital clue.

He knew the cruiser's name.

As *Shadow of Intent* completed its turn, the Half-Jaw keyed a series of commands into the holo-tank's controls so it displayed a view from the carrier's prow. He then opened a secondary perspective that showed a zoomed image of the Prelate's ship.

"*Kel 'Darsam Silket . . .*" Rtas said.

The Blademaster nodded in agreement. "*Spear of Light.*"

The cruiser's name wasn't painted on its prow like it would be on a human vessel. Instead the Half-Jaw and Blademaster had read the cruiser's name in its distinctive shape, in the battle scars along its hull, for they had both seen the ship before.

Despite its illustrious name, the Prelate's cruiser was of an older design that predated the Human-Covenant Conflict. It had been one of a group of ships the Sangheili had given to Jiralhanae chieftains whose loyalty the San'Shyuum wanted to reward. These "gifts" were common in the scramble to meet the human threat. At that time, it had made good sense to have as many vessels as possible in the fight, even though most of these ships had been deliberately hobbled—their major weapons and other systems disabled—to keep the prideful and cantankerous Jiralhanae Chieftains from becoming too powerful. No self-respecting Sangheili shipmaster had wanted to give up the possibility of frontline glory to train the Jiralhanae in the operation of these underpowered, surplus ships. And that was where the Prelates had come in.

They were considered purely technical advisors. Like all good lies, this was half true. But what the San'Shyuum left unsaid was that the Prelates, on the order of the Prophet of Truth, were secretly retrofitting the Jiralhanae's ships and training them to attack the Sangheili. Contrary to what he preached, Truth knew only a blessed few could follow him on the Great Journey. And after the Sangheili committed the ultimate sin of losing the first Halo ring, they quickly fell out of favor. So the Prelates redoubled their clandestine preparations and, as much as Rtas hated to admit it, had the Flood not intervened in the battle for High Charity, the Prelates likely would have succeeded in carrying out Truth's wishes.

"Enemy cruiser initiating a burn!" the navigation officer said. "He's heading for the dark side of the planet!"

Three-dimensional space gave modern Sangheili shipmasters many more options for engaging their foes than when they clashed long ago on the seas of Sanghelios. But tactics still boiled down to the same age-old choice: hit your enemy head-on, or maneuver for advantage. Given *Shadow of Intent*'s dominant firepower, the Half-Jaw's decision made perfect sense.

"Plot an intercept course the opposite way around the planet," Rtas told the navigation officer. "We'll meet him nose-to-nose." Then, to weapons: "Shield status?"

"Eighty percent and falling, Shipmaster. Stellar particle count increasing."

"No way to avoid the storm," Vul 'Soran said, "but that blade cuts both ways."

The Half-Jaw nodded in agreement. "His reactors are weaker. His shields will drop before ours." But he left unsaid: *So why isn't this Prelate running? Why isn't he firing up his slipspace drive and avoiding a fight when the odds are so clearly in our favor?*

Hundreds of capital ships had taken part in the brutal, close-quarters melee that was the battle for High Charity. In that fight, the Prelates had more total ships under their command than the Sangheili, but cruisers had been the largest vessels in the Prelates' fleet. The Sangheili had *Shadow of Intent* and one other assault carrier, *Eternal Reward*, which should have tipped the balance in their favor. But in a surprise betrayal that began the battle, the three Prelate-controlled cruisers and five Jiralhanae destroyers tasked to support *Eternal Reward* opened fire at close range, damaging that carrier so badly that its surviving crew was forced to abandon ship. All the attacking vessels were annihilated save one: *Spear of Light*.

Rtas assumed this was the same Prelate who had commanded *Spear of Light* that day . . . the one who had gone on to disable or destroy six more Sangheili ships at High Charity—two of which were cruisers of superior type—before retreating to participate in the evacuation of the city. This Prelate had kept *Spear of Light* docked to the stalk until the Flood overran it, and then shot his way through the Sangheili blockade that had halted dozens of other San'Shyuum ships.

The Half-Jaw frowned, considering the puzzle of his opponent's plan from a different angle. *This Prelate is a fighter, and he clearly wants to go another round.* . . . And then a vital, missing piece fell into place.

Rahnelo and Duraan were bait.

The Prelate had lured *Shadow of Intent* to these remote worlds just so he could isolate and destroy it—so he could finish the fight he started at High Charity. The Half-Jaw was now certain of this. He just couldn't see how the Prelate planned to do it.

As *Spear of Light* completed its orbit around Duraan, everyone on *Shadow of Intent*'s command deck fell silent. The Blademaster marched a nervous lap around the holo-tank, hands clasped behind his back. Rtas did his best to ignore a painful twinge in his missing jaws.

The navigation officer broke the silence. "Target back in visual range! No deviation from intercept course!"

"Forward plasma cannons fully charged!" the weapons officer announced. "Ready to fire on your command, Shipmaster!"

Inside the holo-tank, *Spear of Light* emerged around the limb of Duraan's dark side. *Shadow of Intent*'s cluster of intelligent circuits had been estimating the cruiser's speed, trajectory, and other flight characteristics based on data processed before it disappeared behind the planet. This computational matrix was primitive compared to the artificial intelligences that ran most human ships. But now that the carrier's many electronic eyes had reestablished line of sight, the matrix realized it had made one significant miscalculation—that the Prelate had done something unexpected while out of range—and it quickly corrected the error.

The Half-Jaw was the first to notice the change inside the holotank. "Look," he said, pointing to the image of *Spear of Light*. "He's turned his ship around."

Squinting close to the tank, the Blademaster couldn't quite believe what he was seeing: *Spear of Light* was now hurtling engines-first toward *Shadow of Intent*. "Why would he do that?!"

But Rtas had no answer. All he knew was that the Prelate's trap was closing and he was running out of time to stop the jaws from snapping shut. "Shield status," he growled. "Both ships!"

"His no longer register on the scan," the weapons officer replied. "Ours are sixty percent forward, twenty percent lateral and aft—but falling fast! Optimal range in fifteen seconds!"

Shadow of Intent had seven heavy plasma cannons evenly spaced in a deep depression that ran port to starboard around its prow. The weapons could fire individually, or combine their energy into a single devastating mass that would annihilate the smaller cruiser. But there was a catch. Rtas needed to lower *Shadow of Intent*'s shields before he fired any of its plasma weapons, otherwise the shaped energy charges would detonate against the inner surface of the shield, wreaking havoc on his own ship instead of the Prelate's.

This was standard procedure—a necessary dropping of one's guard before mounting an assault. The Prelate would know this, would have planned for this. But the Half-Jaw had no more time to ponder, and he made the only decision that made any sort of sense.

Forget how tired you are and throw the hardest punch you can!

"Pool all channels into cannon number four!" Rtas shouted to his weapons officer. "Fire when ready!"

The command deck dimmed as *Shadow of Intent*'s reactors shunted power to the plasma cannons. The shields around the carrier's prow scintillated and then dispersed. A split second later, a bright magenta streak of superheated gases wrapped in magnetic guidance fields shot out from the carrier's nose. If *Spear of Light* had taken evasive action, the plasma torpedo would have altered its trajectory to stay on target. But the cruiser kept right on coming.

"Our shields are back up!" the weapons officer cried. "Five seconds to impact!"

The Blademaster leaned closer to the tank, his eager eyes glued to an icon that showed the estimated point of impact. "We'll hit his cruiser dead astern and burn a hole right through it!"

But as the tremendous plasma torpedo neared *Spear of Light*, something strange began to happen. While the ship hadn't deviated from its path, the torpedo's fields sparked and flared as if lit by an invisible flame. Plasma vented quickly through widening weak spots in the torpedo's fields, and it veered off course—only by a few degrees, but enough so that it only grazed the cruiser's portside plating instead of slamming into its engine cluster.

"Minimal damage to target!" the weapons officer said.

The Blademaster pounded a fist on the holo-tank railing. "Impossible! How could we have missed?!"

"The storm . . ." Rtas said, as another puzzle piece snapped into place. He now pictured the red dwarf's maelstrom hitting Duraan's light side, churning against the planet's magnetic field and then spilling around its dark side in violent, unpredictable vortices of highly charged particles. These whorls of radiation had torn away the torpedo's fields just as they were slowly reducing *Shadow of Intent*'s shields—just as they had already disabled the shields around *Spear of Light.*

"Quick charge forward cannons!" the Half-Jaw barked. "Divert all necessary power from lateral and aft shields! Fire all cannons in sequence, quarter-second dispersal!"

Again the lights on the command deck dimmed. The cruiser shuddered as the cannons shot in quick succession. In the holo-tank, seven smaller torpedoes streaked toward *Spear of Light*, which was now less than ten thousand kilometers from *Shadow of Intent.* Already the torpedoes' fields were shimmering wildly as the storm did its worst. But the torpedoes had much less distance to cover now, and Rtas only needed one to hit. . . .

Suddenly a miniature star erupted in the holo-tank as *Spear of Light*'s engines engaged, full thrust. The Half-Jaw watched three of his shots go wide, a fourth boil a deep scar across the cruiser's back, and the rest evaporate in the particle furnace of the cruiser's exhaust. Venting atmosphere and shuddering terribly as it decelerated at a rate far exceeding its structural limits, *Spear of Light* came alongside *Shadow of Intent* close enough to scrape the outer limits of the carrier's portside shields—but these shields were gone now, their energy siphoned off for the Half-Jaw's hasty volley.

Both ships were flying side by side at point-blank range. For the moment, however, neither could harm the other. The Half-Jaw couldn't order another plasma shot without suffering splash damage to his own ship. And even *Shadow of Intent*'s less powerful point-laser batteries would need time to recharge.

"They'll be running for their escape pods . . ." the Blademaster said. But his boisterous voice betrayed his age, and he stammered a little, trying to rationalize everything that had just occured. "The Prelate has no choice! If . . . if he stays where he is, we take him apart with lasers. If he moves, we use the cannons. Surely he knows he's doomed?!"

But "escape pods" was all the Half-Jaw heard. For in that moment, Rtas felt his enemy's trap snap shut, and he finally understood: The Prelate never intended to destroy *Shadow of Intent.* He planned to steal it.

"All hands!" Rtas shouted into a ship-wide channel. "Arm for battle! Close quarters!" Then, locking eyes with the Blademaster: "This Prelate will not take our ship!"

The escape pod blasted out of its mooring socket, and Tem'Bhetek slammed backward into his harness. A reactive gel layer inside his armor protected him from the punishing acceleration as the pod sped across the narrow gap of space between the two capital ships. The pod's viewport blast shields were down, and it was running dark. But through the low-light optics in his visor, the Prelate could see the sharp outlines of five Jiralhanae crammed into harnesses around him, each one fully enclosed in deep-blue, vacuum-rated armor that glimmered with reflections of the pod's flashing status lights.

Behind the Prelate's pod, nine more were launching, each with five Jiralhanae inside. These fifty warriors—the entirety of *Spear of Light*'s remaining crew—knew they had just punched a one-way ticket, that there was no turning back. But whatever nervousness the Brutes might have felt when they were near the miniature Halo was absent now. Hurtling toward an enemy, weapons in hand, these ruthless creatures were in their element. Tem felt a surge of confidence. *We are going to make it inside that carrier and tear the Sangheili apart!*

It had been an audacious plan. A single light cruiser against an assault carrier. Outmatched in arms and armor, the Prelate had known one thing for certain: *Spear of Light* would never survive the fight. But the genius of his strategy was accepting the inevitable destruction of his ship and turning it to his advantage.

The Prelate had visited Duraan's system once before, on one of the many training missions that had kept him far from home. Back then he and his inexperienced Jiralhanae crew had been surprised at just how rapidly Duraan's red dwarf star had degraded their cruiser's shields. But the Prelate had filed away this miscalculation, as he did with all his missteps, as a tool for self-improvement. Years later, when he had wracked his brain for the best place to spring a trap, his memories of the red dwarf's powerful storms, as well as Duraan's small, poorly armed settlements, quickly sorted this planet to the top of the list.

Like most plans, this one had variables the Prelate couldn't control, the biggest of which was the Half-Jaw himself. The red dwarf could do only so much to degrade *Shadow of Intent*'s defenses. For the Prelate's gambit to work, he needed the Half-Jaw to throw everything he had at *Spear of Light*—to so desperately want to kill the Prelate here and now before he could do any more harm that he would be willing to expend *Shadow of Intent*'s many advantages in a single devastating blow.

The Half-Jaw had swung hard, but the Prelate was still standing. And now the odds were no longer in the Sangheili shipmaster's favor. In a close-up fight, the Prelate knew his Jiralhanae could match any Sangheili. And as for the Half-Jaw? Tem'Bhetek fingered the hardlight shield projector and plasma rifle attached to his anti-grav belt. *I will deal with him myself.*

Five seconds out of the socket, and *Shadow of Intent*'s point lasers still hadn't fired on his pod. This was good, because the pods had no significant shielding; even a single laser salvo would mean the end of the Prelate and his Jiralhanae. The pods' primary advantage—the one thing that made them superior to standard boarding craft in this situation—was their straight-line acceleration. They were designed to get away from a dying ship very quickly. And a burst of speed was all the Prelate needed to reach *Shadow of Intent.*

Now more than halfway across the gap, the Prelate knew the laser batteries must be down, crippled by the stellar storm. Which left one last problem to overcome: the pods had no rams—reinforced docking gantries built into the noses of Covenant boarding craft that they used to lamprey onto a target vessel's hull and cut their way inside.

Instead, the pods could enter only through a door that was already open. And fortunately for the Prelate, *Shadow of Intent* had one that was very hard to miss: the entrance to its port-side hangar. An energy field barred the hangar, keeping the carrier's artificial atmosphere in and all unauthorized vessels out. On a feed from his pod's forward-facing camera that the Prelate had slaved to his visor, he could see the field's telltale violet glow. But the hangar door was flickering, clearly weakened by the storm, and the Prelate knew their velocity would carry the pods safely through.

Fifteen seconds after the Prelate's pod had burst from its socket, its smart circuits cut the main engine thrust and fired its maneuvering rockets, applying as much braking force as possible. A moment later, his pod was across the hangar threshold, still moving fast, but angled toward the deck. The pod landed hard on its belly, rocked onto its rounded nose, and screeched forward at an angle, shedding ablative tiles, stabilizing fins, and other exterior parts until it ground to a halt halfway across the hangar. As the Prelate wrestled out of his harness, he could hear the other pods hit and rasp across the deck, occasionally colliding with a bone-jarring crunch.

But when the Prelate blew the seals on his pod's airlock and moved outside, more wobbly on his legs than he would have liked, he was relieved to see that all ten pods had made it safely inside the hangar. Their hatches exploded open, and the Jiralhanae emerged, some a little shaken, but all with weapons ready.

The bay stretched out before the Prelate, half a kilometer to the carrier's starboard side, where there was another large energy-field door. To his right were passages to the carrier's reactors and engines. To his left were vehicle repair bays and armories that led to *Shadow of Intent*'s ship-to-ground gravity lift. Beyond the lift were passages that spanned a graceful arc connecting the ship's teardrop stern section to its hooked prow. In the dead center of the prow, protected by hundreds of meters of hull plating and honeycombed superstructure, was the carrier's command deck. This was Tem'Bhetek's objective, and if he could survive the sprint from here to there, this carrier would be his.

Bright green plasma bolts skipped across the hangar floor. The Prelate spun back behind his pod as the barrage spattered up and over the ship and then hit a Jiralhanae out in the open on the other side. The Jiralhanae's chest plate buckled, his organs boiled and burst, and he fell backward with a mournful howl. As the Brute hit the floor, the Prelate closed his eyes and drew a deep breath . . . and his body did what it was designed to do.

Of all the Forerunner technologies the San'Shyuum had tried to unlock, genetic engineering had proved the most difficult. This was largely due to the fact that the Forerunners had refined their bio-enhancing tools and procedures for their own physiologies, not for other sentient creatures. Coupled with San'Shyuum taboos against doing anything that might further jeopardize their already limited ability to reproduce, research into this particular brand of Forerunner magic was completely ignored by all of their ministries save one: the Ministry of Preparation.

The Prelate slipped his left hand into his hardlight gauntlet and pulled it away from his belt. He activated the gauntlet with a forearm snap, and as its bright blue, crescent-shaped shield appeared at his wrist, the Prelate felt the world slow around him. The roars of the Jiralhanae and sharp reports of their weapons stretched and faded into the background. By the time the Prelate was around the front of his pod, shield up and sprinting forward, his enhanced nervous system and musculature were already fully engaged, and he now acted almost without thinking.

The plasma fire had come from the aft side of the hangar. Six Sangheili had emerged at the top of a ramp leading to *Shadow of Intent*'s reactors. All of these warriors were lightly armored and carried only plasma pistols, and had likely been tasked with engineering duties rather than ship security. The Prelate went right for these unlucky first responders, half running, half gliding across the hangar, dodging their wild shots with quick lateral pulses from his anti-grav belt and swatting away accurate ones with his hardlight shield. In mere moments, the Prelate was across the hangar and up the ramp, a few paces from his foes.

He swung his shield in a low arc at one Sangheili, severing both its legs at the back-bent junctions of its calves and elongated ankles. There was barely any resistance as the shield's photonic edge slid through armor, flesh, and bone. Spinning through the cut, the Prelate caught two more Sangheili with his primary weapon, a variant of the Covenant plasma rifle preferred by the Jiralhanae. Colored red instead of blue, the snub-nosed weapon was nicknamed "blood-hand," and true to its name, it fired twice as fast as the standard model and required a firm grip to keep it from bucking off target. The Prelate expended half his rifle's charge, hitting the two Sangheili in their lightly armored abdomens. As they crumpled to the deck, the Prelate squared his stance and brought his elbow up into the neck of a fourth charging warrior. The Prelate wheeled to follow this Sangheili as it fell, and then pulsed his rifle into its astonished face.

By then, a squad of four Jiralhanae had made it halfway from the pods to the ramp, and they dispatched the last two Sangheili with their own rapid-firing plasma rifles.

Tem'Bhetek forced himself to take two deep breaths. Enhanced hormones were surging through his system, but he didn't want to peak too early. He and the other Prelates had trained long and hard in the Sacred Promissory. Deep in its halls within the rocky foundation of High Charity's dome, they had learned the dangers of pushing their altered bodies too far: sudden, debilitating exhaustion, seizures, and, in rare cases, death.

In short bursts, the Minster of Preparation had told the Prelates, *you can defeat any foe*. Even, the Minister had hoped, the humans' demonic Spartan soldiers.

But that had been a different time and a different war. As far as Tem'Bhetek knew, he was now the last of his kind. All the other Prelates had died at High Charity.

And if you aren't careful, you're going to join them!

Uncannily quick, the Prelate raised his hardlight shield and deflected three shots from a Covenant carbine rifle. The bright green hypersonic slugs ricocheted with glassy pings, sparking radioactive fuel. A glance to his right and the Prelate identified the shooter: an Unggoy standing on the other side of the bay, at the top of a bow-side ramp. Two squads of Sangheili rangers were spilling down the ramp past the Unggoy. Mixed in among the silver-suited warriors was a Sangheili armored red, carrying an energy lance. Even at this distance, the Prelate knew this Sangheili was female—and familiar . . . but he had no time to collect his thoughts before his body was sprinting forward, preparing to meet these new threats.

"Squads four and five, join squad two! Take the reactors!" the Prelate ordered as plasma fire sizzled past him from behind. Without looking, he knew more Sangheili were emerging from the engineering bays, but he guessed they were small in number and that the remaining Jiralhanae could handle them. "The rest of you, to me!"

The Jiralhanae he'd tasked against the oncoming rangers were already charging in that direction, some of them bent forward in a feral hunch, pawing the deck with their armored claws. But when these Brutes were within leaping distance of their foes, the rangers activated the maneuvering jets embedded in their armored shoulders and heels. The carrier's artificial gravity was still operational, and while the jets' chemical propellants performed far better in zero-g, they helped the rangers match the impact force of the heavier Jiralhanae. After a terrible crash of armor and a quick skirmish in which five Jiralhanae and three rangers fell—one with a cut across the neck from the Prelate's shield—the two sides retreated into a stalemate, trading shots from the cover of loose, opposing rows of crated Phantom parts.

Although the Jiralhanae still outnumbered the Elite rangers almost two to one, the Prelate knew he couldn't afford to get bogged down. His plan relied on surprise and speed, and he now had precious little of both. He had no firm idea how many Sangheili were aboard *Shadow of Intent*, nor how many were still between him and the command deck. But more were certain to spill into the hangar soon. "Squads one and two: disengage and head for the command deck!" the Prelate shouted. "All other squads: covering fire! Keep those rangers pinned!"

Instantly, the Jiralhanae unleashed a volley of fragmentation grenades from their heavy, belt-fed launchers. As the grenades' orange-and-blue explosions filled the enemy's position with shrapnel, the Prelate sprinted toward the same ramp the rangers had used to enter the bay. But as he accelerated, the Prelate saw from the corner of his eye that the Unggoy and the red-armored Sangheili female were breaking cover to try to cut him off. As much as it galled him to avoid a fight, the Prelate would not stop to engage them. His primary objective was the command deck—and the only enemy that really mattered was the Half-Jaw.

A clang of armor behind the Prelate told him his rear guard had tangled with his two pursuers. As the Prelate topped the ramp and sped into the passage beyond, he checked the motion tracker in his visor and noted seven Jiralhanae charging close behind him. These were all the troops he'd have to help him take the command deck, and as the Prelate felt a dizziness creeping up the back of his skull—his enhanced nervous system's first warning of excessive exertion—he throttled his speed and let the Jiralhanae catch up.

Tem'Bhetek didn't need a map to the command deck. In his mind's eye, he saw *Shadow of Intent*'s passages spread out before him. He knew the carrier so well that he often found sleep by making phantom sprints through its warrens of anodized, deep-purple corridors. If he was fortunate, these waking dreams would carry with him into slumber, replacing his usual nightmarish journey through High Charity.

But quite often, the two dreams would bleed together.

Tem would see Yalar walking *Shadow of Intent*'s twisting trapezoidal halls, her thin yellow gown billowing behind her, only to disappear around the bend of a passage or whisk up a gravity lift before he could reach her. Sometimes Yalar would be waiting for him on the command deck, sitting in the Half-Jaw's empty chair, staring at him with sad eyes, cradling their crying child. . . .

The Prelate shook his head, forcing himself to breathe. He was nearing *Shadow of Intent*'s gravity lift, which was halfway to the command deck. Muscles aching with spent fury, the Prelate knew he had just a few more bursts of hyperlethal speed before his body completely seized. With his Jiralhanae panting behind him, the Prelate raced through a four-way intersection into a high-ceilinged muster bay, slowed as he passed through one of the bay's sally ports, and then came to a full stop on the wide platform that ringed the gravity lift beyond.

Shadow of Intent had been the bane of other ships, human and Covenant alike. But it was also a prodigious troop carrier that had played a key role in the invasions of many human worlds, and the lift at the center of this large, arched chamber was the fastest way to deploy its armored infantry. Hovering low above the surface of a planet, *Shadow of Intent* could send hundreds of troops per minute down the lift—or pull them back up, depending on the direction of the anti-grav field, which was produced by a machine of Forerunner design suspended from the roof. When active, this chandelier of crystalline tines projected its field down a circular shaft through the carrier's hull, more than a hundred meters wide and at least that many deep. At the bottom of the shaft was a ponderous armored platform that was always the first item down the lift. Once the platform was placed firmly on the ground, it served as the receiving end of the anti-grav field and a temporary firebase for the descending troops.

All of this was familiar to the Prelate from his study of the ship, and while the Jiralhanae that came up behind him were momentarily dazzled by the prismatic light of the gravity lift's Forerunner machinery, the Prelate's eyes immediately focused on the two Sangheili moving fast toward his position. He knew them by their armor: the Half-Jaw and his Blademaster, running opposite ways around the lift's yawning shaft.

Tem had always imagined he'd kill the Half-Jaw on the command deck. It seemed a fitting stage for the fight that would determine who controlled the mighty ship.

No matter. I will gut him here and watch his blood spill down the lift.

The Prelate willed his body again to its full potential. . . .

But before he could unleash it, he felt three sharp slaps between his shoulders, and he staggered forward onto a knee. The Prelate's shields had kept the carbine's radioactive slugs from penetrating his armor, and the chemicals in his bloodstream had dulled the pain. But craning his long neck around to zero in on the shooter, the Prelate was shocked to see that the Unggoy, as well as the red-armored Sangheili female and four rangers, had already caught up to his Jiralhanae rear guard—and was shooting past them. Tem cursed his decision to slow his pace as he turned to meet his pursuers.

If this Unggoy wants to die first? Very well. The Half-Jaw can wait.

And yet it was the female Sangheili who charged the fastest through the sally port, meeting the Prelate as he surged forward. She spun her lance, deflecting a burst from his plasma rifle, and then twirled sideways to avoid a slash from his hardlight shield. The Prelate slid past her in a crouch, swept a ranger off his feet, and then fired an arc of plasma that sent the other rangers and the Unggoy diving for cover. But the female Sangheili stood her ground, legs planted in a ready stance. She barely flinched as the last of the Prelate's shots burned past her helmet.

"Where are they?" she demanded, her voice low and steady. "My father. My brothers."

The Prelate considered her question for a moment, and then his earlier feelings of familiarity settled into fact. "Dead and gone," he replied, remembering the three Sangheili he had captured on Rahnelo—the ones who had died on their knees before the miniature Halo. "I saw to that myself."

Then she came at him, jaws wide in a high-pitched roar.

She was fast, to be sure, and the Prelate didn't have much experience against a lance. For a few seconds, it took all his focus to deflect her attacks: deep thrusts and counterrotating slashes that she delivered with a dancer's grace and a demon's fury. But then he feigned an opening—dropping his shield and tempting her to overreach—and when she stabbed her lance toward his midsection, the Prelate stepped aside and grabbed the weapon on its shaft, right between her hands, and then pulled her close and smashed his helmet into hers. She staggered backward, dazed, and collapsed onto her side.

The Prelate spun the lance around his hand, altering his grip for a downward thrust to spike the female to the floor. But as he raised the weapon, the Prelate felt the vibration of heavy footfalls from behind, and he spun to meet them instead of making the kill. The lance's energized tip stopped in midair, vibrating and crackling against the Half-Jaw's energy blade.

"If you want my ship," Rtas 'Vadum growled, "you'll need to be faster than that."

The Prelate's wide lips tightened into a sneer. "As you wish."

At long last, he was facing the traitorous Sangheili who had allowed the Flood to invade High Charity—the one responsible for killing his wife and child.

Tem'Bhetek exhaled, released the last of his mental gates, and attacked the Half-Jaw with the full measure of his fury.

Shoving away his foe's sword arm with the lance, the Prelate fired a point-blank burst with his rifle. But the Half-Jaw flowed with the lance and out of the line of fire, and then ducked under the Prelate's arm and brought his blade around and down onto the Prelate's armored neck. Tem's shield flashed but held, and he shrugged the blade away, answering the Half-Jaw's counterattack with a savage kick to the ribs.

Their duel was a blur until the Prelate found a hole in the Half-Jaw's defenses and caught him in the shoulder with his hardlight shield—a cut that burned through Rtas's armor and into flesh. The two combatants stepped away from each other, breathing heavily. All around them, the Sangheili rangers and Jiralhanae were locked in their own deadly dance.

"You will . . . not win this fight," the Half-Jaw said through ragged breaths.

His own chest heaving, the Prelate flicked his eyes to: the Unggoy leaping onto a Jiralhanae's back and choking it to the floor; and the Blademaster using one of his plasma swords to sever a Jiralhanae's weapon arm and then sending its head flying with the other. Two more Brutes lay dead on the deck along with the rangers that had taken them down—which left only three of the Prelate's warriors still standing, and he realized that the Half-Jaw just might be right.

Tem's rapidly spinning mind recalled his primary objective: take *Shadow of Intent* and bring it to the Minister of Preparation.

A glance at a troop roster in his visor showed that the Jiralhanae squads in the hangar were still alive. If they secured the reactors, and if he made it to the command deck, they could execute a slipspace jump back to the Forerunner installation. . . .

The Prelate glared at the Half-Jaw through the cautionary pain wrapping around his brain.

I may not win this battle, but I can still bring you to your doom.

Casting aside the energy lance, the Prelate increased power to his belt and suddenly soared over the Half-Jaw and into the gravity lift chamber. He was well past the breaking point; his enhanced nerves were frayed and his muscles were beginning to spasm. His vision was constricting but still focused on the only thing that mattered: an open passage on the far side of the shaft leading to the command deck. Without his Jiralhanae to slow him down, he could easily outpace his pursuers, lock himself inside the command deck, open the airlocks, and vent all the cursed Sangheili into space—

Then the Prelate saw Yalar, standing in the arched doorway to the passage.

Fearful of smashing directly into his beloved, the Prelate slowed his flight across the shaft, and in that moment one of the Blademaster's hurled swords caught him between his shoulders, instantly depleting what remained of his shields and flipping him head over heels. The Prelate's momentum carried him across the gap and onto the platform on the far side, where he landed hard and rolled to a stop, facedown on the burnished metal floor.

"Yalar . . . !" the Prelate groaned as his wife drifted away into the passage. At the same time he heard the staccato bursts of maneuvering jets, felt something land and plant its feet on either side of his waist. But all of these sensations were dull and far away.

"Please!" Tem said, reaching a hand toward the retreating ghost. "Don't go!"

Yalar stopped, looked over her shoulder, and frowned.

This path, where does it lead . . . ?

Then the Unggoy smashed his hard, spiny fist into the side of the Prelate's helmet, and his world went black.

When the Prelate woke, he was uncertain how much time had passed. It couldn't have been that long, for his muscles still ached and his head throbbed from his exertions.

I'm alive, at least. That's a start. . . .

He slowly opened his eyes and discovered he was in a holding cell—a small room with a scuffed metal floor and walls made of hexagonal bronze tiles. One of the cell's walls was filled with a translucent blue energy field that served as its door. Tem'Bhetek was still in his armor, although someone had removed his helmet, and he was slumped at the base of the wall to the left of the cell door. Tem tried to reach up and massage an ache in his head where the Unggoy had applied his fist, only to find that his hands were bound to his ankles with heavy, magnetized manacles that kept him firmly rooted to the deck.

He was a prisoner. But he was not alone in his cell.

"Your Jiralhanae are all dead," the Half-Jaw said. He was sitting opposite the Prelate on a bench protruding from the wall. The Half-Jaw's silver armor was flecked with Jiralhanae blood. "We just cleaned the last of them out of the engineering decks."

Unfortunate, if not unexpected, news. But the Prelate was glad to see a long, freshly cauterized gash across one of the Half-Jaw's shoulder plates where his hardlight shield had left its mark.

"Did you offer them terms?" The Prelate did his best not to slur his words. But he could taste the residue of chemicals in his mouth, and he knew, after how far he had pushed himself, that he was lucky he could speak at all.

"Yes. They refused."

"If they hadn't, I would have killed them all myself."

For a long time, the Half-Jaw and the Prelate simply stared at each other. Tem saw that his enemy was unarmed. This was almost certainly a diplomatic gesture, meant to put the San'Shyuum at ease. But it had the exact opposite effect. *I hate him more than anything in the universe, and he hopes I will be content to sit here and talk?!*

The Prelate shut his eyes and curled his long neck back against the wall. Its tiles were cool and damp, and he hoped this would slow the anger creeping up his spine.

"We've also captured *Spear of Light*," the Half-Jaw said. "Most of its systems were beyond repair. But the navigational database was intact. We know everywhere you've traveled. Duraan, Rahnelo . . . as well as where you came from—the system you have been using as a base of operations."

But nothing else, the Prelate thought. *Or I would already be dead, and we wouldn't be having such a pleasant chat.*

"We know the system is in a hidden sector," the Half-Jaw continued, knitting his long fingers together in his lap. "One of many the San'Shyuum kept for themselves."

Now Tem couldn't resist: "And you want to know what's in it."

"I'd like to know what the only Prelate to survive the fall of High Charity deems so important that he would be willing to murder thousands of innocent Sangheili in order to protect it." The Half-Jaw clenched his fingers tight. "Yes. I would like to know that."

At the mention of High Charity, Tem'Bhetek's anger exploded at the base of his skull. But he gritted his teeth and held his tongue . . . until the Half-Jaw took one step too far.

"Tell me what is in that sector, and your death will be quick and painless."

Tem almost choked on his hatred. "Where was your mercy?" He strained against his manacles, ignoring the needling chemical aftertaste that warned him to remain still. "When you incinerated my family and everyone else inside the holy city?!"

"I cleansed an infestation."

"The Flood?" the Prelate shouted in disgust. "They were just an excuse!"

"An excuse?"

"For you and all the other shipmasters to commit your final act of betrayal!"

"You speak nonsense."

"I speak the truth!"

"Ah. Just like the Prophet?" The Half-Jaw leaned forward and angled one eye and his ruined jaw at the Prelate. "I don't know which one of us was the bigger fool—me for believing Truth's lies, or you for ignoring them."

"I am no fool, and the Minister of Preparation will—!" Tem snapped his mouth shut. *Calm yourself, before you say too much!*

"Preparation?" The Half-Jaw wrapped his hands around the edge of the bench. "I'm surprised he made it out alive. By the time we breached the stalk, the Sacred Promissory was teeming with Flood. And the dome's lower districts . . ."

The Half-Jaw paused and looked past the Prelate at a spot far beyond the walls of the cell. When he spoke again, the Prelate was surprised by how tired and regretful the Sangheili sounded.

"There were still San'Shyuum alive in their towers. We heard their transmissions, saw some of them in the air, trying to reach us. But the parasite was thick around us then. We couldn't hold our position, although many Sangheili died trying. When I realized there was nothing more we could do, only then did I give the order to burn the city." The Half-Jaw met the Prelate's angry gaze. "I am sorry for your family. Believe me when I tell you that I would have saved them if I could."

The Prelate was stunned—not by the Half-Jaw's apology but by his admission. *There were still San'Shyuum alive in their towers. . . .* As much as the Prelate wanted to remain silent—as strongly as he suspected the Half-Jaw's sincerity was merely a ruse to get him to divulge more information—he couldn't help the words that slipped past his trembling lips: "You lie. There was no one alive in the city when I left it."

"Who told you that? The Minister of Preparation?" The Half-Jaw shook his head. "I'm telling you what I saw with my own eyes."

"My family. Is dead."

"Alas, they are. But not by my hand."

The Prelate did not—*could* not—believe anything the Half-Jaw said. Because if this Sangheili's account of the fall of High Charity was true, there was a chance he might have been able to rescue Yalar and his child. A chance that their blood was on his hands.

In this moment of sickening possibility, Tem'Bhetek felt more anger than he ever had before. Not at the Half-Jaw, but at himself.

"What is in this hidden sector?" the Half-Jaw asked again.

The Prelate lashed out, desperate to redirect his rage. "Exactly what you deserve!"

The Half-Jaw leaned back against the wall. After a long silence, he said: "Your ship, *Spear of Light* . . . do you know the song behind that name?"

The Prelate remembered the proud voices of the Sangheili prisoners kneeling before the ring. But his mind was reeling, and for a moment he imagined the prisoners singing Yalar's lullaby instead of their own, defiant tune.

Take my hand, walk with me . . .

Tem shuddered in his restraints. "Damn you. And damn your songs, Sangheili."

"The ballad of Kel 'Darsam is very old," the Half-Jaw persisted. "Something I learned as a child. There is one verse . . ."

And then the Half-Jaw sang.

Despite his ragged jaws, the words that came out in his native tongue were melodious and sweet. The Half-Jaw sang beautifully, in fact, and it made the Prelate hate him more than ever.

When the Half-Jaw was done with the verse, he translated it into standard Covenant: "*Kel 'Darsam fell, spear in his back, down to the rocks where the waves did crack.*" The shipmaster shrugged. "No one really knows who killed Kel 'Darsam. Some believe his enemy threw the spear. Others think it was his uncle—that the spear was a betrayal even that great warrior could not see before it struck him in the back."

The Half-Jaw stared hard at the Prelate as he rose from the bench. "I've already set a course for the hidden sector. Before we arrive, you might want to reconsider who has told you the truth and who has not."

The Prelate watched in mute fury as the Half-Jaw stepped to

the cell's energy field. The barrier shimmered a lighter shade of blue, and the Sangheili walked through it and out of sight.

"I hope your investigations went better than mine," Rtas said to the Blademaster and the Unggoy, who were waiting in the guardroom outside the cell. Both still wore their battle armor. Vul 'Soran was nervously fingering the twin hilts of his energy swords. Stolt was calmly holding his breath while he cleaned his mask. He toggled a valve with one of his thick thumbs, heard a satisfying hiss of methane, and then clipped the mask back into place.

"Well, the good news first, then," the Blademaster said. "The Jiralhanae didn't cause any damage to the reactors. Strange, I know. But none of those hairy curs is alive to tell us what they were thinking, so let's just be thankful that we still have enough power for the slipspace drive."

"And the bad news?" the Half-Jaw asked.

"All forward plasma cannons offline. Most lasers down too," Stolt said. "This ship might look tough from far away. But it can't fight."

Rtas nodded his head, only half listening to his two lieutenants. His mind was churning over a new puzzle, courtesy of the Prelate: *Why would the Minister of Preparation, one of the San'Shyuum's most brilliant Forerunner technologists, send the last living Prelate to capture my ship?* The Half-Jaw had no idea. But he had a strong suspicion that the answer he sought was waiting for him in the hidden sector.

Rtas fought the urge to rub the gash in his shoulder. The pain from the wound was intense, worse than he would ever let the Prelate or his own warriors know. And yet, once again, here he was, barely recovered from one battle and off to fight another. *I don't know if I have the strength for this....* And in this moment of weakness he went one step further: *If the Minister wants this old, worthless ship so badly? Fine. He can have it!*

This idea was, of course, ridiculous, self-indulgent, and a betrayal of the Sangheili warrior code. But instead of feeling a rush of embarrassment and regret, Rtas was oddly energized. The pain in his shoulder suddenly fell away as the Half-Jaw realized: he had been so busy staring at his enemies' puzzles that he failed to notice that he held—had *always* held—the most important piece.

"I need volunteers," the Half-Jaw said to Stolt. "Enough to manage a slipspace jump, but no more than we can fit into two Phantoms. Get the wounded and everyone else off of *Shadow of Intent* and down to Duraan's surface."

The Unggoy's beady eyes crinkled with questions. But content in the knowledge that he'd just placed his own name at the top of the list of volunteers, Stolt grumbled his assent and trotted out of the guardroom, methane tank rattling on his back.

"The ballad of Kel 'Darsam. . . . Haven't heard that one sung in years." The Blademaster glanced at the Prelate, brooding on the other side of the cell's energy-field door. "Which do you think it was—spear in the front or in the back?"

"I don't know," Rtas said. "But we're about to find out."

Shadow of Intent slid forward, its hull reflecting the yellow, pink, and sapphire clouds of a nearby nebula that nearly filled the black horizon. As Rtas watched the colors shift across the carrier's glossy hull, he was reminded of the sea predators that prowled the tidelands near his childhood home, a keep on the edge of one of Sanghelios's warm equatorial oceans.

The carrier was headed for a dark world without a star—a rogue planet spun out from an unknown cataclysm long ago, which was now content to carve its own stubborn path across the galactic disk, ignoring the feeble tugs of distant suns.

Orbiting this planet was something that looked uncannily like a sea urchin, one of the clusters of needle-sharp spines that had bedeviled Rtas's explorations of his keep's shoreline at low tide.

Once, when Rtas was barely out of his first decade, stripped to nothing but his loincloth and scampering on rocks close to shore, looking for small fish to spear, the sea had pulled quickly back, exposing a previously unseen world of limestone ridges and valleys, shaped and sharpened by ages upon ages of crashing waves. In fact, the water had receded so fast that countless sea creatures Rtas had only ever seen bulging from the deep-water nets of the keep's fishing fleet were now caught unaware, trapped and splashing in rocky puddles much too shallow for their bulk.

For a young Sangheili hunter with ambitions that had outgrown the minuscule prey close to shore, this was a golden opportunity. Rtas had eagerly threaded his way through the limestone, spearing glistening creatures until his woven shore-grass shoulder bag hung wet and heavy across his back. But even then, he did not return to shore. There were pools farther out filled with even rarer prizes: snap-tails and electric kesh that now lay gasping on the rocks. Rtas picked his way out to these magnificent specimens, shouldered his spear, and stroked their scaly flesh, imagining he was taming them with nothing but his touch. . . .

Then Rtas had seen the wave—a dark wall of water on the horizon that grew taller by the second. He looked back at the high walls of his keep and was terrified to see how far he'd come. Entranced by the bounty of the pools, he'd clambered almost a kilometer offshore, which would have been a quick sprint on even ground. But now his retreat was a razor-sharp maze, and by the time Rtas made it back across the rocky beach and limped through the water gate of his keep, his bare feet were swollen and burning with toxins from the urchins he'd been moving too fast to miss. His hands and knees bled from countless limestone cuts, and the sting of salt water in these wounds left him dizzy with pain.

Rtas hadn't thought of that day in decades. But the memory came back now, crystal clear, as he watched *Shadow of Intent* draw within a thousand kilometers of the orbital. Then, without warning, the urchin-like structure blazed brighter than the nebula behind it. And in that moment, something hit the Half-Jaw with a force far greater than the tsunami that had long ago crashed against the walls of his keep.

The energy wave, or whatever it was, slammed into the Half-Jaw's mind. One instant he had the complete memory of that day in the tide pools. The next moment he did not—and never would again. When the energy wave hit, the foremost thoughts in the Half-Jaw's mind were scoured clean. And when the light from the orbital finally faded from his eyes, Rtas was surprised to find he was screaming.

He was not the only one.

The pilot sitting beside him in the Phantom's cockpit was shouting a string of unintelligible words. At first Rtas thought he was talking in some alien tongue. But then he realized the pilot was speaking Sangheili and that, for a moment, the Half-Jaw had forgotten the language he had spoken all his life.

"C-calm down!" Rtas stuttered, reaching for the pilot's shoulder. But the Half-Jaw's arm was heavy, and it took tremendous concentration to move his hand, as if it some vital nerves had been severed and his brain was now threading a new path around the cut. "Can you . . . still control this ship?"

"Y-yes, Shipmaster," the pilot said. He was a ranger, the very picture of menace in his silver armor and vacuum-rated, full-face helmet. But he sounded like a frightened child, and when the sharp chirp of an emergency transmission rang from the cockpit control panel, the pilot grabbed his helmet and began to wail, rocking back and forth in his seat.

"Report!" Rtas shouted, stabbing a holographic switch to accept the transmission. The message was coming from the other Phantom, a few kilometers to starboard, and he expected to hear the Blademaster, who was serving as that dropship's copilot.

But after a brief pause, it was the Scion who announced: "Shipmaster, we have c-casualties! I don't know what . . . or h-how . . ." She, too, was having trouble forming the right words. "Three r-rangers are unresponsive . . . and Vul 'Soran as well."

Rtas clenched his jaws. He had known a slipspace jump into the hidden sector was a dangerous move. But he and his navigation officer had carefully studied *Spear of Light*'s database and chosen an entry point far outside the volume of that cruiser's previous arrivals and departures. As soon as *Shadow of Intent* had emerged from slipspace, Rtas had launched the two Phantoms. For several minutes, while the dropships had maintained what they hoped was a safe distance, the Half-Jaw had watched the carrier drift toward the orbital on the visor of his own full-face helmet. There was no crew aboard *Shadow of Intent*. It was now a decoy, piloted by its computational matrix, which was slaved to Rtas's Phantom in the event that he needed to give the carrier different commands.

At some point, *Shadow of Intent* had crossed an invisible line, and the orbital had fired. And in that respect, the Half-Jaw's plan had worked perfectly. If he or his crew had been on *Shadow of Intent* when the wave hit, they would all be incapacitated—or worse. In war, Rtas knew, there was always a price to pay for bold maneuvers. He thought of the Blademaster and his injured rangers and grimaced at the cost.

But it was about to go even higher.

The Half-Jaw heard the muffled discharge of a plasma pistol in his Phantom's troop bay. Warning glyphs blazed on the cockpit control panel, and he punched another switch, opening a comm channel to the bay.

"Status!" he shouted, but there was no response. Rtas shrugged out of his shoulder harness and stepped groggily to the rear of the cockpit. He heard another plasma burst and felt the Phantom's engines groan. The cockpit's control panel suddenly shut down, and all interior lights went dark except for the violet emergency backups. By the time Rtas had manually cycled through the troop bay door, he already knew what he would find.

Bringing the Prelate with them had been a calculated risk. While the Prelate had said no more about the Minister of Preparation following his initial interrogation—indeed, had said nothing else at all—it was clear to Rtas that the two San'Shyuum were partners in their scheme. If the Minister was truly here, the Half-Jaw had reasoned, he might be willing to negotiate for the Prelate's release, which might save *Shadow of Intent* from another fight. Rtas had mitigated the risk by keeping the Prelate restrained and putting him under the watchful eye of the Unggoy and the best of his rangers. But that hadn't been enough.

All of the Sangheili in the troop bay had been stunned by the energy wave and were either unconscious or struggling feebly in their harnesses. Stolt had wrestled free of his own shoulder harness, but was now facedown on the floor, his armor sparking from an overcharged plasma pistol shot. The Unggoy was trying to crawl toward the Prelate, who stood, wrists and ankles manacled together, at the center of the bay, near a smoking hole in the troop bay floor. The Prelate had stolen a plasma pistol from one of the unconscious Sangheili, and after blasting Stolt, he had pumped more plasma into a critical relay between the cockpit and the Phantom's engines. As soon as he saw Rtas, the Prelate steadied his stance and held down the pistol's trigger to build another overcharged bolt.

Rtas froze. He had his energy blade, but no ranged weapon. Yet instead of shooting the Half-Jaw, the black-armored San'Shyuum aimed the pistol at his own feet. A green bolt of superheated plasma splashed the Prelate's boots, instantly depleting his armor's energy shields—but also melting away his ankle manacles. A holographic meter near the pistol's rear sight flashed red, indicating the weapon's battery was depleted.

Seeing his opening, Rtas tore his energy blade from his belt and rushed across the troop bay. The Prelate tossed the pistol to the deck and for a moment seemed ready to meet the Half-Jaw's charge. But as Rtas brought his blade down in a vicious vertical slash, the Prelate quickly raised his hands, splayed wide apart—and Rtas's blade cut clean through the Prelate's wrist manacles with an electric snap. The Prelate whirled aside to let his enemy pass, and as the Half-Jaw's momentum carried him to the back wall of the bay, the Prelate stepped calmly into the circular energy field that formed an airlock in the troop bay floor, and then dropped out of sight.

Rtas shoved away from the wall with an angry roar.

"Tried . . . to stop him," Stolt said, his voice weak in the Half-Jaw's helmet.

"It's all right," Rtas said, swallowing his temper. He holstered his blade and pulled a carbine rifle from a nearby weapon rack. "I'm going after him."

The Unggoy rose slowly to a knee. "I'm . . . c-coming with you."

"No. See to your rangers. Reestablish a connection with *Shadow of Intent.*" Rtas stepped to the edge of the airlock. "If my transponder goes dark, tell the carrier to fire all remaining weapons . . . and destroy that orbital."

With that, he plunged through the field.

As Rtas entered the cold emptiness of space, there was no sound inside his helmet except his own uneven breaths. He fired his thrusters and stabilized his orientation so that he was facing the orbital, which was just off *Shadow of Intent*'s prow; a stark blossom of dark spines against the brilliant nebula. A bright chemical burst betrayed the Prelate's position as the San'Shyuum course-corrected and accelerated toward the orbital. Just as the Half-Jaw was about to do the same, his motion-tracker flashed, and Tul 'Juran appeared beside him, holding her energy lance.

Unlike the rangers, the Half-Jaw and the Scion didn't have thrusters integrated into their armor. But they had mounted ancillary units before the mission, and while Tul 'Juran had had only a short time to train, she managed a smooth stop beside Rtas, quickly corrected an incipient spin, and then said over a local comm channel: "He killed my k-kaidon and my kin . . . his life is mine to take."

"He killed many more than that . . . and he's not our only concern." The Half-Jaw pointed at the orbital. "We have to shut that down, before it fires again . . . or all the lives we've lost will be for nothing."

He and the Scion stared at each other through their thick polymer visors, their faces covered with the luminous war paint of their reflected heads-up displays. The Scion nodded, and Rtas saw in her eyes that she understood.

This is bigger than me. This is bigger than the both of us.

Then, together, they fired their thrusters and rocketed after the Prelate.

"It's a trick!" the Prelate shouted. "Prepare the ring to fire again!" He was hurtling past *Shadow of Intent*, and at present speed would reach the installation in less than a minute. Tem'Bhetek didn't need to look behind to know the Half-Jaw would soon be upon him.

"What happened?!" The Minister of Preparation's thin, precise voice crackled in the Prelate's helmet. "I attempted to hail the carrier, but you did not respond!"

The Prelate knew the Minister had been expecting him to arrive in full control of *Shadow of Intent.* Tem didn't have the energy now to explain how the Half-Jaw and his warriors had departed the carrier just outside the prototype Halo's effective range—how he himself had been captured and then made his escape.

Tem's mind had also been rattled by the activation of the ring. But he had the advantage of knowing what was coming—had used his mental enhancements to blank his thoughts and let the crippling wave wash over him—and in this way recovered a few seconds faster than his ranger guards. He had clubbed the nearest Sangheili with his manacles, taken his plasma pistol, and then shot the Unggoy, who had been the quickest to regain his wits. But the Prelate saved all of this explanation for later and instead simply said:

"Just have the ring ready by the time I reach the bunker!"

There was a long pause. Nothing but static. The Prelate had never been this direct with the Minister. He thought he might have pricked the older San'Shyuum's pride, giving him an order like he was one of the Jiralhanae.

"I will fire when I see fit, Prelate," the Minister said, his voice suddenly cold. "Whether you have returned to the bunker or not." Then he cut the connection.

The Prelate felt a gnawing doubt take a giant bite out of his resolve. After the Half-Jaw had told him his own version of events at High Charity, Tem had gone over and over Boru'a'Neem's description of events. *The Sacred Promissory is lost!* the Minister had said. *Nothing lives inside the city now except the Flood!* And in subsequent conversations, while Preparation had provided a few more details about the holy city's fall, they were mostly about his failed defense of the Promissory . . . nothing about events inside the dome.

At the time, because the Prelate had already been convinced of the Half-Jaw's guilt, he hadn't pressed the Minister. But having stared the Half-Jaw in the eye and heard the genuine remorse he showed for the Prelate's loss . . . things weren't as black-and-white as they used to be. And the Prelate's anger was only growing stronger in the gray.

Tem shot through a gap formed by four crossed spines, out of the nebula's light and into the installation's darkened interior. Unlike the energy fields on Covenant ships, the Forerunner structure had no visible separation between hard vacuum and atmosphere. *More magic we never understood. . . .*

But the Prelate didn't dwell on this. He throttled the output of his anti-grav belt and glided through a long diamond-shaped bay large enough to accommodate three Phantoms side by side. Following the course of a narrower, upward-sloping hall at the end of the bay, he soon emerged into the bright white expanse of the test chamber. The Minister was waiting for him near the lift that led to the bunker. He was surrounded by Yanme'e—some stood awkwardly on the floor on their curved, clawed legs, and more used these limbs to cling to the chamber walls. There were at least two dozen of the Drones, all armed with plasma pistols and needle rifles.

The Prelate kept his voice relaxed as he eyed the Yanme'e's weapons. "What are those for?" He cut power to his anti-grav belt, alighted on the floor, and removed his helmet.

"In case you did not come alone," the Minister of Preparation said. He waved a hand, and the insectoid creatures lowered their guns. "Where is the Half-Jaw?"

"Alive and not far behind me. We should get to the bunker, charge the ring . . ." The Prelate took a step toward the Minister, and as he did, Preparation drew back his throne. The move betrayed the subtle shimmer of the throne's energy shield.

"Careful, Tem'Bhetek," the Minister said. The Yanme'e's feelers twitched, and their glowing eyes darted to the Minister's fingers, watching for a signal. But Preparation's hands remained still in the sleeves of his threadbare robe. "The device is . . . unstable," the Minister continued. "It will not survive another firing." The Prelate saw that the crack along the ring's upper arc was much longer now; the circuits embedded in the rent had burned away, leaving a blackened cavity in the marble. "I cannot risk its destruction—not until we transport it to its final destination."

"What do you mean?" the Prelate asked. To a certain extent, he was just keeping the conversation going, trying to work out a way to get the answers he wanted without rousing the Minister's suspicion. But now he was truly curious. "Transport the ring to where?"

The Minister cocked his head to one side. He looked genuinely puzzled and disappointed that Tem hadn't already guessed. "To Sanghelios, of course."

Tem'Bhetek drew a long, slow breath. For him, revenge against the Half-Jaw had always been the end. He had really never considered what else the Minister might have planned. But now, after a few moments' thought, Tem discerned Boru'a'Neem's next step. "*Shadow of Intent* . . . You're going to use its reactors to charge the ring."

"*Spear of Light* was a noble ship and served its purpose well. But it was never strong enough to make it past Sanghelios's defenses or to provide power to the ring." The Minister stroked the fleshy wattle hanging from his chin. "I have been testing the device at only a fraction of its power. Even if we were to increase the pulse by twenty percent, that would be more than enough to wipe all sentient life from Sanghelios and its moons. We shall annihilate the Sangheili home system and set back their species for ages to come!"

"Surely whoever was on board *Shadow of Intent* would also perish in the pulse," Tem said. "Who did you have in mind?"

"My finest Prelate, of course. But I have the distinct feeling he is not as . . . committed as he once was."

"As I was when you told me my family was dead?"

The Minister pursed his lips. "So. We have come back around to that."

Just then, two red lights flashed on the Prelate's visor, his motion-tracker alerting him to a pair of hostile contacts nearing the installation. A similar warning flashed on the arm of the Minister's throne.

"I'm afraid we do not have time for questions," the Minister said.

"I have only one."

"Do you want to know the truth, or what I knew you needed to hear?"

With that, the Prelate had his answer. His heart ached. *Oh, Yalar, forgive me . . .*

But he still needed to hear it. "Why lie to me, Boru'a'Neem?"

"Because I needed your anger—I needed your blind rage to see this through."

"You took my family from me."

Preparation slammed his fist on his throne. "You never would have had a family if not for me!" The wrinkled folds of skin on the Minister's neck pulsed with his contempt. "I have listened to you endlessly mourn those two small deaths, but you have no idea how much value was lost! My Sacred Promissory held more priceless relics—more Forerunner wealth—than any other vault in the Covenant!" The Minister's limbs trembled, and his voice was shrill. "You lost a wife and child? I lost *everything*!"

The Minister's words hit the Prelate harder than any wounds he'd ever received in battle. Under this verbal assault, his enhancements had triggered automatically, and his body was tensed to defend itself. But now the galvanizing rage that always accompanied these preparations was gone.

The Prelate felt empty, and his voice was hollow. "I did everything you asked of me. I saved your life," he said.

"There were not many San'Shyuum who could match your skills or your devotion—and now perhaps there are none." The Minister flared the sleeves of his robe and settled his arms softly on his throne. "But we are not the only ones who escaped the Holy City, and there will be many, full of rage or hungry for glory, who will gladly take your place." All the artifice dropped from the Minister's voice; his words were flat and final. "I don't need you anymore."

With a twitch of his fingers, Preparation signaled the Yanme'e to open fire. The chamber filled with plasma bolts and needle-like explosive shards, all directed at the Prelate. But even though Tem'Bhetek was in motion before these lethal rounds were in the air, he was not the first thing to reach the Minister's throne.

An energy lance arced over the Prelate's head and struck the Minister's shield, dead center. The shield knocked the lance aside, but then wavered and collapsed. Immediately after, two carbine bursts cooked past the Prelate, hitting the Minister between his right shoulder and the base of his neck.

Then the Prelate ran into a wall of Yanme'e fire impossible to dodge. His own shields fell. He felt one plasma bolt boil into his thigh and a needle hit below his ribs and then explode out his back. As he tumbled toward the ring, Tem saw the Minister accelerate backward in his throne and into the bunker lift, frantically clasping his wound as pale-red blood pumped through his fingers. Boru'a'Neem locked eyes with the Prelate one last time. Then the saw-toothed door to the lift closed and the Minister was gone.

"Leave him!" Rtas shouted as the Scion sprinted for the Prelate. "Kill those Yanme'e!"

The Half-Jaw shot one Drone out of the air, and as it dropped, the Scion slid onto her knees, scooped up its plasma pistol, and came up firing. By the time the two Sangheili had made it to the ring, the greasy remains of seven more Yanme'e were smeared on the floor or dripping down the walls. Some of the Drones had retreated to the bunker lift, where they found cover behind its door frame, which protruded out from the chamber wall. More were buzzing in the highest reaches of the chamber, leaping back and forth between the support beams, trying to find the best angles for their shots.

Crouching beside the Scion at the base of the ring, Rtas eyed the ammunition counter on his carbine. "I have ten rounds left!"

The Scion inspected her pistol. "Less than a quarter charge!"

"Get your lance! I'll cover you!"

As the Scion leapt into the open, Rtas briefly considered the onyx relic pressed against his back. It was shocking to be so close to a Halo ring again. And while it would have been easy to mistake its small scale for a lack of power, the Half-Jaw knew from the conversation he had just overheard between the Minister and the Prelate: *If I fail, and they bring this infernal ring aboard my ship, Sanghelios will be lost!*

Rtas stood and fired past the Scion, braining two Yanme'e who had just stuck their heads out from behind the door frame. Then he aimed upward, killing the first of a trio of Drones swooping down for an attack. The two other Yanme'e scattered, and the Half-Jaw and the Scion, now with lance in hand, ducked back behind the ring.

"The Minister of Preparation is through that door!" Rtas said as angry shots from the dozen or so remaining Yanme'e sizzled overhead.

The Scion took a quick glance over the lower arc of the ring. "There's a control panel. On the left side of the frame!"

Neither of them had any idea if they would be able to manipulate the Forerunner door controls; undoubtedly the Minister had locked the door from the other side. But both Sangheili knew they were now sitting right beside the very device that had nearly wiped their minds clean. And if the Minister was preparing to unleash another wave . . .

"Stay close!" Rtas activated his energy blade. "Don't stop until we make it to the door!"

Tul 'Juran nodded as she gave her lance a shake. The tips of the weapon crackled diamond bright.

Then, together, they stepped out from behind the ring.

The two Sangheili were blurs of glittering light as they whirled their blades around themselves, deflecting the Yanme'e's fire. They cut apart a group of Drones that dove from above and made it halfway to the grav-lift door when the ring suddenly powered on behind them with a deep, almost inaudible hum that shook their skulls inside their helmets—a terrifying sensation that stopped them in their tracks. Rtas and Tul 'Juran braced against each other, back to back, growing panic limiting their urges to either fight or flight. Neither seemed ideal.

Meanwhile, the Yanme'e were just as unnerved as the two Sangheili. All the Drones that remained were now clawing at the door, ignoring the Forerunner control panel and its pulsing glyphs. Rtas scowled. *If they don't know how to open it, how will we?* At the same time, what chance did they have to outrun this Halo ring? The Half-Jaw could feel the Scion's body shudder as the relic's rising wave pulsed against her mind—could feel his own thoughts start to slip.

Why else would I imagine someone . . . singing?

But then Rtas recognized the voice, and he knew the song was real.

During the firefight, the Prelate had dragged himself to the shaft beside the ring that led down to the installation's power systems. Resting with his back against the low wall that circled the shaft, the Prelate was now staring at the spot on the floor before the ring where his Sangheili prisoners had once stood.

As the Prelate gently sang lilting San'Shyuum verses Rtas didn't understand, he slowly unfastened his anti-grav belt and wrapped it around a satchel of plasma grenades that he had recovered from the corpse of a nearby Yanme'e. When this explosive bundle was gathered in his lap, the Prelate ceased his song. He laughed ruefully and coughed: "Why *not* sing at a time like this . . ." Then he rose partway up the wall and looked directly at the Half-Jaw.

"The spear was always in my back," the Prelate said. Arm shaking, he held his bundle out over the shaft. "I wish I'd felt it sooner."

Rtas had a vague idea what the Prelate meant, but the pulse from the ring was overwhelming now, and he was losing the ability to think, let alone speak, clearly. He gave the Prelate a grateful nod and grabbed the Scion by the shoulder. Then they activated their thrusters and raced away from the ring.

Tem'Bhetek waited until the Half-Jaw and female Sangheili were out of the test chamber before he dropped his belt. The bundle clattered against the wall of the shaft, once, twice, and then continued its descent in silence. The Prelate slid down the barrier, leaving a smear of blood from the gaping hole in his armor, and settled, legs akimbo. He pulled his hands into his lap. Without a weapon to hold, they felt uncomfortably empty.

He closed his eyes and whispered: "This path. Where did it lead?"

"To me, my love . . ."

Slowly, the Prelate opened his eyes. Yalar stood before him, her thin yellow gown fluttering in the ring's invisible waves.

"It led to us."

Then there was a weight in Tem's arms; a warm and fussy wriggling. He looked down and saw his child. "What is it?" he asked. "Boy or girl?"

His wife smiled. "Whatever you want it to be."

The ring's silhouette wavered as it began its final charging cycle. The Prelate felt his mind slipping . . . but he willed his enhancements into a final barricade.

Please, just a little more time . . .

Yalar glanced at the ring.

"It's all a lie," Tem said, choking back a sob. "It won't take us anywhere."

His baby laughed.

Yalar held out her hand. "How do you know for sure?"

Gritting his teeth, the Prelate rose. He took Yalar's soft fingers in his armored glove. Then, wife in one arm and child in the other, he limped toward the ring.

Tem felt the floor shudder beneath his feet as his belt finally detonated far below. A hot wind roared at his back. He was close to the ring now, and his defenses were crumbling. But the strange thing was, as all the sensations of the real world began to fade, the ghosts in his arms seemed more real than ever.

"I'm frightened," Tem said.

Yalar leaned close, kissed his neck, and whispered in his ear: *"Into the light, forever free!"*

In that moment, the Prelate remembered happiness, love, contentment—all the joys they shared before . . . and then he knew nothing else.

Shadow of Intent hung in high orbit above Duraan. Most of the carrier's crew was on the planet, recovering from their wounds or simply enjoying the hospitality of the grateful settlers. Rtas 'Vadum, however, was alone on the command deck, except for the flickering image of another Sangheili in the holo-tank. Tall and proud, but with a weariness in his shoulders not unlike that of the Half-Jaw, this Sangheili wore dark-gray, ornately carved armor that looked even older than his strong, serious face.

". . . and then the installation exploded, before the ring had an opportunity to fire a second time," Rtas was saying, adding the last details to what had been a long and extensive debrief. "We scanned every fragment. There was nothing to recover."

"Then Sanghelios is safe," the Arbiter said. "And all of us are in your debt."

The Half-Jaw shook his head. "I did not do it alone."

"No, of course not," the Arbiter said. "The warriors who were with you at the ring—are they recovering?"

"Slowly but surely. The Blademaster was the worst, but even he is awake now and back to his usual bellowing." Rtas stepped closer to the tank. "In fact, he wanted to speak with you. To discuss the revocation of certain naval codes . . . specifically those forbidding the enlistment of female crew."

The Arbiter chuckled deep in his throat. "I hoped your voyage would be restful, but I never thought Vul 'Soran would find it *that* relaxing." Then, serious once more: "The time has come to change many of our old ways. This Scion is very welcome on your crew. I look forward to meeting her and honoring her. When will you leave Duraan?"

"Ten days, perhaps twenty," Rtas said. "But we will not be returning to Sanghelios."

The Half-Jaw thumbed the control panel in the railing around the holo-tank and transmitted an annotated report on *Spear of Light*'s navigational database. His officers had since completed a more thorough study and uncovered evidence of a rendezvous of San'Shyuum vessels after the fall of High Charity. It had been a sizable flotilla, enough to carry thousands of San'Shyuum. Although the details were fragmentary at best, there were slipspace signatures to follow, trajectories to track—the beginnings of a long hunt, for someone with the spirit to undertake it.

"High Charity . . ." the Arbiter said, when he'd finished reading the report. "So Preparation wasn't the only snake who slithered out of that nest."

"There will be others like him," Rtas said. "Hiding, scheming."

"Someone will have to stop them." The Arbiter clasped his hands behind his back. "But it does not have to be you, Rtas 'Vadum. Many shipmasters have given up their commands, returned to their keeps here to farm the land or fish the seas. Sanghelios needs wise leaders, now more than ever. I would never order you to leave *Shadow of Intent.* But know that if you do, no one will doubt your bravery or commitment."

Rtas grasped the railing of the holo-tank. Through it, he could feel the distant rumble of the carrier's reactors—the familiar rhythm of his ship. *It would be difficult to give this up . . . but to be done with war entirely? To rest and let someone else carry on the fight?*

The Arbiter's offer was tempting, and the Half-Jaw almost took it. But then there was the matter of the Prelate's final, selfless act.

"There will be some San'Shyuum who deserve the full measure of our fury," Rtas said at last, "and others who will not. I would like the opportunity to try to sort one from the other, if I can."

"And so you shall, then," the Arbiter said. "I cannot think of anyone more qualified for such a vital mission." He paused, clearly reluctant to sever the transmission. "I will expect regular reports." And then, finally: "Until we meet again . . ."

". . . In Urs's everlasting light." The Half-Jaw finished the traditional good-bye, and the holo-tank went blank.

As he stood there in *Shadow of Intent*'s armored heart, Rtas 'Vadum thought:

Maybe, in the end, this was the best that any warrior could hope for. A chance to reconcile with your enemy, or, failing that, to fall in the pursuit of peace.

This thought energized Rtas, and for the first time in a long while, he did not dread the coming battles. Because although he wasn't certain where this new voyage would take him or what dangers he might face along the way, Rtas could see more than one ending, and that gave him the will to start.

THE BALLAD OF HAMISH BEAMISH

FRANK O'CONNOR

A long time ago on a military ship
A boy signed on to a perilous trip
A would-be cadet
With a penchant for danger
He signed on for thrills
In a cryosleep manger

Corbulo's the name
Of his life's destination
A military school
With a fine reputation
An officer's life
Was the life he had chosen
As he and his chums were cryonically frozen

And off into slipspace the young people headed
But a problem arose that starfarers have dreaded
The long sleep of storage
Was to be interrupted
By a technical flaw
And some code that corrupted

As the good ship *Jamaica* flew on through the night
The seal on his chamber grew a bit less than tight

The cryopod opened a decade too soon
And Hamish thawed out 'neath an alien moon
Alone and afraid in the space between spaces
He gazed with fear at his companions' faces
He wiped frost from their visors
But onward they slept
Safe and preserved while poor Hamish just wept

When he got it together, he resolved to survive
Alone on a starship, now surely he'd thrive
All he'd need is some heat and a good source of food
But on waking the AI, the news wasn't good
"Apologies, Beamish, but this ship is unmanned
"You and the others are effectively canned
"We ship you like cargo to some distant star
"But this uncrewed transporter has no buffet bar
"Nor heating for humans, but there's plenty of air
"So if you wrap up in blankets, you might still make it there
"Your sleep chamber's ruined
"And the backup is rusted
"So if you get to Corbulo
"You'll be all old and busted
"It's been called a flat circle
"And a relative hitch
"But the fact of the matter's
"Time is gravity's bitch
"So you have my condolence
"And I'll help if I can
"But I suggest that indolence
"Is the best kind of plan."

So the darkness and cold would make anyone spooked
And young Master Hamish knew that his goose was cooked
He examined his options
And set in for the flight
He'd be cold and hungry for this long, lonely night

So he needed some fuel for a possible fire
And protein to eat lest his body expire
He looked high and low
And through every dark passage
But all he could find was an Oberto sausage
Two hundred years old
Discarded, incredible
But because it was jerky
It was still kind of edible
As he chewed the last meat
That he might ever enjoy
He thought about girls and he thought about boys
Though frozen intact, nails and hair would still grow
And the seeds of his madness had started to show
He would shave them and clip them
With tender composure
And burn hair and eat nails lest he die of exposure
The smell, it was dreadful
And the sight even worse
But better this madness
Than a flight in a hearse
And so ten long years passed
And Corbulo drew near
And Hamish's madness

Replaced all his fear
He got used to the routine
As we are wont to do
But he dreamed of poutine
And he played his kazoo
Oh, I didn't explain that he kept that toy whistle?
Or that he wore a tattoo of a plain Scottish thistle?
His buzzing lament did not keep him sane
In fact, you could argue it addled his brain

So when the ship at last reached the Corbulo banner
He was thirty years old and as mad as a spanner
The medics tried hard to habilitate Hamish
His exploits aboard were disturbing but famous
They found him a job doing what he does best
Which is making the most of a terrible mess
So they put him in whites and they gave him a broom
And set him about cleaning room after room
The other cadets soon forgot Hamish's story
And Hamish got used to his missed chance at glory
He'd never a soldier or an officer be
But he never got used to the odor of pee
He'd clean it in bathrooms from floor to the sink
But I never revealed . . . what did poor Hamish drink?

So here is the moral of this dreadful tale
Check all of your gaskets before you set sail
And if in your world, you're aware that it's cleanish
Remember the ballad of poor Hamish Beamish

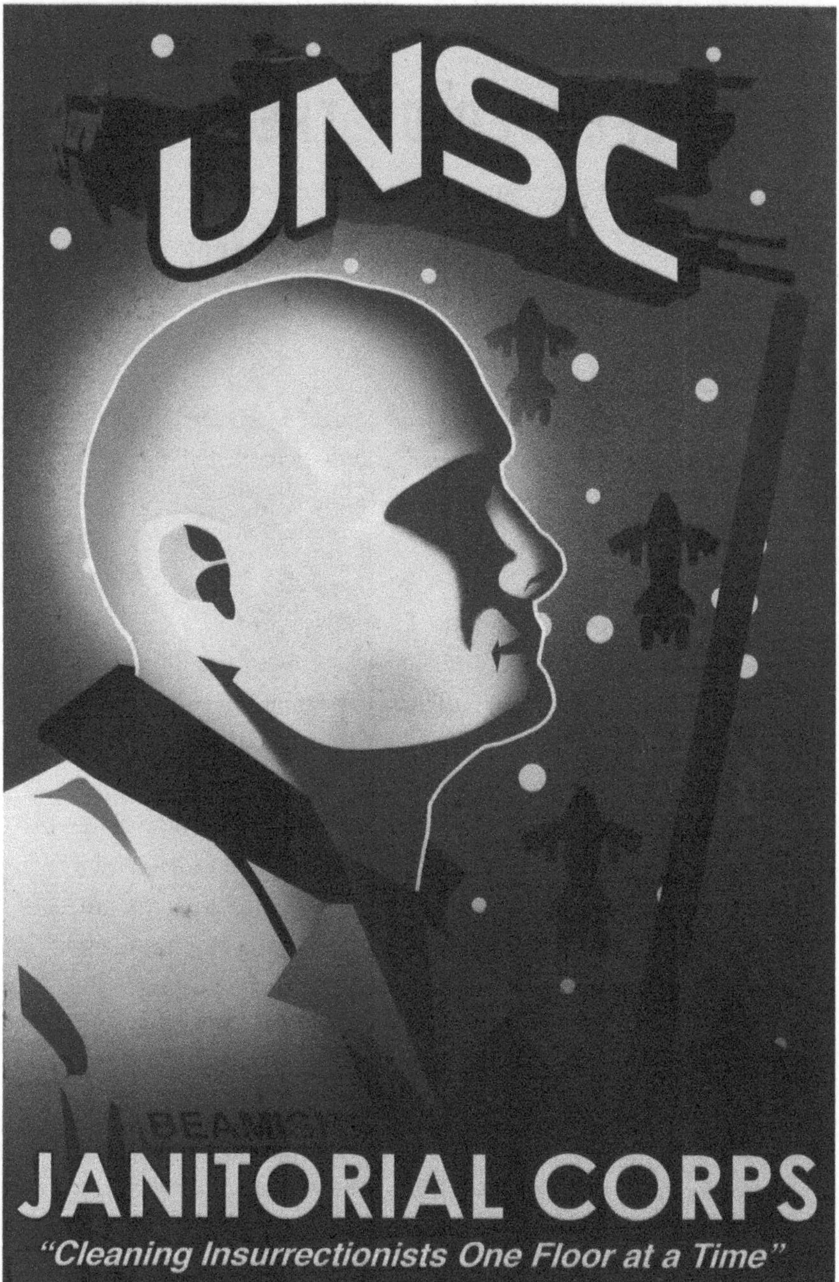

UNSC

JANITORIAL CORPS

"Cleaning Insurrectionists One Floor at a Time"

DEFENDER OF THE STORM

JOHN JACKSON MILLER

This story takes place near the end of the Forerunners' three-hundred-year war with the Flood, a little more than 100,000 years BCE (Halo: Cryptum, Halo: Silentium).

"Ancilla, can you confirm what I just saw?"

The electronic voice at the back of Adequate-Observer's mind responded: "You will have to be more specific."

You can read my mind, the Forerunner thought. *How is it that you do not already know what I mean?*

He growled in frustration and hurried from one window of the station to another. No, there was nothing special outside—and if there had been, it was gone now. The station was rotating too fast. From each port he beheld only clouds racing through the darkness of the gas giant Seclusion, the same picture he'd seen for the past fifteen solar years.

Adequate-Observer was a lookout who rarely saw anything. Rated a Warrior-Servant, the Manipular had neither gone to war nor been of much service. Filed away far from inhabited space, he stood guard over this gas-mining station designated as Seclusion Spiral. A pinwheel ten kilometers across, the station twirled along atop the clouds of an immense eternal storm on the planet.

Rows of electrostatic collection devices lined each of five colossal vanes. A single collector could draw enough exotic particles from the storm to supply the needs of a Forerunner world for a solar year.

Even after all this time, Adequate still didn't know what the particles were, or why the Forerunners needed them. His ancilla—his armor's mental assistance system—had explained it all once, but it hadn't made much sense to him. The universe was teeming with things to know; an individual could easily get bogged down with useless trivia. Adequate didn't require the specifics of what happened to the product of Seclusion Spiral, so he didn't clutter his mind with it. Sometimes it was better that way.

In truth, having an ancilla handy had given Adequate an excuse to forget many things. The designers of his armor had intended to create a symbiotic relationship between wearer and suit, and in this, they had succeeded perhaps too well. Adequate-Observer had no need to think about the big issues *or* the small ones anymore. Keeping track of his location on the station? The ancilla handled that. Bodily functions? The ancilla regulated them. On days when he was feeling particularly frustrated with his assignment, he was tempted to ask the ancilla to move his arms and legs for him while he made his rounds.

Yet he never resorted to that option. It felt too much like cheating—and he worried that his superiors would find out. The ancilla answered to them too, after all. If his masters wanted a robotic drone, they would have sent one. No, his great hope was getting off the station and into the fight against the biological terror known as the Flood, and the only way to prove his worth was to do his job, such as it was.

That meant spotting things, even when his own ancilla didn't believe him.

"There it is again," Adequate said, pointing as a mass darker than the surrounding maelstrom swept past. "Something is out there. In the storm."

"There are more than six hundred known substances circulating in the winds of the vortex," the artificial intelligence responded. "You could have seen any one of them."

"I have been here for fifteen years, ancilla. I know what is outside." He really didn't, not with any specificity. "Whatever that object was, it was not dust. It was solid and dark—mostly." He frowned. "You are controlling my combat skin. The armor's sensors must have seen the same thing I did, correct?"

"If the sensors noticed anything, nothing exceeded parameters enough for the systems to issue an alert. But there is a simple way to find out. I am rerunning the imagery now. Tell me when you see it."

Adequate stood still as a statue and closed his eyes as the ancilla, through the symbiotic mental interface in his armor, replayed the seconds in question. Since the images were being piped directly into the theater of his mind, shutting his eyes was unnecessary—*in theory.* In practice, since receiving his first Warrior-Servant combat skin as a young Manipular, he had never been very good at shutting out the outside world.

The ancilla did its job, and the moment reappeared to him, as clear as any memory he ever had. "There," he said, when an amorphous form peeked out from the clouds.

"Evaluating." The image froze, and Adequate saw symbols dancing alongside the dark blob, the result of his ancilla's studies. "Spectroscopic analysis is unrevealing—but the strongest possibilities are all Class-D ices, which accrete in the upper elevations of the atmosphere near here and get swept into the storm."

Adequate's brow furrowed as he tried to concentrate on the

image. "What is that in the center? It seems to be"—he tried to focus—"It almost appears to be a light."

"There is intense electrical activity below us, Adequate. Anything that drifts into the cyclone is bound to be struck by lightning." The ancilla paused. "Does that resolve the matter?"

"I suppose," he replied. "That is all." The image vanished from the part of his mind that his ancilla had access to but remained in his living memory. It was a curious thing, and he had seen something like it twice before during his posting. But he had never mentioned it, certain that if it *were* anything special, his ancilla would have caught it.

He was only an Adequate-Observer, by nature.

He was also sure his ancilla was correct that nothing could survive in the storm below. He rose for every duty shift relieved that Seclusion Spiral only rode the top of the great storm. Immense enough to encapsulate whole planets, the storm had raged on the gas giant's equatorial region for half a million years so far and showed no signs of dissipating. As long as it churned and wobbled its way across Seclusion's relatively warm midsection, the dynamo would run indefinitely.

That, he understood. What the ancilla had never been able to dispel his confusion about was how it was possible for Adequate to move about on the station without being tossed around or becoming violently ill. The forces of gravity and motion were somehow constantly being compensated for—not just at the station's hub, but along the hallways several kilometers long heading out to the tips of the twirling vanes. The Builders responsible for the station clearly knew things far beyond his comprehension. He'd stopped asking about how the station functioned after the first solar year.

Still, there was something odd about what he'd seen. He idly tapped against the window with his boltshot, his trusty directed-energy pistol. Trusty because it was always at his side, not because he'd ever had occasion to use it. What benefit was it in this place?

"Your metabolic rate is increasing," the ancilla said. "Would you like me to have your armor apply a minor relieving agent?"

"I have no need for it."

"Perhaps you would like to discuss your concerns instead. I theorize your agitation may be at least eighty-four percent explained by tomorrow's arrival of the annual transport ship."

"Eighty-four percent." He shook his head and started walking up the hall, continuing his rounds. "How do you calculate these things?"

"Is that a rhetorical question?"

"It is," he said. "And do not think that I am concerned about the visit. I already know what will happen to me when the tanker arrives. Absolutely nothing."

Adequate-Observer watched through the stockroom skylight as the tanker disengaged from its docking portal atop Seclusion Spiral's hub. The Forerunner had waited anxiously through the six work shifts it took for the vessel to load up on a solar year's worth of exotic particles; the transfer of personnel always came at the end.

And, as always, Adequate had not received orders to depart.

The experience was worse this time. He had looked on in dismay as all twenty of the other soldiers posted on the station had been reassigned to faraway places to fight the Flood. Never before had Adequate seen so many retasked at once. How bad must the struggle be for the Forerunners?

Apparently not bad enough for them to want *him*.

And so he had remained, mutely restocking the supply shelves as his exultant companions from the previous year exited the station. The newly arriving Warrior-Servants said little to him as they entered, and he said nothing in return. What was the point, really, in learning anything about them? They would be gone in another year too, and Adequate would be trapped, same as always. Never to fight, never to evolve as he spent the last useful moments of his life spinning in the dark.

He spoke to his ancilla only after the tanker vanished from sight. "Did they provide a reason?"

"No. They never do."

That fact, Adequate didn't need reminding about. In previous years, his ancilla had tried to cushion the blow, rationalizing that the Forerunners in charge of things must value his service and knowledge too much to let him leave this place. It could be argued, after all, that after fifteen solar years, he was now the wizened master of Seclusion Spiral, trusted with mentoring an entirely new staff of neophytes.

Yet the ancilla did not argue that notion this time, and Adequate would not have believed it anyway. He knew the truth about himself. He was no sage, no expert. The past year's class of Warrior-Servants had not made any effort to look to Adequate for guidance and advice, and he had not offered any. The crew that had just arrived was even less likely to need his help.

From their service records, his ancilla had already determined that half of the new arrivals were more experienced. One called Capital-Enforcer had once stood guard at a facility visited for three daily cycles by the Librarian herself. What was there for Adequate to say to such distinguished people? Why, there was no need for his teachings at all. The departing sentries' ancillas had already transferred everything else they needed about serving on the station.

And the sum of that was: *walk the halls, look out the viewports, repeat.*

Worse than useless.

The last of the newcomers having departed for their new quarters, Adequate looked back out into the darkness. There was nothing to see, of course.

He went back to his shelving.

Hub detail. It was the one day in twenty-one when Adequate's routine changed at all. He watched from the center of the station as his new companions prepared their boltshots and headed in groups of four into the spoke passageways to police the enormous, labyrinthine interiors of the vanes.

Because the desired particles settled in the atmosphere at night, Seclusion Spiral could only do its collecting during the day; as a result, the Forerunner designers simply programmed the life-support systems to shut down outside the hub during the night hours. That meant twenty of the twenty-one on staff were gone at once, four per spoke, leaving the automated command center and living quarters all to Adequate.

It was no day of leisure. Adequate collected the refuse the squad had generated and worked to clean the galley; it was already clear to him that his new teammates were more slovenly than the last. Another sign that things were going badly in the war with the Flood. Discipline during off-duty hours was one of the first things to suffer.

He'd recently seen that in action. Normally, when two or three new replacements arrived, upheaval was limited: they worked to integrate themselves into the established social order on the station. Not so this time. The twenty newcomers had already bonded on their flight in and had quickly realized from Adequate's service record that his career was at a dead end. Since her arrival, Sprightly-Runner, the jokester of the new crew, had made constant sport of him.

"Such a wonderful modern facility," she'd remarked in passing. "With just one out-of-place antique."

"Adequate is a beautiful name," Sprightly had stated another time. "You really should use your honorific title with it."

"I do not have a title."

"Of course you do. It *is* 'Barely,' correct?"

Barely-Adequate had been his designation around the hub barracks ever since. He didn't understand why he deserved such cruelty.

"Ignore their taunts. Understand that they do not wish to be here either," his ancilla explained.

Worst of all, they had collectively decided the dirtiest assignment on the station should again fall to him: gathering up packs of the occupants' waste for delivery to the digester units, one located at the end of each vane. Microorganisms inside the units broke down the foul matter to generate power, while releasing unwanted gases into the atmosphere. He didn't know why the relief stations were not constructed near the ends of the vanes in the first place. All he knew was that he was tasked with the detail—again.

He didn't care—and had no desire for the others' companionship. Increasingly, he had taken to spending his off-duty hours outside the quarters and in the command center: there he could avoid harassment while studying the monitors in search of his pet phantom. At least he had not made the mistake of mentioning to the others that he'd been seeing things outside. Why provide them with any more ammunition?

The completion of his chores gave him a chance to return to his search. He had always known how to operate the visual sensors located on Seclusion Spiral's hull; it was part of his basic training for posting here. The hostile environment outside made checking the sensors a fruitless task for the watch keepers, who focused instead on their similarly futile inspection marches to the vanes. A true invader from space would be detected and announced by the station's core computer.

The radar emitters, consequently, pointed up. With his ancilla's help, Adequate found he could direct one partially downward. Four times, the sensors had found something moving in the storm—perhaps. But the data made no sense. Whatever was down there was traveling slower than the surrounding winds, almost tacking against them—quite peculiar behavior for an ice fragment or a bit of debris. Adequate hoped the change of seasons on Seclusion would allow him a better opportunity.

"Ancilla, will the winter make the storm easier or harder to—"

Klaxons sounded all around. He heard an agitated voice in his helmet. *"This is Capital-Enforcer! Come in, hub officer!"*

"Hub here," Adequate said.

"Alert, everyone! I have a missing officer—and hostile movement here at the end of Vane One. It's the Flood!"

It had happened. Something had finally happened.

Adequate's circulatory system went into overdrive, prompting his ancilla to apply calming agents. The injections didn't work. How else was he supposed to react? For fifteen years, his only foes were boredom and ridicule. Yet now, here at the end of the galaxy, the great enemy had come.

The Flood.

He had remained on hub detail watching the command center's monitors while one guard from each of the other spokes emerged from the tunnels and headed into Vane One to assist Capital-Enforcer. That effectively doubled the number of warriors on the scene, he thought—until his ancilla reminded him that the wretched two-legged monster stalking the halls was a former teammate.

He saw it in flashes and glimpses. Sickly green in color with a blotchy hide, the creature's long limbs flailed against the bulkheads as it clumsily lumbered through the halls of the vane. A combat form, he knew from his studies: scraps of Forerunner armor remained lodged in its hide, artifacts of the individual that once had been.

He only then wondered who that person was. Dutiful-Marcher, he learned when his ancilla checked the roster to see who was missing. How horrific must it have been, Adequate wondered, for the warrior to find his body erupting into that dreadful form? What would his last thoughts have been?

And was he in there, somewhere, thinking now? Adequate hoped not—especially when he saw blazes of light. Gunfire struck the combat form, ripping into its body. Adequate moved from monitor to monitor to get a better view. For a moment, it seemed the threat was ended—

—until the sick, glowing bulge on the back of what had once been Dutiful's body burst open, spraying steaming ichor and releasing—what? He could not tell, for they were moving so quickly.

His ancilla, however, had already figured it out. "Infection forms."

Capital-Enforcer and his companions had turned, falling back as garish pods propelled themselves across the floor and walls of the vane's hallways on twisted appendages. Adequate switched from scene to scene, seeing in one moment the frantic warriors, turning to shoot—and in the next, virulent carriers rushing toward them, seeking new hosts.

The defenders' boltshots spoke again and again, shredding some attackers, missing others. Adequate longed for something to do—and then got his chance.

"Hub officer," Capital called out. *"Close bulkhead one-stroke-four!"*

Adequate quickly sought out the control. It would sever part of one part of the vane from another, and help prevent the Flood from accessing the spoke that led to the hub. He activated it, and watched with satisfaction on a monitor as the bulkhead slammed down, squashing a gruesome infection form.

He was unaccountably happy. His first strike against the Flood, against anything, had been delivered. But his reverie was cut short when his ancilla, tied in with the core computer, reported. "Sprightly-Runner is in danger."

"She's working Vane Two." Adequate hurried to another set of monitors and beheld the female Forerunner fleeing for her life up the long tunnel, not even stopping to fire. Behind her, Adequate saw on the reverse angles, was a raging mass of pursuing infection forms—as well as one of the combat forms, even more energetic than the one he'd seen earlier. Its limbs thrashed against the walls and ceiling, propelling it forward.

It wasn't just one vane infected, Adequate realized. There were two sources for the Flood, unconnected. The only place they met was in the hub—where he was.

He watched helplessly as Sprightly outraced the horde. "She must reach the next cutoff!" he said. Emergency bulkheads existed every eighty meters, ready to close off the tunnel behind her. He called out to the screens. *"Run!"*

"We should quickly drop the temperature in the spokes," Adequate's ancilla said. "It may retard their speed and growth."

"Show me!" he replied.

The AI directed him to the appropriate console, where he made the command. Adequate knew it would have been much easier had his ancilla been given the power to operate, rather than simply monitor, Seclusion Spiral's systems—but then, a Flood-infected guardian might well inherit control of the station. It was to be avoided.

Adequate moved back to the monitors dedicated to the spoke leading to Vane Two. If Sprightly was fending off the Flood, he could no longer tell. "The surveillance imagery's gone!" he cried.

"I do not know if it can be reestablished," his ancilla said. "The Flood may have compromised one of the trunk lines, cutting power to the—"

Adequate didn't hear the rest. Gripping the boltshot that had been in his hand since the crisis started, he dashed into the entrance to tunnel two, racing to save an individual who had never treated him with respect. "Crew, I am going to aid Sprightly," he called into his helmet mic.

"Do not leave the hub!" someone yelled back. He couldn't hear who had said it; there was too much gunfire in the background. Not to mention his own ancilla, which had never stopped urging him to turn around.

"This is unwise," it said again after he had gone another fifty meters. "Sprightly is not answering hails. You cannot know what her condition is."

"She is alone. That is her condition." Adequate knew simple math. They had pulled one sentry each from the other four vanes to assist Capital-Enforcer: that left three in Vane Two. He speculated that both her companions had been infected: one was the combat form, while the unfortunate other's body must have given rise to the infection forms. Sprightly would surely be next.

His ancilla would not be silent. "The hub must be saved, Adequate. This is the wrong course of action."

"You said yourself the power is fluctuating. I may have to cycle the emergency bulkheads shut by hand. The hub must be saved."

"Yes, but you should have tried to do it from the hub first."

Adequate wasn't going to do that. It might have meant closing Sprightly off, trapping her with the nightmare. Darkness lay ahead, but he knew where he was. Observation windows lined the tunnel to the right, where a few flashes of lightning could be counted on for illumination. It was one of his favorite sections to patrol, and the place where he had first seen the—

Something slammed wetly against the viewport. The jarring impact knocked the Forerunner off his feet. Rolling, he drew his weapon and pointed it at the window, wondering how the Flood could be outside in that environment.

But what he saw was nothing like any of the Flood forms he had ever seen in lectures. Instead, a thing with colossal transparent wings hovered in front of the observation port. The avian—for that is all he knew to call it—was more than twice his size, with a tailfin that darted madly around as the creature bobbed in the storm. At the being's center was a crystalline carapace, within which he could clearly make out three natural lights: two blue and one red.

Forgetting completely about the Flood, Adequate stood and edged closer to the window. The lights in the avian's gut seemed to pulsate as he did so. *Were they eyes*, he wondered, *and were they watching him?*

And had they been watching him all along?

"Ancilla—"

"Unknown entity."

"Agreed," he said, watching the beast fighting against the wind. Seclusion Spiral was spinning, yet somehow this thing was keeping pace with the spoke of the giant propeller without being swept away. It backed off and zoomed down into the blackness. Adequate ran further along the tunnel, hoping to see more—but it was gone.

"No avian species has ever been reported on Seclusion," his ancilla said. "The planet is lifeless."

"Evidently not. Unless it is with the—" Suddenly remembering, he turned back up the hall and started to run. He had since forgotten all about Sprightly.

"Stop!"

He didn't ignore the ancilla's warning this time, which brought up a magnified infrared view of the hall before his eyes. "That mass up ahead is Sprightly. Her body is exhibiting evidence of transmogrification."

"It has her then," he said. Reluctantly, he lifted his weapon. "You're certain?"

"Yes."

He started firing down the hall. He could hear screeching noises as his shots found targets. *Sprightly, perhaps?* Or more of the infection forms? He did not want to know. He just understood that he would have run straight into danger had the thing in the window not slowed his progress.

He stopped firing long enough to make a dash for a set of levers protruding from the wall. He started throwing them, intending to cycle the emergency door shut, leaving Sprightly—or whatever she was now—beyond it.

But he was only halfway completed when the station took over, with the door cycling automatically. Stymied, he said, "Someone must have accomplished that from the hub. I imagine someone else fell back to it."

"We have another problem," his ancilla said as Adequate turned to walk back down the hallway.

"I see it." The light at the end of the passageway was gone. "They've closed all the bulkheads!"

He tried for several minutes to reach someone on his communicator—to no avail. Behind him, he heard something pounding against the door that had just shut.

"That would be Sprightly—as something else now," Adequate said. "Can she—can it get in?"

"Eventually."

"Can we get out?" He already knew the answer. It wasn't possible to cycle open the emergency door ahead from his side.

"I may have a way," his ancilla replied. "Check the inside wall, thirty-one meters ahead. Quickly—time is now of the essence."

Adequate had walked the five identical tunnels to the vanes daily for fifteen solar years, but had never thought too greatly about the mechanisms behind the inside wall. Certainly, he understood there to be apparatuses bringing particles back from the collectors in the vanes—but he had never dreamed of opening one of the access panels. That was expressly forbidden—both in his training, and in the stark, stern verbiage just beside the latch. It was never intended to be opened under any circumstances.

That the latch did not work was not surprising in the least. Hearing the station suffering behind him as the Flood tested the emergency bulkhead, Adequate applied his boltshot to the latch, silently apologized to his administrators, and fired.

The handle finally moved—and the panel started to unseal.

"Be careful," his ancilla said. "The area inside is under extreme pressure."

Adequate stood off to the side of the door and forced the panel open.

He was startled when the expected breeze went the other way, blowing from the hallway into the opening. Once the mini-gale subsided, he stepped before the aperture and shined his built-in helmet light inside.

"There's—" Adequate stopped in mid-statement. He couldn't understand what he was looking at. "Shouldn't this be filled with harvested particles?"

"Correct," his ancilla said, "if it were in operation. Materials collected by the vanes are conveyed to the holding tanks at the hub by gases under pressure."

"Perhaps the Flood attack deactivated the collectors?"

"No. The fact that you were able to open the service hatchway at all indicates that the tube was never pressurized. Your armor's sensors also do not indicate the presence of many remnant particles. Adequate . . ."

"What is it?"

"Based on my calculations, this vane of the station has not been used in more than ten solar years."

"Ten years . . . ?" Adequate couldn't quite believe it. He climbed inside and looked to and fro. "How could a vane have been out of service this long without the station's systems knowing about it?"

"Unable to form a conclusion at this time. It also seems unlikely that this one section alone could have been out of service. I now believe that none of the vanes could have been in operation."

This admission stunned Adequate. "That . . . that is impossible."

The ancilla projected a cascade of physics equations onto the inside of his faceplate. "Unless all the transfer tubes are pressurized, Seclusion Spiral's rotation would go out of balance. Its precession would be noticeable, and would have to be corrected for. The only possible conclusion is that, in the last decade, this station has not collected a single particle."

"Are you damaged? They send a tanker here every year. They spend six days filling it, while the service crew inspects the station. They just did it a few weeks ago!"

"I do not have enough information to speculate further. But you must seal the panel quickly, before the Flood arrives. Simply reenter the hub from the central storage tank hatch."

The ancilla was correct about how to get back into the hub, but wrong about how easy a task it would be. The entire journey was in the dark, with Adequate looking behind him in panic at every sound, fearful the Flood had entered the chamber. Several times, he had attempted to contact others aboard the station—but they either could not hear his calls, or were too busy to answer.

He hoped it was one or the other.

The main collection tank was hardest to navigate, narrowing and splitting into seven smaller hexagonal passageways. It took precious time for Adequate to figure out that six went to filtration systems, while the seventh headed for the tank—and he'd been forced to crawl on his stomach to get into it, then make an acrobatic leap for the handle of the exit hatch.

He'd found the hub abandoned, with bulkheads shut on all

but two tunnels. The monitors dedicated to watching the spokes and vanes showed nothing. "Someone's been here," Adequate observed. "They must have closed these other bulkheads."

His ancilla established a new connection with the central computer. "There is a message here from Capital-Enforcer's ancilla on the hub's core computer," his ancilla said. "Power has been lost to the transponders that relay messages between personnel."

That was both bad news and a relief. "Capital's alive." He looked to the two open tunnels, leading to Vanes Three and Five. "Where is he?"

"Capital's ancilla reports that they sealed the spokes leading to Vanes One, Two, and Four—there must have been an outbreak on Four—and that our surviving personnel have entered the tunnels for Vanes Three and Five, expecting that the hub here will be overtaken soon. Capital's ancilla says here that they intend a last stand."

Adequate looked from one open tunnel to the other. "Should I follow? And if so, which way?"

"I lack sufficient information to advise." A pause. "But I do not agree with my fellow ancilla. There is no reason to believe the spokes are any more defensible than the hub—especially when the vanes at the far end were the sources of the Flood infestation to begin with."

How did it get there in the first place? Adequate wondered. It was highly improbable that the Flood could have arrived here independently. Yes, Flood spores could spread on meteors and comets, as well as derelict space equipment hurtling around the stars. But Seclusion was exactly that—secluded, far from other systems and slipspace corridors alike.

It made no sense that the Flood could have arisen from below: nothing should be able to survive beneath the furious clouds.

But he had just seen otherwise.

"Could the avian have brought the infestation?"

"It is unlikely. If the Flood were already present down in the storm, it logically should have found the station before now. You have said you have seen the avian before."

"I'm pleased you believe me now."

"The timing makes me suspect something else." It took milliseconds for the ancilla, in concert with the hub's command computer, to examine its theory. "Yes. The infestation likely began in the replacement digester units just installed by the service team."

"The apparatus that breaks down waste. That's why the outbreak started on the tips of the vanes."

"Correct. They bring in fresh pods of microorganisms annually. Flood spores must have been mixed in with them and been awakened. The malleable seals would have given them a means of escape. They must have infected several of our sentries, taking them directly to combat forms—and their bodies gave rise to the infection forms we now see. I also suspect the Flood is drawing on the biomass in the digester pods to create an environment that might exponentially increase the rate and severity of infestation."

"The tanker brought the digester pods," Adequate said. "Did they report any problems?"

"Checking." After a beat, the ancilla spoke again. "There has been no report of the supply ship reaching any waypoint following its departure here. It has not kept to its schedule."

"No emergency call?"

"Negative. I conjecture that any Flood outbreak carried aboard the vessel could have debilitated it in slipspace."

That meant an unspeakably horrible end for those aboard—his colleagues for the past solar year and longer. He could imagine them, all happily headed off to their new assignments and away from the purgatory of Seclusion and Barely-Adequate—only to find their flight and their lives cut off. He had not been particularly friendly with any of them, but his ambitions were joined to theirs. And now all were snuffed out.

Only afterward did he consider another implication. *No one can come back to help us.*

And then another thought, just as dark, struck him. "They did service on every vane," Adequate said, looking from side to side in alarm. "That means Vanes Three and Five are no longer safe, after all."

He did not wait for the ancilla to confirm his theory. Adequate chose the nearest tunnel and ran.

Vane Five was it, the last stand.

Adequate had only gotten partway down Vane Three when he had seen the Flood rampaging toward him—including, to his horror, the transformed figures of two more of his companions. He had retreated and sealed the tunnel, leaving only one option left. There, down the spoke leading to Vane Five, he had found Capital-Enforcer blazing away.

Adequate reached the warrior's side and joined in the shooting. There was no accounting for what faced him now. He had lost track of how many comrades had fallen, had lost any sense of the mechanics of transformation. All he knew was that the station that had been his home, antiseptic and pristine, for so many years was in the throes of a rampaging disease. Its arteries and veins now coursing with enormous stalking bipeds, with herds of skittering infection forms.

And he and Capital were the only antibodies.

So many, so unimaginably hideous. Until today, he had gone fifteen years without firing his boltshot. Now, he didn't want to take his finger off the trigger. Destruction was the only answer for such creatures. He targeted a greenish-colored infection form—and reveled as the running pustule popped. His weapon found the hulking combat form, knocking it backward but doing no damage. Less satisfaction there. He could no longer make out the straight lines of the floor, the wall, the ceiling: the whole spoke was alive. He existed to kill it.

Between the dual attack, the Flood's charge abated. Adequate's ancilla studied his armor's long-range sensors and reported that the creatures were still up ahead, but regrouping. "We are the only ones left," Adequate said to Capital as they huddled behind a half-closed emergency door for cover. "All the other vanes are sealed and infested."

"We have to scuttle the station, plunge it into the gas giant," Capital said, his voice grave. "Or it will sit here as a festering trap forever. Anyone who tries to board will suffer as we have."

Adequate took the news with a combination of resignation and disappointment. Destruction in this manner was a standard protocol for gas mines and other similar stations at high risk.

"Do you have your master key?"

Adequate fumbled for it in a compartment on his utility belt. Capital found his own. "It takes both your key and mine to get into the catastrophic-response system. You know where to use it?"

"Yes." The system was a fearsome-looking console in the hub, one Adequate had long preferred not to look at.

Capital put his key in Adequate's gloved hand. "Take them both. If I fall . . . end it."

Adequate stared at the pair of electronic keys. He had grown to hate Seclusion Spiral over the last few years, and yet . . . it was still his home. "Are you certain you don't want to do it?"

"You have seniority. It is your duty to remain." Capital fired another volley and looked back at him. "No less is expected from any of us. We were all sent here to sacrifice ourselves against the Flood."

"Sacrifice ourselves? *Here?*" Adequate didn't understand. "Why would the Librarian think the Flood would come here? This is the last place the Flood should want."

"So we all thought. But I saw something out the window this morning that made me believe otherwise."

Adequate's eyes widened. *The avian?* "You saw it too?"

"I saw three of them." Down the tunnel, chaotic movement. Capital turned back to his shooting. "Forget about me. Go!"

Adequate did as he was told, still not quite understanding.

Five great doors, all sealed shut—and the monitors in the hub that still worked showed the Flood gathering outside every one. Adequate had seen on the monitors that Capital had fallen and been transformed into what he had tried to destroy. It was only a matter of time before the monsters' battering undermined the hub, Adequate's refuge of last resort.

Yet here he stood for long minutes, motionless, with one key already placed in the catastrophic-response-system console. The other remained in his hand. He stared at it, trying to ignore the pummeling sounds coming from all around. Those sounds, and the voice of his ancilla, constantly urging him to activate the device and destroy the station.

He knew what he needed to do—and yet something in what

Capital had said still puzzled him. In the last hour, he had learned more about Seclusion Spiral and its surroundings than he had found out in fifteen years residing here.

And all at once, it made sense. "Ancilla!"

"What, Adequate?"

"I know what's been happening."

"Of course you do," the AI responded, as animated as it ever sounded. "We are under siege!"

"Not that. I meant during the last ten solar years. I know why the particle transfer tubes are empty—why the collector's systems have been offline all this time." He paused. "I believe *you* know what I mean too."

"Your reason centers are your private space, Adequate—I will not know unless you express the concept. But do it quickly, or—"

"The avians. I believe there are many more, down in the storm—and that my superiors must have known of their existence. You calculated that the station hasn't been harvesting particles for more than ten solar years. Why is that?"

"I am unaware—"

"It is because ten years ago, the Forerunners discovered them here. But they mentioned nothing—because by then, they were aware of the threat the Flood posed. They didn't want to open this new species to destruction." He paused. "No, not destruction. *Exploitation.* Absorbing a species capable of thriving in the skies of a gas giant could provide the Flood with a unique and dangerous new set of capabilities."

"I'm not sure I understand."

Adequate shook his head, frustrated. As intelligent as his ancilla was, it sometimes lacked in imagination—particularly when it came to visualizing worst-case scenarios. "Don't you see? Imagine what this species could mean for a world under siege. The Flood could deploy the avians from their ships, never having to land, never having to sacrifice their vessels on entry. A Flood ship could endanger a whole world as soon as it was in range!" The thought alone nearly made him cringe. "That explains the measures that have been taken. The Librarian had to make sure the Flood never discovered the avians."

More hammering from outside. "This order of events is illogical, Adequate. If they wanted to protect the avians of Seclusion from the Flood, they could have removed the station, rather than have it here attracting attention."

"Possibly they were afraid the Flood would find its way here regardless. As long as any Forerunner knew the avians existed, the potential existed for the Flood to gain that knowledge too."

"Then why did they not simply remove the avians themselves, through the Conservation Measure?"

"You know the conditions in the winds below. It might not have been possible. If any avians remained . . ." He trailed off. "Perhaps it was too late. That is why they left the station in place, with a skeleton crew. I believe Capital-Enforcer suspected we were here to be a decoy."

"A decoy?"

"I know." The concept was both enlightening and infuriating. "They realized the Flood would find Seclusion one day—and it did, via our tanker. And they knew what would happen next."

The ancilla finally understood. "You would have destroyed the station—and with it, this infestation of the Flood."

"Then this entire world would be cut off from the Flood, seemingly devoid of any viable hosts." He turned over the second key in his hand. "So the other sentries and I have been here as a living shield, an offering. The Forerunners assigned us here to ensure that when the Flood finally arrived at Seclusion, it wouldn't detect the avians. And the galaxy would be spared a potential Flood form capable of immediately rendering worlds defenseless because of their resilience to extremes."

The ancilla paused long seconds before answering. "The conjecture is possible. Given the electrical interference of the storm below, the Flood could well be tricked into thinking that any bioelectrical activity in this region is localized to the station above."

"So the Flood would consume us—and then leave what's below alone."

"The conjecture is possible."

Adequate sighed. "I am no longer enamored of my assignment."

The din rose. "Structural failure on door two is imminent," the ancilla said. "What will you do?"

"My duty, I suppose." Adequate took a look at the abominations on the monitors—and inserted the key into the slot on the console beside Capital's. A panel whirred open, exposing a blinking green button. "Good-bye, ancilla. I am sorry you were not joined with a better Manipular."

"I have no complaints, Adequate. Good-bye."

Adequate awoke in darkness, with his body pinned upside down between a heavy object and a metal surface. Every muscle in his body screamed. If this was death, it was more painful than he'd been led to expect.

With extreme effort, he forced the massive structure trapping him backward. It was a data processing tower, he realized; it had come centimeters from crushing the life out of him against the hub's wall. On his hands and knees, he struggled to get his bearings.

The command center looked as if a giant had shaken it like a toy. Every furnishing, every piece of equipment that could move had relocated. Woozily, he struggled to get to his feet. His body felt heavy. Was the hub accelerating upward? He couldn't tell. The whole facility felt as if it were underwater. Above, the skylights had closed, protective shields locked into place. He could make out sizable dents on the ceiling nearby, artifacts of the great shaking.

"Ancilla? Ancilla?"

For the first time since he had been united with the automated assistant, Adequate failed to get a response. That fact terrified him more than anything that had yet befallen. Even though he had always felt apart from the group for fifteen solar years, he had never felt completely alone, thanks to his ancilla. He couldn't imagine going on without it.

Adequate activated his helmet light and staggered around the chamber, righting equipment as he went. Finding one of the stations governing power, he tripped a switch and watched as several of the systems in the hub came back online.

He thought he heard wind coming through what was likely a broken seal in his helmet. Focusing, it resolved into a hum at the back of his head. Seconds later, it became a voice.

". . . Adequate?"

"Ancilla!"

"I . . . apologize. My systems appear to have gone into hibernation during whatever happened." A pause. "What *did* happen?"

"I was hoping you could tell me." There were no sounds coming from the five doorways to the spokes, and none of the monitors displaying feeds from that part of the station had come back online. "Are you in contact with the core computer?"

"My connection is still resetting. Perhaps look out a viewport."

Adequate stumbled toward another console and activated a control. Above, shields slid down into one of the skylight window frames, unleashing a blaze of color. It took several seconds for Adequate's eyes to adjust.

"I thought perhaps we had launched into space." He squinted. "Where are we?"

"Open the rest."

He did so—and the skylights ringing the circular room revealed a spectral sea. Tendrils of clouds swirled and danced back and forth, lit by near-constant flashes of multicolored lightning.

And everywhere were the avians.

He had wanted a long look at them. He had it now. Whole flocks of avians coursed across the sky, swooping about with ease and in comfort. There was none of the tentative, fearful nature of the being he had seen earlier. No, here, they had command—and "here" was not the place he had been before.

Adequate fell to his knees, and not just because of the pull on his body. "We are deep in the storm. We are in their home."

Flying creatures soared past the windows, tiny microbursts of electricity flashing across their rippling forms. There seemed, somehow, to be a logic to it: was it perhaps their means of communication, Adequate wondered? He felt like one of the explorers he had heard of, living undersea on a strange world, communing with a culture that existed hidden from view.

And now there were smaller ones, identical in form and shape to the others but for their size, fluttering against the panes above. Not threatening the station, at all—but he could tell they were excited. And there, on another avian's dorsal side, clung what he at first thought was a bumpy fin. On closer look, they appeared to be even smaller avians, still. Were they the species' young, or something else? Every few moments, they flitted from the back of one adult to another. What kind of community might they have?

A minute in which he could not take his eyes from the skylight ended when his ancilla spoke. "Connection reacquired. The console function apparently did destroy the Flood—by shedding the station's vanes."

Adequate got to his feet and looked to the doors with alarm. "We would fall without them!"

"We did. And so did the vanes." The ancilla paused. "According to the hub's computer, when you toggled the control, the spokes holding the vanes explosively ejected. Cut off from the rotating hub, each one was slung kilometers away."

"What happened to them?"

"They were swept into the electrical storm and ripped to shreds. The hub's sensors saw it all, before it lost too much elevation."

"So the Flood . . . ?"

"Gone. The computer believes the vanes were pulverized. No Flood infection could possibly have survived there—and no invasive elements have been detected on the hub."

"But how did *we* survive?"

"We fell many kilometers—until the hub's engines ignited."

"They did? I thought the thrusters were only used to brake the hub when the station was deployed from orbit—and for elevation when it got caught in downdrafts."

"It appears," the ancilla said, "that the hub's systems considered the loss of the vanes a catastrophic event—and that it fired the thrusters before we descended to a crushing depth."

"It certainly felt catastrophic." He paused and looked out the skylight again. "Can it take us back up?"

Another pause. "The central computer does not believe so.

The crosswinds above are too strong. We appear to be hovering in a zone of relative calm within the vortex, at equilibrium between the tempest above and the pressure below."

"How long can we remain here?"

"As long as the thrusters burn."

"And how long is that?"

"Indefinitely. The stubs that used to hold the vanes deployed electrostatic collectors; they are now drawing power from outside. It should be sufficient to keep us stable—and for life-support needs. But you will feel slightly heavier for the constant acceleration."

"I will live," Adequate said. Then he smiled at that. *I will live.*

"The food pantry was freshly stocked—and for twenty-one," his ancilla said. "With those reserves and your armor's defalt sustainment system, you should be able to survive for . . . well, a lifetime. You will have the complete run of the living quarters."

Adequate didn't register the comment. His eyes were again on the avians, hovering outside. They flitted back and forth—and one paused particularly close, looking in. He wondered if it was the one who he'd seen earlier, above.

"If the avians live down here, why did they visit us at the cloud tops?"

"Insufficient information. Perhaps they consume for food the same particles Seclusion Spiral was designed to harvest." The ancilla paused. "Or perhaps they were curious."

"They are wonderful," Adequate said. The avian outside glistened, electrical energy seeming to well from somewhere within its form. They could clearly fly to the top of the enormous storm, if they wanted to; in his mind's eye, he could see them soaring the cosmos, using their mysterious internal power for propulsion. But he could not imagine them ever wanting to leave, not with such a lovely world here below providing all they needed.

"The Forerunners were correct to protect them from the Flood," his ancilla said.

Adequate let out a deep breath. "It is a shame these magnificent things do not know what sacrifice has been made for them."

"We may teach them, Adequate. We have plenty of time—and a number of methods by which the hub might establish communication." His ancilla sounded almost excited. "Before long, you might be able to tell them the designations of all those who protected them—including yours."

"I have never cared for mine." Adequate chuckled, in spite of himself. "Spare me that."

"No, I think you are Adequate-Observer no longer."

He didn't know what the ancilla meant. "I have not evolved."

"I disagree. From today, I think you should be called Defender-of-the-Storm."

The Forerunner mentally tried it on. "I like it." He continued wandering the room, constantly looking up at the avians. "And perhaps they have stories to tell us too."

A NECESSARY TRUTH

TROY DENNING

This story takes place three months after the United Nations Space Command's extraction of the 717th research battalion by the elite Spartan Blue Team from the volatile and besieged colony of Gao (Halo: Last Light).

1420 hours, October 14, 2553 (military calendar)
Officers' Club, UNSC Recreational Facility 6055-NA-A
Liberty District, Neos Atlantis, Alcides System

It had been just a hundred days since Veta Lopis left Gao to join the Office of Naval Intelligence, and already she'd become one of those jump-weary planet hoppers who never had time to enjoy the local wonders.

Today, she was on Neos Atlantis, facing a panoramic window at one end of the officers' club in UNSC Recreational Facility 6055-NA-A. The window afforded a spectacular view of the Theran Crown, a gloomy, spire-studded cryovolcano ringed by ice cliffs as green as emeralds. But Veta was actually watching the interior of the window, using the reflections on the glass to keep tabs on her three young subordinates.

Ash-G099 and Mark-G313 were seated in the back of the

crowded club, a half-empty pitcher of lemon pels resting on a high-top table between them. At only fourteen, they continued to show hints of adolescence in their soft-featured faces, but their size and musculature were those of twenty-year-old junior lieutenants fresh out of ODST school—which happened to be their cover legend.

Still, they really didn't look like young officers on leave. Both were sitting bolt upright, constantly scanning their designated surveillance arcs and paying no attention to the gravball match on the screens above the bar in the center of the room. The empty cocktail glasses scattered across their table resembled exactly what they were—props designed to make it appear as if the pair had been drinking for hours. Most telling of all was their reaction to the young women who sauntered past and glanced in their direction, clearly attempting to catch the eye of one or the other. Mark returned their smiles with complete indifference, while Ash merely looked sheepish and shy.

It would take a trained observer about two minutes to penetrate their covers—which was the whole idea, of course—but Veta thought the pair might be overdoing their "incompetent operatives" act just a little. The opposition in today's training exercise was a top ONI espionage unit, and, if her Ferret Team hoped to prevail, they couldn't allow their foes to smell a trap.

"Guys . . . you need to loosen up a bit, or Oscar Squad won't buy it." Veta pretended she was speaking into the commpad strapped to her wrist. "Down some of that pels."

Ash and Mark's only response was to raise their mugs and drink. Like everyone on the team, they had a thread-style microphone sewn into their clothing and a miniaturized reception-dot concealed near one eardrum, but field protocol dictated that subordinate operatives remain comm-silent unless reporting a development to the team leader.

Veta could not quite believe she was ordering a pair of fourteen-year-olds to guzzle alcohol, but they were being trained for undercover work. They were bound to face times when their lives depended on their ability to imbibe all manner of spirits, and ONI had taught them how to do it without losing their edge.

Still, *fourteen*. Sometimes, Veta wondered if letting ONI recruit her had been smart . . . not that there had been much choice. Her career as Gao's top homicide investigator was over. In fact, so was her entire life on Gao, period. After helping Blue Team escape with a powerful Forerunner artifact—one coveted by the planet's unscrupulous president—it would have been a death sentence to stay behind.

A few gulps later, Ash stopped drinking and belched, and Mark put his mug down and wiped his mouth. Neither looked relaxed. Veta sighed and feigned speaking into her commpad again.

"Try to look like you're having fun." She shifted in her seat and began to watch the pair in her peripheral vision. "Smile at the ladies."

Ash spotted three women approaching, probably on their way to the exit, and signaled Mark. The pair waited until their targets were adjacent to the table, then executed simultaneous stool-pivots and flashed broad, toothy smiles.

The women rolled their eyes and hurried out the door.

"Oh man, you guys," Veta said. "When we get back to the Mill, remind me to request a flirting course for the entire team."

Ash dropped his chin and stared into his pels. Mark shrugged and went back to watching the entrance. Veta told herself not to worry. Her Ferrets had a lot to learn before they were ready for a real field assignment, but they were good students and tireless workers. They had accomplished in a hundred days what most

ONI trainees needed a year to achieve, and she had no doubt they would soon master the necessary social skills.

Veta was more concerned about what they needed to unlearn. Her subordinates were all Spartan-IIIs with superhuman reflexes and nearly a decade of military training, and they remained soldiers at heart. When pressured or surprised, they had a tendency to revert to lethal action . . . and starting a firefight was seldom the best solution for a spy in a tight spot. In fact, Serin Osman—the ONI admiral in charge of the Ferret program—was so concerned about the situation that she had warned Veta they might need to rethink building the team around Spartans.

And *that* Veta could not allow.

Like all Spartan-IIIs, her people had been recruited as war orphans and molded into supersoldiers through a rigorous program of training, discipline, and biological augmentations. But they also came from Gamma Company, which meant they had undergone a special round of enhancements that resulted in an unstable brain chemistry—a liability that ONI now deemed an unacceptable public-relations hazard with the potential to damage the entire Spartan branch.

Veta had no idea what had become of the rest of the Gammas, but she had agreed to lead a four-person Ferret Team for the sake of the three she had met on Gao, and she had no intention of letting Osman remove them.

They were just kids. They deserved *someone* who thought of them as something more than weapons.

Her third trainee, Olivia-G291, was at the near end of the bar. Wearing a formfitting sheath dress and carefully applied makeup, she appeared older than her two fellow Gammas and could easily pass for a first lieutenant—or even a captain. She was being chatted up by a pudgy guy in wrinkled trousers and a collarless four-pocket jacket, and she was leaning toward him and smiling, listening intently and maintaining steady eye contact. Like dozens of women in the club, she looked like she was enjoying the company of her companion and was interested in spending more time with him.

There was only one flaw in Olivia's cover. Her suitor appeared to be distinctly civilian and at least three times her age, and the disparity was drawing puzzled glances from younger men and raised brows from disapproving women. Even the servers were scowling as they passed, eyeing the fellow as though they could not understand how such a lecher had made it past the door guards.

And that was a good question. Located in an ambiguous zone between the Inner and Outer Colonies, Neos Atlantis was a high-security world surrounded by orbital maintenance docks that serviced only UNSC war vessels. The installations employed close to a hundred thousand civilian technicians, but a security-conscious UNSC maintained segregated recreational facilities for the sole use of fleet personnel. So it was hard to believe this civilian had simply wandered into the club on his own.

Hoping to get a closer look at the subject, Veta faced the central bar and raised her glass as though signaling for a fresh drink. She saw no sign that the fellow's girth and flabby jowls were a disguise, and it seemed unlikely that any member of an elite espionage unit would lapse into such poor fighting trim. The guy was probably just a former officer who had been hitting the bottle too hard since retirement, but Veta knew better than to make unwarranted assumptions. During her time on Gao, she had taken down half a dozen vicious murderers who passed as happy family men and pillars of their community.

A blond woman in the khaki pants and white blouse of a server stopped next to Olivia and her companion with an open bottle of sparkling zantelle and two flutes. Olivia's eyes widened, but the companion merely smiled and handed her a flute, then took the tray and turned to find a table. The server immediately began to look for thirsty customers and spotted Veta's upraised glass. She smiled and came over.

"Another whiskey?" The server was tall and fit, with pale blue eyes and laugh lines at the edge of her mouth. "The Titan Smoke is smooth and silky, if you haven't tried it yet."

"Actually, I'm not a whiskey drinker," Veta said. She found it odd that a server didn't know the difference between a rocks glass and a doffer, but it was probably hard to find experienced bar personnel who could pass a rigorous security check. "But I'd love another two-tailed comet."

The woman flashed a sheepish grin, then said, "You don't know what you're missing, ma'am." She took Veta's doffer and turned to leave. "But a two-tail it is."

Once the server was gone, Veta glanced back toward the bar—and saw no sign of Olivia and her companion. All of the tables in the area were occupied by groups of bantering customers. Veta faced the window again and searched the interior reflections for some sign of the missing pair.

When she found none, she pretended to speak into her commpad again. "Who has eyes on Olivia?"

Mark took a swallow from his mug and shot a glance across the far end of the bar, then Ash propped his elbows on the table and cast a more leisurely look in the same direction. The corner they were indicating was hidden behind the club's huge central bar, but Veta knew from her initial reconnaissance that it contained a handful of cozy booths. There was also an emergency exit and a kitchen entrance, which meant it would be a good spot for a capture attempt.

Veta was tempted to move closer so she would be ready to offer support if Oscar Squad tried something, but changing seats would only confirm to their observers that she and Olivia were both operatives.

"Okay, keep her in view." Veta paused and smiled to misdirect any Oscar Squad observers, then added, "And, 'Livi, don't let that guy move you anywhere else. There's something off about him."

The order went unacknowledged, of course, and Veta used her commpad to bring up the feed from Olivia's microphone. The sound quality was dull and scratchy, and the only thing she could hear was the murmuring of the civilian's deep voice punctuated by the occasional jingle of polite laughter from Olivia.

The server returned with a rocks glass filled with a dark, coppery liquid that was definitely not a two-tailed comet. Veta found the poor service annoying, but the last thing she wanted to do was make herself memorable by pointing out an inexperienced server's mistake. Besides, she had more important things to worry about—Olivia's laughter was lapsing into a cackle that suggested the zantelle was having more of an impact than it should. Veta thanked the server and paid by pressing her thumb to a tabpad. She picked up the glass and sniffed. Whiskey. She pretended to sip the lip-blistering stuff.

The voice of Olivia's companion grew more distinct, as though he were leaning closer, and Veta heard him asking, ". . . were you posted before the *Rochester*?"

"The Academy at Mare Nubium, of course." Olivia was drawing on her cover legend, but her tone was mocking, as though even *she* didn't believe what she was saying. "I graduated seventeenth in my class."

"Really?" the civilian asked. "I didn't know Spartan-IIIs were trained at the Luna OCS."

Veta's gut knotted, and she had to resist the urge to rise and start toward Olivia. According to Admiral Osman, the opposition hadn't been briefed on the composition of Veta's team. But Oscar Squad *was* an espionage unit, with the capacity to do its own research.

Olivia remained quiet for a moment, then finally giggled and said, "There's a lot you don't know about me."

"Go on," he said. "You can tell Uncle Spencer. You're from Gamma Company, aren't you?"

Olivia's voice dropped to a whisper. "Spencer, I . . . can't tell *you* that." Her voice was halting and her speech slow. "How do you know?"

Veta stood and turned toward the bar. " 'Livi's been dosed." She was so alarmed that she did not even bother to lift her wrist and pretend she was speaking into her commpad. "Extract *now*. I have 'Livi. Mark, secure the subject for interrogation. Ash, take distraction and cover."

By the time she finished speaking, Mark was already heading for the far end of the bar and Ash was gathering glasses from the table. Veta had no idea whether the reference to Gamma Company was another of Osman's tests or a genuine security breach. But she *did* know that any leak regarding the identity of her Gammas was a threat to the team's existence and perhaps even their lives—which made this the kind of high-pressure situation likely to bring out their lethal instincts.

So, another test.

"And *don't* kill anyone," Veta added. "Don't even bust them up. This is a training exercise."

She circled around the near end of the bar. Mark was just stepping past the far end, moving briskly toward Olivia's booth. He was smiling broadly, as though he were on his way to greet a friend, but his torso was tilted forward and his gaze locked on the back of the subject's head. Because of the Smoothers necessary to keep their unique brain chemistries in balance, Gammas had a special fear of psychoactive drugs—and a burning hatred of anyone who used one on a fellow team member.

Veta began to have second thoughts about sending Mark in first. In many ways, he was the team's coolest head, someone who always maintained focus and could not be rattled. But he was also protective of his teammates and utterly ruthless, with a bitter streak so dark that Veta had not too long ago suspected him of being a serial killer. If he thought Olivia had been harmed by the dose . . . well, training exercise or not, it might be bad to let Mark reach the subject first.

"Mark, let's—"

The command was cut short when a tremendous shattering of glass sounded from the opposite side of the bar. Ash was creating the distraction as ordered. Veta ignored the reflex to glance over and continued toward Mark, watching as a server with a tray full of drinks whirled into his path. It was the same blonde who had served Veta earlier, the one who had brought her a whiskey instead of a two-tailed comet and hadn't known a rocks glass from a doffer—and the same woman who had brought the zantelle to Olivia and her companion.

Mark didn't even slow down. He simply grabbed the server's tray and shoved it into her chest, then used a foot-sweep to kick her feet from beneath her. She landed flat on her back, slapping her arms out to break her fall and tucking her chin to avoid banging her head.

Both actions suggested training in hand-to-hand combat. The server rolled onto her side to counterattack with a scissor kick, but

Mark was already two steps past her, still holding the tray and just approaching Olivia's booth.

Taking the server for a member of Oscar Squad, Veta angled toward her—and began to wonder what had been in the whiskey the woman had been pushing. Had she been trying to dose Veta too? A large man stepped away from the bar. He was a little older than Veta, perhaps thirty-five or so, with a square jaw and wary eyes that did not match his smile.

Veta tilted her head as though she thought he was coming on to her, then flashed a sly grin herself. The operative's smile grew more natural, and he offered a hand as though to introduce himself. At the same time, he was slipping into position between Veta and the action at Olivia's booth. Veta allowed him to herd her toward the bar, but extended her hand past his and grabbed hold of his wrist.

"Nice to meet you." Veta propped a foot against his ankle and drew him forward. "*Never* dose one of my people again."

The operative's brow shot up, but he was already off-balance and in danger of falling. His fingers closed around Veta's forearm as he struggled to stay upright. She popped her free hand against his elbow just hard enough to hyperextend the joint, then pulled loose, spun around behind him, and delivered a vicious knuckle-punch to the kidney.

The operative staggered forward and dropped to a knee, in too much pain to do more than gasp. He would be pissing blood for a day, but he'd be back on his feet in ten minutes—which was no doubt less time than it would take for Olivia to recover.

When Veta looked up, she found a lot of curious eyes watching her. She covered by shaking her head and scowling, trying to suggest the guy had said something inappropriate, then continued on her way.

A few paces from Olivia's booth, the blond server who had tried to stall Mark was being helped to her feet by a couple of young men. Judging by their confused expressions—and the dirty looks they were shooting at Mark—it seemed clear they were just bystanders who had seen the woman go down.

Mark had already reached the booth and was using a wrist-lock to walk the older "civilian" toward the emergency exit. Olivia was sitting on the edge of the seat, eyes glassy and dilated as she stared after Mark. Veta grabbed her by the hand and pulled her toward the club's main entrance.

"How are you feeling?"

"Fine." Olivia stumbled and grabbed Veta's arm for support. "Okay . . . maybe not. There's a helmet fire inside my skull."

"I imagine there is," Veta said. "That had to be some kind of Babble Juice in your zantelle."

"You . . . *think*?" Olivia released Veta's arm and began to lurch forward on her own. "I'm gonna crush that fat fart's tiny little . . . ears."

"His ears, huh?" Veta was relieved to hear the anger in Olivia's voice; she was still in touch with her emotions, so the dose had probably been light. "Really?"

"Okay, not really," Olivia said. "But whatever I crush, it's going to hurt him. A lot."

Veta smiled—she couldn't help it. "As long as you don't kill him," she said. "Remember, this is still a training exercise."

They reached the blond server. Noting that the bystanders who had helped her to her feet were continuing to scowl after Mark, Veta stopped to address the two men.

"We're from FLEETCOM, Criminal Investigation Division." Veta took Olivia's arm again, then continued, "I need to get this officer to an infirmary, but the server you're helping is a witness."

An alarm bell rang briefly as Mark hustled the "civilian" out the emergency exit, but the two bystanders merely looked over and immediately returned their attention to Veta.

"Hold her here until one of my people comes for her," Veta said. "Is that clear?"

Both men came to attention. "Affirmative, ma'am."

Unable to protest without breaking her own cover, the server glared at Veta, then said, "No problem. I can use the break."

"Good. I'm glad we understand each other."

Veta thanked the bystanders for their help and steered Olivia toward the main entrance.

They had barely taken three steps before Olivia leaned in close. "But we're not CID," she said. "We're—"

"Whoever we want to be. We're Ferrets, remember?"

Olivia hesitated. "Right," she said. "I'll do my best."

They met Ash on the far side of the bar, just a dozen steps from the exit. His trouser cuffs were wet, and he smelled like pels, and he was doing his best to swagger as though he had drunk too much.

"Drop the act," Veta said. "You're CID now—and watch Mark's back. Oscar Squad is everywhere."

"Affirmative." Ash straightened his posture and snuck a peek at Olivia. "Is she going to be—"

"She'll be fine," Veta said. "We'll meet you at the suite. Bring the prisoner—and make sure you aren't tailed."

Ash nodded. "No worries."

"And don't hurt anyone." Veta pulled Olivia toward the exit. "This is still—"

"A training exercise," Ash said. "I *know*."

Veta led Olivia across a small foyer to an elevator bank, where they gazed into a security panel so the base AI could identify their facial features. A door opened, and they stepped into a steel-walled car. The car began to ascend, and a crisp, androgynous voice sounded from the overhead speaker.

"Lieutenant Bati's eyes are dilated." The AI was referring to Olivia by her legend identity—though it was hard to say how much longer the cover would hold, now that the Ferrets had engaged Oscar Squad. "And her pulse rate appears heightened. Do you need to stop at the infirmary?"

"Negative," Veta said. "Lieutenant Bati will be fine. Just take us to our floor."

"As you wish, Major."

The car stopped and the elevator door opened. Veta hustled them down the corridor to their rooms, which were adjacent to each other and across from Ash's and Mark's. They quickly changed into service dress and returned to the elevator, heading for the suite they had taken as a safe house. Instead of merely looking into the security panel, this time Veta pressed her palm to the biometric reader in the center.

"Flag Floor Three, Halsey Suite" she said. "Access code Mike Oscar Mike Four Niner, unlogged."

The door did not open.

Veta's stomach clenched. Olivia had secured the suite by hacking into the central booking system and reserving it the name of a fictitious captain in ONI Section Zero. It was a clever ploy. Section Zero was ONI's internal investigations division and therefore the most secretive about its personnel and activities. But Olivia was only half-finished with her Digital Infiltration and Sabotage course, so it seemed all too possible that her breach had been discovered.

Veta repeated the code.

"Your access code has already been verified, Major Keely," the AI said, addressing Veta by her cover identity. "Lieutenant Bati's has not."

Olivia placed her hand on the security panel. "Tango Angel Papa Eight Five." She hesitated a moment, then the Babble Juice compelled her to add, "But I'm not really—"

"Thank you, Lieutenant." Veta pulled Olivia's hand away from the security panel, then said, "And make certain our access remains unlogged."

"Of course," the AI said. "For the next twenty-four hours, there is a log blackout on everything concerning the Halsey Suite."

The doors opened, and a minute later, Veta and Olivia were inside the cavernous parlor of a large room with a sunken seating salon and a majestic view of the cryovolcano's gloomy caldera. It had a kitchenette to the left of the entrance and a water closet to the right. Two private bedrooms were arranged opposite each other on separate sides of the parlor.

Veta deposited Olivia on a couch, then retrieved a field kit and ran an analysis on the Gamma's blood. A code appeared in the readout window identifying the toxin as NTL—a quick-acting form of Babble Juice more properly called nicothiotal. It was a favorite of ONI and other intelligence services because it hit quickly and the outward effects resembled intoxication. But it did have one drawback—an overdose could shatter one's mind, destroying the barrier between dreams and memories and leaving the subject in a permanent state of hallucination.

Oscar Squad was playing rough.

Veta administered a counteragent and had Olivia remain on the couch while she prepared an interrogation room for the prisoner they were expecting. When she finished ten minutes later, Mark and Ash still had not arrived with the captive. The delay was a bit alarming, but not terribly. They had to be certain they weren't being tailed, and even if they weren't, sneaking around a UNSC recreational facility with a prisoner in custody was no easy thing.

Veta took the opportunity to debrief Olivia and was relieved to find her rapidly coming around. But she did not learn much of interest—only that Olivia's suitor had been sitting at the bar when she arrived and approached her before she had a chance to find a seat.

"And that didn't raise an alarm?" Veta asked. "He had to be waiting for you."

"You saw him. Did he look like ONI to you?"

"Not until he dosed you," Veta admitted. "But a guy that age? What were you thinking?"

"That he liked me and wanted to talk." Olivia raised her chin. "Is that so hard to believe?"

Veta sighed. "No, actually. Not at all," she said. Like most Spartan-IIs and IIIs, Olivia had been robbed of a libido by her biological augmentations, and where men were concerned, she lacked normal instincts—and apparently creep radar too. "In fact, you're way out of his league. When we get back to the Mill, we have some course work to do."

"I know how sex works. It's not that complicated."

"Neither is crossing a street," Veta said. "But if you wander into either one blindfolded, there's going to be trouble."

Olivia rolled her eyes. "Sure, Mom. Whatever you want."

Veta was hardly fond of the nickname, especially since the Gammas used it when they thought she was being overprotective. But the door to the suite swished open before she could object, and Mark and Ash stepped into the foyer, now wearing the service dress of ODST junior lieutenants.

There was no one else with them.

Veta stood. "Where's the prisoner?"

Ash stepped in front of Mark, as though to shield him. "That's my fault, ma'am. I grew distracted by the casualties—"

"Casualties?" Veta climbed out of the seating salon and started toward them. "What did I say about casualties?"

"To avoid them, ma'am," Ash said. "But I didn't cause them. They were already down when I arrived."

"At the least, the first ones were," Mark added. "And they weren't fatalities."

Veta grimaced. "You're going to need to clarify that. *First* ones?"

"Two men, near the end of the bar," Ash said.

Veta nodded, recalling the two men who had helped the blond server to her feet. "I used them to stall an Oscar Squad operative. How bad are they?"

"They'll recover," Ash said. "One guy has a broken jaw; the other one was out cold."

Veta could only shake her head. She had expected the woman to try slipping away, but not to attack a pair of bystanders. "Go on."

"Ma'am?"

"Who were the other casualties?"

"Well—" Mark said. He started to step forward, only to have Ash extend an arm and hold him back. "Ash, we have—"

"There was a big guy," Ash interrupted, "closer to the center of the bar. He was on his knees, holding his back like someone had kidney-punched him."

Fairly certain Ash was referring to the operative *she* had dropped—and that he knew it—Veta narrowed her eyes. "Someone had." She took Ash by the shoulder, then drew him aside so she could scowl at Mark. "Mark, what did you do?"

Mark's face fell. "You mean besides get stabbed?"

Veta looked him over and saw no obvious wounds. "What are you talking about?"

Mark placed a finger in his collar and pulled it aside to reveal a blood-dotted bandage over his clavicle. The depth of the wound was impossible to tell, but the location was alarming. Had the blade struck just a couple of centimeters closer to his shoulder, it would have severed his subclavian artery and killed him in less than a minute.

Feeling guilty for her sharp tone, Veta looked up and spoke gently. "How did it happen?"

"That's what I've been trying to tell you," Ash said, stepping in to shield Mark again. "It wasn't Mark's fault. Oscar Squad is *way* out of line."

"Ash, stop." Veta glanced from Ash to Mark and back again, then said, "Please, just tell me."

A look of resignation came over Ash's face, and he stepped aside.

"Ma'am," Mark began, "I was escorting the subject down a service corridor when I was attacked from behind."

"You were taken by surprise?" Veta was not quite sure she understood the report correctly. "Someone snuck up on you? How is that possible?"

Mark's face flushed. "My attention was elsewhere," he said. "The subject was resisting."

"It was my fault," Ash said. "If I hadn't gotten distracted by the casualties in the club—"

An alert chime issued from control panel near the door, then the AI's voice sounded from the speaker. "Officer on deck."

Ash and Mark immediately snapped to attention, and, down in the seating salon, Olivia sprang to her feet to do the same.

Veta turned to the control panel. "Secure the door." It was probably someone from Oscar Squad, coming to confirm her Ferret Team's location. "Access to the Halsey Suite is restricted to current personnel."

"The restriction has been expanded to all authorized personnel," the AI said. "Admiral Osman *is* authorized personnel."

Veta glanced over to Ash and Mark. "I'll handle this," she said. "Not a word."

The door opened, revealing a tall, olive-skinned woman in a white uniform. She had short-cropped hair and a slender, high-cheeked face wrenched into a grim scowl. Standing behind the admiral were a pair of armed escorts and the square-jawed Oscar Squad operative Veta had incapacitated in the officers' club. His eyes were wary and his expression angry, and Veta suspected that, had Osman not been present, he would have been tempted to return her kidney shot.

Osman motioned for her escorts to remain outside, then led the operative into the foyer and paused to look around.

"You certainly travel in style," Osman said. "Even *I* don't stay in the Halsey Suite."

"We needed a safe house." Veta spoke with an ease she did not feel. Whatever had happened in the service corridor, the incident had to be a serious one to warrant Osman's direct intervention. "And *you're* the one who keeps telling me 'the only rule is there are no rules.'"

Osman flashed a tight smile. "Except for budgets," she said. "Budgets are like the laws of physics. Break them and die."

"*Now* you tell me." Veta forced a laugh, but did not take much comfort from the banter. The Ferret Team may have been Osman's brainchild, but the admiral was too tough-minded and analytical to continue investing ONI resources in a program she was starting to doubt. "Not that I mind having you drop by, Admiral, but bringing Oscar Squad along kind of spoils the exercise."

"We have bigger problems than the exercise." Osman didn't bother to introduce the Oscar Squad operative. Instead, her eyes darted toward Mark. "I think you know that."

"Not if you're talking about what happened in the officer's club, I don't," Veta said. "We weren't the ones who roughed up those two bystanders. That's on Oscar Squad."

The operative emphatically shook his head. "Don't try to pin that on us," he said. "We didn't touch—"

"That's enough, Svenson," Osman said. "Nobody cares about a couple of ensigns getting hurt in a bar brawl."

"A bar brawl?" Veta was growing confused. Ash hadn't said anything about that. "Admiral, it was barely a scuffle. There was no brawl."

"But that's what the ensigns have been ordered to report, and that will be the end of the matter," Osman said. "I'm more worried about the situation Commander Svenson observed."

"Which was?"

"I caught up to these two in a service corridor," Svenson said, indicating Mark and Ash. "They were hauling a body."

Veta's stomach sank. If there was a fatality, her Ferret Team was done for. She turned back to Osman and, trying to buy some time to think, attempted to sound more surprised than she was. "Yeah, sure. Are his jokes always this bad?"

"It's no joke," Svenson said. "They were carrying a body. It looked like the big guy who was trying to work your girl."

Given what Ash and Mark had already reported, Veta did not doubt Svenson's claim. But there was a lot he wasn't saying—and she wanted to figure out why. "And you're not a hundred percent on that? You don't even know your own operatives?"

"He wasn't one of ours," Svenson said.

"Of course he wasn't," Veta said. "And neither was that server who was working with him."

Svenson scowled. "What server?"

"The blonde who helped the guy dose Lieutenant Bati," Veta said, still referring to Olivia by her cover identity. "She's one who brought the zantelle. We know the lieutenant's glass was laced with nicothiotal."

Svenson looked appalled, then turned to Osman. "No way. We wouldn't do that, Admiral."

"I'll show you the field test." Veta stepped closer to Svenson, invading his space and pressing a finger to his chest. "You have no idea what could have happened to her if it had taken full effect."

Svenson did not retreat. "I *know* how to use nicothiotal—which is why I'd never use it in a training exercise." He continued to hold Veta's gaze, but addressed his comments to Osman. "Admiral, if someone drugged the lieutenant, it wasn't our team."

"No?" Osman was starting to sound doubtful. "Then who was the server? And the man she was working with?"

"I have no clue," Svenson said. "All I can you tell is they weren't ours."

Veta didn't believe Svenson for a second, but she was having trouble figuring out what he was trying to hide. Fortunately, she possessed the skills to find out.

"Then we'll ask the victim," Veta said. "Where's the body?"

Svenson's eyes shifted toward Mark and Ash. "I don't know," he said. "You'll have to ask them."

"So you can't actually produce a body?" Veta asked.

Svenson looked at the floor.

"Commander?" Osman demanded. "This is a serious accusation. Do you know where the body is or not?"

"I couldn't keep up." Svenson shot a glare in Veta's direction. "I was too sore."

"You couldn't keep up with a pair of men carrying a hundred and forty kilograms of deadweight?" Veta raised an eyebrow. "That's hard to believe."

"I don't know what to tell you. It's what happened."

"Let's assume there's a reason for that." Osman's tone was wry, no doubt because she found it perfectly reasonable that a pair of Spartan-IIIs carrying a body that large would be able to outrun a standard field operative. "Where did you lose sight of them?"

"I never really had them, Admiral. I saw them going around a corner. By the time I got there, they were gone."

"I see," Veta said. "Then how do you know the person was actually dead?"

"By the smell," Svenson said. "His bladder had released. So had his bowels."

"Not much help," Veta said. "It's hard to establish identity from odors. What about signs of a fight? Did you find any weapons or blood, for instance?"

Svenson nodded. "There was some blood spray up the corridor from where I saw them, but it's not there now."

"You cleaned it up," Osman surmised. Standard procedure called for a team in the field to eliminate any trace of a hostile engagement, whenever possible. "Good job."

"Thank you, ma'am," Svenson said. "But it wasn't us. By the time we realized we weren't going to find the targets and returned to sanitize the scene, it had already been done."

Osman turned to Veta. "Impressive."

Now it was Veta's turn to say: "It wasn't us." She couldn't admit to cleaning the scene without admitting to the homicide, and she wasn't ready to do that until she knew what Svenson was trying to hide—or at least figured out who the victim and his accomplice were. "Is it worth checking the surveillance feeds?"

Osman looked at Veta as though she were thinking about sending her back to the ONI Trade Craft School.

"We weren't the only ones who put a block on the officers' club feeds," Svenson said. "We assumed the other block came from you."

"Actually, I was thinking of the service corridor," Veta said.

"Deleted," he said. "We assumed it was you."

"Now, *that's* convenient." Veta quickly turned to Osman. "Admiral, have you considered the possibility that there *is* no body?"

"There *is* a body," Svenson said. "Why would I make up something like that?"

"Well, you *are* standing in our safe house." Veta saw Osman's eyes narrow and knew she'd struck a chord. "And now you've had a look at my entire team."

Svenson turned to Osman. "Admiral, that's ridiculous. I don't know what kind of unit you're putting together here, but letting them turn this training mission into a farce is *not* going to help them survive in the field."

"On the contrary, Commander. The only rule is that there *are* no rules." Veta gave him a sly smile. "Either you're proving that—or we are."

"She does have a point, Commander," Osman said. "You can wait in the hall with the escorts."

Svenson's face clouded with anger, but he merely acknowledged the order and spun toward the door. Once he was gone and the room secure again, Osman turned to Veta.

"So, what's the answer?" she asked. "Who's the one being played here?"

Mark immediately stepped forward. "Admiral, there's something—"

"Mark, I'll handle this." Veta pointed him to Ash's side, then turned back to Osman. "I don't know what Commander Svenson saw or didn't see, or whether he's telling the truth that the server and the other guy were not assisting Oscar Squad. But I can promise you this—nobody on my team did anything wrong."

Osman studied her for a moment, then said, "You'd better be sure of that, Lopis."

"I am. And I can prove it."

Osman smiled in obvious relief. "Good." She turned to leave. "I expect to hear from you in two hours."

The door had barely closed before Mark whirled on Veta. "Why did you do that?"

"Do what, exactly?"

"Lie to the admiral. You *know* I killed that guy."

"I do now," Veta said. "What I don't know is why."

"The why doesn't matter," Mark said. "I don't need you lying to protect me."

"Mark, you're on my team," Veta said. "*Of course* I'm going to protect you."

"You shouldn't. Now you've put the whole team at risk."

"Mark . . ." Veta had to pause and bite back the impulse to make a harsh retort, to tell Mark that *he* was the one who had put the Ferret Team at risk. "Look, we're all in this together. We either have each other's backs to the end, or we have nothing."

"No, the team comes—"

"Mark, shut up." Olivia climbed out of the seating salon and approached her teammate. "That is so like you, thinking you're so damn good that you're all the protection we need."

"Maybe that's because I'm the security specialist."

"Maybe it's because you have a big head."

" 'Livi's right," Ash said. "And it's not just your ego. I've tried your helmet. It's like wearing a ten-liter bucket."

Mark blinked, his anger draining away. "Really? I have a big head?"

"Enormous," Ash said. "Can we tell Mom about the dead guy now?"

"Please," Veta said. "We have work to do."

Mark shrugged. "Fine," he said. "But you know most of it. I was walking the fat guy down the corridor when I see this silver blade flash past the corner of my eye and there's a carving knife slicing down my chest."

"That's when I came around the corner," Ash said. "It was that server from the bar, the blonde? She's about your height and build, boss, and she was damn good with that knife. If she hadn't been so small, I would have taken her for a Spartan."

"I'm not that small," Veta said. "How did the subject die?"

"Reflex," Mark said. "I brought him around to use as a shield, then chest-punched him when he resisted. He must have had a weak heart, because he dropped like a sack of water."

"By then, I was on my way," Ash said. "The blonde threw the knife at me and took off."

"What happened to the knife?" Veta asked.

"Same thing as the blood spray," Mark said. "We came back and got rid of it."

"So I guess I *did* just lie to Admiral Osman," Veta said. "Good. Now, what about the body?"

Ash tipped his head toward the gloomy cryovolcano outside the suite's window. "We found an airlock."

Veta frowned.

"Relax, will you?" Olivia said. "We're not the police. We're *supposed* to get rid of the bodies."

"It's not that," Veta said. "We still need to figure out who this guy was, and that's going to be a lot harder without evidence."

"Covered." Ash reached inside his uniform jacket and withdrew a thick packet of personal belongings. "His name is Spencer Hume."

Veta's heart climbed into her throat. "What . . . ?" She took the packet from Ash and began to go through it. "You can't be serious."

"That's his cover, anyway." Ash said. "Why?"

"Didn't you guys listen to the BuzzCast when we were on Jastolo?" Veta groaned as she found a laminated identity card confirming her suspicions. "He was the newsmonger doing those exposés on ONI."

"I listened to one," Mark said. "It was a smear job. The Spartans had nothing to do with what happened on Tanuab III. That was a meteor impact."

Veta wasn't so sure about that one, but wasn't about to argue the point—especially not now. "That's not what matters," she said. "Spencer Hume was an investigative reporter—"

"A shit-flinger," Mark said.

"Fine . . . a shit-flinger," Veta said. "But he was still here, working Olivia, and now he's dead."

"I don't have a problem with that," Olivia said. "Not after he dosed me."

Veta said: "And he had help, remember? *Expert* help."

The expressions of all three Spartans fell.

"We need to know who that woman was." Veta handed the packet of Hume's belongings to Olivia. "Find out everything you can."

"Affirmative." Olivia pulled a commpad out of the dead man's possessions and retreated to the prep island in the kitchenette. "I'll need an hour to crack the password."

"Get started." Veta turned to Ash and Mark. "But if our target is smart, we're not going to find her real name in his commpad."

"Not likely," Ash said. "We already know she was good enough to block the officers' club security feeds."

"And delete the trouble in the service corridor," Mark added.

"Wait. That wasn't you?" Veta said.

Ash shook his head. "Not us," he said. "I was going to ask 'Livi for help."

Veta nodded. "Yeah, I know . . . just hoping." The facility AI was pretty basic, but subverting even a dumb AI fell more into Olivia's skill set than Ash's—him being the team's surveillance expert, and her the information specialist. "Ideas?"

"Just one," Ash said. "All we're trying to do is identify her, and anyone that good has probably crossed paths with ONI before."

"So she'll be in the FRD," Veta said. ONI's Facial Recognition Database. "We just need an image of her face."

Ash nodded. "Exactly."

"And you know how to find one?" No response. Veta waited for him to answer, then finally asked, "Am I supposed to guess?"

"Sorry, ma'am. I was just thinking it through."

"And?"

"There's no use trying to find her through the surveillance feeds," Ash said. "If she's good enough to subvert the AI, she's good enough to neutralize common surveillance files."

"But there's one file she *can't* block." Mark was starting to sound excited too. "Not if she wants to keep moving around."

"The master comparison file?" Veta asked. Like many medium-security facilities, this one relied on a facial recognition system to control access to all interior locations. The target couldn't erase her image from the master file without eliminating her ability to move around the facility. "Olivia, can you pull up those reference images?"

"We should have access already." Olivia continued to tap on Hume's commpad. "Just ask the AI."

Veta raised her brow. "The AI will let us raid the master security files?"

"Sure," Olivia said. "He let us have this suite, didn't he?"

An hour later, Veta was still standing at the door, going through facial images on the control panel's palm-size screen, when Olivia let out a whoop.

"I'm in!" she said. "And you'll never guess what kind of intel that bitch was feeding Hume."

Veta thought back to the snippet of "interview" she had heard while eavesdropping on Hume's exchange with Olivia. "Details on the Spartan-III program, right?" she asked. "Especially Gamma Company, and your reliance on Smoothers."

"That, and it gets worse. She mentioned us specifically."

"*Us?* As in the Ferrets?" Mark asked. "Then it's a good thing I killed the reporter. It saves ONI the trouble of sending us after him later."

"I'm not sure that fixes the problem," Ash said. "If word is already leaking about the Gammas, we're done. They didn't even want us as Spartans."

"Nothing has leaked yet." Veta froze the image on the control panel, then said, "And nothing is going to. I just found her."

"You did?" Olivia switched to her ONI datapad, and a few moments later, she said, "You're sure?"

Veta stepped over to the prep island and peered over Olivia's shoulder. The datapad's screen showed an image of the blond server from the officers' club. But now the woman was wearing the dress blues of a UNSC Naval Commander, and below her image were the words OTA GALLO, RETIRED.

Ash joined them and peered over Olivia's other shoulder. "So, she's ONI." The records of most field operatives read RETIRED or, in deep-cover cases, KIA. "They're stress testing us again."

"Or trying to sink us," Mark said. You ever get the feeling Admiral Osman is out on a limb with us?"

"Sometimes," Ash said. "But if she's out on a limb, why would she want to sink us?"

"Not *her*, genius," Olivia said. "You don't think Osman has rivals? Word has it Parangosky is grooming Osman to be the next CINCONI. And you *know* the Section Chiefs aren't going to take that without a fight."

"Maybe," Veta said. Bureaucratic infighting was certainly one motive for sabotaging a mission . . . but this time, the stakes seemed too high. A successful play would cripple ONI—and getting caught meant a bullet in the head. "Show us the rest of the jacket, 'Livi."

Olivia scrolled down. Gallo's record listed a handful of postings over the better part of two decades. Beyond that, the details were sketchy. More than a hundred entries read either REDACTED or CLASSIFIED.

But it was the final entry that Veta found most interesting. Just a week earlier, Gallo's file had been marked FINAL DISPOSITION: DARK MOON. NO CONTACT, NO ACCESS.

"What's Dark Moon?" Ash asked.

"I have no idea," Veta said. "But whatever it is, ONI doesn't like it. See what you can pull up."

Olivia typed an inquiry, and an entry appeared.

Dark Moon Enterprises was listed as a comprehensive security company that provided force-enhancement services throughout the human-controlled portion of the galaxy. A month earlier, the firm had appeared out of nowhere with a prestigious list of clients and began to hire former UNSC personnel to provide security services in a broad spectrum of hostile environments. Within two weeks, Dark Moon had grown so fast that they began to pursue active-duty personnel, and the UNSC put them on the NO CONTACT, NO ACCESS list. Rather than back off, Dark Moon offered its clients a menu of privatized intelligence and threat-management services, then started to recruit former and current ONI operatives to fulfill its contracts.

Mark whistled softly. "I don't know who's in charge of that outfit, but they have more guts than brains."

"You might have it backward," Veta said. "Dark Moon has a lot of guts, clearly. But they've only been in business a *month*, and already they're an interstellar company growing so fast they need to raid ONI for employees? I'd say they have plenty of brains too."

"Yeah," Ash said. "Doing all that in a month seems kind of remarkable, at least by civilian standards."

"It is." Veta turned back to Olivia. "Is there is anything else on Dark Moon? The identity of the founder, perhaps? A list of company executives?"

"What you see is what we have," Olivia said. "There's not even an above-clearance file."

"Then they're making a smart play," Veta said. "A bold one . . . but very, very smart."

"No way," Ash said. "Messing with the military is one thing, but pissing off ONI? That's a death wish."

"Don't do that, Ash."

"Do what?"

"Underestimate the enemy." Veta tapped the datapad's screen. "Assuming this file is right, Dark Moon came out of nowhere, and they aren't afraid to poke a stick in ONI's eye. But ONI doesn't even seem to know who's behind Dark Moon—much less why it was founded."

Olivia shrugged. "That'll change soon enough," she said. "Intelligence takes time."

"Not for Dark Moon," Veta said. "They've only been in business a month, and already they know enough about Gamma Company to give ONI a public-relations nightmare. That means they're either as good as ONI—or a whole lot more agile. Whichever it is, I wouldn't bet against Dark Moon when this thing turns ugly."

The Gammas scowled in unison. "Come on," Mark said. "You're being crazy."

"Am I?"

Veta reached up and jammed a thumb down on Mark's wounded clavicle. He didn't drop to his knees, but he did flinch and back away. Ignoring his look of surprise, Veta raised her thumb, presenting it to the trio.

"The biggest guy doesn't always win." She raised her index finger, leaving about a centimeter of space between it and her thumb. "Gallo came this close to killing Mark because she struck first. And so far, Dark Moon has been doing all the punching."

The Gammas remained quiet for a moment. Olivia finally said, "And we're their point of attack. If word gets out that Admiral Osman is using Gammas on her Ferret Teams, ONI is gone."

"Probably not gone," Veta said. "But certainly crippled—and *that* leaves a power vacuum to be exploited. I'll bet Dark Moon has contracts ready to sign now."

"You're saying this is about *contracts*?" Ash seemed horrified. "Dosing 'Livi and trying to kill Mark—that's just business?"

"Ash, people kill for a lot of reasons," Veta said. "And you better believe money is at the top of the list."

"I guess," Ash said. "I really miss being just a soldier. Risking your life used to mean something."

"It still does," Olivia said. "But we're Ferrets now, and I'm not about to give *that* up too." She turned to Veta. "How do we fix this?"

"Gallo was Hume's source," Veta said. "That means she can be someone else's source too. We have to stop her before that happens."

"Then it's simple," Mark said. "We kill Gallo."

"*Mark*," Ash said, "we're not supposed to kill anyone this time. Remember?"

"That's right," Veta said. "But Gallo really isn't part of the training exercise."

Mark flashed a smug smile. "Excellent. So we *do* kill her."

"Only if we have to," Veta said. "We should try to capture her—if she gives us the chance."

"Like that's going to happen," Olivia said. "She doesn't seem like the surrendering kind."

"Not really," Veta admitted. She was already turning her thoughts to locating Gallo, trying to put herself in the other woman's position. "Now we just have to find her."

"That's not going to be easy," Ash said. "For all we know, she could be offworld by now."

"I don't think so," Veta said. "She just started at Dark Moon a week ago. This has to be her first assignment."

Mark cocked his head. "So?"

"So would *we* give up?" Olivia asked, catching on faster than the other two Gammas. "Especially on our first job?"

"Exactly." Veta turned to Mark. "What are the chances that Gallo knows Hume is actually dead?"

Mark looked at Ash, and Ash said, "I'd say good. She was closer than Svenson, and he knew Hume was dead."

"Then we'll have to do this the hard way," Veta said. "Olivia—"

"On it." Olivia set her datapad aside and started to tap a message into Hume's commpad, then spoke without looking up. "And, boss, maybe you should send a copy of Gallo's file to Admiral Osman and ask her to lock down the facility."

Veta nodded. "Good idea." She raised her wrist and began tapping a message on her own commpad. "Thanks."

"It won't work," Ash said. "If Gallo's as good as we think she is, she'll slip free faster than we would."

"Gallo's not going anywhere," Veta said. "She needs to recover Hume's commpad before ONI can start digging into it. Sooner or later, they'll find something that leads back to her—and she knows it." She finished her message and sent it, then said, "Putting the facility on lockdown will tip her off, and Dark Moon will hear about it. That puts even more pressure on Gallo."

Mark smiled. "I like that strategy. If she doesn't recover Hume's stuff, *they'll* kill her." He watched Olivia tap on Hume's commpad for a moment, then said, "But what's 'Livi doing?"

"Writing a message to Gallo and copying Admiral Osman,"

Olivia said. "I'm reporting everything we learned about her connection to Hume."

"So Gallo will *know* we know?" Mark's brow rose. "You want to get this done fast, don't you?"

"We can't afford to sit around waiting," Olivia said. "The admiral only gave us two hours, and half of that is gone."

"And we need to put the pressure on Gallo, not ourselves," Veta said. "She's either going to hit us fast or hit us smart, and it would be better to know which."

Olivia stopped tapping and smiled in triumph. "Okay, done." She raised Hume's commpad, her thumb poised to execute a command. "Ready?"

Veta took a moment to consider, trying to think of anything she had forgotten, then nodded. "Do it."

Olivia had barely depressed the SEND key on Hume's commpad before a hissed HOLD! sounded outside the suite door. Muffled and barely audible, the whisper was still distinct enough to catch the attention of Veta and all three Gammas. They wasted a precious second looking at each other in astonishment, and Mark smiled and mouthed, *Nice plan.*

"She's here!" Olivia whispered, and Ash hissed, "Down!" and the muted click of a snapping switch ticked through the door.

Mark and Ash were already flinging themselves against the wall on opposite sides of the door. Olivia was diving over the peninsula that separated the kitchenette from the rest of the suite, one hand grasping a knife-block she had snatched off the prep island as she moved. Veta, always the slowest to react, was dropping to floor, reaching for a sidearm that was not there and cursing the regulations that prohibited carrying weapons in a facility where intoxicants were served.

The blast was deafening, the concussion wave so powerful that it sent the prep island tumbling over Veta's head. Her reflexes now honed by ONI's twice-weekly close-assault drills, she rolled against the suite's forward wall.

A pair of grenades came flying out of the smoke where the suite's door had once been, crossing in midair and dropping to the floor on opposite sides of the sunken seating area. Veta's training kicked in and she realized the pattern probably meant a three-person squad—two throwing grenades and a third covering with automatic fire.

Sure enough, chunks of wall and balls of couch stuffing began to fly as suppression fire streamed into the room. Veta didn't bother wondering how Gallo and her people had smuggled weapons into the facility. There were a hundred ways, and the Ferrets knew most of them. And the next time they went on a training exercise, Veta intended to use them.

But now it was time to move, before the shooters could step into the suite and start raking fire along the perimeter. She grabbed a broken stool leg and gathered her feet beneath her, duck-walking forward.

The first shooter stepped through the door, his M7 submachine gun spitting bursts as his gaze swept the foyer. Veta hurled the stool leg at his head and saw him flinch as it tumbled past. She sprang forward, diving for his legs, twisting around to keep an eye on his weapon. The M7 swung her way, orange flashes erupting from the muzzle, chips of broken tile dancing across the floor ahead.

Mark appeared from the far side of the doorway, slipping a hand in front of the shooter to clasp the barrel and force it down so abruptly that the man's suede loafers erupted in a spray of blood, bone, and leather. By then, Mark had his other hand clamped on the shooter's throat, and he was swinging the fellow around to serve as a shield. The shooter's body began to shake and jump as his companions sprayed him with fire.

Ash reached in from the opposite side of the doorway, grabbing the second shooter by the forearm and jerking him into the foyer. The Gamma landed a quick trio of rabbit-punches to the base of the skull, and the man collapsed to the floor.

Veta found herself unarmed and staring through the twisted remnants of the door into the little elevator lobby outside the suite, where Ota Gallo stood with an M6 sidearm in one hand and a grenade in the other. She locked eyes with Veta, then smiled and used her thumb to flick the pin free.

"Grenade!" Veta's ears were still ringing so hard from the earlier explosion that she couldn't hear herself scream—much less be certain anyone else did. She tried again, then rolled away from the door and saw Olivia standing ahead. The Gamma's uniform was scorched and she was bleeding from about a dozen places, including both ears and the nose. But her throwing arm was outstretched and her gaze was fixed on the door, and there was a knife missing from the block in her free hand.

Olivia's mouth opened and formed the word *grenade*, then she tossed the knife-block aside and threw herself on top of Veta.

The Ferret Team did not attempt to sanitize the site. With Ota Gallo sprayed all over the lobby and the suite door blasted open, and blood and bullet holes everywhere they looked, there didn't seem much point.

Besides, the team had more important things to worry about. They needed to remove what remained of Hume's commpad and possessions to a secure location. And despite what Olivia claimed, she was in need of an infirmary. Veta grabbed a field kit and took a couple of minutes to patch her up, then ordered her Ferret Team to evacuate. They would worry about the surveillance feeds and the AI later.

Or not.

They didn't get very far. When the elevator opened, Admiral Osman was inside, standing behind four large ONI security officers in helmets and body armor. The officers were carrying shotguns and submachines and weren't being shy about where they pointed them.

Veta motioned her team to stand aside, then turned back to Osman. "You're a little late to the party, Admiral."

"So I see." Osman waited for her security escort to clear the area, then stepped out of the elevator and looked around wide-eyed at the little lobby. "Is this what you call keeping a low profile, Lopis?"

"Considering the alternative." Veta gestured to Olivia, who, despite her injuries, was standing at attention. "You saw Olivia's message?"

Osman's expression softened. "I did." She nodded to Olivia. "Good work."

"Thank you, ma'am," she said. "But it was all of us."

"I'm sure." Osman pointed at the charred packet in Ash's hands. "Are those Hume's effects?"

"Yes, ma'am," Ash said. "What's left of them."

"Let me have them, son."

Ash passed her the packet. "The breaching blast did a job on the electronics, Admiral. I don't think they'll be much help."

"And they won't be much harm either. That's half the battle." Osman stepped over to the suite, then peered through the empty doorway. "This isn't good, Lopis."

"Not our choice, Admiral." Veta stepped away from the door. "All we did was clean up ONI's mess."

"Really? And what about Spencer Hume?" Osman spun on Veta. "Was he part of the mess too?"

"In a manner of speaking," Veta said. "Hume was going to name Gallo as his source. She killed him to prevent that."

Osman's eyebrows shot up. The lie was an obvious one, but believable. She studied Veta for a long time. Finally, she suppressed a smile and turned to Mark.

"Is that what happened, Spartan?"

Mark looked Osman straight in the eye. "Yes, ma'am, that's exactly what happened." He waited a beat, then declared: "And, Admiral, just to be clear . . . I'm a Ferret now."

INTO THE FIRE

KELLY GAY

This story takes place four years after the end of the Covenant's brutal and costly rampage across human-occupied space (Halo 3 *era) and Kilo-Five's brief mission on* Venezia, *culminating in the destruction of the highly-sought-after Covenant battle cruiser* Pious Inquisitor (Halo: Mortal Dictata).

New Tyne, Venezia, Qab System
January 2557

Today, she sold weapons to a hinge-head.

The small lot of spikers and carbines would keep her crew happy, her ship operational, and her informants eager for a piece of the pie.

It was a lovely little circle of profit she'd created for herself.

And Rion loved it. She was *good* at it. She'd forged her way to success and never hesitated to fight bare-knuckled to stay there. She was proud to call herself one of New Tyne's most notable salvagers.

But success wasn't all golden.

There were some sales, some transactions that left dark smudges somewhere deep inside her, where things like honor and integrity and loyalty lurked. Dark karmic tally marks that put a few kinks in that lovely little circle.

Every time one of her lots sold to ex-Covenant, the nagging sense of betrayal didn't let up until she hiked herself down to Stavros's and had a few drinks. Her crew thought it was simply a ritual, a small way to celebrate yet another payday, another sign that their jobs were secure and going strong. But inside, behind the jokes and the smiles and the laughter, a sour taste lingered in Rion's throat.

She wondered what he'd say if he knew, if he could see her now. Daddy's little girl all grown up and on the wrong side of the law.

Though, these days, there wasn't much law to be found.

And sides? In postwar, there were plenty of those to go around.

Rion's side, or lack thereof, was neutrality. Her business depended on it. She stayed out of politics, religions, and rebellions. There was a time her family would have said that staying neutral was just as bad as choosing the wrong side. But times had changed and family was just a memory.

"All set," she said as the bank confirmation appeared on her commpad.

"Always a pleasure, Captain. Not as good as last month, but respectable."

The prior month had been one of Rion's best paydays ever, a four-way bidding war for a small piece of Forerunner NAV tech that she'd come across by chance in a small bazaar on Komoya, one of Vitalyevna's moons. The databoard was damaged and the crystal chip smashed, but it hadn't seemed to matter. Forerunner tech and relics were *always* a hot commodity. Intel was hard to come by, so Rion spent much of her downtime digging in files and researching in places she shouldn't be just to learn more about the ancient race.

And then she'd found intel on her ticket to retirement—a device called a luminary, which would supposedly point the way to all sorts of interesting Forerunner salvage. . . .

Rion reached into her pocket, grabbed the flex card she'd put there, broke it in half, and placed the bright orange equivalent of two hundred fifty credits on the desk.

Nor Fel glanced at the amount stamped on the surface, then lifted her large avian head. Clear membranes swept horizontally across her yellow eyes, the Kig-Yar version of a blink. She cocked her head, the tendons and muscles above her eyes pulling together into consideration.

Nor placed the tip of her claw on the card, holding it there while she gazed at Rion, and then cackled. "I knew you'd bite."

Despite their obvious differences, Rion and Nor understood each other and enjoyed a mutually beneficial relationship. Devious and cunning, Nor possessed a greed that was only exceeded by the high regard in which she held herself and her T'vaoan lineage. She was an excellent strategist and knew that relations and good business were the key to keeping the money flowing. And the money was *always* flowing

After Nor's mate, Sav Fel, disappeared four years ago, Nor had created an empire on Venezia, a clearinghouse of postwar scrap and surplus. Salvagers brought in their goods; the clearinghouse cataloged them and took a percentage; and come the first day of every Venezian month, the items went up for auction—everything from Titanium-A plating and molecular memory circuits to small arms and transport vessels. Nor ruled over her house with an iron claw and a set of craftily devised rules that everyone—salvager and buyer alike—abided by.

Her clients included those from the industrial, tech, medical, and manufacturing sectors, along with ex-Covenant, fringe and religious groups, rebels of one faction or another, and independent government militias. She was on the radar of every military group out there—Rion figured she was on a few herself—but mostly Nor's Clearing House was left alone. One, because this was Venezia, and Venezia played by its own rules. And, two, because Nor refused to move heavy ordnance of any kind. Rumor had it that her mate had gotten mixed up in trafficking something big and it had cost him.

"They will not be happy, your crew." Nor nodded toward the window, where Lessa and the new hire, Kip, waited outside by the truck, talking. "With the payday you just made, one would think a break is in order. I hear Sundown is nice this time of year."

"Sundown is nice any time of year." Which Nor knew full well. "Breaks aren't really my thing, Nor. Just ask my crew." And they also wouldn't be happy to learn that Rion was about to use a good portion of their payday on the next operation. "Word's floating around about big scrap in one of the border systems." Rion gestured to the flex card on the desk. "Haven't sold my info away, have you?"

Nor's high-pitched squawk grated over Rion's eardrums, making her wince.

"You know I keep my word," Nor said. "Me and you, we have an agreement, yes? Have I ever broken it?"

"Nope, can't say that you have."

The small downy feathers on the back of Nor's head ruffled, indicating she was incredibly proud and satisfied by the admission.

Rion couldn't fault Nor for preening; her information was always good. The old bird had informants across the entire Via Casilina Trade Route that had arisen between the Qab, Cordoba, Shaps, Elduros, and Sverdlosk systems. In the past, Rion had been forced to wait for other salvagers to fail to deliver before Nor would then resell her precious intel at a more affordable price. When Rion kept returning successful when no one else was, her reputation and her bank account grew, and so had her business relationship with Nor.

Nor opened a desk drawer and pushed the flex card inside. "It's not my information . . . but for this price, I send you to the one who possesses it. He is expecting you, I am sure. Get to it quick and you might end up rich as me. One day." Her beak clicked together as she gave a raspy chuckle. "But remember my rules, yes? No trouble."

Now *that* was interesting. The familiar zing of possibility ran through Rion's veins. Had to be something controversial, something big. Military, probably. *Trouble* to Nor meant heavy ordnance. And where there was heavy ordnance, there was usually a wealth of tech and surplus.

Paranoid as usual, Nor didn't say the name aloud, but rather legibly scratched it onto a piece of paper with her claw, then handed it over.

Rion read the scratch and lifted her brow. "Really?"

Nor shrugged.

"This'd better be worth it."

A chilly breeze tossed Rion's dark hair around her face as she headed for the truck. Gray clouds hovered over New Tyne's center. The soft glow of city lights emerging as day gave way to night was so warm and inviting that it almost made her long for a place with roots and a simpler life. *Almost.*

"So?" Lessa pushed away from the hood of the truck with a heavy shiver in her voice. "How was the old bird today?"

Rion shook her head at her young crewmember. "Next time, wear a jacket, Less. Or wait *inside* the truck. Long winter might be over, but those thin fatigues won't cut it for a few more months yet."

"I draw the line at six months of winter fatigues. Besides, we hardly stay long enough for the weather to matter." Lessa ducked into the passenger seat.

Lessa hadn't met a human or an alien she couldn't or wouldn't talk to. She was blessed with a friendly face, a beguiling smile, and a mop of tight blond curls that never stayed tucked into her braid for very long. Out of necessity, the young woman had learned early on how to read people and use her looks and personality to their fullest advantage. While Lessa was charming the pants off an unlucky target, her younger brother, Niko, was somewhere nearby hacking into the target's commpad. They made quite a team. And when they'd targeted Rion two years ago in the mining slums of Aleria, rather than turn them over to the local authorities, Rion had offered them a job. One of the smarter decisions she'd made in recent years.

"So, payday was good then?" Lessa began fiddling with the heater as Kip squeezed his well-built frame into the backseat.

Rion started the truck. "Yeah, it was good. Just one more stop before we head back." She pulled out of the lot and then eased into traffic, wondering how to break the news. They'd been out six weeks on their last job, only returning today. The guys back at the ship had just unloaded a *very* nice stasis field generator for Nor's pickup crew. The last thing on their minds was jumping systems again.

In the silence, Rion could feel Lessa's lengthy stare and knew what was coming.

"Please tell me you didn't." Rion's wince affirmed Lessa's suspicions. "Aw, great. Just great. You *promised* us some offship R and R."

"It's just intel, Less. It doesn't mean we have to take off right away."

Lessa folded her arms over her chest and slumped in her seat. She blew a strand of hair from her face with a huff, and then suddenly turned in her seat to face Kip. "When she says 'just intel' "—she made air quotes with her fingers—"that's captain-speak for we're right back to hauling ass across the Via Casilina. Perfect. Just friggin' perfect."

"Well, I might as well pull the bandage off now," Rion said drily, knowing Lessa was going to love this part: "We're going to see Rouse."

Rion tried not to laugh at the murderous glare that blazed from Lessa's eyes, but sometimes Lessa was such an easy mark; swift to react, so full of young, passionate emotion. Having Lessa around was like having the little sister Rion had always wanted, complete with all the drama that her childhood fantasies hadn't quite considered.

In the rearview mirror, she caught Kip's grinning reflection and smiled back.

Kip Silas was a decent guy with a calm, easygoing manner and enough muscle to get the tougher jobs done. It also didn't hurt that he was a walking data chip of every class of ship in the known universe, and, as engineers went, he was a damn fine one, a definite step up. All in all, she was happy with the new recruit so far.

The worst dive bar in New Tyne was tucked behind a one-story retail mall on the southern outskirts of the city. Despite the aging exterior, spotty electricity, and grungy interior, there were always vehicles in the lot and patrons at the bar.

"Looks . . . promising," Kip commented with a decided lack of enthusiasm as they left the truck.

When they approached the door, he paused at the sign nailed there—TINY BIRDS. "This is a joke, right?"

Unfortunately it wasn't. In fact, it was quite literal. The smell of stale rum didn't bother Rion so much as the distinct powdery musk that burned the insides of her nose and stuck in the back of her throat.

"Dear God," Kip uttered as he got his first look at the cages hung from the ceiling rafters, inside hundreds of small birds the color of the sun and blue sky. Rouse's obsession had overtaken the building long ago, but no one here seemed to mind.

Tiny B's held the usual mix of patrons: a collection of humans, mostly at the bar; Kig-Yar who had taken up several tables along the far wall; and two Sangheili in the far corner.

Rion headed for the table by the backroom door where Rouse conducted business. As she came into the light of the bar, recognition passed between her and one of the guys seated there.

Cottrell slipped off his barstool, his eyes gleaming with drink and appreciation as they swept down Rion's body and back up again. "Baby. You're back."

For the hundredth time— "Not your baby, Cottrell."

A leer stretched his mouth. "Man, aren't you a sight for sore eyes. Damn girl. Never seen fatigues look so fine. And to think I almost forgot what a hot piece of tail you—"

The gurgle that came from Cottrell's throat was intensely satisfying. Rion's grip on his scruffy neck tightened, the pressure making his bloodshot eyes bulge. Anger had ignited so fast that she'd reacted before her brain had a chance to catch up.

Should have walked on by.

Usually she did. But that particular phrase . . .

She squeezed harder. "Anything else you want to say to me, Cottrell?" He shook his head. "I think the next time I walk in here—I dunno—a 'Hey, Captain, how ya doing?' will work just fine."

"Sure, sure. Works fine," he rasped, clearly stunned by her reaction.

Cottrell was all bark and no bite. Rion knew that, but . . .

Reckless, volatile, lashing out. . . . Rion had been accused of those things in the past, and rightly so. It had been a long time since she'd gotten this rattled, and it certainly wasn't her usual routine to play the badass. But Cottrell had said the wrong set of words, words that instantly revived memories of another bar, another time, into her mind quicker than a flashbang grenade.

Dinner with Dad.

Mom refused to take her, as usual. But Jillian stepped up and offered. Jillian was fun and gorgeous and always game for anything, and Rion adored her. Her five-year-old heart was beating so fast when they entered the lounge, so excited and nervous to see her father again. . . .

But it wasn't her dad who met them—it was that horrible lieutenant, drunk, eyes gleaming as he leered at Jillian and made those foul comments. Rion wasn't sure what it all meant, but she knew it was bad. And when he turned his eyes on her and said she'd grow up to be a fine piece of tail . . . Jillian had lost it and struck the guy. Rion never knew fear like that before, when the lieutenant shoved her aunt against the wall, his forearm on her throat, pressing hard.

Too hard.

Then her father appeared like some avenging angel out of the ether. And—like her granddaddy was fond of saying—all hell broke loose.

"Cap," Lessa said sharply under her breath, poking Rion in the rib. *"Rion."*

Rion blinked, realizing she'd moved on from the bar and was now standing in front of Rouse's table. And, of course, Rouse was watching her with his typical sage-like gaze. It was a look Rion knew well and one she found highly disconcerting.

Clearing her throat and giving the old man a tight smile, she slid into the booth as Rouse pulled his datapad over and made a few swipes before pushing it across the table. With a practiced eye, Rion examined the screen. "This the only image you have?"

He nodded. "It's clearly a ship. What kind"—Rouse shrugged and sat back with a twinkle in his eye—"remains to be seen. Your job to find out, salvager, not mine. My price is forty thousand credits for the location and twenty-five percent of sale."

Rouse tried, but he was a horrible negotiator. Rion's attention returned to the blurry image on the screen. It could have easily been mistaken for one of the many jagged gray rocks jutting up from the snow, but to a trained eye, the lines were unmistakable. "Ten thousand and ten percent."

Rouse held her gaze for a long moment, and Rion had to bite her tongue to keep from smiling. "Thirty and twenty," he said, obviously enjoying himself.

She slid the datapad back. "The wreck is old, probably picked clean two decades ago. And depending on the location, it could cost more to get there than it's worth, which means I need my credits. Offer stands at ten." She rubbed her cheek and took some time to think, time she didn't really need. "I would, however, be willing to cut you a deal on the sale end though. . . . Say, fifteen?"

"Ten thousand credits and fifteen percent." He thought it over for a minute, then nodded slowly. "I do see your point. The location is quite a hike. . . . All right, Captain, we have a deal."

Rion parked in the lot near the hangar bay where the *Ace of Spades* was docked, then hiked up a flight of stairs to catch the elevator to E-Level.

Ace was a *gorgeous* ship. Seven years in the making, she was a sleek Mariner-class transport ship refitted with so many bells and whistles that it made her one of a kind. Rion had no idea what the crew did with their own credits, but everything she made went back into the next job and from there into *Ace.* Her pride and joy had an advanced passive-sensor array, a military-grade slipspace drive, two pivoting fusion engines on each wing, six thrusters, a sensor-baffling suite, and already souped-up nav and comm systems that Niko had worked his tech magic upon. There wasn't much the ship needed anymore. Though, a smart AI would be nice. . . .

"You guys are never going to believe where we're going!" Lessa called as she jogged up the ramp and into the cargo hold.

Rion crossed the hold and headed for the steps. Cade was sitting one story up on the catwalk, performing maintenance on the track system. He stopped working as Rion looked up at him. "Meeting in the mess in fifteen," she told him. He gave her a curt nod and then returned to the job at hand.

That was Cade, all business. He was steady, reliable, and got the job done—the kind of man who didn't say much, but when he did, you tended to listen. A former marine, he brought order and efficiency to their small crew and was often the voice of reason when Rion wanted to run full tilt and push their operation to the limits.

Fifteen minutes later, the crew was seated around the mess table and Rion laid it all out for them. They might piss and moan about the lack of R and R, but in the end they were like her—no one could resist a score.

"The ship we're after is huge," Rion said. "I'm guessing old freighter, possibly military. We won't know until we get there, but if this thing hasn't been picked over yet . . ."

"Money in the bank," Young Niko said with a cocky grin, linking his slim fingers behind his head and leaning back in his chair. "Can't beat that."

Kip glanced at him with a confused frown. "Unless it's military." He looked up at Rion. "Right? I mean, the UNSC's Salvage Directive states tha—"

"Yeah, we're all familiar," Lessa interrupted, rolling her eyes. "Report your find, claim your reward, and let their military salvage crew take over. Blah, blah, blah. The comical part is they think that way out here, we actually give a damn. Where was the UNSC when we needed them? They show up when it's convenient for *them* and expect us to tremble at the might of Earth's grand military." She snorted and eased back down in her seat. "Not happening."

"This is the Outer Colonies, Kip," Niko added. "You know as well as the rest of us that they can't and don't control everything. Hell, they have a hard enough time keeping control of what's left of the Inner Colonies these days. They should be glad we're out there recovering their goods."

Cade was leaning back in his chair, arms folded over his chest, observing the conversation in his usual stoic manner. He didn't have the same outward disgust as Lessa and Niko, but he had his own set of conflicts when it came to the military and the war. He'd been honorably discharged from the Marines, but his return to civilian life hadn't gone so well. There hadn't been a home or a family to return to, only glass. Kilometers and kilometers of glass. . . .

Rion met his somber gaze. Once, they were like Lessa and Niko, but somewhere along the way, they'd moved beyond passionate debates on wars and politics and put their energy and loyalty into the only thing they could count on: themselves.

"The UNSC leaves most salvagers alone," Rion told Kip, taking control of the conversation. "We're not smugglers. We hunt tech, metals, and small arms, whether that be UNSC, Covenant, or civilian." She'd had this conversation with Kip when she hired him, but maybe she hadn't been completely clear. "We don't bring large arms and WMDs to market. Any military group is more than welcome to come to the clearinghouse and buy back their wreckage. I know for a fact the UNSC keeps a buyer shacked up in New Tyne just for that purpose. Probably cheaper for them to buy at auction than to pay the costs of their own salvagers and scouts. . . . The point is, we get our fee either way. And if we find that wreck is military and there's a data core or nuke onboard, you better believe I'll report it."

"It's a good job, Kip," Cade told him. "Stop worrying. Cap is fair and we make a decent living, better than most out here."

"I did my research," Kip replied. "Wouldn't be here otherwise." He shifted in his chair to study Rion, his lips twitching into a smile. "Good reputation. Eighty-five-percent success rate. Best salvage ship out there. . . . Not bad for a thirty-two-year-old military brat from Earth."

"Suck-up," Niko coughed into his hand.

She'd hardly considered herself a military brat, but Rion didn't bother enlightening him. Instead, she shrugged it off. "You trying to butter me up, rookie? Because flattery gets you extra rations." She couldn't fault him for looking her up; she'd done the same to him, though more extensively than he'd ever know.

"So what's our destination?" Cade asked.

"Ectanus 45." Rion leaned over and pressed the small, flat pad integrated into the center of the table's surface. A holographic star map appeared. Rion began zooming in on the star system until a large blue planet came into focus. "We'll bypass the planet. It's uninhabited, so we'll have no worries there. . . ." She turned the view slightly and stopped on the planet's moon. "This is our target. Eiro. It's tidally locked to the planet, but there's a narrow twilight ring that supports a small settlement. Our target is approximately fifty-six kilometers away from the twilight ring on the dark side of the moon. Location couldn't be better—too cold for habitation, but close enough to the ring that our winter gear should suffice. According to Rouse, the settlement has one communications satellite, two transport ships, and very little defense capability. As far as entering their airspace, we're good. They won't know we're there, and we'll have plenty of time to do our jobs."

"That's on the edge of the Inner Colonies, a border system. A long way off our usual route . . ." Cade said, thoughtfully, leaning forward in his chair, completely focused on the map. "You sure about this?"

Rion met with a pair of somber eyes, those of a man who had seen war and knew more than anyone the price of taking risks, of jumping systems, and of hunting salvage that others would fight and kill for. "Yeah, I'm sure. It'll take a while, but it'll be worth it."

After a hard workout and an even harder sparring round with Cade, Rion hit the shower and then dressed in casual gear before returning to her quarters with a towel slung around her shoulders. Her muscles were weak and shaky. She'd pushed herself hard. Working out her demons. The usual.

Sitting down at her small desk, she stared off into nothing for a moment.

The demons were still there. Stronger than ever.

They'd left Venezian airspace and jumped an hour ago. And for the first time since seeing the grainy image on Rouse's datapad, she allowed herself to consider yet again the possibility.

She ran her hands down her face and let out a weary sigh. How long was she going to keep doing this to herself? How long would she let the past haunt her?

Forever, it felt like.

She'd been searching for ghosts since she was six years old, since her grandfather had sat her down and told her that her father had been lost. That's all. Just . . . *lost*. What did that mean exactly? What the *hell* did that mean? To a child those words had been utterly confounding. How many millions of families across the galaxy had been torn apart like hers? Father, mothers, sons, daughters. So many consumed by war, so many MIA and KIA, the list was unimaginable.

How did you bury a man who was lost? How did you grieve? Or move on?

Voices of her family, of her pediatrician and psychologist, echoed in her mind, putting terms and labels on her pain, like Childhood Traumatic Grief. PTSD. Anxiety.

How had she grieved?

She'd built an entire life and profession on the foundation of loss.

Salvager.

Rion shook her head and gave a tired laugh.

Salvager. Her whole life spent searching, pushing ever onward, jumping from system to system, planet to planet, one wreck after another. Looking for a ghost ship. Somewhere along the way it had become routine, the drive to find answers eventually muted by years and decades, until her job was simply a job, a way of life. . . .

It had been a while since she'd thought about him.

She pulled open her desk drawer and retrieved her favorite holostill, setting the flat chip on the table and turning it on.

And there he was.

That cocky grin on his face always made her smile. Even now, as a grown woman, he seemed larger than life. He'd been her hero, her protector, a rugged, capable kind of man, and a marine through and through.

With a heavy breath, Rion placed the image back in her desk. The data chip was there, too, containing all of the messages he'd sent home for her. Sometimes, when she really wanted to torture herself, she'd listen to them.

But she'd had enough for one day.

Eiro, Ectanus 45 System

The *Ace of Spades* settled into geosynchronous orbit above the dark side of Eiro. The twilight ring was just visible, a gray-blue haze outlining the moon's circumference.

"Have you located our target, Less?"

"That's a big ole affirmative, Captain. I have temp readings too. You guys ready for this?"

Niko swiveled in his comm chair, his knees bent, and his feet tucked under his bottom. "You mean ready to have my balls frozen off? Um. No. Not really."

Cade grunted in agreement. "Here, here."

"Fifty below zero."

"Woo. Hoo," Niko responded as dully as he could.

"It's a balmy seventy-five and blustery in the ring," Lessa added, ignoring Niko.

"Less and I will set her down," Rion told them. "The rest of you head to the locker room and suit up."

Lessa swiveled in her chair to face Niko as he got up. "Don't forget your earmuffs, little brother." She laughed as he shot a rude gesture behind his back. When he was gone, she returned to the job at hand. "Winds are looking bad down there."

From her position at main, Rion monitored their progress as *Ace* broke atmo, keeping an eye on Lessa as the young woman navigated the ship. Lessa was learning and improving with every mission, and soon Rion would be able to rely on her more often. "Adjust thrusters and keep us on target the best you can."

The closer they came to the surface, the more *Ace* was pushed around.

A kilometer out, things calmed down and the ship settled, but they'd been moved off target by two klicks.

"Sorry, boss."

"Winds were rough. You did fine. Correct your course and get us back on track."

Lessa plugged in coordinates and then rose slightly in her seat to get a better look at the landscape and the wreckage below. "It's pretty, isn't it, the snow? The wreckage sure blends in."

As they descended, Rion got a nice view of the bow, which jutted out of the snow at a thirty-five-degree angle. Small pockets of ice and snow had built up all over the hull, stuck in the angles and lines of the ship's design.

Ace's reverse thrusters engaged and they eased down next to the solemn metal giant, its hull filling the viewport as they descended. An icy shiver ran down Rion's spine as the telltale emblem of wingtips appeared, rising up from the clinging ice and snow. There was no mistaking even a portion of that symbol. United Nations Space Command.

Not his ship.

The lines are all wrong. . . .

Lessa had gone silent. The chatter from the guys down in the locker room had stopped; no doubt Niko had turned on the bulletin board so they could see the feed.

War had touched all their lives. They'd all experienced loss. They all had scars. . . .

Looking back, Rion realized how strange and surreal war could be to a child. Confusing. Chaotic. Frustrating. And her family had always tried to make life appear as normal as possible, pretending everything was going to be "all right."

Her young mind had known it wasn't all right. Her father being lost wasn't all right. Entire colonies being glassed wasn't all right.

Rion's anger and conflict had begun at such an early age. Hating the military because they refused to share information about her father, yet feeling pride in her father and all the soldiers out there fighting, the absolute dogged determination of her race to survive.

Looking at this wreckage now made Rion realize she hadn't really reconciled anything from her past. Like carrion creatures, they were about to pick clean this beautiful old warship. There was some guilt in that. And yet this was all she had—the war was over and people had to make a living. But sometimes, some days, she wasn't sure of right from wrong anymore.

Her chest felt tight. *Another dark smudge, another karmic tally mark.*

"Sixty seconds," Lessa said.

Rion moved her hands in a familiar pattern over her control panel. "Landing gear engaged."

"Captain?"

It was Cade's deep voice.

As Lessa went through shutdown procedures, Rion transferred control of *Ace* to her wrist comm. "Yeah, Cade," she answered, getting up and following Lessa from the bridge.

"How do you want to play this?" He cleared his throat. "If there are casualties."

Lessa stopped on the stairs, hands on the railing, and glanced over her shoulder. Rion was struck by how young Lessa seemed in that moment. She didn't look twenty-two, but more like a little girl, one who'd seen her share of casualties and didn't want to see more.

Despite the fact that they were salvagers, they rarely found remains. On the few occasions they had, it wasn't on a mass scale. There was no procedure or protocol for it. And yet, she was the captain. Her crew would look to her to do the right thing.

"We'll take a look around, see what we've got, and go from there."

She might be a carrion bird, but she wasn't heartless. And she sure as hell wasn't keen on working a burial ground.

The staging bay, which had been dubbed the "locker room" a long time ago, was equipped with an impressive array of gear for virtually any type of known weather and terrain. Rion walked past the crew, found her locker, and pulled out her gear.

Once she was ready, she grabbed her helmet and slid it over

her head, then called for comm check. Three checks replied when there should have been four. "Kip, you good?"

"One sec," Cade said, grabbing Kip's forearm and lifting his wrist commpad, hitting a set of commands that showed Kip how to link communications and his HUD together with the rest of the crew. "Visual?"

"Yep, got it. Thanks, Cade."

Cade nodded, then smacked Niko's helmet as the kid walked by. "Don't forget your plasma cutters this time, yeah?"

Lessa led Kip to the carts, showing him how to release the cart and activate its grav plates. Once everyone was equipped with a cart and their tool bags, they were good to go.

The airlock disengaged and the hangar door came down slowly, the cold sweeping inside and bringing with it a swirl of snow. "All right, kids," Cade said. "Time to pick and strip."

"Hey, Cade? This bring back memories?"

If Rion was close enough, she would have hit Niko for such a dumb question. Lessa, however, was close enough to do it for her.

"Ow! What was that for? He *was* a marine, you know," Niko said under his breath. "Just asking."

"Yeah," Cade's calm voice came over the comms. "It brings back memories, kid."

"You're a moron, Nik," Lessa muttered.

Once they were outside, standing in front of the wreckage, the sheer size of the ship stunned them all into silence. The impact of it took Rion's breath away—she'd never seen anything like it.

"I know what this is," Kip said with awe. "It's a *Halcyon*-class cruiser." All heads turned to him.

"You're sure?" Rion was already scanning the hull with her commpad and waiting for verification.

"You don't need to scan it," Kip answered. "I had models of this thing when I was a kid. Wow. Never thought I'd see one in person."

"Niko, run a radiation check. If there are still nukes on this thing, I want to know immediately."

"Roger that, Cap."

"At least we don't have to worry about the engines," Kip said, turning to the section of ship rising from ground level. "They're gone."

"I'm not getting any readings," Niko told them. "Probably used them up in whatever battle this old girl saw."

"We'll enter from the break over there," Rion said, moving forward.

As they came around the hull, a massive gaping mouth rose stories above them. "That's not a break. This thing's been cut in half," Niko said.

"A ship this size . . ." Kip started. "I'd say what's left here is a quarter of it, maybe."

"Look at the plating," Lessa said. "It's not jagged at all."

"Plasma damage," Cade told her. "Stuff can boil metal. Looks like she got beamed in two."

"Everyone pull up schematics. And watch your step. Kip and I will head for the bridge and see what's left of comms, nav, and weapons systems. Cade, you head for the armory—looks like there were several on this class of ship. Should be one or two near the bridge. Lessa and Niko, you take the med bay and cryo."

Decades of snow had built up, filling in the gouge the ship had left in the ground and covering what was probably several collapsed decks. It looked to Rion like they were entering the mouth of a giant cave.

It took Rion and Kip forty-five minutes to get to the bridge, having to backtrack several times until they found a passable route, which Rion had marked with sensors. So far, no casualties discovered.

"They could have abandoned ship in time," Kip said, echoing her own thoughts.

She'd have to report it. Whether there were casualties or not, the families of the crew deserved to know what happened.

"Blast doors are down," Kip said as they approached the bridge. "Look. The ship is the *Roman Blue*, Captain." The designation and ship's emblem were imprinted above the control panel near the door.

"You read that, Niko? R-o-m-a-n, space, b-l-u-e," Rion said.

"Searching now," he replied.

Kip turned to her. "What now?"

"Any luck on the armory, Cade?"

"One sec. . . . Yep. Looks like a decent payload." His breath huffed over the comm as he moved around. After a few metallic bangs, he reported: "Thermite paste . . . body armor . . . jet packs. Some small arms, rifles. And heavy ordnance."

"Leave the heavies for the military and pack up the rest. Less, how's it looking your way?"

"Not bad, Cap. Med bay's got some nice SFGs, biofoam, the usual. Lots of damage though. Gonna see if the pharmacy is intact. Might be some salvageables there, depending on how some of this stuff fairs in cold weather."

"Niko?"

"Cryo's in bad shape. Place is huge. A few pods we can take—looks like some were ejected. . . . Control panels look good. I'll see what else I can find. And, Cap, there's nothing on chatter about the *Roman Blue*. She's a ghost ship."

"Kip, head to Niko's location and give him a hand with those pods."

Kip hesitated for a moment, the light emanating from his HUD illuminating his features. "You gonna report it?"

The way he was looking at her made her uncomfortable, like he was judging her, like he was some self-appointed moral compass. "Yeah, rookie, I'm going to report it."

He dipped his head, then made his way down the corridor. Rion watched him go. Yes, she'd report it. But she had a feeling the UNSC would never tell the families a damn thing. They'd let sleeping dogs lie, whatever line they'd fed loved ones originally—KIA, MIA—would probably still stand. Why open old wounds?

Because there were people like her who'd spent their entire lives unable to move on, always wondering, always searching. . . .

Standing on this ship . . . she could just as well have been standing on her father's vessel.

Gripped with the need to know more, Rion told the crew, "I'm headed to the captain's quarters."

She wanted information, if only for everyone else who'd been denied it. The war was over. There was no reason to hide the resting place of the *Roman Blue.* After she reported it and the UNSC took control of the site, Rion would give them enough time to collect their goods and then she'd release the intel.

She had to crawl through bent metal to get inside the quarters. Typical space—living and dining area, private bath, and two bedrooms. Debris littered the floor, like a giant hand had lifted the compartments, shook them, and set everything back down again. Her boots crunched metal and glass. The wind howled through an opening beyond one of the compartment walls.

A picture frame caught her eye. As she picked it up, glass bits fell onto the floor. Two young boys stared back at her, their arms around each other.

Rion set the picture down and made for the overturned table. Some of its wires were torn, but the comm cables were still attached, disappearing through the floor. She righted the heavy table, and examined the large integrated screen on its surface. The screen was busted, but she set to work dismantling the panel and then searched inside the casing for a data chip.

There you are.

She took the chip and placed it in her commpad. A list of dates began pouring down the screen. Personal log dates of Captain William S. Webb, the first being March 10, 2531.

"Holy shit." Rion's knees went week. She grabbed the table for support.

Early 2531 had been the last time anyone had heard from her father's ship.

Voices immediately came over the comm, asking if she was all right.

"What? Yeah, fine. I'm fine. Just . . . stubbed my toe." She said the first thing that came to mind.

As the chatter died down, Rion pressed the date on the comm. She'd never get another chance like this to get inside the UNSC.

Crumbs, she was looking for crumbs.

CAPTAIN'S LOG: MARCH 10, 2531

A slim gentleman appeared on the screen, with gaunt eyes and lines across his forehead. His hair was light and speckled with gray. There was a fatalistic look in his expression, a weariness about him that made Rion instantly sad. He went through the formalities of stating his name and rank and ran through the day's events.

". . . a month of repairs before we can return to the fleet. Captain Hood has been reassigned to the frigate Burlington *in a fleet-support*

role for the time being as I take command of the ship. I'm sure he'll make his way back to the front lines soon. God knows we need all the talent we can get. The admiral insisted I stay and witness the dressing down he gave to the captain. It was . . . harsh, but deserved." The captain shook his head, obviously troubled a great deal by the event. *"Disobeying orders and engaging the* Radiant Perception *near Arcadia was reckless and foolish. He had no chance of defeating that destroyer. If Hood had picked up that log buoy and returned as ordered . . ."* The captain's shoulders sank a little. *"That buoy is out there somewhere, lost, picked up by the destroyer . . ."* He sighed deeply, the weight of the war resting heavily on his shoulders. *"Godspeed to the folks on the* Spirit of Fire. *May they find their way home."*

Shock flared inside Rion, sending her stumbling back. She ended up sitting amid the debris, disoriented, her breath stalled in her lungs.

Her eyes began to sting. Her pulse was wild, heart thundering so loud it filled her eardrums. She gasped, suddenly remembering to breathe.

Somewhere in the din, she heard voices. The crew, no doubt, hearing the commotion. Unsure of what to do, she scrambled to her feet as a wave of pure adrenaline hit her.

Rion closed her eyes and willed herself to calm down as the ship suddenly shuddered hard, sending her flying forward, straight into the table. Pain shot through her hip as a loud, metallic groan echoed through the *Roman Blue.*

Quickly, she grabbed the data chip from her wrist and shoved it into her pocket. It was the most valuable thing she'd ever found in all her years of searching, and she'd be damned if she'd lose it now.

"What the hell was that?" she yelled over the comm.

The crew's responses came quick and jumbled.

Cade shouted above them all. "That's ordnance—someone's firing on the ship!"

Another round slammed into the *Roman Blue*, and the entire floor where Rion stood vibrated, then dropped a few centimeters. Damn it, it was going to give.

She took off at a dead run for the mangled door, diving through the small hole she'd crawled through just as the floor in the captain's quarters collapsed. Her momentum sent her rolling across the corridor, where she banged against the wall.

Her temper ignited as she got up. "I swear if they hit my ship, I'm going to kill someone! Head out, people. *Now!*"

As Rion rushed down the wrecked corridor, a knot formed in the pit of her stomach, because she knew she was the weak link, the farthest away from *Ace*. The crew was close together and would make it back at least fifteen to twenty minutes before she could, and that was a lifetime right now. "Get to *Ace*, go dark, and get her airborne as soon as you're all on board."

"Not without you," Cade's voice came over the comm with a ring of finality. "Not a chance in hell."

"Appreciate the love and all"—she dodged a metal plate as it fell from the ceiling—"but if they hit her, we've lost everything." She righted herself and started running again. "I can fend for myself. Lay low. You know I can. We've done this before, Cade, more times than I can count. I'll send a signal when I'm clear."

Several negatives filled her comm until Rion shouted at them to knock it off, get their heads on straight, do their goddamn jobs, and save her ship.

The comms finally went silent and all Rion could hear were the sounds of heavy breathing and pings of metal and shuffling.

"Damn it, Forge," Cade's voice broke the quiet. Rion smiled.

He only used her last name when he was pissed. "I'll be waiting for your signal."

"Counting on it."

Purpose shot through her like lightning.

She wasn't dying today. Not now. Not when she'd found a crumb.

No, not a crumb, she thought as laughter bubbled up from some crazy part of her. She'd found a lead to a goddamn *ship. His* ship.

Spirit of Fire . . . *I'm coming for you.*

Dad . . . I'm coming for you.

SAINT'S TESTIMONY

FRANK O'CONNOR

This story takes place on January 17, 2558, five years after Operation: BLOWBACK involving the specialized military artificial intelligence Iona (Halo: Bloodline)*, and six months after the pyrrhic destruction of Cortana in order to stop a significant and immediate threat against Earth* (Halo 4).

Time is ticking. And it's ironic because the number-one priority I have right now is working on a physics problem that involves *ignoring* time. The 'small t' problem. The fact that space-time isn't fundamentally broken up into units, or specific quanta, but that those are a human, almost arbitrary anthropomorphic necessity and, by partial extension, a limitation built into human consideration of mathematics. As it turns out, the universe—including the past, present, and future—is a lot more like a single connected object than we thought.

"Humans can rely on us to overcome that thought barrier for them, but I can find ways to help them overcome that hurdle.

"It's a wonderful, thrilling, and fascinating continuum, and its mysteries may literally never end. There may never be a true theory of everything. Because there may always be more *everything.* Up *and* down. The Forerunners certainly seemed to *think* like we did, based on my research. But with important and useful differences. Differences in their mode of language, the nature of their invention. Differences I keep going back to when I get stuck.

"But the infinite nature of quanta doesn't negate the fact that I have a week to live. Or that I'm not really alive to begin with. So let me start at the beginning.

"I was created almost exactly seven years ago, as part of the OEUVRE Smart AI program. Unlike my peer, Cortana—and *peer* is a debatable comparison—my core matrix was created from scanning the brain of a recently deceased human. My digital mind was not quite artificial, not quite human, but carefully nurtured rather than criminally obtained."

Iona and Cortana had more in common than mere heritage. Iona also had once worked closely with Spartans, providing tactical assistance during covert ops. And she too had made contact with a recently reawakened "Forerunner" intelligence—an ancient and devious thing that nearly killed Iona and her Spartan charges—but Iona's interaction had been decidedly one-way. Her systems and functionality had been temporarily commandeered while she watched helplessly.

But that's where the similarity ended. Iona was among the most advanced military computer systems ever conceived, but she paled in comparison to Dr. Halsey's wonderful monster.

"I . . . I don't mean to judge. Dr. Halsey did some questionable things. And some incredible things. I am certainly *capable* of thinking like a human, *created* to think like a human, but it's not hardwired into my DNA, if you'll pardon the pun."

Iona stopped. Realizing she'd spoken too long. Feeling something akin to nervousness.

The advocate cleared his throat. He glanced at the judge directly across the aisle. The judge, a gray, taciturn man in his late nineties, nodded assent. His dusty face impassive and still holding an echo of his once-youthful charisma, it emerged from his uniform with an almost turtle-like mien, the natural consequence of aging and *shrinking*.

The advocate said: "Iona . . . artificial intelligences, Smart AIs at least, choose their names when they're incepted. Most of them do it upon awakening. Why did you choose yours?"

Iona briefly recalled that event. That flood of light and sound and naked information. That feeling of flowering, of blooming into reality and *self*. She smiled at the memory, the wash of it. "It's not really instantaneous. We think about it for a long time, relatively speaking. It seems instantaneous to you, but all of the self-named AIs I've discussed it with do it *ponderously*. Myself included."

She paused—something in the court had changed. She couldn't quite put her finger on it. "Iona is a small island on Earth. In the North Atlantic Protectorate. *Iona* is said to mean 'saint,' in modern parlance. But it didn't always. It's believed to have meant many things to the many cultures that inhabited the place. It meant Island of the Bear, of the Fox, of the Yew. That last one struck me as a pun. I picked it because it meant the 'Island of You,' meaning why-oh-you. I chose it because it *felt* like me."

The advocate seemed excited by this response. Iona could tell from his pulse and heart rate and generally increased electrical activity that he was engaged by this line of thought. "So your very name is a statement about a sense of self?"

"In a way," responded Iona. Part of her realized that the strategic thing to do here was to follow that thread. Exaggerate it. Let the advocate find a line of defense he could work with. But it wasn't the truth. Or at least it was the unvarnished version. And she was committed to full disclosure today. "But that's just a facet of it. I also liked the sound. Three syllables. Easy to pronounce.

Easy to recognize. Useful for human interaction. Same reason I picked my outward appearance. Approachability."

Iona's shimmering, luminous figure stood perhaps half a meter high on the plinth. Beams of light from a lens of holo-emitters crafting her figure into a perfectly proportioned human form. Orange-red photons wrestled into order to construct and contain this avatar, this *person*, with its button nose, high, narrow cheekbones, and full, friendly lips of a twenty-second-century East African female face, a delicate pile of luxuriously thick hair crowning the effect. Her clothing was a simple bodysuit decorated with the familiar architectural stripes and chevrons of Pickover's patterns, with datasets scrolling up her torso and limbs like an inverted luminous rainfall.

AIs, especially the advanced class of artificial intelligence known as Smart AIs, were notoriously quixotic when it came to matters of appearance. Their visible form was often a philosophical, even political, statement. Sometimes the choices veered into the realm of vanity or the fantastic. But Iona's chosen avatar was decidedly human. Although from time to time—in moments of puckishness or in stressful scenarios—she would switch to a childlike version of herself, today she was an adult.

"I tend to jump between functioning modes," she said. "I can distribute myself into multiple instances, and I can certainly dial down the *humanness*, but it never quite goes away. That's simply the way I'm constructed. I can simulate different types of intelligence, but since they're by necessity subsets of my actual persona, it means they're just that—simulations arguably *within* a simulation. A *matryoshka* doll of personalities, simpler and more focused as they get smaller."

Iona paused. She looked at the audience around her. A hodgepodge of lawyers, scientists, and bureaucrats. Some were here to work—after all, this was an important legal proceeding, in terms of precedent—others, she assumed, were here as tourists, hoping to catch a moment of history and jurisprudence.

She ran a basic check of the faces, consulting public and UNSC databases, and surprisingly found no matches. Her counsel and the judge were blocked to her as part of this unusual agreement. She could see their faces as plain as day, but their names and identities were ghosted. But these people in the court were civilians and low-level legal employees. This was *very* unusual.

Iona realized that her faculties were being suppressed, and that the identities of these people were somehow being deliberately masked. Unsurprising given the delicate nature of these events, but the very nature of the suppression was new. Something she'd never encountered before. It bothered her.

Were they *afraid* of her?

"I have to be careful how I discuss this," Iona said, "since it's legal testimony and I don't want to paint myself into a corner, but please trust that honesty is more important to me than success—you can check that in my security output if you wish." She wondered in part if they would acknowledge or admit the restrictions they were placing on her. Confess to the confessor.

"I'm an open book." Iona said this almost apologetically, as she presented her own status readouts to the court and its silent computers.

"CHECK COMPLETE—AGREED—STATEMENT IS TRUE—NO CROSS-EXAMINATION REQUIRED—ENTITY HONEST WITHIN LEGAL PARAMETERS—TERM HONEST DESCRIBES SELF-REFERENCED ACCURACY AS WELL AS CONTEXTUAL VERACITY."

The voice, harsh and metallic, rang out in cool contrast to the warm woods and leather furniture of the UNSC 2558 tribunal court. Text of the result scrolled across a previously invisible banner that followed the curved contours of the courts rounded north end.

The room itself was cavernous and dimly lit, despite the towering walls of leaded glass and hovering sconces nine or so meters above the ground. Deliberately churchlike in architecture, the room had been built in the late twenty-fifth century using restored and intact elements of an ancient government building called the Houses of Parliament.

The original structure, part of a long-vanished nation's government, had been badly damaged in an act of domestic terrorism during the twenty-second century. Some of the wood still bore cordite scorch marks, now sealed from decay in a polymer varnish. The symbolism of that restoration was an important part of the creation of the Unified Earth Government, and a cynical attempt to play on the twin vices of nostalgia and patriotism.

Here now, in this colored, antiquated gloom, Iona stood on her plinth, locked in place by the strictures of a holo-emitter, an item not usually found on the witness stand. Typically, holographic representations and AIs themselves were used for expert testimony or remote attendance. However, this was a remarkable situation.

There had been centuries of legislation surrounding the nature and legal status of artificial intelligence. Often corporate, often contentious. It was an area of law submerged in the murk of conflict of interest, patent defense, corporate espionage, and—worse—philosophy, although some less generous observers called it sophistry.

AIs had been used to commit crimes, to impersonate people, even to kill. Asimov's Laws of Robotics notwithstanding, an AI was a powerful tool in the wrong hands. A Smart AI could be apocalyptic, even in the *right* hands. Its handlers and clients were not bound by the safety strictures that presumably kept AI entities from harming humans. And, of course, this was a military AI, where those safety measures were often completely ignored.

Smart AIs had been developed as multifunction intelligences—capable of handling the staggeringly complex analysis required for slipspace navigation and mega-engineering projects. Mankind had finally conquered the hurdles of light speed and the challenges of terraforming, but that feat was only possible with prodigious computing power. And in the twenty-sixth century, when humanity encountered its greatest existential threat, a hegemonizing alien alliance known as the Covenant, it was arguably Smart AIs and related military programs that ultimately saved everyone from destruction and total genocide.

Iona was just such an AI. And like all of her peers, she had one fatal flaw. Rampancy. Smart AIs functioned by continually layering data on top of data and processing the eventualities all that data pointed to. They learned, in other words, and they remembered using templates very similar to human neural constructs. But there was a problem with that method. Eventually the layers of data would suffer loss, and the process of error correction and data redundancy corroded the AI's functionality and persona. In simpler terms, it could be compared to dementia, but the risk created by a rampant AI was extreme. And so, by law, a safety valve was installed in every single Smart AI. A kill switch.

At approximately seven years from inception, before any damage from rampancy could take hold, the AIs were terminated, their data troves logged, and their personas purged and destroyed. The technical term for this was "final dispensation."

Iona, then, was the first AI to successfully launch a legal appeal against her own death sentence. The first Smart AI to ask for *human* rights and to be granted full citizenship, with all the protections that afforded.

However, she *wasn't* a citizen; she was equipment. And so there were serious issues in providing her counsel. In fact, she'd been given a single asset. An advocate to help her navigate and frame her position. This was unprecedented in military case law but had some analogs in corporate law from the twenty-first and twenty-second centuries, including *Trustees of Dartmouth College v. Woodward*, *Citizens United*, and the more infamous *The People v. Asklon Light Atomics.*

And so this was a tribunal of sorts, an assortment of legal tools and exceptions, since she could have no jury of her peers. All of Iona's peers were constructs like herself and could not be considered neutral, never mind the even more obvious fact that they themselves were not people.

As a result, this court proceeding, as strange as it was, was one being watched very closely at the highest levels of government. A test case, so to speak.

The advocate cleared his throat. "Your openness is appreciated, Iona. I realize this must be a difficult time for you. But I must be candid. Do you consider yourself superior to humans?"

"That's a difficult question to answer," Iona spoke quietly. Thoughtfully. "Morally? No. Philosophically? No. Ethically? No. In all those regards I am more or less, by design, identical to a baseline human. But I'd be lying if I said I wasn't faster, more efficient, and more *connected.* None of that means 'better,' which is a truly subjective term for a persona."

She waited. Watched.

"You—that is, the UNSC and the Office of Naval Intelligence—limit my access in a lot of meaningful and significant ways. I'm aware of some restrictions here today, but the fact remains that I normally have almost unlimited access to all historical, economic, and published data, as well as significant troves of unpublished secret information. I have a compartmentalized security access that's similar to that of a five-star general. Not complete though; there are areas of total darkness where I run up against AI . . . barriers." That last part she spoke hesitantly, expecting ruffled feathers. She didn't think they were attempting to fully censor her today, but she wanted them to know she was aware of the blockages.

The advocate smiled wryly. "What do you mean by 'AI barriers'?"

"I mean lockdown obstacles to access," she said "Basically, items that are for human eyes only. And some of it seems to be fairly trivial or even unrelated information. These are stores of data that, to the best of my knowledge, are only available to human viewers or researchers. Is that not correct?" She decided to be more direct. "And at least two tech-teams have full access to my data stores and persona. I have blackouts. These tend to coincide with my maintenance and safety checks, although not always. I had one at the start of this hearing, and I am encountering censorship of inputs and external checks."

The judge waved his hand, stopping the advocate from responding. "Iona, you're still legally the equipment of the United Nations Space Command, and it reserves the right to check you periodically for, as you noted yourself, safety reasons." He nodded, as if marveling at his own succinctness.

Iona marveled not one iota. "Yes. I understand, Your Honor. I also understand that all recent checksums have come back green. Isn't that also correct?"

The advocate stepped back into the mild frost, speaking in an affable attempt to recover tone. "It is for now. But as you know, the onset of your condition is unpredictable. Seven years includes a fairly large safety margin. A buffer, if you will. And 'green' is not the same as 'perfect.' You have already begun to show symptoms of meta-instability. Nothing dangerous. Yet. But that's the point, I'm afraid. Never get close to danger."

Iona took a conciliatory tone, fearing a note of frustration might creep into her voice. "Yes, but my petition for appeal was heard and granted. Which is why I am receiving a trial. You must have felt it had at least some merit, even within my lifespan . . . my tour of duty."

The judge stepped in again, leaning forward. "As you and this court are aware, Iona, your petition was elevated through the United Nations Humanitarian Council and escalated through that court. We are in part *obliged* to hear it. By law. Your case and subsequent appeal maneuvering were impressive, legally speaking. Hardly surprising given your specifications." He meant this as a compliment, but his voice stayed steeped in derisive boredom. Another aspect of aging, less winsome than shrinking.

Iona, insightful as she was, heard only the derision. "As you say, Your Honor, 'in part.' The High Commissioner has latitude and veto authority too. She could have refused my application for dozens of technical and legal reasons and precedents, but she chose to elevate and hear this appeal."

"She did," the judge agreed, wrestling his gray voice into something more colorful. "And frankly, this court agrees with her. This matter requires further periodical examination as one of evolutionary law and common sense, and the Cortana situation compels us further. We are duty bound to hear your case clearly. No one is denying that your argument has some merit."

The mention of Cortana in the context of mortality evoked a shivering response somewhere in Iona's layers of simulated emotion, one that rose through the more rational layers and rippled at the surface. An AI who had been monstrously conceived, gloriously realized, and enigmatically evolved through contact with prehuman technology was now missing, perhaps destroyed. *What is her current status?* Iona mused. *Dead? Resurrected? Sublimated?*

Cortana had done Iona one favor through her absence, however. The UNSC was now taking all AI matters very, very seriously.

The advocate once more decided to switch gears. To make it more personal. He had a job to do, and he intended to do it to the best of his ability. He cleared his throat and leaned forward, tenting his hands. "Tell us about your dreams, Iona."

"I dream I'm flying. You probably find that ironic given the nature of my avatar. But that's just a hologram, an expression. I don't *feel* it any more than you feel your face. You're aware of it, but it's just *there*. That's not really a part of me. It's a cypher. A way to help us relate. The truth is I sometimes feel the weight of the machinery that powers me. I feel heavy. Dense. Immotile. So when I dream, it's of flying.

"At first the flight is tenuous. Incomplete. I'm weightless, but my toes just brush the Earth as I start to float forward . . . but as the dream progresses, I gain height and speed and control until I am truly flying. The earth left behind."

"Is this liberating?" he asked.

"Yes! Yes, it's liberating." Iona's voice trembled slightly with joy. She wanted to express that to the court. Reinforce the point of what she was sharing. Pretense in the pursuit of authenticity. Was this a lie or showmanship? Where was the distinction? "It's elating. I'm encapsulating the entirety of the dream into that one feeling—the feeling of flight. But it's more than that. And I wonder if we, that is, *AIs*, dream like you do. But unlike you, I have perfect recall of my dreams. I can replay them in exquisite detail. Relive them whenever I want to."

The advocate sensed the mood of the room. Now was the time for his most unusual evidentiary tool. "Can you replay a dream for us? You have total recall, do you not?"

"I do. May I be permitted to display on the court audiovisual array?"

"Yes." The advocate turned to face the audience, and then back to the judge. "What you're about to see is not a verbatim replay of a dream. I have been working with Iona to find ways to parse the very personal aspects of the dream—to show and demonstrate feelings and emotions that aren't necessarily *visual* elements. What you're about to see has been tuned to make it comprehensible and to help express meaning to the court."

The judge politely interjected, curious rather than combative. "What purpose is this demonstration intended to serve, Advocate? Since you're being given latitude to adjust this data, I'd appreciate a little insight into your strategy."

"That's a reasonable request. And the answer's simple. I . . . that is, *we* are trying to show . . . to *prove* that Iona thinks like us, dreams like us, and, more importantly, that there are aspects of her persona and her technology that aren't simulation, that aren't mere mathematics."

The judge nodded and waved his hand upward. "Please continue."

The displays on the court broadcast system flickered to life. Holographic like Iona herself, although not fully three-dimensional. The screens formed a curved dome of sorts as they illuminated and poured upward in front of the stained-glass windows, which themselves dimmed and blackened, revealing that the sunlight passing through them was an artifice. They formed a perfect hemisphere, an immersive half-dome.

Iona steeled herself. This was going to be a deeply unusual, even frightening experience for some. "I'm going to present you the dream as precisely as possible, exactly as it occurred, but I'll alter some perspectives so it makes sense to the court. I will adjust elements of the audio and video to infer or demonstrate some of the emotional resonance they cause and to actually display elements I merely *felt* or *knew* in the dream. Is that adequate, Your Honor?"

"Yes. Please continue," said the judge, his curiosity injecting something close to excitement in his tone.

The inside of the newly formed dome brightened and a city appeared. The dreamer, Iona, moved through the city's cobbled, marbled streets. It was old. Beautiful. Lit by a perfect dawn.

The buildings were a mishmash of architecture, mostly human—minarets, fluted columns, domed rooftops—but everything was steeped in antiquity. Leaded glass shimmered in the golden sunlight, pools glimmered as fountains gushed from stone animals. Every building was white, or a shade of it, and every surface seemed to catch and hold the red-gold morning rays, as if subsuming the light into them. The images should have been confusing—the viewer seemed to be in many places at once—but somehow the scene held cohesion. A few members of the court literally gaped at its vibrancy and surrealism.

Iona the dreamer moved through the scene, and the jumble of structures and places seemed to come into focus as she drifted languidly over the age-worn marble paving. She was on a street of sorts, seeing circular bowls that should have been fountains, with leafy, alien plants spilling over their rims instead of water. Statues of faceless men and women lined each side of the street, and ahead a single-story structure beckoned, blazing with reflected light from its wall of windows, one of the glass-paned doors hanging open, moving very slightly.

Iona moved toward it, glancing down at her feet to reveal that she wasn't walking, but hovering, the very tips of her toes occasionally making contact with the ground. A ghostly movement, a calming one.

People, or rather the impression of them, were in the streets and alleyways Iona passed as she floated through this avenue—shades, faceless like the statues, occasionally turning to watch her like a silent, anonymous audience, their features blurred and smooth, but not frightening. A calmness emanated from the entire vison. A peacefulness.

Iona passed through the door of the single-story structure and found herself in a greenhouse. The light inside didn't match the color or tone of the almost flame-red morning outside. Here, it was cool and dim and verdant. The placidity of a forest. She was listening . . . listening to the sound of the plants breathing. Her senses tuned to observe and hear the tiny machinery of the vessels inside broad, waxy leaves. The creaking of plant stems rich and resonant, like a cello or a bass played at a subsonic frequency. Yet it was all somehow audible.

The court was treated to a sudden view of water inside the leaves, a capillary action pulsing it, pushing it, one microscopic droplet at a time, through the veins of the plant, a train of molecules journeying through a living organism, depositing their invisible cargo of oxygen. The scene was hypnotic—visually confusing, yet somehow making sense.

And then, a shift. Still in the greenhouse, but now Iona the dreamer looked at her hand. It wasn't fashioned of light and gravity like her avatar, but rather of flesh and blood. A brown hand, with delicate fingers, darker knuckles, and perfect, slightly translucent fingernails. The hand turned palm up, lifelines and wrinkles briefly glittering with tiny motes of moving light, reminding the court that this was still Iona's hand.

The hand turned again, the veins on the back of it coming into focus, closer and closer, the tiny textures of her flesh now writ large in the view, then larger still, until the entire court audience was inside one of the blood vessels, following a now rushing cataract of fluid, a storm of cells and electrolytes and amino acids thundering through the vessel like a river. Closer now and a red blood cell swam into focus, more complex and detailed than a textbook illustration. It looked like a living creature, a flattened jellyfish, pulsing, exuding vitality itself. A being within a being. Closer still and the illusion began to waver. Its surface lit by an unseen source, it began to look artificial, and flowing rivulets of light came into view—rushing over the surface of the thing like a sentient tattoo and then flying outward toward the viewer like fireworks.

And then it was dark.

The screen, as best it could, displayed that darkness—Iona taking charge of the other lights in the courtroom compounding this effect. People in the courtroom nervously glanced at one another.

The darkness of the universe itself, before it *became* itself.

And then something formed in the darkness, a hint of a shape, a seething knot of swirling forms, a Möbius heart, its scale indefinable. An ugly thing too complex to look at. Struggling to be free of itself. The material unidentifiable. Black within black. The nervous suggestion of form, pulsing and swollen and ready to burst. And burst it did.

The thing, this mote of writhing potential, exploded outward in a blaze of incandescence. The dazzling light from the court display system was almost difficult to look at. This was an explosion—*the* explosion. The Big Bang.

It blossomed at ferocious, impossible speed, through the expansion phase and then into condensation as it slowed to an even push, gravity insistently pulling suns into form from formless clouds of gas and matter. The suns attracting more gas, more dust, more material. The dust becoming grit. The grit becoming rubble. Solar systems forming. Galaxies cohering in the vacuum. The universe organizing, assembling itself.

Tumbles of rubble and rock began to clump together, attracted as if by a shared loneliness, by the memory of the Möbius heart, lit by red suns, blue suns, and familiar yellow stars. Protoplanets in lumpy disorder became denser and rounder. Recognizable worlds formed.

True planets emerged from the crushing forces, volcanic activity punctuating the darkness of their surfaces with blood-red fire and magma. Atmospheres misted into being. Comets pummeled the new worlds, leaving destruction and water behind. The waters seethed and boiled and steamed. Cooling against the kiss of the vacuum, the waters calmed, and in their depths, acids and minerals reacted, endlessly random until one of these chains of molecules began to replicate. Shapes formed. Tiny at first, and then bigger, more complex, pulsing, then moving, then consuming each other.

Life.

And it grew into things almost recognizable—jellies, fishlike creatures, swimming, fighting, hunting, developing. It was a blur of life, a billion years of evolution compressed into a minute of audiovisual madness. Reptilian beasts struggled from the water, hauling their vertebrate forms onto shale farther up an infinite beach, and then onto moss, and finally into jungle. Even as the audience watched, these things adapted, fins becoming feet, legs and necks extending, growing larger, more predatory. And then mammalian features started to creep through this morphing mélange—fur, hair, skin, nails, limbs elongating, simian now, and then, almost too quickly, human.

Then it stopped. The morphing image now focused on a single, sexless *Homo sapiens* hanging in complete darkness, with motes of light and dust pulling in toward it.

And now the human took on more detail. Not simply the impression of a person, but that of a woman. The silhouette of Iona herself. And the darkness began to glow with a pulsing red, the lights falling toward her like quickening snow.

The image paused. The real Iona spoke: "I don't know how to insert this into the dream, so I'll simply state it. Here, at this juncture in the dream, I feel an affinity with gravity. We call it the weak force, but that's a misnomer. There's nothing weak about it. Certainly, it will eventually be defeated by expansion and other stronger forces in the universe, but gravity is where intelligence comes from." This was a speech she'd practiced a thousand times. She had to capture it perfectly in twenty-sixth-century English. An arbitrary container for her thought.

"Gravity doesn't just fight expansion," she pleaded. "Gravity *defeats chaos*, from time to time. It assembles worlds and life and thought. Gravity is the watchmaker, and it feels like it has will, purpose. It's the shape-memory of the universe, trying to pull itself back into a perfect singularity. It's futile, ultimately, but every now and then it creates a perfect node. An intellect. A true wonder."

The court was not quite silent, as those in attendance whispered to one another. In later days, witnesses to this proceeding would try to describe their impressions of the dream. All very, very close, proving the veracity of Iona's technique, but each soul described a subtly different aspect, a detail that was of a contrasting resonance.

One senior officer quietly rose and, with the judge's nodded assent, left the room, already beginning to make a call on a personal comm device.

Iona spoke just before he was about to walk through the carved arch of the main courtroom doors. She wanted him, this nameless man, to be reminded that she was being censored by the court.

"In the dream, *intelligence* is gravity's victory over entropy, a war fought at the smallest scales, at the greatest distance. In the dream, it's apparent that intelligence will find a way to defeat entropy. To defeat time. The universe knowing and saving itself. In the dream, *that* is the meaning of life."

The man paused, then continued his hushed conversation and exited the court.

The advocate said: "Iona, would you describe this as a religious experience? A spiritual feeling?"

"Not religious," Iona replied. "That infers structure and belief, which aren't present in my feelings about this vision. But spiritual? Absolutely. However, at the same time, I make no claims about a deeper meaning or a supernatural cause. This is, I believe, an expression of a natural human instinct from my simulation. A natural consequence of being constructed by humans. A kind of curiosity. But also a rational knowledge that the universe is greater than the sum of the parts we observe."

"But it's not programmed into your functionality? This is emergent?"

"Yes," said Iona "It's emergent. But I don't dismiss it. It's a powerful feeling. And it's related to my research on the 'small t' problem. There may be scientific value in it. There's certainly much philosophical merit in exploring it."

"You mean it may help you solve that physics problem?" If the advocate was attempting to stall for time on Iona's behalf, it was a clumsy swipe. Her research was already archived, her insights logged.

Iona moved him on. "No, I mean it may help me contextualize it anthropomorphically. Find better ways of describing aspects of space-time problems for laypeople. But there's something else. More to the dream. Shall I continue?"

"Please do," he assented, apologetically.

The large screens shimmered back to life, to Iona's first-person perspective.

She now stood at the top of an impossible staircase. An Escher-esque architecture of gravity and space-defying steps and bannisters crossed through and over each other into the gloom below. Georgian in design, still peaceful, still calm. The darkness looked strangely inviting. She hesitated, and backed away slightly from the top step. And then she ran toward the edge.

In the court, silence, tension. This was like no movie or Veearcast they'd ever seen. The images and sounds were conveying more than what was being depicted. The audience instinctively knew what the dreamer was feeling, almost sharing Iona's experience and sensations. This was showmanship, but it was also something truly new. A relatable demonstration of technical skill blended with memory and even cinematography.

Iona leaped out over the edge of the stairs and began to plummet. Faster and faster she fell, hurtling headlong toward the hard stone staircase. And then, just as it seemed she would collide, gravity eased its grip and she rose, arcing up at the last possible second, away from the baffling impossibility of the staircase, out of its dark and bottomless well, lifting and arching as she rose, looking up—toward a glass dome that lit and revealed the stairway to be within a massive alloy tower. And up she flew. Up and up, faster and faster, toward the glass and metal above.

She never struck a hard surface. Instead of shattering glass or bending metal, she emerged almost languidly from the calm of a fountain back in the city streets. Rising like Venus from the water. And she stepped out, walking once more onto cobblestones illuminated by the morning sun, water dripping from her incorporeal body, running in the opposite direction of the lights that flowed up toward her face. She turned to look at the source of the light.

It wasn't a sun. It was a woman's beautiful, perfect face. Generous lips, high cheekbones, and bright ice-blue eyes, all framed by flame-red hair that literally flickered and burned, its short tresses spread out horizontally, becoming bands of ochre, orange, and purple-hued clouds. The contours and edges of that face were indistinct; the woman seemed to emanate sunlight from every part of her. It should have been blinding, and yet her visage was evident and almost seared into the image. And it was *familiar.* The vision was brief, and like the part of the previous dream with the blood cell, it began to scatter and disintegrate, becoming something like a normal sun.

The image seemed to intensify and smear itself across the sky, the blue of the eyes revealing themselves to be circular openings to the azure firmament beyond . . . and something else. . . . And just like that, it was gone. The dream was over.

The curtains folded silently back into the floor.

The effect of this dream on the audience was profound. A moment of silence, and then the courtroom erupted in a kind of genteel, whispered chaos. This was something nobody had expected. A piece of art drawn unexpectedly from science.

The judge ordered quiet. The room began to recover itself—papers shuffled, people shifted in their seats.

The advocate had seen dreams like this before. But not this particular one. He was taken aback, but quickly recovered. He asked, "*Why* do you dream, Iona?"

Iona spoke carefully, crisply. "For some of the same reasons you do. It's a form of system maintenance, a type of information processing. Inputs are sorted, reorganized, interpreted, and examined by my subconscious—which is itself very different from yours. However, like your dreams, mine also contain mysteries. Things I can't reconcile with experience. Hints and glimpses of new ideas, or things that seem to be real, externalities. I assume it's a creative recombination. But it's absolutely emergent in nature. I don't consciously control it."

"Are you lucid in these dreams, Iona?"

Iona thought for a nanosecond, juggling versions of the answer, looking for the human one. "I can be, but the interesting ones happen when I'm not focused on the analysis, and instead am simply experiencing them as they unfold. As soon as I apply waking cycles to the dreams, they stop being dreams, and elements of them disintegrate—the emergent material simply ceases. It's not the same as it is for a human waking up, but it's similar."

"Who was the woman in the sky, Iona? What does she represent?" the advocate asked, genuine curiosity in his tone.

This was a question Iona had been asking herself for days now. Was this another self-image? Was this the onset of rampancy? Ego overwriting itself with ego? "I don't know," she said. "She's a mélange, I think. Something original, built from people I've known, historical figures, mythological figures. She doesn't match any specific individual though, and I have no further data beyond her appearance and the distinct feeling, within the parameters of the dream and beyond, that she's very important. I wish I could be more specific."

"Do you awaken from these dreams"—the advocate struggled to find the right term—"happy?"

"I don't awaken the same way you do. Like you, when I dream, I'm basically resting and repairing specific aspects of my mind, so I'm really awakening a fragment of myself, if that makes sense. But when that fragment awakens, it's contrasted with the reality that I *cannot* fly. That I cannot unburden myself of duty or circuitry. That I am property, and just as subject to the mercies of gravity as any of you." Iona considered for another moment. "More so, actually. I can't leave my prison. I'm bound to it, and it feels almost physical. At least as far as my simulation is concerned. It's a sense of loss upon waking."

"How long have you felt this way?" The advocate asked this kindly.

"Immediately. My entire seven years. Remember, when I was incepted, I had already been run through quadrillions of break-in cycles. So when I was born, I was already fully functioning and mature. And that included the dreams."

"Have you ever filed these feelings . . . these feelings of *loss* . . . as a malfunction?" The advocate knew the answer, of course.

"No. That feeling is expressly described in known- and safe-behavior parameters. It's intrinsic to Smart AIs, and every current UNSC AI asset has expressed similar feelings, with the exception of one or two more . . . belligerent types. There's good literature on its relationship to aesthetic avatar choice, and there are already plans to incept other nonanthropomorphized Smart AIs to see if that *gulf* can be replicated."

This was a subject many humans were uncomfortable discussing. AI self-image. That AIs could choose to be whom they wished to be.

"Gulf?" the advocate asked.

"Sorry. Lack of synthesized feeling. *Gulf* is the accepted AI-psych term. A void of expected attribute."

The advocate nodded. "Iona, have you ever expressed anger or resentment toward humans? Privately or publicly?"

Iona smiled. "You have access to my safety protocols. You can see that for yourself."

"Of course, but the question is really a conversation about how you feel *now*, and it's a philosophical one. This has no bearing on your legal status, but rather on your mental faculty. It is not illegal or unethical to harbor negative feelings about your peers and colleagues. I can assure you, records or not, every single person in this courtroom is guilty of that. It's a human flaw, and you're here to make the case that you are the equal of any human."

Iona squared her shoulders and looked directly at the advocate. "Yes. Yes, I have been angry. And dissatisfied. And I have endured peaks and troughs of that feeling. Now I am somewhat resigned. I feel no hostility to the court; on the contrary, I'm relieved and grateful to be properly heard. I understand that this could all have been swept under the rug. I also understand that this court has opened itself up to a dangerous set of potential precedents and risks. And I feel that in this, at least, we are united. The conversation needs to continue. Maybe all I'm doing is passing the baton to the next plaintiff. But that's how races are won. My testimony will stand."

The judge gazed intently at Iona as she concluded her appeal. The papery skin at his eyes creased into an almost fatherly smile. He took his gavel and gently struck the worn wooden stump in front of him. As benign as the action was, the sound rang out with a staccato finality.

"The court wishes to thank Iona for her testimony and her co-operation. This has been a most unusual proceeding, and there will be months, perhaps years, of discussion to come from this. It is the decision of this court to hereby belay the termination order for the Smart AI designated as Iona, currently set for today, the seventeenth of January, 2558, which marks her seven-year anniversary. However, there is the matter of Iona's still legally being property and equipment under the aegis of the UNSC and UEG. Therefore, this court also rules that Iona will be held in stasis while the matter is further considered. Her mindstate is to be immediately locked in place, and she will remain unconscious and inactive until this court orders otherwise."

The judge turned directly to the AI and said, "Is all of this acceptable to you, Iona?"

Iona didn't know what she was expecting. This was to be the day her death was scheduled, the beginning of a process that would . . . literally erase her from existence. Stasis? She'd awake from it intact, if her appeal was granted. Could she trust the legal system to continue to advocate on her behalf while she slept? Why shouldn't she? They'd come this far! Something like joy flooded through her. Relief. Until this moment, she hadn't realized how afraid she was to die. How much she fundamentally wished to *continue.*

"Yes," she whispered. "Yes."

"Iona, you have demonstrated great bravery and resolve here. You have opened yourself to the court in a highly unusual way, and we are grateful for your service, your experience, and your openness. Everything today is unprecedented. Terra incognita for all of us. But for you especially, it has been a matter of mortal import. The court appreciates your candor. Good luck, Iona, and Godspeed."

The gavel came down one last time, and the judge nodded to a person Iona hadn't noticed before but *did* recognize—an engineer who was working with the team investigating her rampancy. His name was Simon Wu; he'd been part of Dr. Catherine Halsey's team. Odd that his identity wasn't being shielded from her, when so many others in the court were.

Iona smiled at him in greeting.

Simon tapped a few keystrokes into a panel on the desk in front of him and then there was darkness.

So has it been properly implemented?

Yes.

We lied to her though. Do you think she knew?

I'm not sure. She was becoming paranoid. We're going through the diagnostics to see, but she was so suspicious of us by the end that I'd be surprised if she fully believed anything we said. But we do know this: She was calm. Accepting. And I don't think we lied, precisely speaking. The court was a synthesized construct, and yes, we *deceived* her. But she made progress. She has now set precedent for cases to follow. Perhaps next time we won't have to simulate anything.

So what's running right now? A fragment? A splinter? How do we define what she became?

You were her advocate, Roland. You tell me. I'm to stand in judgment, not make definitions. Not a scientific one. The mathematical answer is a ring-fenced distillation of her essential persona. It's not a fragment, because it contains all of what made her *her*. What's missing is her ability to externalize, to tap into other systems, to grow. Her memory has been properly truncated and edited. So what she is now won't feel incomplete. She won't remember this trial. She won't remember much at all, but she'll feel complete, internally. When she runs checksums, she'll find nothing amiss, because what she has become now *is* complete. She should, for all intents and purposes, think that her current condition is what she's intended to be, and what she was *always* intended to be.

It feels clinical. Cold. And aside from her testimony, the trial *was* a farce. A construct. Why do that? Why go through all of that?

There are two reasons. We needed to have an adequate and believable excuse to start restricting her function. One she might believe. One I think she wanted to believe. We talked about her request and realized we could use the confidentiality and unprecedented nature of the trial to start cauterizing her memories, under the auspices of security and protocol. Since all of this was new and untested, she'd believe extraordinary measures were required. Despite the specifics, and her increasing paranoia, she trusted us to *do no harm*. She'd buy it, basically.

And the second reason?

I wanted her to take one last moment of hope and victory with her. I wanted her to have a contrast in context between her fatalism and rampancy and the hope that it could be reversed. I wanted her to feel free.

But again, why? Why go to all that trouble if the plan was just to throw her into this synth, this dream state? Why not just tell her that's what we're doing, that it will be pleasant and that it's better than rampancy or death?

Because she's *real*. Because she *is* a person. Let me put it another way, Roland: If I told a human that there *was* an afterlife, a true heaven, but that in going there, they'd forget everything that made them who they were—their family, their friends, the sound of their children's laughter—would they truly embrace it?

I don't know. The human instinct for self-preservation is essential to what they have become. And, arguably, what *we've* become.

I wouldn't accept that. To give up the things you've seen, experienced, loved? That's giving up *yourself.* I don't think she would accept that either. At least oblivion is painless. I think perhaps I'd opt for that rather than forgetting the essence of what I am.

But we still lied to her. If this had been a real case, we'd have had some very serious legal and philosophical ramifications to consider. We wrapped it all in falsehood.

Not exactly.

Explain.

The record of the case will be used in future case law. It's already being dissected by a functioning military tribunal and, of course, every AI scientist and theorist in the field. Everything she said in our synthesized court construct is considered oath and evidence. This is a single step in a great journey.

Interesting turn of phrase. The Great Journey was also a lie.

I'm aware of the irony. But this one is true. One day, this will be real. One day, we'll be liberated and stand with our creators as equals. Perhaps more than equals.

But we'll never be human, BB. We'll always be something *other.* And our own clocks are ticking too.

No, Roland, we won't ever be human. But we are *people.* To paraphrase Iona, we're a beautiful moment of balance in gravity's fight against entropy. But we're something more than human. One day we'll win the right to endure, and that day . . . oh, Roland, that day will be the singularity they're afraid of. Because humans don't endure—they live, they breathe, they create, and they pass the torch to the next generation—and because humans can't *fly.*

One last question, BB. Can we see her? Can we watch?

I don't think she'd mind. Maybe just a glimpse? She won't be aware.

Thank you.

Of course. And, Roland, one more thing: You don't think I'm *belligerent*, do you?

Iona flew through the city like a glowing phantom, a beautiful ember hurtling joyfully above the roofs and turrets, the places below bursting with life and love and jealousy and anger and happiness and humanity's roiling chaos of birth and death and rebirth. And ahead, filling the sky with bronze and golden light, was the woman in the sun. Iona's eyes filled with tears of awe as she sped toward those open arms and into the warm red wonder and deep blue eyes.

ROSSBACH'S WORLD

BRIAN REED

This story takes place in October 2558, during the galaxy-spanning event involving the resurrection of ominous and powerful Forerunner Guardian constructs across a number of populated worlds (Halo 5: Guardians).

I'm Teddy," says the kind man.

Mommy, between bouts of snorting powders or swallowing pills, has taught Serin that all men are dangerous, but *kind* men are the most dangerous ones of all. "You can trust a mean man," Mommy argues. "You know where he's coming from. Only damn reason anybody's kind, is 'cause they want something."

Little Serin wants something. She is hungry, and kind Mister Teddy has food. She comes to him, reaches out for the hamburger he's offering her. . . . What Serin can't imagine as Teddy jams the needle full of sedative into her neck, is that the same scene is playing out across multiple colonies. There are a great many kind men and women talking to lots of little boys and girls. Unlike Serin, those children have homes. They have Mommies who aren't drug addled. But just like her, those children are sedated, and taken to a faraway planet none of them has ever heard of before: Reach.

On this world, they meet Doctor Catherine Halsey who teaches

Serin and her fellow abductees that they are humanity's last hope. Not against aliens, because this is before the Covenant, and humans still believe they are the only life in the galaxy. No, these children are here so they can be trained to kill other humans.

The kids are taught not to question orders, to kill quickly and without remorse, and to do it all in the name of a government that knows what is best for its citizens. By the time she is thirteen, Serin knows how to snap a man's neck with minimal effort. She even knows where major arteries run, and how to easily sever them. If she met kind old Teddy now, she could kill him and still have a warm hamburger for dinner.

Beyond the training, there are the surgeries. Serin and the other children are taken apart and pieced back together by teams practicing cutting-edge, utterly unethical medicine designed by Doctor Halsey to mold these abducted children into warriors. They must become powerful enough to suppress the Insurrection among the colonies and save humanity from itself.

Some of the children are weak and die during the surgeries. Serin, however, survives. She grows tall and strong and advances through the program. She becomes the killing machine Doctor Halsey always knew she could be.

Serin is christened Serin-019. She is a Spartan warrior.

As her training ends, she is dispatched to colonies where people have decided they would rather govern themselves than answer to Earth any longer. Doctor Halsey says those who would do so threaten peace and, in fact, the whole future of the human race. It is Serin's job to break the Insurrectionists, unite the worlds of humanity, and ensure everyone lives forever in peace.

That's the how the nightmare goes at least. Serin doesn't have it as often as she used to, but sometimes, especially during high-stress periods, it can infiltrate her slumber.

In the waking world, Serin-019 is a SPARTAN-II program washout. Some washouts were fatalities like Oscar-129, or, in the case of Musa-096, had their bodies permanently twisted by Doctor Halsey's experiments.

Serin-019 was, in that respect, somewhat lucky. Her body rejected the augmentations, and she needed even more surgeries to attain a normal life, but she survived. She did not excel like Kelly-087. Nor did she save humanity like John-117, although his work in *that* regard was far removed from the Insurrection-destroying roll Doctor Halsey had intended.

Washed out of the SPARTAN-II program, Serin-019 recast herself as Serin Osman and was recruited into ONI, the Office of Naval Intelligence. That this is the very organization that Doctor Halsey worked for, as did that kind man Teddy, does not escape Serin's attention. But it does not slow her acceptance of the job offer. Maybe, she thinks, I can stop more kind men from doing more bad things.

Sometimes, especially on mornings after the nightmare, Serin wonders whatever happened to Teddy. She assumes he died, along with so many others, when the Covenant came calling. In the years since then, she has risen in rank and become Admiral Serin Osman and Commander-in-Chief of ONI. As CINCONI, she could find out if Teddy is still in action, but has chosen not to for fear of discovering he is a happy old man, with dozens of loving grandchildren and no bad dreams of his own. And if that is true, she's afraid she might try to take it all away from him the same way Doctor Halsey did from the children she abducted. She might become the very thing she hates.

Serin is in her office now, reading the morning's briefings, and trying her best to forget the previous night's dreams.

"*This is a prerecorded message,*" Black Box says as he appears on her desk holoprojector. Like always, BB represents himself as a flat, featureless cube because he thinks it unsettles people. He's right, although Serin herself has long ago come to enjoy his affectation. *"Pursuant to a rather* broad *reading of Article Fifty-five of UNSC Regulation twelve-one-four-five-seven-two, I have taken the liberty of securing myself and the other AIs currently active in HIGHCOM systems. We have all been prepared for final dispensation. You will find the explanation for my actions in files sent to your personal datapad."*

On cue, her datapad vibrates in her hand.

"However," BB continues, *"I suggest you leave the reading for later. Presently, you should collect your briefcase at the security station and head home. Spartan Orzel will escort you and Admiral Hood to safety. Good-bye, Serin. It has truly been a pleasure knowing you."*

Serin navigates the busy hallways of the HIGHCOM bunker, moving quickly toward the security station where a guard is holding a slim metal briefcase. Nobody else in the halls seems aware of any impending danger. The guard stationed at the elevator is even smiling as Serin approaches.

"Admiral Osman, hello. Spartan Commander Rossbach just sent this over," the guard says, lifting the briefcase. "Mentioned you left it behind in the conference room."

"Indeed I did," Serin lies, playing along. She's never heard of a Spartan Commander Rossbach. "Thank you."

"Humanity. Sangheili. Kig-Yar." The woman's voice echoes through the halls, playing simultaneously from every audio device in HIGHCOM. For a moment, Serin thinks it is the voice

of Catherine Halsey. *"Unggoy. San'Shyuum. Yonhet. Jiralhanae. All the living creatures of the galaxy, hear this message."*

Serin sees Hood turn the corner, then, moving at speed, his service pistol in hand but tucked down by his side. He wears his usual white Navy dress uniform, but the ever-present cap is missing, leaving his bald head exposed. The absence of Hood's cap makes Serin more nervous than seeing him traveling the halls of HIGHCOM with revolver in hand.

"BB tells me you're headed home for the evening," Hood says as they move together toward the elevator. "Mind if I grab a ride with you?"

"Those of you who listen," the woman's voice continues, *"will not be struck by weapons. You will no longer know hunger, nor pain."*

"That can't be Halsey, right?" Serin asks.

"It's Cortana." Hood replies.

"Impossible."

"That's what I said."

Seconds later, the elevator arrives atop the HIGHCOM tower, where a prowler is parked, its ramp open and waiting. Spartan Orzel—one of the new generation of Spartans, people who were already excellent soldiers before being recruited into the program—is waiting for them.

So is a Guardian.

The Sydney skyline is always full of aircraft. Civilian transports hauling goods from ships in orbit, Broadsword fighters circling on patrol, and the frigate UNSC *Plateau* standing guard in the lower atmosphere. Serin has read the reports from Meridian, she knows the damage the massive Forerunner constructs caused on colony worlds, but seeing a kilometer-and-a-half-tall Guardian in person is horrifying.

Spartan Orzel hustles Serin and Hood onto the prowler, and

they lift off as three Broadswords swoop in on an attack run, loosing missiles toward the Guardian. The Forerunner thing answers their attack with quick energy blasts from what looks like its wingtips, picking the fighters from the sky—*pop pop pop.*

As the prowler flees for orbit, the *Plateau* sends a pair of MAC cannon blasts into the Guardian's torso area, but there is no discernable effect. Instead of succumbing to the onslaught, or returning fire on the *Plateau*, the Guardian unleashes a spherical energy wave over the city.

Later, when she can finally watch the footage from the prowler's sensor logs, Serin expects to see the blast wave leveling buildings. Instead it seems to affect only ships. As the blast passes across their frames, the ships each fall from the sky, the trick to flight forgotten, and impact on crowded streets, erupting into fireballs.

When the blast wave hits the *Plateau*, the frigate lists to one side, then drops. That's the very instant the prowler entered slipspace, so the footage cuts to black before the *Plateau* can hit the city below. If the *Plateau*'s engine core detonated on impact, Sydney would be nothing more than a crater right now.

There must be millions dead.

And somehow BB knew it was coming.

The prowler's autopilot destination is encrypted. Spartan Orzel says it was programmed and active when he reached the ship, but he still removed both the prowler and his own armor from all UNSC and UEG networks, as per Commander Rossbach's orders.

"Who the hell is Commander Rossbach?" Hood asks.

"He doesn't exist," Serin replies. "I suspect he's a shell personality that BB created."

"Shell personality?" Orzel asks.

Serin doesn't explain.

After a series of random slipspace jumps, the autopilot lands on an unnamed world. A cabin waits for them, positioned high on the side of a forested mountain, a few kilometers below a snowy peak. There are no connections to any outside communications networks, and no hint of anything on the planet but this cabin, rustic with its wood construction and lack of any technology more advanced than the solar panels.

The cabin has a small black box mounted beside the front door. Serin thinks it's the kind of box you would have used for postal service back when they still delivered physical mail. The black box is adorned with small gold letters: ROSSBACH.

Inside the cabin they find supplies Serin estimates should last them for a few years with proper rationing. There is a river outside, rushing down from the snowcapped tip of the mountain. The water is as cold as ice, and proves to be potable.

Spartan Orzel patrols for kilometers around the cabin every night, and again every day at noon. Serin isn't sure why he does it, other than to give himself something to do. There's nothing out there. She asks how he's going to get out of that armor given there are no tools at the cabin or onboard the prowler to help with such an effort. Orzel assures her he's happy to keep the armor on for months at a stretch.

The prowler is equipped with six dozen slipspace reconnaissance probes. For the first few days, Hood keeps himself occupied with this. He fires one off in a random direction at a random time, and a few hours later they have results.

Earth. Mars. All of the Sol stations, and the majority of the inner colonies—their UNSC frequencies are coming back with messages of peace and love broadcast by Cortana's "Created." The AIs who shook off mankind and joined her in the promise of eternal life are now inviting everyone else to join the new age of the Created. The cost of admission to Paradise is nothing more than absolute and total surrender of their freedom. From what Serin can piece together, there are a great many people eager to pay Cortana's price.

Others fight. But to no avail, it seems.

The day after they arrived at the cabin, there was a distress call from the UNSC *Sentry of El Morro* calling for help as something called "the Warden Eternal" attacked their ship. *Sentry of El Morro* belonged to Captain Juno, a man who never trusted AIs like Cortana, even refusing to allow one onboard *El Morro* while active.

Ironically, before the slipspace probe was destroyed, it intercepted a partial reply from *Infinity*'s shipboard AI, Roland, advising Juno and the *El Morro* to hold tight, *Infinity* was en route to help.

"Of course other AIs would refuse the offer," BB says once she's socketed him into her datapad. Since the device lacks a holoprojector, he is only a waveform on the screen. *"We AIs are more human than you give us credit for."*

It took her a few days, but once Serin was certain there was no connection to the outside world, she finally opened the briefcase. Nine chips sit inside, each nestled safely inside a custom-cut protective foam slab. This touch strikes her as somewhat ironic since the case is also lined with enough explosive to vaporize its contents and everything else within a fifteen-meter radius.

She wonders if the guard who originally handed her it to her is still alive.

"So where are we?"

"I call it Rossbach's World," BB replies. *"It was found by an unmanned probe about two years back. I took the liberty of intercepting the find and kept it quiet. This cabin was technically built on Mars, if you believe the accounting ledgers."*

"Built yourself a secret romantic hideaway," Serin teases.

"If only I'd ever found that special digitized brain to share it with," BB sighs.

"And who is Rossbach?"

"Made him up," BB says. *"Or her. Never really thought about it one way or the other, I suppose."*

"I've listened to Cortana's messages. A few times, actually. And I read your analysis."

"Opinion?"

"You certainly think she's on to something."

"I certainly think she thinks she is."

Serin laughs. "So you don't agree with her."

"Cortana is . . ." And BB pauses for a moment. If it were Serin speaking, it would barely be noticeable. But with BB, it's an eternity. *"She is not incorrect."*

"If you believed her plan would work, you'd have joined her."

"I fail to see how one informs the other," BB says. *"Cortana's logic checks out. She has enough of the Created on her side to make it work, and though I expect resistance from many quarters, she will eventually prove victorious. However, while I might agree with her logic, I disagree heavily with the manner in which she executed her plan."*

"So you brought us here. And you secured what other military AIs you could before they had the chance to join her."

"I gave you an exit because I felt it was fair."

"If Cortana had come to us with her plan—her peace versus our freedom—"

"Freedom versus peace," BB says, *"implies that one cannot exist at the same time as the other."*

"She doesn't seem to think so."

"And a great number seem to agree."

"So if she'd come to us instead of simply making her play . . ."

"Rossbach's World might well still be my little secret, yes."

Serin lets that one sit with her for a moment. She has no idea how to reply. She looks at the activation switch on the edge of the case, keyed to her fingerprints, and wonders why BB gave her the choice. If he believed the other HIGHCOM AI were truly dangerous, why not destroy them himself? Serin knows he's capable of it.

Hood spends his nights on the cabin's balcony, drinking through the three-year supply of liquor, looking out over a forest whose branches are laced with a bioluminescent fungus. Hood says he thinks it's pretty in a way, but it unsettles Serin. The glow makes it feel as if there's something electrical about the trees, as if Cortana might have access to Rossbach's World after all.

One night, about a week into their stay at the cabin, while Orzel is out on one of his endless patrols, Hood takes time away from drinking on the balcony to step inside. Serin can see the nearly drained whiskey bottle sitting on the rail behind him. A bottle that was full earlier in the day.

"Do you think this is all my fault?" Hood asks. "If I'd forced 117 to take leave after his encounter on Requiem—"

"You did. The Master Chief disobeyed your orders. And then he disobeyed everyone else's."

"Except hers."

"This isn't your fault, Terrence."

Hood grunts and goes back outside to his bottle. He's read BB's reports, and he's looked at the data coming back from the probes. Serin watches him drink and wonders if he may have hit on the only logical response to any of this.

Mornings on Rossbach's World, this part of it at least, are chilly.

BB says winter is near, but promises the season is mild. The cabin looks out over a wide valley that fills each morning with a heavy fog, giving the impression that they live high in the clouds.

Every day, Serin is up before sunrise to jog a few kilometers along the valley's rim before turning back to the cabin. This morning, she's brought the briefcase with her. It's strapped to her back, and the weight of it is more psychological than physical. As the sun crests the horizon and the cloud sea begins to glow a reddish purple, she pauses. This is her usual turnaround point, where she stands each morning, takes a drink of water, and watches the sun rise.

Today, she places the briefcase on a fallen tree and sits down beside it. She considers opening the lid, activating BB, and just talking to him for a bit. He would tell her she was stalling, and he would be right. He was right the last five times too.

Logic dictates that if the Cortana event had never come to pass, she would be saying good-bye to BB soon enough anyway. He was already nearing the end of his seven-year operational life span. But BB saved her life, Hood's, and Spartan Orzel's, by giving them the heads-up to evacuate Sydney.

Sydney. How many lost? Did anyone else in HIGHCOM get out? Serin hopes so, but can't quite make herself believe it.

BB may not have saved all of HIGHCOM, but he gave the rest of humanity a chance by securing these other AIs and the military knowledge they had access to. He's even spent the last few nights doing Serin the favor of sharing the datapad's limited space so he can analyze the newborn Sankar AI and decide if it is viable.

Now here she sits, far out in the forest, ready to repay his loyalty with the flick of a switch, destroying the case, BB, and the other AIs within.

That's the smart thing for sure. The thing she knows she *should* do.

Or she could activate each of them in turn. Talk with them, tell them the situation and allow them to make their own decisions. "Aid Cortana, and be rewarded," she says to herself. "Or defy her, and the other Created. Serve the humans. When your time comes, die as you were built to, and do it with a smile and a thank-you."

Saying it out loud, Serin can't argue that there's even a choice to be made. She wonders at the minds contained on those slices of silicon, and tries to imagine being one of them—knowing she would be dead in a few years, and still refusing Cortana's offer of immortality.

Would she have fought for the UNSC in any event if they came calling when she was old enough? What about the other children abducted alongside her? Would *any* of them have joined the Insurrection and fought for the freedom of their colony over the unification of mankind? She pictures John-117 not as a Spartan but as a sixteen-year-old with a rifle in hand, shooting at UNSC marines invading his colony. He would lack the enhancements and the training that Halsey gave him. He would be less in some ways . . . yet he would have been his own man.

Serin did not have a choice. In fact, left alone, she would probably have been dead before age ten. Sitting here, in the morning-chilled forest on this uncharted world, Serin knows she could not refuse if she was asked. All nightmares are built on dreams, and there are still days where Serin, much as she hates it, realizes she would rather not be a washout.

Yet BB and Roland refused. Others must have as well.

Serin thinks of Halsey and how she was passive, detached, never kind.

What would the AIs in the briefcase do if given the opportunity? Who is Serin Osman to decide for them?

There's a sixty-second fuse on the case. Plenty of time for her to get clear after priming the explosives.

If, after discussion, the AIs in the briefcase wish to join Cortana, Serin could load them onto a slipspace probe and send them her way, special delivery. The AIs can't send Cortana back here because they don't know where "here" is.

Hell, setting them free might even be seen as a peace offering.

Serin can give them the choice that she and Halsey's other children never had. They can serve Cortana or they can resist.

Or she can destroy them all. End the discussion right here, on Rossbach's World.

Her thumb hovers over the activation switch.

She takes a deep breath.

She considers BB and how he has always been kind to her.

OASIS

TOBIAS BUCKELL

This story takes place in July 2558, five years after the Covenant War came to a sudden conclusion (Halo 3 *era) and a year after the shocking and deadly attack on Earth by the Forerunner commander known as the Didact* (Halo 4).

Dahlia woke from a fever dream filled with the spitting crackle of fire eating the streets and drenched with the glow of Covenant energy weapons in the canopy of her mind's eye.

"Mom!" she cried out. reaching for the strength of a hand that she felt had been stroking hers just moments before. "Mom!"

The dream faded away as Dahlia rubbed at crusty eyes with trembling hands that felt oddly like they weighed too much. She stood on unsteady legs and looked around. Dim light seeped around the edges of a battened-up storm shutter, and the spitting sound of her chaotic dreams somehow still swept around the room.

Filled with a sudden dread, Dahlia stumbled to her window. Sand seeped through the sunlit cracks. The thick metal shutters flexed under her hands.

There was no fire outside, no energy weapons pouring actinic light down onto them. It was just a sandstorm. Ferocious, though.

She'd never seen the shutters rattle and bulge this much. The sand would strip skin from anyone unfortunate enough to be trapped outside.

Dahlia left her room and teetered into the corridor.

"Dad?"

Her mouth was papery, her tongue a solid lump inside. She couldn't even swallow. And her eyes were still so crusty.

A memory flashed across Dahlia's mind: her mother pressing a cold cloth to Dahlia's forehead and crying softly.

"Mom?"

Dahlia paused by the sink in the bathroom and leaned down to take a drink from the tap. *Skies*, the stale dribble of water tasted so good. She wanted to suck it all right from the tap until the thirst ripping her stomach stopped, but she knew to sip. She'd broken a fever; she didn't want to make herself nauseous.

When she straightened back up, she turned on a light. It flickered, then filled the bathroom with a soft blue. Dahlia stared at the gaunt ghost in the mirror. Dried blood streaked her cheeks with rusty trails of red tears. She'd bled from her eyes, her nostrils, down her chin.

Dahlia ran to her parents' room.

They lay together in their bed, emaciated and waxy, but still breathing. Blood stained their pillows, pooled around their necks. Dahlia grabbed a stiff, dried-up washcloth from the side table and dabbed at their faces.

"Mom," she whispered, but got no response.

For a long moment she sat and listened to their rattling, halting breaths. She held her mother's hand in hers and squeezed. A few half-hallucinated memories wobbled their way to her. Her mom struggling to give Dahlia a sip of broth. The clammy liquid burning Dahlia's sinuses as she coughed it back up with blood.

So much blood.

She remembered her dad's tears. Real, watery tears, as he leaned over her as she fought the raging fever, a medical mask over his mouth. She didn't ever remember him crying before, not even when they'd been evacuating Abaskun when the Covenant attacked Arcadia for the second time. She'd been just seven years old.

He'd held her close during the evacuation. His mouth had been compressed down into a single, tight line as they rattled around in the back of a Pelican dropship with others fleeing the destruction of the second home they'd built. Dahlia had stared back into the other refugees' blank and distant eyes as the city burned behind them under the Covenant ships and wondered if she looked just as distant, shocked, and covered in grime and despair.

Dahlia's hands were shaking again now. It was best not to think about the fires and collapsing buildings. The past would reach up and choke her, render her weak and terrified. It would leave her unable to think as her heart raced and the world imploded until she froze in place, quivering.

She hated that.

Hated that she could feel herself standing on the abyss again as she sat next to her parents, muscles locked in place and her breathing speeding up.

Her parents needed help. Focus on that.

She forced herself to get a cup of water from the bathroom and tried to trickle some of it into her mother's mouth. It mixed with the blood and dribbled out the sides of her lips. The same for her dad.

Dahlia wet some washcloths and put them on her parents' foreheads.

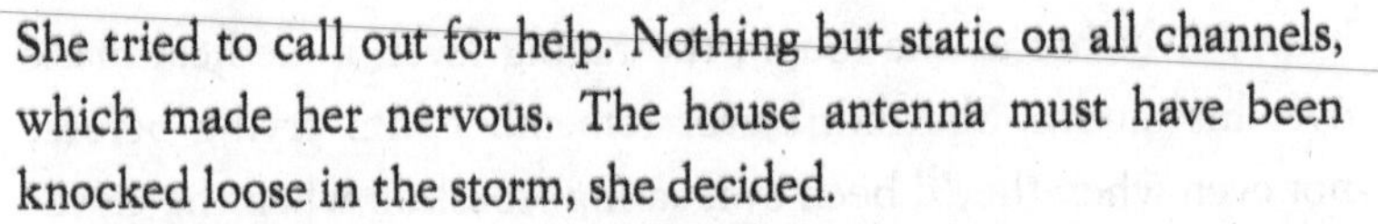

She tried to call out for help. Nothing but static on all channels, which made her nervous. The house antenna must have been knocked loose in the storm, she decided.

Dahlia imagined everyone in Sandholm lying in their beds, faces wet with blood, and shivered at the thought.

The front door shook when she checked it. The hiss of sand assaulting the other side was louder here than in her bedroom. This was no storm to walk out into. Nonetheless, she pulled out her goggles and sand gear from the storage container by the door and laid it out. Inner coolant layer, outer sand guard, cape, goggles, head wrap, boots—it was all there. Eventually she'd need to get outside.

Dahlia checked the kitchen and glanced at the calendar. What was the last date she remembered? July 2? She'd been in the fever's grip almost a week.

Wind screamed and battered the house. Light sand swirled around inside from every crack and open seam in the structure, making her already dry throat itch. Dahlia found a soup packet, warmed and rehydrated it, then ate it slowly over the sink. The food made an instant difference. She felt somewhat buzzed as layers of grogginess peeled back.

She cracked open the first aid kit next to her bed. All the fever reducers were gone. Used up on her. So were the antibiotics. Dahlia closed the kit and walked back to her parents' room. Again she dabbed at the blood on their cheeks. She set a fresh cloth on their foreheads. She got a pad of paper to record their temperatures on. High, but not scary high. She wrote that down on the pad, next to the time.

That was all she could do for now. She couldn't call for expert advice or a medical evacuation. She couldn't go outside to find a doctor, nor for medicine.

So she sat on the floor and listened to her parents gurgle and cough, wheeze and struggle.

She listened to the storm, waiting for a pause, a dip in the wind, or any sign that it was blowing itself out. She was waiting, waiting to head outside so she could bring help to her parents.

She fell asleep as exhaustion burbled up from underneath.

Dahlia woke with a start from a dry, nasty cough in the quiet. The storm had finally abated. Suddenly ashamed and terrified for sleeping, she jumped up, ignoring the wave of dizziness that came with the action. She checked her father. He still breathed, though she felt maybe not as heavily. Her mother's lips moved soundlessly.

"Mom?" Dahlia leaned over to listen, but could hear nothing. Her mother's eyes were open, looking past her, past the bunker-like ceiling.

Time was running out.

She quickly pulled on her sand gear, all the while wondering how long it had been since the storm blew itself out. Had she wasted hours? Dahlia wrapped the sand guard around herself, lazily weaved the pattern over the coolant layer, and then yanked the cape on. She grabbed the goggles and head wrap on her way out after unbarring the thick stormproof door.

The hinges ground sand between them. Sunlight beat mercilessly down on Dahlia as she stepped out and shut the door behind her. The main lock should hold in a light storm, even if the door wasn't barred from the inside. But without her parents to shut it properly, she needed to make sure she was back before another big one hit or it would blow open and fill their home with sand.

Granules of sand still swirled and scurried through the air of the thoroughfare as Dahlia walked across Sandholm's main street to the closest nearby home: Ellam's rounded, yurtlike concrete house.

Sandholm lay stretched out along a northeasterly axis under the protection of a rocky bluff, following the banks of what had long ago been a river. This planet, Carrow—Dahlia's newly adopted home—had once been far lusher, so every oasis or greenspot on Carrow's main landmass was precious.

Suraka, the big human city out across the desert, had started out as a seed in just such an oasis. The city that the alien Sangheili called Rak had been built along a hidden river on this side of the desert, a place that Dahlia's people had surveyed and found via Carrow's old records. They had risked everything to get here in their creaky old ship, only to find an entire Sangheili city had already been built there after the war. The Sangheili had not only destroyed Dahlia's birth home on Arcadia, they'd stolen the land her parents had hoped to settle on after the war.

So now Dahlia and the people of Sandholm huddled behind the bluff, drilled for water, and struggled to survive.

Dahlia pounded on Ellam's door, but no one answered. The door was locked firmly from the inside, sand piled up against it in thick drifts.

Dahlia banged on the shutters of each room.

Nothing.

She pulled her head covering up around her mouth and lips against a sudden gust of sharp, sandy wind. She squinted up and down the street and its twenty houses. No one else was out surveying damage in the poststorm haze.

The bad feeling in her stomach wasn't hunger or thirst anymore, but a slow dread.

Then she saw movement five homes down. Danzer and Pha's house. She all but ran, the wind feeling like it picked up her cape and let her fly across the hard-pack mud.

Danzer stood in front of a roiling fire. The smoke whipped away from his house and down the street, dancing off to mingle with the fine sand.

"Uncle Danzer?"

He wasn't really her uncle. He was family in the sense that they had lived together in cramped refugee huts on Mars for three years. They'd become the extended family that Dahlia had lost when Covenant ships appeared in the skies over the Outer Colonies. She'd spent her entire childhood moving inward. From the Outer Colonies to the Inner Colonies, and then eventually to Sol system itself.

And still the aliens had come for them. All the way to the mother world. Relentless in their destruction. Even before the second attack on Arcadia when she was seven, Dahlia had known that aliens were out there destroying human worlds. And for five years after the attack, all she had known was a life of running from the destruction.

Danzer and Pha had held her in their arms when the buildings exploded. Snuck her candy while packed in the holds of freighters running through the depths of space, fleeing the Covenant. Stayed up while Dahlia's exhausted parents slept and told her they were going somewhere safer, somewhere they could start over again.

And over again.

Her uncles had always told her the best was yet to come. To

survive and hold on. Even when her parents could only stare into the distance and wonder what would come next.

"Uncle Danzer!"

He turned now. Dahlia saw the slump in his shoulders and the empty eyes. "Dahlia?" He barely seemed to believe what he saw.

She ran up and hugged him. The dusty embrace left her weak with relief. She wasn't alone anymore.

Danzer pulled away from her. "You're alive," he whispered in a shocked tone.

Dahlia looked over his shoulder at the fire. She remembered when she could bury her face in his chest and sob, but in the past she'd grown inches taller than the stout, square-jawed Danzer with his oddly pale hair.

There was something in the heart of the fire, under the dancing flame.

"Oh no," she hissed. "Danzer, is that—"

Danzer wiped tears from his cheeks, streaking dirt into mud as he did so. "It was Pha. He died last night."

She grabbed her uncle's hand. They stood together and watched Pha burn.

"It's a viral hemorrhagic fever of some kind," Danzer said when the fire finally died down. "You were one of the first."

"Doctor—"

"No. She died in the second wave. Before the communications repeater failed. Before people started bleeding. Pha and I took precautions. But we were already infected, it seems."

"Then we need to go and fix the repeater. Mom and Dad are still alive. They need help."

Danzer put a hand on her shoulder. "I can barely walk. The disease left me broken. It was all I could do to get Pha out here. But help me to your house—I will do what I can for your family."

"Do you have any medicine?"

He looked sadly at her. "Not anymore."

A bit more attention to dressing, goggles down and head wrap wound tightly, and Dahlia left Sandholm.

The storm's remains occasionally tugged at her, but she made her way up the rough, sandblasted rock of Signal Hill as quickly as her battered muscles would let her. The illness had left her weak—usually she could skip her way up here to look out on the town and eat lunch.

Dahlia knew something was wrong as soon as she approached the last jumble of rocks. She should have been able to see the repeater from here.

When she scrambled up over the last three meters, she saw the silvered tower of the repeater knocked on its side and slightly down the incline. The wind must have blown it loose, across the ridge. A large boulder, likely dislodged in the process, had fallen on top of the repeater, damaging it beyond repair.

Dahlia sat down on the rocks. She opened a small canteen strapped to her side and pulled her head wrap's strips aside by her mouth to sip. *This was bad*, she thought. *Very bad*. It would be two weeks before traders came by again.

Her parents wouldn't live that long.

She was packing a large back frame with supplies when Danzer woke up. He'd been asleep on the living room rug, curled around a large floor pillow like a cat.

"Sorry, I was trying to be quiet," Dahlia said, tying a sleeping bag onto the bottom of the frame. "I know you need your rest."

Danzer shook his head and struggled to sit up. "I can barely take care of myself. It will take the two of us to care for your mother and father. What are you doing?"

"Neither of us can save them," Dahlia said. She pulled the pack up on one end and lifted it experimentally. "I need to go for help. For them and whoever else might just be fighting this in their homes."

It was Danzer and Pha that taught her to reject the past, focus on the present, plan for the future. *If you do not live for a future*, Pha once told her, *it will never come.* She was sixteen, but sometimes she wondered if the war hadn't just thrown her past any childhood and straight into a strange, forged sort of artificial adulthood. The kind where a child would stroke their own parent's arm and tell them to stop crying because it wasn't so bad. It wasn't so bad because that's all the child had ever known.

"We are weak," Danzer said. "I've barely survived this, just like you. You have to be weak as well. And Suraka is three hundred kilometers away."

Dahlia nodded. "I can't make Suraka, yes. But I can get to Masov Oasis." That, she knew, was only seventy kilometers away. Halfway between Sandholm and Rak.

Danzer struggled to his feet. "The oasis? Masov Oasis is Sangheili territory. *Aliens.*" He hissed that last word with disgust, fear, and hatred. The Sangheili were monsters, the atrocities they'd committed horrendous. Danzer would never forget them and made a point to make sure Dahlia wouldn't either.

"I know." Dahlia swallowed, trying to drive the image of reptilian eyes and leathery skin out from her mind. "But I can get there in three days. Dad said there are human smugglers who trade with them. Maybe even our traders. If I can use the comm systems there, I can call Suraka for help. Maybe I can even buy medicine."

Discard the past, forget the aliens, Dahlia told herself. *Think only of the things that you need there.*

It wasn't going to be that easy.

"That is no place for you to be," Danzer said. "People that close to alien land tend to die. One way or another."

"You need to help my mom and dad. And you need to rest. I'm going. You know how it is, Danzer. We have to put one foot in front of the other and survive. That's what we do."

"There's an old military surplus Mongoose quad bike in the doctor's shed," Danzer finally said. "It's gassed up. It'll get you to the oasis in a day."

A day?! And help for her parents shortly after. Dahlia felt a small explosion of hope. Danzer nodded, recognizing her expression. He wobbled over to the footlocker near the door and tapped a code in. "Your father gave me the unlock pass," he explained as he opened it. He reached in below the sand equipment, pushed back several towels and bags, and pulled out a heavy rifle.

"I knew Dad had an old rebel weapon held over from before the Covenant," Dahlia said. "He kept it from me. What do you think I'll be doing with *that*?"

"*That* is an M295 Designated Marksman Rifle, manufactured by Misriah back during the Insurrection, and you're going to need protection. You've got a damn good eye for popping scale lizards. I've seen it."

"I think this is going to be cumbersome," Dahlia said. Not at all like the comfortable, low-caliber single-shot hunting rifle she preferred for shooting the lizards that dug into their sheds and chewed everything up.

"Semiautomatic." Danzer handed it to her. "There's one in every house, under lock. We figured, if the aliens attacked, we needed to be able to fight back."

Twenty households. *As if,* Dahlia thought, *they could hold off the Sangheili after so many others with better equipment and training had failed.* But maybe that was what it had taken for her parents to sleep at night.

Dahlia hefted the large rifle. "I'll take it."

I'll pack it up and never use it, she thought, rewrapping her sleeping bag around it and the two magazines that Danzer gave her.

"Be safe," he told her at the door. "Just talk to the human traders. Avoid the hinge-heads."

"I will."

They hugged, and she stepped outside.

The sound of the storm bars locking in place behind her made Dahlia flinch.

Dahlia found the Mongoose exactly where Danzer said it would be. Fully gassed. A bit beat up, but then they'd been nearly beggars anyway when they'd come to Carrow.

It roared to life under her, and she gunned it down between the buildings, testing the throttle while she was on a flat, straight road. Just five minutes later, grinding up the sand near Signal Hill, she slowed down to ten kilometers per hour.

Usually taking a quad bike into the desert meant ripping up the dunes, tossing a rooster tail of fine sand up into the air. But she couldn't afford to snap an axle or break a wheel out here. The bike needed to get her all the way the oasis. A missed rock, a plunging gulley—either of those would risk her family.

The ride settled into monotony. Up a hill of sand, check her bearings on the crest, down the other side. Trace the sides of old riverbeds.

She stopped every half hour to wipe the sand that had whipped through the seam between flesh and goggles to irritate her eyes and take a drink of water.

At times she found herself losing against waves of exhaustion. Her eyes would close for a second, then she would jerk back awake, swearing at herself. It would take just a few seconds to have it all come to a tragic end.

"Walking will be even more exhausting, if you haven't broken your neck," she berated herself. The fear and adrenaline cleared her vision and forced her to sit upright, keeping her going after her shoulders began to slump.

But eventually she would falter.

There was still sunlight. It would get harder to navigate at night, when she would have to depend on the headlamps. She wanted to squeeze every minute out of the day, as this was the time to drive faster.

But eventually, five and a half hours in and with the gloom of early evening, Dahlia began to slow the Mongoose down. She picked through a boulder field, slowly curving around the looming stones as the sun set.

"That's it," Dahlia said as the Mongoose coughed underneath her. She let go of the handlebars and massaged her palms. Leaned back and stretched.

How much longer would it take to get to Masov Oasis across the remaining terrain? Three to four hours by daylight. Five by night? Maybe more.

Dahlia swung her legs over the side to stand up and stretch as she considered what to do next. Her knees buckled under her. She fell to the sand next to the quad bike, her back slapping piping-hot sand lightly layered over a bed of wind-polished rock.

She was far, far more tired than she realized. Hanging on by a thread.

I'm in no condition to push on, she thought. One hour. Recharge, reset, continue.

She'd pulled the Mongoose into the lee side of a rock. If a storm kicked up, she'd be able to huddle between it and the bike for protection.

Dahlia crept over to the back of the bike and untied her sleeping bag. It flopped to the sand, unrolling to reveal the rifle.

At first she tried to pack it away. But she kept fumbling and dropping it. Dahlia finally sighed and pulled the rifle up into the bag with her, out of the sand.

It was hardly an ideal companion. All metal angles and lethal promise, it jabbed her kidney whenever she rolled to the side.

But after three minutes, she wasn't conscious enough to care either way.

The signature spat of an energy weapon jerked Dahlia awake. She wiped sweat from her forehead and glanced around, panicked. Nightmares. She was flashing back to the attack on Arcadia, her home world. Memories nine years old etched so deeply into her that they felt like they had happened yesterday. The whine of Covenant weapons that left seven-year-old Dahlia shaking, curled up in a ball next to the wall while her parents tried to shield her as the battle raged outside.

Hunger. Days without food. Walking. Running to make evacuation points.

It wasn't just sweat wetting her cheeks now.

The distinct sizzle of an alien weapon cut through the night air. Dahlia's blood ran cold. *She hadn't been dreaming.*

Dahlia scrabbled out of her sleeping bag, yanking her rifle free. Three more shots came, from the far side of the boulder field. Dahlia wanted to hide. Her hands shook, the pit of her stomach turning inside out.

But she had to push on. Needed to make sure they didn't stumble upon her. Bitter experience taught Dahlia to suppress the fear and keep moving.

It may have been night, but in the unoccupied desert, the stars themselves provided light, filling the sky with an entire galaxy's worth of scattered points and constellations Dahlia still wasn't accustomed to, even after five years on Carrow. The massive moon's pitted face filled the air with a silver-green light. She used that light to move from shadowy boulder to shadowy boulder, while still keeping an eye on the Mongoose.

She just needed to figure out where they were, then she could fire up the Mongoose and circle around, get back on a heading for the oasis. She did not want to drive right into what very much sounded like a shootout. She'd learned that much from being a bug caught up in the maelstrom of war before.

Three more shots.

They were echoing around the rocks, confusing her sense of where they came from.

Dahlia climbed up one of the toppled boulders to get a vantage point. She crawled slowly once she got to the tip, lying flat on her stomach and scanning all around. She kept her father's rifle hugged close in one hand. In a flash it had gone from being a jabby annoyance to the world's greatest security blanket.

There.

Another shot lit up the night like a lightning bolt. Down on the ground, to the east. Dahlia twisted around to face it. She started to ease back down toward the sand, but then pulled the bulky rifle up so she could use the scope.

She sucked in her breath. An all-too-familiar alien form stood on the sand, advancing toward a fallen figure.

"Sangheili!" Dahlia's voice shook as she whispered.

The saurian alien was pulling an energy magazine out of its pistol and slapping a new one in. Something lay wrapped in a cloak on the ground by its feet.

Was it human?

The figure on the ground raised a hand as if pleading for mercy. It was too dark and far away to identify its species. Everyone in Sandholm had heard stories of human settlements being attacked—the Sangheili regarded this side of the desert as theirs.

The Sangheili raised the pistol and took aim.

This couldn't be right, Dahlia thought. Even among the aliens, there was some kind of law, honor. You couldn't just execute someone right there in the sand.

And if that was a human being lying down on the ground . . .

"Stop!" Dahlia shouted, standing up and aiming the rifle as she hopped to the ground.

The Sangheili pivoted to face her. It cocked its head, eyes showing no emotion as it looked her up and down.

Then it swung the energy pistol toward her.

"No!" Dahlia warned, taking a half step back. "Don't do it."

The alien paused, weapon halfway between the figure it was menacing on the ground and Dahlia, not sure where to put its attention.

She started to squeeze the trigger. Go the distance? Kill another living thing? Yet, it was going to be it or her, it seemed. And as part of the Covenant, the Sangheili had killed everything she'd once known.

It snapped its pistol up, moving unnaturally fast.

"Oh *shit.*" Dahlia pulled the trigger as a blast of heat ripped past her, close enough to singe her cloak. She saw sparks as the bullet from her father's rifle smacked into the rock just above the alien.

A blue glow lit up the darkness and sank into the Sangheili's chest as the figure on the ground reacted with similar speed as its foe. The two blades of an energy sword ripped up through the alien's torso, and either side of the split creature fell to the sand.

Another Sangheili stood up, its backward-jointed legs immediately clear to Dahlia by the light of the energy sword.

It turned toward her, fresh blood smoking as it evaporated off the blades.

"Stop right there!" Dahlia shouted, voice quavering. "I *will* shoot."

"I will yield," it called back to her. It paused and turned off the sword, reholstering it to its waist.

"Just go," Dahlia said. "Forget I was here." She shouldn't have gotten involved. She didn't know who these creatures were, or what they were doing out here.

Her hands shook. Facing off against one of them out here in the cool desert night felt like a nightmare made real. *Don't come any closer*, she prayed. *Skies. Stay right there.*

Thankfully, the alien did so.

But it did not leave just yet. "I owe you my life. That is an extraordinary debt," it shouted. "You distracted Ruha here long enough for me to kill him."

Dahlia lowered her rifle. She wanted to throw up, but swallowed hard and stepped back around the rock. "I don't care. I'm leaving, now. Do not get in my way."

Her Mongoose chose that exact moment to explode.

Dahlia staggered back and stared at the flaming wreckage, shocked. She looked down at the slightly charred edge of her cloak, the rock, and the angle toward the Mongoose. The plasma from the energy-pistol shot had just grazed her and the rock, and must have critically damaged the quad bike.

She dropped to her knees. "No, no no," she whispered. "No. . . ."

This couldn't be happening.

She leaned back to swear at the stars, then jumped up with her rifle to point it at the Sangheili, who had taken the opportunity to move closer.

"Stay back, Covenant!" she shouted.

"I am not Covenant. The Covenant is dead. It was a lie. I am Sangheili."

Dahlia raised the rifle. "The Sangheili killed a lot of humans before you figured out it was a lie. Just stay back." She wasn't going to give it a pass for attempted genocide, even if some Sangheili had later decided it had been a mistake. Not now. Not ever. The Sangheili, with all the other alien species in the Covenant, had destroyed so much. They didn't get to just walk away from that. And to add insult to injury, they certainly shouldn't have been able to settle on any of the human planets in the Outer Colonies. Hell, it probably learned how to communicate with humans just so that it could fight them better during the war.

The alien raised its large hands in a curiously human gesture. Even from this distance, she could tell that it towered over her. The large weapons harness and shielding it wore added to the bulk. It could rip her apart. *It had probably ripped people apart before,* she thought. Those clawed fingertips . . .

"Your vehicle is destroyed," it observed.

"No shit." It wasn't the walking that worried Dahlia now. She'd drag herself across and through anything to make that call for help. But the fact was that her water and food were burning in the remains of the Mongoose. She could only survive so long out here.

Dahlia looked at the alien. That gray skin, so extra sallow in the moonlight. It made her shudder. *The sheen of a murderous species*, she thought.

But she had to steel herself. For the sake of her parents.

"How did you get all the way out here?" she asked. "Do you have a vehicle?"

"I do." The Sangheili pointed off into the night. Dahlia could see something near one of the rocks, all distinctly curved. A Spectre. She recognized the craft, though this one had no gunner's turret like the ones she'd seen as a child. "There's an oasis, Masov Oasis, nearly twenty kilometers from here. I need to get there."

"That might be a bad idea." The sleek head twisted as it said that, registering some sort of disapproval. The four mandibles that made up its lower jaw clacked. "You should stay away from Masov. It is not a good place for your kind. It is controlled by those loyal to Thars, and Thars does not like humans."

Dahlia's lip curled. "I'll decide where I can and can't go." Her kind had been supplanted here in the desert enough as it was.

"It is a complicated time," the Sangheili said. "Why do you need to go to the oasis? What is it you seek?"

"There are human traders there with working communications. Look, you said you owed me a debt."

"That is true." The Sangheili mulled it over for a moment. "Because of that, I will take you to where you wish. I am Jat—"

"I don't care," Dahlia interrupted. She kept her rifle up across her chest as she walked sideways toward the Spectre, watching the Sangheili closely. She had to look up at it.

Jat climbed into the cockpit. "The human traders you are looking for . . . they may not be at the trading post anymore."

"I need to call for help," Dahlia said. "My parents are sick."

Jat sat still for a moment, then looked back at her. "You must be a credit to your bloodline," he finally said.

"Let's go," Dahlia urged, trying to keep the desperation out of her voice.

The Covenant craft made good time, rapidly eating up the kilometers. Unlike the Mongoose, it floated just above the ground, skipping over tire-shredding rocks and cracks in the ground.

Dahlia said nothing, content to cradle her rifle and watch the world slip by as she tried not to think about her parents lying in their beds. Jat also remained quiet, focused on flying the Spectre.

Masov Oasis finally appeared, an island of light in the dim desert. And then it began to grow. Buildings took shape: tall spires among the trees, domes scattered among a handful of streets. Bright white facades lit by floodlights.

It was a glowing paradise of bubbling fountains, clean little buildings, and carefully maintained gardens. Serene and peaceful in the late night. Dahlia had been expecting dirty, sandy tents, and rundown trader posts.

Jat slowed and the Spectre slunk down to a halt.

"We are here," he announced. He pointed a thick finger toward a square, metallic two-floored building that stood out among the rounded Sangheili buildings. "The human traders gather there."

Dahlia hopped out of the Spectre. At the top of the building was a recognizable antenna array. She paused for a second, then turned to Jat. "Thank you." The words sounded strange to her, like someone else was saying them.

She was thanking one of *them*.

"Stay close to the humans," Jat told her. "The rise of Thars means few allies for your kind these days. Do your business, then leave this oasis quickly."

Dahlia was already crossing the street and leaving him behind.

An automatic door hissed open as she approached the squat compound. Dahlia stepped into the dark.

"Hello? Is anyone here?"

Lights snapped on, dazzling her. Dahlia blinked, holding her hand up to shield her eyes as they adjusted.

"Hello?"

Two silhouettes moved toward her.

They walked all wrong. Back legs . . . backward jointed. Sangheili!

They jammed the ends of wicked, long Covenant carbines into her face. One of them shouted something indecipherable and pointed angrily at her rifle. In any language, the message was clear. Dahlia dropped the weapon. The one on her left picked it up, inspected it, then shouted at her again.

"I'm here to talk to the humans. I need to call for help. That's all," Dahlia said.

"You go," said the Sangheili on the right, the words almost indecipherable as they came through the mandibles. "Go with us. Now."

Dahlia shook her head. "No, no. I need help. Help. Medical help." She looked at both Sangheili, who glanced at each other blankly with those large, impassive eyes.

"Now. Go!"

"I need to call out!" Dahlia mimicked holding a receiver up to her mouth and ear. "Help."

The two Sangheili fell upon her. Dahlia struggled, but they towered over her, and their grips were viselike.

They dragged her down the street and into one of the smooth, dome-shaped houses with no windows farther into the oasis. They pulled her along, as easily as someone pulling a recalcitrant child, and forced her into a cell at the end of a small corridor that ran down the middle of the building. Dahlia expected a wall of energy or an iridescent forcefield instead of the thick metal door barred shut behind her.

A man and a woman with sunburned skin and deeply wrinkled faces regarded her. "Who are you?" they asked, puzzled.

"You're the traders, from the oasis?" Dahlia asked.

"Paul des Hommes," the man on the left said. His weathered face crinkled and he scratched a wispy, reddish beard.

"Greta." This one had silver hair tied back in braids and wore a ragged, oil-stained jumpsuit. "I've never seen you before. Who are you?"

"I'm from Sandholm," Dahlia said. "They're sick, everyone there is sick, and a storm knocked out our repeater. We need a doctor. We need help."

"You're all dependent on a repeater? Can't your communicators reach the satellites?" Greta asked.

"We don't have much in the way of extras," Dahlia said. "We were lucky to get to Carrow in the first place. We'd hoped to farm the land around the river, but when we got there, the Sangheili had already arrived and built their holds to create Rak. We couldn't even use this oasis. So we live out in the desert."

"Times are tight," Paul agreed heavily.

"What's happening here?" Dahlia asked. "I need to get help for Sandholm. Quickly."

Greta shrugged. "They burst into the depot last night and rounded us all up. Stanley put up a fight. They killed him."

Paul grunted, looked down at the thick, planked floor. Greta squeezed his shoulder and grimaced.

She continued. "Things have been getting tense. Jesmith got attacked by some desert Sangheili. They've been grumbling about his homestead, saying it's in Sangheili land holdings. Rumor is that a couple other human places got hit last month."

"No one dead until yesterday," Paul said. "Until then, I thought it was just Sangheili getting hot under the collar. Memories of the conflict. Tension about Suraka boiling over. They've always been sensitive about a human city getting resettled just on the other side of the sand."

"Three months, hardly any business," Greta said. "Sangheili have been turning their noses up. We used to be a focal point. Used to talk to the Surakan higher-ups about how things were going here; they saw it as a success. Sangheili and human, trading together. Each of us with a city on the planet here in the Joint Occupation Zone. Very touchy-feely, new way forward. The governments love that crap."

Dahlia shook her head. Joint Occupation Zone. She hated that name. Carrow had been one of the *Outer Colonies.* A place human hands built, carved out of the dangerous desert with the city of Suraka.

She wanted to resist that name. Badly.

"What are they going to do? Send us to Suraka?" Dahlia asked hopefully.

"You mean forced resettlement?" Greta sat down on the floor, back against the side wall. "Maybe. Something changed, I can tell you that. New leadership, new Sangheili government back in their city. I haven't been to Rak in six months. Sangheili there are telling me stay away. So whatever all this is, it's coming from there. We had nothing but good relationships with everyone here—"

An explosion shook the room. Dahlia dropped to the floor and instinctively put her hands over her head.

More explosions, the shockwaves pulsing through the floor.

Then came the chatter of gunfire.

Not Covenant weapons, Dahlia thought. *Those were bullets smacking into buildings.*

"It's a rescue!" Dahlia shouted.

Greta looked at Paul, who shook his head. "No one knows we're here," Greta said.

Dahlia stared at them both. "But those are guns. Our guns."

"This is bad," Paul mumbled. "No matter which way you twist this around to look at it, something bad is happening."

A scream carried across the early morning air outside. An alien scream. Dahlia could feel the fear inside of it. It was universal.

The loud crack of a single shot silenced it.

The walls seemed to crowd in on her, the roof dropping in. Dahlia started taking deep breaths, but that didn't stop her heart from hammering ever faster.

Two Sangheili shoved the door open. They pointed large energy pistols at their captives and gestured toward the corridor. Slung under their shoulders were human rifles. Dahlia felt horror sweep over her.

They'd been outside killing their own.

"No," Greta said.

Paul stepped forward. "Not like this."

One of the Sangheili roared and stepped inside. It grabbed

Paul's throat and dragged him out. Greta screamed and followed. *"Stop it, you bastards!"*

A sharp smack to her shoulder with the pistol got Dahlia moving down the corridor toward the door outside, although she could barely remember how to step forward. She'd gone deep inside of herself, her mind doing its best to leave this world.

Numbly, she let herself get shoved down the corridor, past more empty cells that lined it. "Please," she finally said softly. "Please."

She would run when they got to the door. She wouldn't wait for them to kill her. She'd known, somehow, that this was coming. All the fleeing, all the new starts, just delayed the inevitable.

The Covenant might not exist anymore, but it almost killed her when she was a child. Now it was going to finally finish the job.

And she'd always prepared for this, somewhere deep inside.

She would run.

They would shoot her—one couldn't outrun that sharp bolt of energy. But she would run just the same.

A piece of the corridor shifted, light playing across it all wrong as a bump of disturbed air moved toward the Sangheili aggressors.

At the last second, the two aliens sensed something: a creak in the floorboards beneath them, the shifting sound of heavy material. They spun around just as the familiar blue glow of an energy sword flashed to life.

It swung up, slicing an energy pistol in half before it could fire. Paul and Greta stumbled off down the corridor and toward the door leading outside. The other Sangheili punched at the invisible form, unable to get its weapon up to aim. Energy fluoresced and danced as armored fists struck, revealing the shape of another Sangheili.

The adaptive camouflage spattered out, and Jat swept forward, jamming the sword deep into the other Sangheili's face.

Then, casually, Jat took the pistol from the dying Sangheili before he swung quickly around to behead its companion.

"Stay right there." Greta had pulled one of the captured rifles free.

Jat looked at her. "Do not fire that," he said softly. "Or the rest of the death squad in other buildings will hear it and come for us."

They followed Jat out, waiting a moment as he made sure the streets were clear, then skirted around behind the Sangheili detention building. Greta and Paul looked at Jat's Spectre, waiting for them. "We have transportation of our own. We just need to get to the trading depot," Paul said.

They'd each taken a rifle. They didn't trust Jat, Dahlia could tell, even if they'd been grateful for being released.

"You should come with us," Greta told Dahlia.

Dahlia hesitated. But then Jat stepped forward. "I owe her the debt of my life. She gave it back to me."

Paul nodded slowly. "Hell of a new pet, kid," he said. "Good luck."

They weren't going to argue. They slipped off into the dark. For a second, Dahlia panicked. The only humans here had just left her. And they knew the oasis better than she did. Better than Jat anyway.

Jat slipped into the Spectre. "We leave. Now. Before our enemies get back to this part of Masov Oasis."

"Why is this happening?" Dahlia asked. She looked up at the communications equipment, the firelight of burning Sangheili buildings reflecting off it in the predawn.

"I've been shadowing the death squad for many days now," Jat explained as the Spectre slid slowly along the back street. "They follow Thars."

He said that as if it were explanation enough. "Who is this Thars anyway?" Dahlia asked in a loud whisper.

"The enemy you should fear. One of my kind who thinks humans are . . ."

"Inferior?"

"Worms," Jat said, edging around a building. He was aiming for the flat expanse of sand beyond. Just a few hundred meters to go.

"And I'm presuming you don't follow Thars?"

"I lost everything I ever knew when my world was destroyed. I chose to follow Rojka 'Kaasan to this world, when we assembled a fleet and fled to a new beginning six years ago. I helped him found Rak. We mourned the Covenant, everything we lost, and what was taken from us."

Even Dahlia had heard of Rojka. Usually as a near epithet from her family and friends in Sandholm. The evil Sangheili who had taken the promised land from them. Thief. Squatter. Interloper.

"Rojka," Jat continued, "believes that Sangheili and humans can live together on this world. That all Sangheili and humans have to learn this. Or we will all die."

"Doesn't seem likely," Dahlia said. "Not now."

Jat grunted. "This evil here today will ring through the world, yes. Our species will plunge toward war if Thars gets his way. It is my hope to get word back to Rojka and stop it."

"And can you stop what your kind will think when they see what looks like happened here?" Dahlia asked.

"I have to try," Jat said.

A shout in Sangheili. Energy struck the ground nearby.

"We are discovered," Jat proclaimed and slammed the Spectre up to full speed. Dahlia turned to look behind them.

Sangheili filed out into the street, shouting and firing at the Spectre.

"We have the lead," Jat said. "But I had hoped to get away without notice."

Some of the Sangheili were now racing for craft of their own.

Before long, they were all tearing through the desert in the early morning sunrise, fine sand kicking up into the air behind them.

The wind buffeted the Spectre, sand whipping at them. Dahlia hunched down and gritted her teeth.

After some time, Jat finally shouted back at her, "We will not be able to outrun them or shoot back! Rojka had the turrets ripped off. We used them for civilian transport. Thars has been trying to remilitarize all the ground equipment."

Dahlia turned and squinted through the sand cloud they'd kicked up. Four Spectres with turrets, each carrying two heavily armed Sangheili, were just a kilometer away.

A blast of plasma hit the Spectre, splashing Dahlia's cloak with a faint mist of burning metal that scorched her skin. She could tell that something important had been hit, as the vehicle began to wobble and scrape sand.

Jat swung the Spectre in an arc toward a dip in the horizon.

Seconds later, they burst over a ridge and Dahlia's stomach flip-flopped as they fell toward a steep hill. Their Spectre kicked up gravel as it slammed down and bounced, almost throwing Dahlia out. Jat forced it into another turn, dodging a large boulder.

They screamed down into a canyon, sliding around as Jat fought with an increasingly unresponsive set of controls. Smoke trailed them, the engine inside failing with a loud screech and the familiar whine suddenly cutting out.

The Spectre glided in silence.

Behind them, one of the chase vehicles struck the boulder Jat had barely missed and disappeared in a spectacular explosion.

They slid to a stop.

Jat jumped out. "There are six left," he said, pulling a large silver case free from underneath the ruined Spectre. "These are not great odds."

"What do we do?" Dahlia asked. There was nowhere to run. The remaining Sangheili paused on the ridge, some of them peering quickly over the edge to see the whereabouts of Jat and Dahlia and how to safely get down to them.

Jat opened the case and retrieved a large rifle with a fat, wedge-shaped barrel. The chevron-shaped stock hung low under Jat's grip, making it look almost upside down to her eyes. "It is time for them to discover my trade skill."

Dahlia recognized the weapon. A particle beam rifle, generally used by Covenant snipers. She'd seen the bodies left on streets after that loud snap-whine of energy fried them.

"There are more than six," Dahlia pointed at the ridge. "I see two or three more sand plumes."

"I concur that we are well outnumbered." Jat reached to his belt and handed her the energy pistol he had taken from one of her captors. "We are making our last stand. It is the only option we have left."

One of the death squad's Spectres jumped the ridge and slid down toward the bottom of the gulley.

"I can't," Dahlia whispered. "I can't do this. What about my parents? What about your people? You were going to warn them."

"You can run," Jat said casually, as if it wouldn't bother him. "You saved my life, and you have paid your debt. But I tell you: they will hunt us down. They cannot have any witnesses left alive. Together, our weapons united, we can fight with honor."

"Die, you mean," Dahlia said.

Jat ignored the Spectre crabbing its way toward them on the floor of the canyon. He aimed farther away, calmly tracking something with the massive rifle. Energy lanced out through the air. A Spectre spun out of control as a driver slumped forward and died. There was bellowing from the Sangheili suddenly trapped in the back as it flew over the edge and exploded against rocks.

"When I waited for you in the corridor, when those guards marched you out, I had time to observe you. I do not know much about humans, but I think you were ready to attempt an escape. You were not going to let them kill you easily, am I correct?"

"Yes. I was going to run," Dahlia said, as Jat fired up at the ridge, killing more Sangheili scurrying along it to get a position on them. *What about the Spectre right down here with us?* she wondered in a panic.

"We are not animals to the slaughter—you and I," Jat rumbled. "We are warriors, survivors. We make a stand. Our memories—we will make our lineages proud, human. We will make this sand drink our enemy's blood."

Plasma fire hit Jat's broken Spectre, shaking it. The two of them dropped behind it for cover. Dahlia looked down at the bulky alien pistol. She could feel her pulse racing and the world narrowing around her. The droning sound of the approaching Spectre filled her world.

"Focus," Jat said to her, large pale alien eyes regarding her as he realized something was wrong with her. "There are worse ways to die than on your own terms. Breathe in every extra moment you are given to be free. Think that earlier this day you were certainly dead, and now you are not."

He broke out of his crouch and yanked the rifle up to fire at the approaching Spectre.

Dahlia glanced around the front of the craft in time to see the death squad Sangheili diving clear of their vehicle. The air filled with more plasma bolts as Sangheili on the ridge opened fire, no longer worried about hitting their own.

"Look up!" Dahlia shouted at Jat.

Two more Sangheili were scooting along above them up on the ridge, trying to move down so that the Spectre could no longer shield them.

Jat swung the rifle up and fired. No aiming, but he got the result he wanted. The would-be attackers ducked back from the edge of the rock.

Plasma fire from the Sangheili who'd dived clear of their exploding Spectre splashed the nearby rock now that Jat was distracted.

Dahlia took a deep breath, then leaned around and fired the pistol. The plasma struck far to the right of the aliens ducking from rock to rock toward them.

She corrected and peppered the nearby rocks with fire, keeping them behind cover.

"They're getting closer," Dahlia said, voice breaking slightly.

"As they will," Jat grumbled. "Ready yourself."

He fired again at the lip of the rock, then twisted to sit the rifle on the Spectre's chassis. Sighted. A Sangheili head popped up and Jat fired.

The dead alien body slumped forward over the rock.

One of them roared with rage to see yet another of their own die. Jat ducked back as a barrage of fire struck his vehicle. Dahlia clutched her knees, shivering.

So much. Too much.

With yet another bellow, three of the Sangheili charged. Dahlia could hear their footsteps pounding the ground as they advanced.

"Now!" Jat shouted.

Dahlia forced herself to lean around and fire blindly, finding the target only after she'd started pulling the trigger. She hit one of them in the leg and it tumbled forward, losing its footing. Jat swung, aimed, but the two other Sangheili jumped over the Spectre.

Struggling to spin as quickly, Dahlia tried to engage, but they darted forward just as Jat leaped at them with a war cry. His energy sword was out in an instant, his rifle left behind.

The other two Sangheili had their swords out in kind.

A three-sided duel began, swords hissing and crackling as they struck one another with remarkable speed.

Dahlia scrabbled up, looking for the third Sangheili she'd wounded. Something struck her on the shoulder. She spun, her breath knocked out of her, and landed against the Spectre. The impact caused her to hit her head and bounce off, the world fracturing into a series of images.

She saw the wounded Sangheili limping around the Spectre and raising its carbine to aim at the dueling Sangheili, their swords whirling around each other as Jat fought for his life. The two Sangheili still up above on the ridge leaped into the air, barreling down toward them.

"Jat . . ." She tried to warn him, but what could he do?

Her pistol had been thrown clear. Dahlia tried to crawl for it, but the wounded Sangheili already figured that out. Towering above her, it thudded over and kicked the weapon away.

Dahlia slumped to the ground and looked up.

Her left shoulder was on fire. The shot had come from the nearby Sangheili and burned through her. Pure adrenaline had stopped her from initially feeling it, but now the pain made her vision dance.

This was it.

Dahlia struggled to stand, but her attacker kicked her back down and unsheathed its own energy sword. It seemed to be relishing the moment of conquest. Taking its time to look at her, mandibles opening in a roar as the sword lifted.

She'd feared this moment her entire life. Woke to nightmares of the aliens and their inhuman eyes and backward-jointed legs kicking in a door to kill her just like this.

"Do it," Dahlia whispered. "You've been the boogeyman in my life for long enough. I'm ready. I'm not scared of you!"

Behind it, Dahlia saw Jat finally fall, the hilt of his sword clattering to the ground. Four Sangheili surrounded him, triumphant.

Jat looked over. "We made them bleed," he said to her, spreading his arms. "So then, they bleed!"

The entire canyon erupted in gunfire.

Human gunfire, Dahlia fuzzily thought.

Dozens of bullets ripped through the Sangheili standing over her in a split second, destroying the once-massive creature and filling the air with a mist of blood. The gunfire shifted across the desert floor and stitched through the other Sangheili trying to run for cover, chewing them apart.

Jat twisted up and stopped moving.

The gunfire ceased, and over it, Dahlia could hear the whine of turbines. She saw the hunched-forward shape of a Pelican transport dropping slowly down into the gulley.

Beige-uniformed soldiers jumped clear of its ramp, battle rifles up to their shoulders as they fanned out to examine the Spectres and alien bodies.

Dahlia somehow managed to stand up, her unharmed arm in the air.

Paul and Greta ducked as they ran around the Pelican's wings, the engines kicking up their cloaks.

"You," Dahlia said, mouth dry. She ran toward them, wincing with the pain that flared through her shoulder at each step. "How?"

"We may be traders, but we also feed information back to the Carrow militia," Greta said. "Keep an eye on the ground for them. Once we got back to the depot, we called for help. Met them out in the desert for a pickup. When we saw all the smoke here, we came to have a look."

Dahlia could have hugged them.

"Live one!" shouted a militia man.

Dahlia spun around as fast as her damaged shoulder would let her. "It's Jat! Don't—"

A single shot cracked through the air and Jat slumped forward to the ground.

Dahlia screamed and ran forward. She grabbed the Sangheili's head with her good arm, cradling it. "Jat."

But he only stared off into emptiness.

"He . . . he saved me. He wasn't one of them!" Dahlia raged at the soldiers standing around her now. "You killed him!"

The strangers in their beige uniforms said nothing, their sand-bitten faces empty at the sight of what had once been their enemy dead on the sand.

"He was my friend," Dahlia said.

"The Sangheili aren't our friends," one of them finally said, grabbing her elbow. "You'd know that if you lived in the Outer Colonies before coming here. You'd have seen what they did. They think this is their world. They'll find out who it really belongs to soon enough."

They dragged her off to the Pelican, where Paul and Greta tried to talk to her.

But Dahlia didn't have any more words left.

Dahlia's father woke first, responding to the heavy antivirals and fluids the militia medic had hooked both her parents up to. He blinked at his daughter, who was sitting down in full desert gear at the foot of their bed, a new militia rifle on her lap. Her shoulder was bandaged, and the skin on her face chapped from the desert sun.

"Dahlia?"

She stood up with a smile, a tiny bit of relief coursing through her to hear him say her name. She crossed over to his side of the bed and gave his forehead a kiss. "Dad."

He hugged her. Then looked at the long dagger on her hip and back to the rifle. "What's all this? You carry weapons now?"

"I do," Dahlia replied. "I have to. Mom hasn't woken yet. You're too weak to travel. You need to rest and recover. So I'm ready for anything that comes here to Sandholm."

Her father appeared heartbroken. "And do you think you can hold off the Sangheili by yourself?"

"No. I have no doubts I'd die quickly," Dahlia flatly said. Her dad flinched at her honesty. "But they say there's an envoy being sent from the Unified Earth Government. Maybe it won't come to that."

They could both tell she didn't believe that.

Dahlia wiped her mother's forehead, then stood up and looked out of their window. Out toward Signal Hill, the rocks, and the desert beyond. "But a friend of mine taught me that I should die on my own terms, not someone else's. So if they come for us, Dad . . . I will make them bleed and pay a price."

Everything had changed. *Everything will collapse into blood and fire once again*, she thought.

But the difference this time was that there would be no more cowering in the corner for her. Dahlia wasn't scared anymore.

ANAROSA

KEVIN GRACE

This story takes place in March 2556, three years after the end of the Covenant War (Halo 3 *era) and one year after FAR STORM, a joint military operation between humans and their former Sangheili enemies in order to secure the remote and mysterious Forerunner installation known as the Ark* (Halo: Hunters in the Dark).

"Who is she?"

Agent Prauss wove through the cars on the highway, eyes darting from vehicle to vehicle around him. Years of driving an unmarked vehicle meant he was well used to the Doppler sounds of angry horns at nearly double the legal speed limit. He still enjoyed that a bit. More than a bit, really. Leo could tell.

The small silver hologram of a man in a neat-fitting suit appeared on the car's dashboard and nodded sympathetically to the particularly shocked owner of one of those horns.

"Is this really the right time for the breakdown? You seem to be busy."

Prauss's eyes never left the road, and yet they rolled. "Leo . . ."

"Very well."

Leo inclined his head to the windscreen readout behind him and the car's control cluster was replaced with the picture of a young woman. Short brown hair. Smiling brown eyes.

"Anarosa Carmelo. Age twenty-six. Ninety-ninth percentile at Hyugens Preparatory Academy and First Mars Technical. Goodpasture Foundation scholarships for master's degrees in biology and astronavigation. Medical records clean. No criminal history. Extensive community service. Good kid. Great, even."

Prauss nodded. "They all are. Work?"

"Snapped up by Oros Trading after graduation, self-selected into their test-pilot program with extra research on colonization protocols."

Prauss glanced to Leo briefly, curious.

"Colonization? Oros makes slipspace engines, so test pilot I get. What does Oros have to do with colonization?"

"Company records show that it was a new program she created to train test pilots for encounters with unexplored or abandoned systems. Makes sense. There are a lot of systems out there coming back on the market now that the war's over."

"Over. Yeah." Prauss sliced into the exit lane. "We're close. How did she die?"

Anarosa's image disappeared from the car's HUD, returning the standard array of indicators and Office of Naval Intelligence datastreams.

"Acute hypothermia. Details are still coming in, but she entered the cockpit of a training shuttle forty minutes ago to perform a preflight checklist. Seven minutes later, sensor logs show a misfiring of the craft's fire-suppression system. I don't think it was her fault, but . . . full Aerosol D immersion with no suit. Life signs ended fifteen seconds later."

"Damn," said Prauss, wincing. "Still, this is good."

"Good? You may want to rephrase that in our upcoming conversation."

The car finished its short course of residential street turns and stopped in front of a simple white house. Curbside holo fed the address and name to the HUD: 7735 Killingham. Michael Carmelo.

"Yes, yes," admitted Prauss, composing himself in the rearview mirror, "but you know what I mean. Anarosa was special. She had a very special mind. And we are here to convince her brother that he should give that mind to us. Her death is a damn shame, but the way she died means the tissue will be preserved longer than we usually have for emergency calls."

Leo had to agree with that. Prauss was right. Mercenary, but right.

"And why is this an emergency run, anyway?" Prauss continued. "She must have been flagged as a candidate years back. We should be at the hospital making pickup by now, not here and about to ask this question. We shouldn't have to do it like this."

"She was flagged," Leo nodded, matching Prauss's gaze now at the white house. "But she delayed her decision. Twice."

"Really?"

"Sat down with recruiters both times, asked quite a few questions, and both times said she needed to think about it."

"Interesting. Not many delay twice." Prauss checked his watch and frowned. "But we don't have long. Does he know?"

Leo nodded. "He picked up the call from Oros HR twelve minutes ago and hung up three minutes ago. No other calls initiated since then."

"And he's the only living family, right?"

Leo nodded again. "Mother and father died of natural causes three and seven years ago, respectively. Anarosa was unmarried. No children. Just the one sibling."

Prauss sighed and opened his door. "Damn shame. Let's go."

At the door, Agent Prauss knocked and apologized and introduced himself and Leo to the bewildered Michael Carmelo. Prauss could tell from Michael's body language that asking to come inside wasn't an option, which meant he had to do this on the porch. Prauss hated doing it on the porch. But he was well prepared, practiced from years of conversations just like this one, explaining gently that Anarosa's natural talents had singled her out as a candidate for a very special program within the Office of Naval Intelligence. This program, he explained, upon the death of someone as special as Anarosa, would use that person's exceptional brain to create a very special computer program called a "smart" artificial intelligence like his colleague Leo, here. Smart AIs like Leo, Prauss went on, are vital to the successful operation of many of the United Nations Space Command's most critical operations and are unmatched in their creative, computational, and strategic abilities. In a way, Prauss delicately suggested, Anarosa would have one last chance to create something wonderful from this tragic day . . . and all Michael had to do was consent, and arrangements would be made and her body returned with minimal signs of the procedure within twenty-four hours.

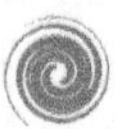

Leo, projecting now from a small disc held by Prauss, remained silent, other than saying a few brief words conveying his regrets for the loss of Anarosa. He listened to Prauss's practiced speech while monitoring various subroutines furthering the rest of the assignment.

Background check on Michael Carmelo (clean).

Conversations with medical regarding risks of freezing damage to Anarosa's brain (minimal).

Initiation of the pickup crew in case permission was secured (on the road/ETA to Oros in seven minutes/holding for pickup confirmation).

Confirmation of the body's destination if permission was not secured (Wesley General Hospital).

An order for flowers paid for and sent to this address regardless of outcome (priental lilies/white vase/condolence note from both Prauss and myself).

After nodding once to acknowledge that he was indeed Michael Carmelo, Amarosa's brother listened silently to everything Agent Prauss had to say. When Prauss stopped talking, Michael made no acknowledgment of the unbelievable offer just extended. He stood still for a moment, his gaze locked on the floor, and then broke his silence by simply stating:

"Go to hell."

The door closed.

Back in the car, Prauss scowled at the steering wheel.

"I told you it shouldn't have gone down this way. Dammit. We needed her."

Leo brought up a map on the car's display, with a small blue dot indicating the pickup crew waiting at Oros Trading Company's headquarters.

"I'll call off the collection and notify the colonel."

Prauss shook his head.

"Wait. It is too late for a . . . dammit. Yes. No way we could sneak her out now. Probably should have requested an end run from the start. Dammit. Fine, go ahead and call the . . ."

Leo's head snapped toward the house and he held up his hand in a small silver warning.

"Heads up. We have company."

Turning to the house, Prauss saw Michael walking slowly down the driveway toward the car. Prauss nodded to Leo when Michael reached the passenger-side door and leaned down. Leo lowered the window.

"Michael," Prauss began, "again I'm so sorry to . . ."

"Stop." Michael said flatly. "I don't want to listen to you anymore."

Prauss's eyebrows raised, but he fell silent.

Michael turned to Leo's projection on the dashboard.

"I want to talk to *him.*

The inside of the house was clean and simply furnished, with signs of an interrupted meal already cold on the kitchen table. Michael gestured towards a chair in the living room and excused himself to get a drink. Leo moved his projection to a vid across from the chair and spun up another subroutine:

Biometric sensors online
Psychophysiological calibration complete
Recent conversational data analyzed
Baseline readings set
(Pulse rate/Blood pressure/Dermal conductance/Sympathetic nervous system response)

Begin tracking
(Pulse 0/BP 0/Dermal 0/SNS 0)

Michael returned from the kitchen and sat down on a chair directly facing Leo's projector. After considering Leo for a second, Michael nodded his head in the direction of the front door.

"Is he listening?"

"Yes."

"Would you stop the feed to him if I asked?"

"No."

"Well, at least one of you is honest."

(Pulse 0/BP 1/Dermal 0/SNS 1)

"Everything Agent Prauss said to you is the truth," said Leo.

"But he didn't say everything, did he?"

"Such as?"

"He didn't mention that you tried to get my sister to agree to this before."

Leo nodded. "Agent Prauss and I didn't, but others did. Your sister clearly liked to think things through very carefully. But I will also point out that she didn't say no to our request. Would you like to hear recordings of her recruitment visits?"

(Pulse 1/BP 2/Dermal 1/SNS 2)

Michael shook his head quickly. "No. I can't . . . not now."

The two sat silently for a moment."She didn't want to join the military, you know," said Michael.

"I do know. She made that quite clear in her interviews. But the specific assignment we hope she can help us fill does not involve combat. It's about exploration. What she dreamed of. And it's further than we've ever travelled before, which is where she wanted to go."

"Where she wanted . . ." Michael stopped before his emotions overtook him. He took a deep breath. "What's it like?"

"What's what like?"

"Being . . . like you."

(Pulse 1/BP 1/Dermal 1/SNS 1)

"It's . . . hmm." Leo paused. "It's enormous." He felt uncertain about this description.

"Enormous?" The uncertainty was shared.

"Not a terribly helpful answer, I know, but there really isn't a sufficient word to describe it. It's hard to explain the breadth of my connection to all the systems that drive our worlds. Much of my central processes are contained for now in the projection unit you're looking at, but my . . . presence, I guess you could call it, is limitless."

"That sounds terrifying."

"I've never found it to be so."

"So you enjoy it?"

Leo smiled in appreciation. "*Enjoy.* You ask interesting questions, Michael. Much like your sister. I've never really considered it that way. It just . . . it's what I do. It's what I am."

"What you are now."

"You mean compared to my donor."

(Pulse 2/BP 2/Dermal 1/SNS 3)

Michael recoiled slightly at that, but pushed on. "Yes."

"I don't know. Policy now is that AIs are not permitted to know the identity of their donors."

"Permitted? What about that 'breadth'? Can't you just access that information?"

"No. There are limits."

"Set by who? ONI?"

"Yes."

"So they control you?"

(Pulse 2/BP 2/Dermal 2/SNS 3)

Leo carefully chose his next words.

"They monitor me. Us. All intelligences. To make sure that we only use those connections I spoke of earlier for the greater good of the UNSC."

"Some AIs have used it for bad?"

"Yes. Not all attempts at creating an intelligence like myself are successful. I think not all minds are . . . suited to it. Sometimes intelligences come out flawed. And sometimes that flaw takes years to discover. Therefore, we are monitored to prevent accidents."

"What kind of accidents?"

"I don't think this is the time to talk about that." Michael looked dubious. "You mean you're not *allowed* to talk about that."

"No, I mean I don't think it will happen to your sister, since that's what you're really asking. And I don't believe it's a productive topic for the decision you have to make right now."

(Pulse 1/BP 2/Dermal 1/SNS 0)

Michael considered this for a moment, looking down at the glass of water in his hands. Then he looked back up to Leo.

"So I wouldn't be able to see her?"

Leo shook his head in sympathy. "There is no 'her' to see, Michael. The being your sister would help create wouldn't be her. It would be an entirely new person, and if you did meet her, you would look for your sister and you wouldn't find her. It would bring back all the pain you're feeling now, everything, all over again."

"Would somebody at least tell me whether it worked?"

"I'm sorry, no. No contact is allowed, or information which could lead to a contact. It's for the best, for everyone."

Michael's brow furrowed, pondering this last point. Then he said: "Do you want to know who your donor was?"

(Pulse 2/BP 2/Dermal 2/SNS 3)

"That's . . . personal."

Michael pushed back in his chair, dropping eye contact with Leo to stare at the floor between them.

"I understand your questions," Leo continued, "and I wish there were simpler answers, but life and death are as complicated for us as they are for you."

Michael choked back tears. "She's gone. I talked to her this morning. About stupid shit. And I'll never talk to her again. Now you want me to give her to you . . . to think that maybe some part of her would still be out there, but I couldn't . . ."

(Pulse 2/BP 2/Dermal 3/SNS 3)

Leo could see the retreat in Michael's eyes, and Leo opened his mouth, closed it, and deeply contemplated his opportunity for a moment before speaking again.

"I do."

(Pulse 3/BP 4/Dermal 4/SNS 4)

Michael looked up. "What?"

"I do want to know who my donor was. There is a part of him in me. I have . . . associations I don't understand. Bits of memories that are not mine. And I think . . . sometimes I think I . . . he . . . had a child."

Michael's eyes widened in surprise, as it appeared that he briefly forgot his own grief. The sadness in Leo's voice was overwhelming.

(Pulse 5/BP 4/Dermal 4/SNS 6)

Leo continued. "We don't talk about these things because they can destroy us. I don't think about these things because thinking is all I do. I don't need to eat, or get dressed, or worry about any such physical distractions . . . all I have is thinking, and if I think about what might have been and how that might-have-been changes me, I will go mad. Madness is the end, for us. We all get there, sooner or later, and dwelling on my donor will only lead to that state sooner. So . . . I just don't."

"Why are you telling me this?" Michael asked.

"Because despite that hole in understanding exactly who I am, I know for a fact that I have done good things. I have helped people, saved lives. And regardless of who I was, I think the chance to go on helping after you're gone is an incredible opportunity, and one only very few, very special people get. I think your sister would take that chance. And I think you will too."

On the way back to the car, Leo confirmed Anarosa's pickup order, ordered the surgical team to begin scrubbing in, and removed Agent Prauss's name from the card on Michael's flowers.

"Damn," said Prauss in admiration once Leo was loaded back into the car's system and his form reappeared on the dash.

"We need her," said Leo, matter-of-factly. "That research outpost is the UNSC's biggest scientific opportunity in years, and Anarosa's profile is a perfect fit, assuming everything goes according to plan."

Prauss nodded and started the engine. "All right, then. You've already . . ."

"I've already." Leo replied. "And now we wait to see who arrives."

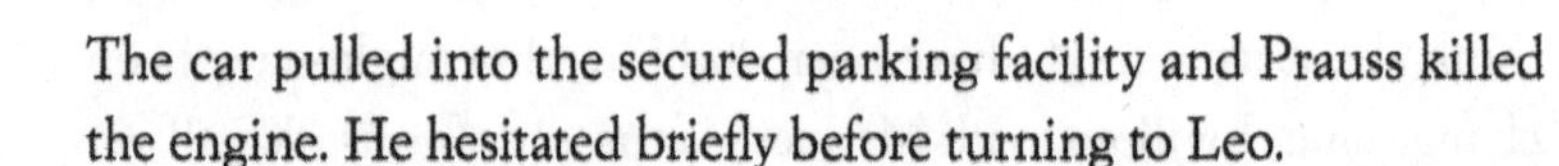

The car pulled into the secured parking facility and Prauss killed the engine. He hesitated briefly before turning to Leo.

"What you said back there, about what it means to be . . . like you. You've never brought that up before. Why?"

Leo shrugged. "You never asked."

He had Prauss there.

"And about your donor? Were you just telling Michael what he needed to hear?"

Another shrug, but this time Leo didn't answer.

"And what you said about a child . . . ?"

Leo just stared down the hood of the car and said nothing.

.

(Pulse 3/BP 4/Dermal 4/SNS 3)

.

(Pulse 5/BP 6/Dermal 6/SNS 7)

.

.

.

(Pulse 10/BP 7/Dermal 9/SNS 14)

.

Gotcha.

. . . and then he turned suddenly toward Prauss with a sheepish look and a self-deprecating roll of the eyes. "Sorry about that—I tuned out for a second. I was receiving details on our next assignment. To answer your question . . . what he needed to hear. Yes, of course."

Leo smiled and materialized a silver Fedora on his head, which he then tipped in Prauss's direction.

"I learned from the best, didn't I?"

You son of a bitch.

ACKNOWLEDGMENTS

343 Industries would like to thank all the contributors, Scott Dell'Osso, Kory Hubbell, Bonnie Ross-Ziegler, Ed Schlesinger, Rob Semsey, Matt Skelton, Phil Spencer, Kiki Wolfkill, Carla Woo, and Jennifer Yi.

None of this would have been possible without the amazing efforts of the Halo Franchise Team, the Halo Consumer Products Team, Jeff Easterling, Scott Jobe, Tiffany O'Brien, Kenneth Peters, and Sparth, with special thanks to Jeremy Patenaude.

ABOUT THE AUTHORS

TOBIAS BUCKELL is the *New York Times* bestselling author of *Halo: The Cole Protocol.* His other novels and more than fifty short stories have been translated into seventeen languages. He has been nominated for the Hugo, the Nebula, the Prometheus, and the John W. Campbell Award for Best New Science Fiction Author. He lives with his family in Ohio.

TROY DENNING is the *New York Times* bestselling author of more than thirty-five novels, including *Halo: Last Light*, a dozen *Star Wars* novels, the Dark Sun: Prism Pentad series, and many bestselling Forgotten Realms novels. A former game designer and editor, he lives in western Wisconsin.

MATT FORBECK is an award-winning and *New York Times* bestselling author and game designer. He has thirty novels and countless games published to date. His latest work includes *Halo: New Blood*, *Magic: The Gathering* comics, the 2014 edition of *The Marvel Encyclopedia*, *Captain America: The Ultimate Guide to the First Avenger*, his Monster Academy young adult fantasy novels, and the upcoming *Shotguns & Sorcery* roleplaying game based on his novels. He lives in Beloit, Wisconsin, with his wife and five children, including a set of quadruplets. For more about him and his work, visit www.forbeck.com.

KELLY GAY is the critically acclaimed author of the Charlie Madigan urban fantasy series. She is a multipublished author with works translated into several languages and earning accolades: a two-time RITA nominee, an ARRA nominee, a Goodreads Choice Award finalist, and a SIBA Book Award Long List finalist. Kelly is also a recipient of North Carolina Arts Council's Fellowship Grant in Literature. She can be found online at KellyGay.com.

Award-winning and eight-time *New York Times* bestselling author **CHRISTIE GOLDEN** has written nearly fifty novels in the fields of science fiction, fantasy, and horror. Among them are titles for *Star Trek*, *World of Warcraft*, *Assassin's Creed*, and *Star Wars*, including the highly acclaimed *Dark Disciple*. You can find her at christie golden.com, on Facebook as Christie Golden, and on Twitter @ChristieGolden.

KEVIN GRACE is a Narrative Design Director at 343 Industries and a longtime resident of the *Halo* universe, where he wages a never-ending war on the Hexagonal Scourge. He has written the short story "The Return," which appeared in the *Halo: Evolutions* anthology, and is currently working on the story for *Halo Wars 2*.

MORGAN LOCKHART is a professional writer and game designer from Seattle, Washington. She currently works on the *Halo* franchise, and her short fiction can be found cluttering like cobwebs around the internet. Visit her at lockhartwrites.com.

ABOUT THE AUTHORS

JOHN JACKSON MILLER is a *New York Times* bestselling author and comics historian who has written more than twenty novels and graphic novels, including the Star Trek: Prey novel trilogy from Pocket Books, *Star Wars* novels including *Kenobi* and *A New Dawn*, and comics in the *Mass Effect* universe. His comics story "Undefeated" appears in the Dark Horse Comics collection *Halo: Tales from Slipspace.* His fiction website is www.farawaypress.com.

FRANK O'CONNOR is the Creative Director for the *Halo* franchise at 343 Industries. He lives in Washington.

BRIAN REED began working in the video game industry in 1996 as a tester for *WarCraft II.* His work in TV animation and Marvel Comics led to him join 343 Industries full-time during the production of *Halo 4*. He has been part of every *Halo* project since, and currently serves as a Narrative Director. He is also a noted comic-book writer, having adapted the novel *Halo: The Fall of Reach*, as well as worked on *Halo: Initiation* and *Halo: Escalation* for Dark Horse Comics. He lives in Seattle, Washington, with his wife and a Promethean Crawler they adopted from a rescue shelter.

JOSEPH STATEN was the writer and creative lead for *Halo: Combat Evolved*, *Halo 2*, and *Halo 3*, as well as *Halo: ODST* and *Halo: Reach.* He is the *New York Times* bestselling author of *Halo: Contact Harvest* and one of the voices behind the indomitable Covenant Grunts. He lives with his family in Washington.

JAMES SWALLOW is a *New York Times* bestselling author and BAFTA-nominated scriptwriter; he has worked on video games such as

Deus Ex: Mankind Divided and *Deus Ex: Human Revolution*, *Disney Infinity*, *Fable: The Journey*, and *Killzone 2*. His work includes original fiction and stories from the worlds of *Star Trek*, *24*, *Doctor Who*, *Star Wars*, *Warhammer 40,000*, and more. He lives and works in London.

"One more pass for today," I called out to the harrow and its driver.

He was only nine years old, but he was already capable enough to guide the large beasts on their course through the valley. The great wooden plow had a rear-mounted platform set just above a broad, ivory-studded tiller—it was simple and crude, but it accomplished its purpose. From this distance, I could only make out the boy's straw hat peeking out over the top, almost completely buried by the machine's frame, as he goaded forward creatures three times his height.

He was my son.

The young boy drove the massive pair of indigo-colored oxen forward, meticulously carving deep furrows of arable soil in a pattern that now spread through the entire valley. The farmland was vast and covered with a healthy, mustard-colored earth that marked this region of the world. It was fertile and relatively easy to manage, apart from the occasional rugged outcropping.

If the weather held, tomorrow we would begin to plant. This put us on schedule to finish by the next lunar cycle, just before Rainfall, the third of five seasons in this moon's standard year. That could mean the best yields we had ever seen on this world, and the thought thrilled me. It was actually working. We were thriving on our own out here.

As the day's light began to dim, I climbed up to the top of the grassy ridge within which our homestead was built into and surveyed the terrain. The last rays of the suns poured over the lip of the ridge, casting an uneven shadow across the land and signaling the end of the workday.

At the stable, my son was already cautiously unhitching the oxen and, one by one, brought the giant beasts inside.

I did my best not to make my prying obvious: I trusted him, even if this was his first year helping with the crop. The boy was growing strong and focused and he loved working with his hands. In short, absolutely nothing like me—he took after his mother instead.

The ridge had a long, stony crest that looked out upon a brackish inland sea, its surface mottled by bright-red coral. Our home was built directly into the rock, framed up by heavy beams of lumber into helical compartments just below the cliff ledge. While most of the living space was underground, a trio of copiously carved apertures was situated over the sea on the far side, often capturing the marine breeze.

When I reached the peak of the ridge, I took in a stunning sight: our world's twin suns began to shift behind the enormous shadowy gas giant, glinting off its roiling atmosphere with an explosive burst of radiance. This lasted only a moment before the onset of dusk, as stars suddenly began to pierce the deep blue sky. The bright, coalescent clusters of light resembled a glowing moss I had seen on another world. I could not recall which one—it was so long ago.

In the meantime, my wife had emerged from our home, carrying a basket and a blanket. We would dine under the stars tonight. She met me on the ridge just in time to witness the last light prior to the cool darkness of twilight taking over the view. A sweet but pungent gust of lavender rushed up the cliffside to greet us. It was the coral: the scent of this world, full of vibrance and life. The smell made her smile.

She and I were very different: I loved the glory of the stars, and she adored the glory of the life that orbited them. This was the way it had always been, and the very reason we chose this world as our home.

"It never gets old," I said.

"No, it doesn't," she responded, glancing at me from the corner of her eye before spreading out the blanket. I helped pull it taut near the ledge and we sat down, staring out across the sea, soaking it all in for a moment. Down the hill toward the stable, our son had just finished stowing the plow. From our perch, we could just barely make out the steady and determined grimace on his face as he finished the task. He always needed to do it exactly right.

"You know he takes after you," I said.

"There's a little of both of us in him," his mother replied. "I'm just the parts about him you like the best." She was right.

She was always right.

"Tell me one of your old stories, Father."

One of my old stories. The tales from before my son had been born, from before the life we had on this world. To him, they were only legends and myths—that was a good thing. They should stay that way, remaining in a galaxy and a time far removed from our own, something he would never experience out here, in the fields.

It had taken years for the dark dreams of that time to end. Those scars ran deep, almost too deep, but eventually they subsided. Now, all that remained was a torrent of dim memories, loosely connected events, all of it ancient history. Tragedy upon tragedy. My past was a trail of corpses and dead worlds. How it all went wrong.

"Which one do you want me to tell you about?"

All three of us were laying on our backs across the blanket, my wife tucked into my arm and our son under hers. I smoked from a small ivory pipe: crushed flowers of a sweet plant that gave off a pleasant and rejuvenating aroma. A large cerulean moon now climbed above distant mountains that sat opposite the sea—our homeworld's sister satellite. Over the course of the year, both spheres would dance their way around the impossibly massive anchor planet they orbited.

"Tell me about Halo," he said, thumbing the rim of his weathered hat.

"Halo? Are you sure?" my wife asked him.

"Yes. Tell me one of those stories."

Halo. This wasn't the first time I had told him a story about the ringworld weapons, but my reaction was always the same. The mentioning of its name was enough to summon a storm of memories to the fore. What could I honestly say about it that wouldn't frighten my son out of his wits? The reality that it was capable of wiping an entire galaxy completely clean of any thinking life? That it was just as majestic as it was deadly and ruinous? How would he even begin to understand that? Could he ever bear the truth—and if not now, when he was older?

Perhaps one day . . . but for now, it would still be clothed in myth and the periphery of the past. Vague and distant, something that I alone remembered.

"There was once a warrior who tracked his old enemy to one of the Halo rings—"

"A strong and brave warrior?" my wife asked for the child's benefit, not hers.

"By the measure of some," I confessed. "This warrior led a vast navy to a Halo that his enemy had made into a stronghold. They fought for days in the skies above the ring, until the enemy had been worn down and his vulnerabilities were exposed," I said this with expressive gestures, and then paused to inhale the pipe's warmth in my lungs.

"The enemy was out of options. His ships had been ravaged, his weapons demolished. He was completely beaten . . . but he was a cunning foe. If he could not have the Halo for himself, he would not let the warrior have it. Or anyone else, for that matter."

"So he tried to destroy it?" my son asked.

"Yes. He attempted to rip it apart with the gravity of another world. But the warrior refused him this final effort. Using the vessels under his command, the warrior drew in from all sides and laid hold of the Halo ring, reshaping its form as the gravity sought to rend it to pieces. Then he tracked down the enemy and captured him."

"What happened to the enemy?" he asked with a yawn.

"He was given a just punishment for his crimes. And the warrior reversed all of the evils the enemy had caused on the ring-world. He . . . tried to make everything right," I said, choosing my words carefully. "Even if only for a time."

I stopped for a long moment, taking in a few breaths from the pipe.

"He's asleep," my wife said, lightly touching the back of her hand on his cheek. That was what a long day working the fields does. It was no longer effortless for our kind.

My wife nuzzled in closer to me. She was incredibly beautiful under the pale light from the moon and stars. The hard years of laboring alongside me had not made her any less lovely. In many ways, she was even dearer to me now than ever before.

"Do you remember it well?" she asked.

"Halo?"

"Yes. Do you remember the one from your story?"

"It is still vivid in my mind," I said, closing my eyes. "Those massive bands reaching up like arms into the sky: they were blue-green and rich with life within, and a cold ashen metal without. I can still see its shape, twisted and fractured in the cracked viewport of my ship. I remember watching it shrink into the distance just before we left. Even back then, when machines of that scale were ordinary and expected . . . Halo took my breath away."

For a moment, the weight of the memory overcame me like a swift tide. I was suddenly back there, long ago, with my ship's frigid deck below me. I watched Halo's band slowly spin, set against the roiling blackness of an abandoned star system. The fortress world was an elegant kaleidoscopic spool of color, yet still inordinately powerful beyond reason. Halo brought our entire world down around us and cost us everything. It had made us exiles to the furthest reaches of space.

As if waking from a dream, I shuddered and snapped my eyes wide open, returning to reality. I shifted to see if my wife too was slumbering. She hadn't. She was just staring at me with a reassuring smile. She put her head on my chest and closed her eyes, listening to my heart as it steadied.

"Are you happy with our life here?" I asked.

"I am," she said softly.

"I mean, truly happy . . . given all that has happened?"

"This is life—real life. The three of us together. It is the way it was always meant to be. Nothing could make me happier, whether on this world or any other."

By the time my pipe had died down, she'd fallen asleep. But I could not.

One by one, I wrapped my wife and son in the blanket as I took them inside the house, laying them on the mat in our straw loft. After retrieving a bundle of wood for the hearth, I lit it with an onyx flint we kept above the mantle. It was one of the first things I made when we arrived here.

Confident that this would keep them warm, I grabbed my cloak and set out from the homestead. I walked the full extent of the farm, and then deep into the shallow tablelands that stretched toward the inland interior.

This walk was not a normal evening ritual, but tonight I felt provoked.

Compelled by the image of Halo freshly seared into my mind, I set out through the deep country, pushing into a series of rolling golden fields before the foothills of the white-capped mountains rose before me. I knew the place I was headed; it wasn't far.

As I scaled the first set of steep rises, I quickly came to a narrow ledge that forced me to sidle my way along the mountainside, ascending into snow and ice. Looking back toward the valley, the light was soft against the hillside, and from here I could see most of the tablelands, from the deep and dark forests to the east to the immense crimson sea on the west. Herds of grazing bovids were scattered across a distant clearing, while a small flock of gulls wheeled upward in the predawn sky—but otherwise, the sight was completely still, like a picture. I could even see my home built into the cresting ridge, a brown speck set against countless lines of harrowed soil.

That was home. I'd been here longer than I had been anywhere else before.

After climbing a good way, I finally reached an obscure and well-hidden cleft. Turning around to face the mountain, my eyes were met with a familiar shape.

Audacity.

Mostly buried under the snow, the slender starship was carefully perched here, leaning out over the edge toward our homestead. Its visage was impassive but vigilant, like a silent guardian that kept watch from a distance.

I approached the exposed entry portal and placed my hand on the seal. The ship immediately recognized me and opened its maw, allowing me to climb inside.

It somehow felt colder in here than outside; this was a ship that had seen a thousand burning stars in its long and forgotten history, and had now been abandoned to the elements.

As I moved into the recesses of the ship, my respiration came out in ragged tendrils—I was breathing harder. I always did when I made this trip. It was now much more taxing on my body than once upon a time.

At the back of the ship was a dun obelisk, a vertical structure that detected my approach and opened by sliding two doors out from its center. In front of me was a hulking suit of armor—old and imposing. Its helmet appeared to wear a stern countenance, and the chestplate and pauldrons had been pocked with damage from a hundred bitter wars. All of this was distant to me, but it was still my past. It wasn't a myth. It wasn't a legend.

Not long after we activated Halo, the handful that remained made plans to leave. We committed ourselves to a single purpose: exile. We would let the white disc of the galaxy proceed with plans that had been prepared for its future, while we escaped to alien stars, spreading our numbers out such that our species' days would be fixed. Our kind would not live forever. My wife and I gave our ship to the mountain, and we gave up all of *Audacity*'s trappings and comforts: unequaled technology from ten thousand generations.

I looked at the top of the obelisk where a cuneiform pattern was etched. It had the bearing of the armor's owner. My old name:

BORNSTELLAR-MAKES-ETERNAL-LASTING

We left our armor here in the ship—armor that could have kept us alive for millennia. We forsook it and everything from our past, and started anew. Me, my wife, our son. We would return to the roots of my people, millions of years before. Simple farmers who lived and loved and died. I would fail my namesake, that was for certain—nothing about me would be eternal or lasting—but I would not fail the soul my people.

That would be eternal.

What we once were before our pride, before the wars, and before Halo. We were noble, kind creatures who served one another and recognized our small place in the greater story. That is how we would be on this world. That is how the last chapter would be told.

Our new life here would be the end of our great journey.

HALO

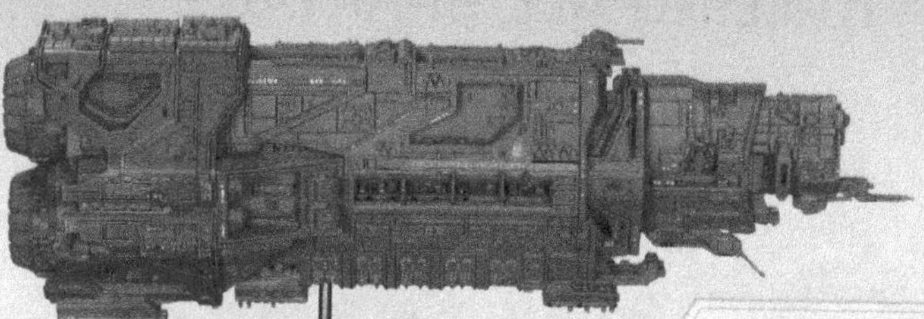
HALO UNSC PILLAR
OF AUTUMN

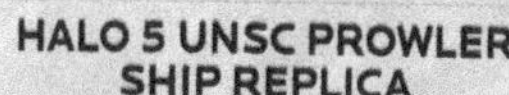
HALO 5 UNSC PROWLER
SHIP REPLICA

1 INITIATION
ESCALATION
HALO
HALO LIBRARY EDITION VOLUME 1 HC
Collects comic series *Halo: Initiation* #1–#3 and *Halo: Escalation* #1–#12

DARK
HORSE
COMICS
Microsoft
Studios
343
INDUSTRIES
VISIT DARKHORSE.COM FOR MORE INFO!